THE *List*

YVETTE GEER

TRYST
A CAYÉLLE IMPRINT

THE *List*

Cayélle Publishing/Tryst Imprint
Lancaster, California USA
www.CayellePublishing.com

Orders by U.S. trade bookstores and wholesalers. Please contact Freadom Distribution:
Tel: (833) 229-3553 ext. 813 or email: Freadom@Cayelle.com

Categories: 1. Romance 2. Multicultural 3. African-American Romance
Printed in the United States of America
Cover Art by Robin Ludwig Design, Inc.
Interior Design & Typesetting by Ampersand Book Interiors

ISBN: 978-1-952404-15-3 [paperback]
ISBN: 978-1-952404-16-0 [eBook]

Library of Congress Control Number 2020940408

TRYST
A CAYÉLLE IMPRINT

CHAPTER

One

"C'MON YOU TWO, WE NEED TO GET GOING."
Shane Rawlings stood up and tried to block out the constant pinging from the nearby slot machines. Seated at the square-shaped bar at the Bellagio Hotel in Las Vegas, secondhand cigarette smoke singed his nostrils, the faint hint of ash lingering on his tongue with every breath. Waitresses in black mini-skirts and white, short-sleeved shirts carried trays of drinks through the crowd.

As soon as Shane, his younger sister Sallie, and his best friend Liam arrived in Vegas, Sallie had decided they would drink in the hotel casino and maybe gamble a little.

"It's been an hour, and we have a lot more to see."

"I don't wanna go yet." Sallie lifted her third tequila shot to her lips.

Shane grabbed the shot glass from her hand and set the drink on the counter.

"Hey," she said, slurring. "You're such a Debbie downer."

"A Debbie what?"

Liam gulped down his rum and Coke. "It means you like to spoil all the fun, man."

"Aren't you two ready to hit the Strip?"

"It's like…like six somethin', right? It's earrrrly. I'm not drunk. I ate some crackers in my room before we came down here."

"You are so buzzed right now." Shane grinned, shaking his head at his sister. "We have a lot more to see." He had the entire evening to show his sister and Liam the infamous Las Vegas strip. The underground malls of the casinos, the nightclubs, the live bands, the gondola rides on the canal. He'd leave out the edgy strip clubs, the members-only sex venues (of which he'd cancelled his membership) and the private poker games. His sister needn't know *that* side of Vegas. "It's your birthday and we have all night."

"My twenty-fifth birthday." She simulated a drum roll on the counter with both hands. She glanced up at Shane with a lopsided grin. "And I'm gonna get in sooo much trouble out here."

"Probably," Shane said. "But you're done here."

She groaned. "Okay, okay."

"He's right." Liam pushed his empty glass away. "We've got all night and we've got our sober tour guide who knows Vegas all too well."

Shane gulped down half of his glass of water. Nope, he wasn't about to explain the endless parties in the penthouse, the half-naked women, the meaningless interludes night after night. He'd lost three hundred thousand dollars and gained four hundred thousand from secret poker games with the wealthy elite. Vegas had allowed him moments of amnesia, to forget the obedient Shane, the Wall Street magic money man who spun millions on his fingers.

The new Shane's life was a stretch from Vegas, from his rowdy personal life, and financially thriving business world. A world long gone.

Sallie gazed around the casino floor; her brown eyes wide. "Thanks for doing this, bro. I know you haven't been here for a few years."

"It's not a problem, Sallie. You're my favorite sister, and it's your birthday."

"I'm your *only* sister." She giggled then squirmed in her jacket. "Is it me, or is it hot in here?"

Liam chuckled. "She's definitely buzzed. We better go."

Shane pushed his half-full glass of water toward Sallie. "Drink that."

She pouted but drank the rest of his water.

Shane signaled to the bartender, a slender woman in a white tank top and tight black jeans, her wheat colored hair tied up in a long ponytail.

She walked over and gave Shane a long, lazy smile, then glanced down at the empty glasses. "Did you need another drink, sweetie?"

"Just closing the tab."

"Would you like anything else?"

Shane recognized the glint in her eyes, promising a wild night of sex and a swift exit in the morning.

The old Shane would've complied, but not the new one.

"I'm good." He retrieved his credit card and handed it to her.

She maintained their silent gaze, allowing him the opportunity to reconsider.

The surrounding machines continued their mantra.

Ping, ping, ping.

Shane gave a pleasant smile, but his eyes flashed a solid "no."

"If you change your mind," she leaned in close, her full cleavage on display, "let me know." She headed to the register.

Liam shoved his shoulder. "What the hell is wrong with you? Did you not catch that I-wanna-go-home-with-you vibe? You're a high school teacher, not a priest."

"I'm not ready."

"It's been six months," Sallie piped in, drawing her raven hair into a loose bun. "You changed yourself, you changed your life, and she didn't want the new you. She was stupid to let you go. I think you've grieved long enough."

His sister called it grieving, but Shane referred to the whole "Heather event" not as the simple death of a relationship, but a full-blown nuclear explosion. Their friends, her clothing, all the furnishings in his apartment, disappeared the night she'd dumped him. Grieving wasn't the word he'd use. He thought of two alternate words. Blistering rage.

Liam stood up. "You need to get back on the bull."

Liam and Shane were best friends since high school, opposites from the day they met that fateful first day in the tenth grade. Liam, with his chocolate skin, hazel eyes and facial hair was doted on by females, invited to every party, and endowed with so much athletic talent, he'd earned a scholarship to USC.

Shane on the other hand, was pale, skinny, reserved, far from the sports scene. He threw himself into his studies and females only paid him attention in their efforts to get closer to Liam. Shane's world transformed after college. He ran five miles a day, vigorously worked out in the gym, and eventually transformed himself into a young man with a tanned, toned body. He'd switched his glasses for contacts and filled his closet with designer suits.

"I agree with Liam. Time to get back on the bull. Shane, are you blocking me out again?"

His sister's voice yanked him to the present. "No. I heard every word you said."

"And what did I ask?"

He faced his sister, her brown eyes challenging him. She folded her arms across her chest, one brow lifted.

"You asked if I was blocking you out again."

"And before that?"

"You didn't *ask* me anything before that."

"Aha! I did say something before that."

"What you said before that was a statement, *not* a question."

Sallie eyed him closely, a staring contest she mostly lost. Today would be no exception. Shane met his sister's fierce glare with a neutral expression. One that said he could go all day with a bland look on his face, his eyes unwavering.

Sallie frowned and averted her gaze. "Damn you, Shane!"

He laughed. "Stop trying so hard."

"Are you a smart-ass with your students too?"

"I'm nicer to them."

Sallie squinted at him, and Shane just smiled. He led them out of the casino and into the garage. Dry, summer heat smothered his lungs.

Liam hung back, walking beside Shane as Sallie strode ahead. "You really okay, man?"

"I'm fine," Shane said.

"Good. You switched it up on everyone, stepped out on your own. Teaching kids, molding young minds. From who you were, to who you are now? Inspiring, man." He slapped Shane on the back. "If she couldn't see that, she wasn't worth it."

"Inspiring? Look at you, Doctor Blackwell. Football scholarship. Med student, now ER doc."

"Are you two done?" Sallie said. "I'd like to go now."

They'd reached the car. Shane pressed the FOB to unlock the doors.

"You still coming to my son's birthday party next Saturday?" Liam slid into the back seat.

"Of course. What kind of godfather would I be if I didn't show up? And what do one-year-olds like anyway?" Shane climbed into the driver's seat and Sallie hopped into the passenger's side.

"Anything they can chew on," Sallie said.

Liam laughed. "She's right."

Grinning, Shane started the engine, the dashboard flickering blue, the radio kicking on a Taylor Swift song.

Liam clicked his seatbelt in place. "And Shane, you gotta bring a date."

"My brother would have to be dating first," Sallie taunted, buckling in. "And he's not."

"That's okay. I've been thinking about it and I've got the solution for that." He dug into his back pocket and retrieved a piece of paper. He unfolded the paper and waved it at Shane. "I created this list just for you. It's gonna help you get your mojo back."

Shane snatched the paper and skimmed the list and read aloud the first task. "*Conquer your fear. Noboru?* You realize Noboru can get me killed?"

"Not if you do it right."

"Really?"

"It's a minor technicality."

"What, or who, is Noboru?" Sallie asked, snatching the paper from Shane. She read over the list. "Oooh, there's some juicy stuff on here."

Shane grabbed it back.

Liam pressed on. "I know what I'm doing. These tasks are all designed to get you back out there and increase your likability with the opposite sex. If you follow my instructions, you'll reach the bottom three items on the list with no problems."

"This is your guaranteed way to get a girl?"

"Guaranteed to get you out of the house. The first step to meeting someone special."

"I'm assuming this is how you got your wife?"

Liam smirked. "Naw, I didn't need any list. I've got skills. My mojo is intact. This is all about you."

Shane handed the paper back to Liam. Only Liam would hatch a half-baked, well intentioned stunt to return Shane to the dating scene. Liam's motto, *go big, win big*. "The last time you thought of something this crazy I was grounded for an entire summer."

"Hey, we were seventeen and I told you to grab Mrs. Grayson's dog so I could sneak over there to see her daughter, Marianne. The damn dog barked at everything. I didn't tell you to run off with it."

"I didn't run off with the dog—the moment I opened the gate to grab her, she escaped."

"See? Not my fault. That was all you. Marianne and I still helped you find her."

"As you should have."

"All that growling and yapping she did when people walked by? She was no dog; that was Satan. Damn little ankle biter."

Shane raised his right hand, the scar near his thumb still evident. "She bit more than ankles and I have the mark to prove it. So, although I appreciate the effort on this list of yours, no thank you. I think my mojo is just fine."

"I'm telling you man. Follow the list, meet the girl of your dreams. You know me."

"Go big, win big," they said simultaneously. Dating again? His stomach squirmed at the notion of another woman worming into his world, into his heart. Shane would let Liam down gently later. No more grand schemes to force him back into society. "We're focusing on Sallie's dreams right now." He eased out of the parking spot, circling the garage, maneuvering down the exit ramp and on to the street. "I'm taking you both to a bar off the strip that makes the best mojitos."

Liam sighed, understanding the conversation was paused for now. "Fine. Let's check out these mojitos."

Sallie clapped her heads excitedly. "Mojitos. Love it."

Shane reveled in the slump of his sister's shoulders, her eyes glazed with a mixture of complete abandon and unbridled glee. Usually Sallie maintained control, minimal excitement, concealing all emotions, just as their mother had raised them. A birthday celebration in Las Vegas loosened his sister's composure; he rarely witnessed this side of Sallie Rawlings.

She stared out the passenger window at the array of red and white blinking lights. Fully lit hotels towered over them, casinos flashing neon signs, people clustered on the sidewalk. "This is so cool."

"Yeah it is."

Liam leaned forward in his seat. "Happy birthday, Sallie."

"Happy birthday, little sis."

"Thanks, guys."

Shane suddenly blinked at the blinding light ahead.

Headlights.

A red pickup truck had jumped the yellow line.

Time slowed, seconds like minutes. Sallie screamed and Shane instinctively covered his sister's torso with his right arm like a man-made seatbelt. Panic rose in his throat; fear scraped his insides. He shoved the emotions aside, focused on the two most important people in the car and tried swerving to the left, but it was too late. Both vehicles collided head on.

Metal crumpled, Shane's face smashed into the airbag, and glass shattered, particles peppering his face. He jerked forward against the seatbelt as the car spun, rammed into a second vehicle, and catapulted into the air, flipping repeatedly. Heather's final words rushed through him.

I've found someone better than you.

He jolted against the seatbelt and tried to look at his sister. Her arms dangled over her head as the vehicle wound upside down. Her eyes were closed, her head swaying as the car then rolled upright. Like floating, they hadn't reached the ground yet. Liam grunted in the back seat then gave a small moan. The pressure on Shane's chest deepened.

He thought of Liam, the mischief in his eyes often getting them both in trouble as teens. He saw Sallie's smile, that kid-like wonder as she stared out the window. An emotional freedom she hadn't experienced in twenty-five years. All of it about to be erased because some idiot literally crossed the line.

Shane gasped for air, the vice like grip on his chest tightening as the car crashed against something hard mid-air then slammed into the ground.

Everything went black.

Two

Ten months later...

HE RV'S AIR CONDITIONER HUMMED LOUDLY, the blast of cold air protecting Emma Jacobs from the humid Florida heat. The searing orange glow of the setting sun blanketed the interior of the RV. With summer long gone and the winter holidays a fading memory, Emma had looked forward to the new year. A chance to reinvent herself, to forgive, and allow, second chances.

She gazed at the dozen yellow roses gathered in the glass vase in the middle of the small table and sighed heavily. Six weeks into the new year and now a debacle was splashed all over social media and the tabloids for the world to see.

Seated at the compact dining booth of her trailer, her temporary home for the last month, she lowered her gaze to the dozen text messages on her cell phone, scrolling slowly through each one. All came from the same man, Jordyn Mars, action movie star extraordinaire.

Things will be different.
I don't want anyone else but you.
Please, give me, give us, another chance.
Meet me for dinner tonight. At the house. We can talk through this.

She'd imagined dozens of ways to spend Valentine's Day.

Dining by candlelight. Slow dancing barefoot on the beach under the moonlit sky, crashing waves the only music. She would've enjoyed a relaxing day at the spa for two. Or watching a movie together at the drive-in, a bucket of popcorn in hand.

Not this.

Her personal assistant, Luci Holt, held up a tabloid with both hands, the photo plastered on the cover making it clear that any chance of reconciliation was effectively killed. "Can I assume this means you two are *not* getting back together?"

Wearing the Armani black button shirt Emma bought for his birthday and a pair of smoky gray slacks, Jordyn graced the cover of the tabloid. He leaned against the driver's side door of his black Mercedes, a woman standing between his legs in a thin striped black and white dress, the fabric tight as skin. Her waist, a size four, her bottom two firm cantaloupes, her breasts full, barely contained by the plunging neckline, she oozed sex appeal and slutty availability. Smooth, slender legs stood firm on cherry red stilettos and her sleek, dark brown hair draped down her back, providing the perfect picture for one of those shampoo commercials.

An uninvited photographer had snuck in and gotten closer to Jordyn, into Emma's front yard in a place that should've been firmly private, and she wondered at the lack of security. Nobody should've

been able to get past the tall, black wrought-iron fence lined with four-foot high bushes and climbing hydrangea winding across the gated wood door entrance. The dedicated photographer had likely earned a hefty paycheck for such a prized image.

The woman's mouth fused with Jordyn's lips in a fiery kiss. She'd laced her fingers together at the back of his bald head. Jordyn's large hands squeezed her ass.

Emma latched onto the single word destined to change her life. Printed in the largest font she'd ever seen, in gleaming white letters above Jordyn's illicit make-out scene.

Caught!

Jordyn had mistakenly assumed his privacy remained intact in the brick driveway of the five-thousand-square foot Hollywood Hills mansion he shared with Emma.

Luci studied the photo, her gaze shifting back to Emma. "Sorry, Emma. I know he was trying to win you back." She glanced at the yellow roses. "Shall I toss these?"

After his last dalliance, Jordyn begged for a second chance and Emma demanded a trial separation. Now this. His indiscretion splashed all over the tabloids on the most romantic day of the year. The public had been kept in the dark by his initial infidelity. Three months apart, three months of roses, three months of heartfelt cards and sentimental texts to win her back, gain her trust, and restore their year-long relationship.

The air conditioner droned softly, the cool breeze sweeping away the early evening humidity. Goosebumps prickled her flesh, and she shivered, nausea rolling over her in waves. The new scandal would become sound bites for entertainment news and late-night television. Everyone scrutinizing her next move.

She, one of America's celebrated actresses, was romantically attached to the gorgeous, macho, monogamously challenged Jordyn Mars.

Take him back or kick him out?

"What are you thinking right now?" Luci asked.

"I'm an idiot." Emma shoved the vase aside. "This is what he calls working things out?"

"Counseling failed?"

"He attended one session then made excuses why he couldn't make the others. Why did I even waste my time?"

"You thought he changed."

Emma turned toward the trailer's window, watching as the sun set across the Florida skyline. Not that she hadn't contemplated dating again. Every man looking her way reminded her of Jordyn. That swaggering smile, those charming eyes.

"You two ever have a deep conversation?"

"You mean talk about his childhood and mine? Our wants and dreams, stuff like that?"

Luci nodded.

"No." She and Jordyn attended film premieres, exclusive parties, networking events. Emma scrambled to remember a conversation with him that didn't involve the entertainment industry. Her brain produced images of her asking Jordyn about his life before Hollywood. "I tried, but he was always vague or blew it off. I just thought he was sensitive about it. I guess he needed a stepping stool for his career, not a real girlfriend." She blinked back tears and heaved in a shaky breath. "I can't believe this is really happening."

Hollywood's favorite couple. Emma, the respected actress beginning her twelfth major motion picture, and Jordyn Mars, the action hero movie star. Jordyn said from the start their pairing was beneficial. Emma established legitimacy for him. A driven woman, she remembered names and faces, she networked. Their union produced a movie for him and an opportunity to direct. His latest movie, *Rush Kill,* premiered next week.

"I couldn't even see I was being played." She hunched over and tapped her forehead on the table three times. "Stupid, stupid, stupid." She choked back the sobs in his throat. Duped by a con artist and the whole world watching.

"You were willing to go to counseling, to forgive him. It takes a strong person to do that."

"He begged for a second chance, crying and apologizing, practically on his hands and knees."

"He's an actor."

Emma looked up at Luci. "You're right. Greatest performance ever." Luci gently rubbed her back and Emma closed her eyes. "You know what? There's no such thing as 'the one.' It's all crap."

Luci removed her hand from Emma's back. "You were good to him and he didn't deserve it."

"No, he didn't."

"Emma, all of this will pass. The press, Jordyn, this whole incident. And one day some guy will come along who will be perfect for you."

"No such thing."

"It exists."

"It's a fairytale. And I need to start thinking about real life." Emma sat up as several tears trickled down her face. She wiped her moist cheeks with the heels of her hands.

Luci sighed. "The press is gonna smother the hell out of you."

"I know." Staring out the window again, Emma noticed people hustling past her trailer window on their way to the parking lot. The production staff hauled away parts of the set, caterers carried boxes of uneaten food, wardrobe people rolled racks of clothes toward white vans behind her trailer.

Later, everyone would attend the wrap-up party. Emma normally made brief appearances at the wrap up parties but stared at the image of the tabloid cover and reconsidered.

Her phone buzzed, vibrating the tabletop. She didn't bother to look at it.

"Emma?" Luci said quietly.

Her phone buzzed again, and she glanced at the screen.

Jordyn. She hoped he'd packed up his clothes, gathered the few belongings he'd brought into their relationship, and disappeared.

She snatched up her phone and skimmed Jordyn's five new text messages.

This is silly.

Don't believe the public.

You're the only one I want.

I refuse to give up on us.

Please, come home.

Home? She wanted him out of her home. The house she'd paid for that he'd moved into. Out, out, out. Emma stood up, charged to the back of her trailer and grabbed her jacket off the bed. Jordyn had dug in, prepared for a confrontation. Emma didn't have the willpower for the ensuing showdown.

"I need to figure this out."

"What do you need me to do?" Luci grabbed the notepad from her back pocket.

"I'll have to figure out how to handle this mess with Jordyn, the press and the fans. But not right now."

"You need a break? I'm with you."

"Call Suzanne. Tell her to make a quick statement to the press that Jordyn and I have been separated for months."

Luci scribbled on her notepad. "Nothing about remaining close friends?"

Emma slipped into her jacket. "Hell no." The time had come for a new direction, not back to a house inhabited by Jordyn and surrounded by reporters, anxious for a snapshot of a distraught Emma. "It's time for a little trip away from everyone."

"Where we goin'? Somewhere tropical?"

"Not even close. We need a hideout and I've got something in mind."

CHAPTER

Three

Lying on his back, Shane opened his eyes. He stared-up at the ceiling, the room enveloped in darkness. His alarm chimed loudly, and he reached over with one hand shutting it off. Daylight wouldn't be for another two hours.

He blinked a few times, rested his arms at his side, wondered what life might've been had he chosen a different birthday venue for his little sister, Sallie.

Skiing in Lake Tahoe.

Eating dinner in a swanky, five-star San Francisco restaurant.

Anything but Las Vegas.

He sighed.

Wall Street Shane had vanished, but after Vegas, the new Shane disappeared as well. Only the quiet man remained. No more laughter, no jokes, no smiles.

As it should be.

And Sallie still wanted him at her engagement party.

Shane heaved in a long breath, sat upright, and flicked on the bedside lamp. No matter how he felt about being stuffed in a room filled with mostly strangers, Sallie needed him, and he owed her.

He jumped out of bed and started the day with his usual routine. Five miles on the treadmill, a hot shower, and a bowl of oatmeal with a half glass of orange juice. Seated at the end of the dining room table, he ate slowly, thinking about Sallie's recovery. She'd lost her left foot. Liam had lost much more.

Shane released another exasperated breath.

Did she really need him at this party?

After breakfast, he skimmed through his closet, picked out a brown plaid button shirt and tan Dockers. He brushed his teeth, combed his hair, hoping his cell phone would ring and Sallie would absolve him of his responsibility to appear.

His phone sat silent.

A bottle of Seven-Up in hand, he returned to the table, eased into the head chair, and graded several quizzes from his students. His red pen struck the pages more times than he'd like.

What did his class not understand about Shakespeare? They hadn't even begun Romeo and Juliet, and if these tests were any indication, the next lesson would be a disaster.

By noon, Shane locked up his condo and trudged downstairs.

His sister hadn't called.

He stopped at the wall of mailboxes at the bottom of the stairs and retrieved his mail, a collection of bills and sales papers. One envelope stood out from the stack. Not a bill and no return address. Shane opened the envelope. He pulled out a picture of him and Liam, standing in the halls of their high school, Liam with that famous smile that always captured the ladies. Shane had tried to smile, but came across with a quirky, awkward grin. He recognized the photo from their high school yearbook.

Shane flipped the photo over, hoping to find a handwritten message, anything to understand why this had been sent to him. The back of the photo was blank.

He pulled a folded piece of paper and an index card from the envelope. He unfolded the lined paper, revealing a letter neatly written.

Dear Shane,

You've been through so much and in the process, you've locked yourself away, something Liam never wanted. You are now being challenged to finish Liam's list, to rediscover the positive parts of the old Shane. This is not a prank, but a request from a concerned citizen who cared for Liam as much as you did. You'll receive one card a week. Complete eleven tasks per Liam's wish and when you're done, I'll reveal who I am (it's not who you think). Get started!

Sincerely, the Last Person You'd Suspect.

Shane read and reread the letter.

Sincerely, the Last Person You'd Suspect? Who the hell was that?

It had to be Liam's wife, Amari. Maybe she'd found the list. Or a hard push from his sister Sallie. She'd known about the list. He glanced up at the street, beyond the glass door. Was he being watched?

Shane remembered Liam's list, a ten-step plan to immerse Shane back into society and hopefully win the heart of a woman along the way. A guaranteed plan to get his "mojo" back. At the time Shane had scanned the list and scoffed at the idea. Amari and Sallie couldn't possibly conjure up something this elaborate, knowing that even the mention of Liam's name aloud caused his throat to swell, his eyes to burn with fury. At fate. At himself. Whoever had done this couldn't possibly know what was on that list—hell, even Shane could only remember a few.

He looked at the index card. "Task One" was printed on the front. He flipped the card over and read the back.

Conquer your fear (Noboru).

The first item on Liam's original list. Shane realized whoever had done this knew exactly what they were doing.

———

"Sallie, what is this?" Shane slid the envelope toward his sister who was seated next to him.

They were on the second floor of Nazini's, an Italian restaurant on Bainbridge Island roughly ten miles from Seattle. Large windows offered a crisp, clean view of Puget Sound. Neatly arranged fruit, sliced meats, sushi rolls, and cream puffs covered platters on the white table-cloth-covered buffet table. Waiters stood at opposite ends of the table in cherry red button shirts and black pants, ready to replenish the diminishing food supply. Additional waiters filtered through the crowd of family members, refilling champagne flutes.

Shane had chosen a table near the window, in the corner, away from the Rawlings clan, and his soon to be brother-in-law's relatives. Various conversations drummed through the dining area, background noise which Shane struggled to ignore.

"What is what?" Sallie picked up the envelope and opened it. She pulled out the letter, the picture, and the index card. She stared at the picture then glanced up at Shane. "What is this?"

"That's what I'm asking you. Someone sent that to me by mail, no return address, just this challenge for me to finish Liam's list. Did you do this?"

Sallie read the letter and slowly shook her head. "It's not me."

"What about Amari?"

"I don't know, maybe."

"Can you call and ask?"

Sallie stared at him. "You haven't talked to Amari in months. Why don't you call her?"

He couldn't look Liam's wife in the eyes, hear her voice, knowing he'd been the cause of something that shredded both their lives. "Sallie, please." He hated the faint whine in his voice.

She slipped the contents back into the envelope. "Fine, I'll ask her. But honestly, I think you should do what it says. Finish the list."

"What?"

"He wouldn't have wanted you living like this. Closed off, bitter, angry."

Shane didn't respond.

"I miss Liam every day. But I miss my brother too, and I want my brother back. The one with the wisecracks, who knew how to laugh."

"He died," Shane snapped.

"No," Sallie shot back. "*Liam* died."

Liam. Their childhood friendship. The adult milestones. The tragedy that followed. Liam hadn't survived Las Vegas. "I don't want to talk about it, Sallie."

"I know you didn't go to the funeral but—"

"I said I don't want to talk about it."

"Have you been to the gravesite?"

Shane didn't answer. He hadn't.

She heaved in a long breath. "Not talking about it is like not dealing with it. You'll never heal unless you deal with this."

"You're relentless."

"I'm your sister and I want what's best for you. If this is what Liam wanted, why not do it?"

"Enough," Shane said sharply. He sighed heavily. Sallie didn't deserve his simmering anger; she deserved only happiness for her upcoming nuptials. He hadn't believed she'd ever settle down. He looked across the room at his future brother-in-law, Patrick, chatting among a small number of male cousins. The men were around the same age, early to mid-thirties, all with careers in corporate environments. Stockbrokers. Investment bankers. Financial consultants. He let out a weary sigh. "I'm sorry. This is your day, your moment. I'm not going to ruin that with my issues. Let's talk about something else?"

Sallie stared hard at him; the conversation parked for the moment but far from finished.

Shane shifted in his chair and glanced around the room. Some of the faces he recognized, most he didn't. "I shouldn't even be here."

"It's my engagement party. My older brother has to be here. I'm wearing a dress and everything. And you know how I feel about that."

He analyzed her soft yellow sundress, her raven hair sweeping across her bare shoulders. He remembered his baby sister in jeans, sweaters and riding boots. "That is surprising." She'd enjoyed digging in the dirt and catching bugs far more than playing dress up with the neighborhood girls. He lowered his eyes to her sandaled foot. Sallie wiggled the toes of her right foot, her left foot replaced by a titanium prosthetic. A stark reminder of their Las Vegas collision nearly a year ago. He shook away the memories, forced his brain to the present. "I know how much you hate dresses. You know you're wearing one to the wedding, right?"

Sallie narrowed her eyes at him and pushed a plate of Bavarian cream puffs in his direction. "Don't think I didn't try to get Mom to agree to a pants suit instead. Something glittery and white. A compromise. Of course, I lost that battle."

"You've got a younger brother too." Shane said as he jerked his thumb over his shoulder at their brother Mercer. He was discussing the latest healthcare technology with their Uncle Phil. Mercer became the doctor in the family. Their parents had been so proud, thankful Shane's so-called "foolish" decisions hadn't rubbed off on his younger brother.

Sallie glanced at Mercer, then back at Shane. "And I love you both, very much." She picked up his uneaten cream puff.

Shane huffed with a half-smile. "So, you say." He nudged the plate aside. "I should go."

"No. Stay. How often do I get to see you?"

"Every holiday and whenever Mom forces me over."

"Exactly. I should be so grateful."

"You know I don't mean it like that." He fumbled with his fingers uncertain what to say. Isolation comforted him and he basked in the silence. "It's just hard for me to be around people. You know things haven't been the same since—"

Sallie covered his mouth with her hand. "It's time to join the living now." She studied his plaid button shirt and tan dockers. "These clothes aren't helping."

Shane stretched his arms out. "There's nothing wrong with my clothes. I look fine."

"I want you to look hot. Women like hot and you need to get laid."

"What?" His eyes widened. Sex talk with his sister? An absolute no.

"You're so damn grumpy. When's the last time you had some?"

"Had some what?" Shane's self-imposed exile meant his social interaction nosedived. "Do I really need to say it?"

"Is this conversation really necessary?"

"Can we just get rid of the nerdy schoolteacher look?" Sallie plucked at the collar of his shirt. "You've been pushing that for two years now."

Shane groaned. "And it works for me."

"Yeah, it screams 'hi-ladies-I-have-issues.'"

"And what does your look say?"

"I'm gorgeous and happy. What happened to all those designer clothes you used to wear? Calvin Klein, Kenneth Cole. Where are they at?"

"Where they belong. At the back of my closet."

"You know you could wear those after work. On a date. At the bar?"

"If I were trying to date, which I'm not. And I'm not big on bars anymore."

"Whatever." Sallie rolled her eyes. "At least shave." She gazed to the group of men huddled near the exit. "Uh-oh. Patrick's going to come over here at some point and ask you to watch a mixed martial arts fight at your place. You know, guy stuff."

He frowned. "I don't want the guys coming over."

She tapped his chest with one palm, pouting, mock empathy creasing the corner of her eyes. "Then you shouldn't have bought a sixty-inch flat screen TV."

The *old* Shane purchased the massive television, a present to himself at the time for raking in several million dollars for his clients in one day. Now he rarely used the damn thing.

"So, what do we have here?" Patrick's best man, Dorian Verselle, slid into a seat across from Shane and Sallie.

Dorian had the beach-boy-next-door good looks. Curly blonde hair, blue eyes, arms and legs bulging, a muscled chest stretched beneath a shirt one size too small for his frame. His cocky grin did not, Shane noticed, melt Sallie into gooey puddles of admiration. She shuddered at the sight of him and rolled her eyes. "What do you want, Dorian?"

Dorian leaned back in his chair, feigning offense. "Why wouldn't I just wanna come over and hang out with my best friend's future wife?"

"Why *would* you hang out with your best friend's future wife?" Sallie countered.

Dorian nodded at Shane as if the two shared a secret. "Shane, my man."

Shane stared grimly at the man across the table from him. He didn't care much for Dorian, a man with a high-performance silver sports car and fast women. Dorian thrived on attention and craved the status of the wealthy. Pretty similar, unfortunately, to the old Shane Rawlings. He was grateful Sallie had fallen hard for Dorian's best friend instead. Patrick was a far better choice, and a better man, than Dorian could ever hope to be.

"There's a huge pay-per-view mixed martial arts fight coming up. What do you think about a little soiree at your place with the fellas? We'll bring the beer."

Anxiety rushed over him at the prospect of a group of people in his condo, all drinking. Asking questions, making conversation, paying attention to him as the host. "I don't—"

"Want you guys to bring too much beer over," Sallie said. "Patrick's gonna be there, right?"

Dorian nodded. "Yeah, of course."

"Good." Sallie put her arm around Shane's shoulder and squeezed. "Great bonding time between my future husband and my brother, don't you think?"

"I guess so," Dorian said, studying them.

Shane opened his mouth to lecture his sister. He didn't want a bunch of people in his place, and he sure as hell didn't want Dorian, but Sallie's pleading eyes unraveled his firm no. "Okay," he said at last. "But something small, not a lot of people."

Dorian held his hands up. "Just a few guys and Patrick." His cell phone rang, and he answered, holding it close against his ear. He rose from the chair, gave Shane and Sallie a backhanded goodbye and headed to the exit.

Shane pointed at Dorian's empty chair. "The last time you talked me into letting those two over, things didn't go so well"

"I know Dorian gets a little out of control sometimes."

"He had sex with his date in my closet and threw up on my kitchen floor."

"Let's not dwell on that. Patrick had a talk with him. It won't happen again."

"Damn right it won't."

"Besides, you've got that list to work on."

"You really want me to complete this list?"

"Absolutely." Sallie patted him on the leg. "So, I suggest you get started big brother."

CHAPTER

Four

*E*MMA SAT ON THE BRICK PORCH OF THE COLO-
nial one-story home she'd rented, cradling a steaming cup of
tea with both hands. She welcomed the warmth steaming her face,
raised the ceramic mug to her mouth and sipped. Lowering the mug,
she gazed around the expansive front yard. Morning light filtered
through the branches of towering Douglas Firs and sunlight spilled
across the grass. A eucalyptus tree anchored one side of the neatly
trimmed and vibrantly green lawn. A gravel driveway led to the garage
on the side of the house. Boxlike bushes lined the porch. A dozen
eucalyptus trees flanked the street twenty yards away, providing a
veil of privacy.

The nearest neighbor lived two miles away. Emma had asked for
privacy and found it. Bainbridge Island, in the heart of the Pacific
northwest, less than an hour from Seattle, Washington.

Her phone buzzed. She slid it from her jean pocket, stared at the screen, and answered.

"Hello, Suzanne," she said.

"Hello, my favorite client."

Emma snorted. Suzanne had at least a dozen high profile actors and actresses on her roster. She called them all her favorites.

"So, you made it?"

"Yes, thank you." Emma sipped her tea. No paparazzi skulking behind the massive tree trunks. No suspicious vehicles camped out across the street from the house. She and Luci had each packed one carryon bag, one suitcase, and hopped on the last flight to Seattle. A vehicle had already been rented through a third party and was waiting in the airport parking garage. They hopped a ferry to Bainbridge Island. Upon arrival, they got into the rental car and drove through a series of winding roads with immense, clustered trees shielding the sunlight until they reached a clearing overlooking Puget Sound. A summer house Suzanne called "Project Vanish."

"No one knows about that place," Suzanne said.

"It's beautiful," Emma said. "And so serene. Thank you, Suzanne, for arranging this."

"It better be for what you're paying, and the strings I had to pull. The guy I hired is very discreet and was able to procure the house from a friend of a friend sort of thing."

"And no one's going to find out?"

"The house, the car, none of it is in yours, Luci's, or my name. The man I used is damn good at what he does, and he gets paid well because of it. So, if he says no one knows about that place, no one knows."

The press didn't know her whereabouts now, but eventually they would. Someone always talked. She remained grateful for the current hideaway. "Well, thank you Suzanne."

"You're welcome." Suzanne sounded pleased with herself. "And don't look at this as such a bad thing. Remember—"

"There is no such thing as bad publicity," Emma said.

"Good girl. I'll check on you in a few days. Smooches."

And just like that, Suzanne hung up.

Emma tucked her phone into her pocket, stood up and stared up at the clear azure sky, smiling at the birds chirping overhead. She finished her tea and went inside.

The interior of the colonial home boasted three bedrooms, an office, family room, formal dining area, and gourmet kitchen. Hardwood floors, area rugs, and craftsman style furniture in earthy brown shades gave the home a warm, inviting appeal.

Emma stood in front of the refrigerator, eyeing an old plastic bottle of Italian dressing and a half-filled jar of grape jelly. She rustled through the kitchen cabinets, searching for anything edible. Finding the cabinets barren, she placed both hands on her hips. First order of business, buy groceries.

Emma took the car keys from the counter and headed for the door. She'd driven by a small market ten miles down the road the previous night. She'd start there.

She swung open the driver's side door and hesitated. Luci usually did the grocery shopping, as Emma's overbooked scheduled didn't allow for these normal, everyday tasks. Shopping at the town market would've been an easier feat for Luci, but she was asleep in their vacation hideaway. Entangled in eight-hundred-thread-count sheets and beneath a down comforter so fluffy she might float up to the ceiling, Luci wasn't going anywhere.

The scenic drive lasted ten minutes before Emma saw the marketplace sign. She parked and reached for the sunglasses on the passenger seat of the car. She found her black beanie on the back seat and tugged it over her head. Emma flipped the visor down, studying her

reflection in the overhead mirror. She didn't look like a movie star, just an ordinary newcomer. No one would notice her, as long as she kept her head down and focused on the mission.

Food.

The small grocery store contained the usual assortment of boxed and canned goods. Cold items lined the freezers along the side and back walls. Two cash registers at the front of the shop. Emma grabbed a black basket and perused the first narrow aisle filled with cereal items and condiments. She paused at the array of cereal boxes, picking up her favorite sugar-coated cereal, and dropped it into the basket. The door chimed, signaling new customers. Emma filled her basket and stood in line at the front counter. The old lady in front of her slowly counted out every dime and nickel to pay her bill.

Emma inhaled a long breath and scanned the shop again. A teenage couple argued outside the store's front window. The boy appeared to be sixteen, his scruffy brown hair pushed upwards away from his forehead. He was scrawny, wearing a black leather jacket, black shirt and dark blue jeans. His brows furrowed together as he listened to the girl standing in front of him.

The girl appeared to be the same age, sixteen, but she didn't match him, not with her sun kissed, golden locks falling to her shoulders. An oversized gray sweater hung limply off her thin frame. The fierce movements of her mouth indicated an unpleasant rant. She waved her arms, emphasizing her disagreement. Lips clamped together, eyebrows raised, the girl hesitated and took a backwards step.

The boy opened his mouth to talk, but the girl seized the silence, cutting off whatever he intended to say. She spoke too fast for an outsider to read lips.

Emma huffed at the dramatics, at the heightened performance of two teens still oblivious to the rest of the world. "How can anyone that young be so angry?"

"I see it all the time," a male voice said from behind her.

Emma glanced back and saw a man holding a six-pack of Seven-Up. At least six feet tall, his broad shoulders and solid build filled his navy blue, plaid button collar shirt and tan Dockers. The smell of cologne and soap tickled her nostrils. Clean shaven, with trimmed, damp black hair, his green eyes blazed back at her.

Emma blinked and darted her gaze back to the front window. Embarrassed by her ogling, she cleared her throat and tried to sound casual. "I wonder what she's saying."

"I hate you." The man emphasized in a high-pitched voice clearly meant to sound like the girl outside. "I never wanna see you again."

Emma chuckled.

The boy finally got the chance to speak and pitched his explanation.

Emma grinned and glanced back at the man. "We don't have to do this," she said, her voice as deep as she could make it sound, coming from a sixteen-year-old boy.

"I saw you talking to Amber."

"She means nothing."

"You just wanna be around your stupid friends all day."

Emma stifled a laugh. "They're immature, they don't understand. You're everything to me. I can't study, I can't *think* without you near me."

"Really?" the man asked in a crooning tone.

The boy focused on the girl's face. He rattled on, grasping her hand, pleading. Emma could only imagine. What did he want? Forgiveness? A second chance? To just be friends?

"There will never be anyone else like you. Ever," Emma said. "I love you, Becky." Maybe her name was Agnes or Naomi, but to Emma the girl looked more like a "Becky."

Becky hesitated, but did not remove her hand from the boy's grasp. Her cheeks lifted upward in a tiny smile.

"I love you sooooo much," the man said, his voice still lathered in a heightened female twang.

Emma didn't know the guy, but his firm declaration made her a believer.

The girl and boy stepped away from the window and strolled across the street, holding hands and smiling at one another as though their spat had never happened.

Emma shook her head. "Young love. Unbelievable."

"Tell me about it," he said and nodded. "I get to see that every day."

Emma stared at him, confused.

"I teach at the high school." He extended his free hand to Emma. "I'm Shane."

She accepted his handshake. "Emma."

The petite older woman in front of Emma finally finished paying her bill. Emma stepped forward and placed her groceries on the counter. The cashier rang each item. Emma looked outside, at the place where the two young lovers once stood. They reminded her of Jordyn, how charming he'd been in the beginning, treating her as if she were the only person in the world, as though no other woman, no other life existed. Except there'd been many other women and a whole other world that Jordyn yearned for, and one which Emma distanced herself from. Lavish, late-night parties, nightclub adventures, and hobnobbing with the wealthy elite.

"Everything seems so over the top when you're that age," she said absently.

"Completely over the top," he said. "And I've seen those two before, they do this all the time."

"They have no idea." Emma sighed.

"What?" Shane adjusted the six pack in his hand. "You don't believe in true love?"

She grunted.

The cashier rang the last item, and the machine displayed Emma's total in green digital numbers. "Twenty-eight ten."

Instantly Emma realized the one item she'd forgotten to grab on her way out the door.

Her purse.

Still sitting on the kitchen table.

She shoved her hands in her back pocket hoping to find a twenty-dollar bill.

Nothing.

"Oh no." She tried the other pocket.

More nothing.

"Everything okay?" Shane asked as Emma checked her front jean pockets and back pockets once more.

She looked up at him, thankful the shame and embarrassment on her face was hidden behind her bumblebee sunglasses. She gulped and flopped her hands to her sides. "I left my purse at home."

The cashier narrowed his eyes at her, ready to scold. Two people stood in line behind Shane. One fidgeted anxiously, the other swayed back and forth peering at the cashier.

She opened her mouth to apologize, for having to return later to pay for the food in her basket.

"Here, Tim," Shane said, sliding his six-pack of soda onto the counter and handed the cashier two twenty-dollar bills. "Put it all together."

Tim accepted the cash, the register pinged, and he shoved the money into the open drawer. He handed the change to Shane but shot Emma a disapproving look. Tim bagged the groceries and Shane hoisted both bags in his arms, then stepped aside allowing Emma to exit the store first.

"Why did you do that?"

"Do what? Pay for your groceries?"

His voice had deepened, a sexy velvety baritone, awakening every nerve ending within her. She tried to block the tingling sensations skipping across her skin. Hormones and lust; a lethal combination. One Emma would not entertain.

"I appreciate what you did, but it wasn't necessary."

He lifted up the corner of his lips in an inquisitive smile. "You're not from around here."

"Not even close." Emma stalked to her rental car. Like another Jordyn, Shane had swooped in with his freshly showered scent and damp raven hair, his emerald eyes just as curious about her as she was about him. Was their conversation in the store friendly banter or an opening for Shane to sway her defenses?

His soapy fragrance tickled her nose, igniting other parts of her body she'd thought long dead. Her stomach fluttered and her heart thudded dully.

"I didn't need rescuing. Especially from some attractive guy with a killer smile and those damn, distracting green eyes. I'm not falling for it."

"You find me attractive?"

"Are you even listening to me?"

"Only the parts that don't sound crazy."

"I'm not crazy, I'm pissed off." She snatched the bags from him, and he watched her, bemused, as she struggled to balance both bags within her grasp.

"Are you okay?"

"Don't I look okay?" she snapped. *No, I'm not. All I can think of is Jordyn's face. His unassuming smile. How special he said I was. Lies.* "So how can I reach you to pay you back?"

"Don't worry about it. It's on the house."

"What is it that you want?"

"I don't want anything."

"You don't want me to pay you back? That makes no sense. Everyone wants something." Her mother also taught her that invaluable lesson. "And guys want a piece of everything. No matter who they step on."

"That's a huge generalization. You don't even know me." Shane held her gaze.

She gulped at the intensity in his eyes but kept her voice firm. "I don't need to. You're a man, it's not that difficult."

"Do you always insult people trying to help you?"

They stood in the exact spot as the arguing teenage couple.

Emma jerked open the passenger car door, almost dropped the bags, then steadied herself and shoved the bags in the front seat. Jordyn didn't buy groceries, didn't buy opera tickets, he rarely bought anything. Emma had been so eager to please him; she'd failed to see the con. A year of her life and money wasted on a man sneaking around with other women. Never again. She slammed the passenger door shut and marched around to the other side.

Shane pointed at the bags. "You know, my—"

"Whatever it is, I don't wanna know. I'm not even like this. I don't normally insult people because I'm reliable, friendly Emma. The one who fully supports your career growth and can be the perfect trophy girlfriend when required. I'm not confrontational. I do whatever I'm asked. Wouldn't that make me an awesome girlfriend?"

"What?"

"Noooo. It makes me gullible and silly. I've embarrassed myself in front of the whole world and now you."

"I don't understand."

"Nothing to understand, Shane. You're good-looking."

"Back to that again."

"You're funny too, but you're not good for me."

"*Are* we in a relationship?"

"Thank you for helping me, I'm leaving now."

"But," he looked down at the bags. "You have—"

"Nothing more to say to me." She slid into the driver's seat. "Reliable, friendly, gullible Emma has left the building." She yanked the door shut, revved the engine and sped away.

CHAPTER

Five

"OKAY, SO WHAT DID YOU DO?" LUCI ASKED EMMA later that afternoon. She snuggled into the corner of the oversized couch, frowning as she waited for Emma's answer.

Emma felt guilty and shifted at the end of the couch. She faced the forty-inch flat screen television, concentrating on the ending credits rolling up the screen. She struggled to focus on the words, the piercing gaze of Shane's emerald eyes haunting her.

Luci raised her feet up onto the couch and sat cross-legged. "Spill."

Emma leaned her head back and looked up at the ceiling. She winced at her harsh tone, remembering how Shane had held her grocery bags and gazed at her in pure wonder. "I went to the store this morning to buy groceries."

"You went to the store? I guess there's a first time for everything."

"Very funny. There was this guy there."

"Oooh, okay. Keep going."

Emma recognized Luci's did-Emma-meet-a-new-man yet tone. She playfully tossed the pillow at her. "Don't say it like that. This isn't a dirty story."

"So, you didn't have hot sex in the storage room with some guy you just met?" Luci reached for the red plastic bowl of popcorn on the coffee table and put it on her lap. "Not that I've done that before or anything." She averted her eyes with a wide smile.

Emma laughed. "You're sooo bad. I don't think sex with a strange man is going to help my current situation."

Luci pointed a finger at her. "It's great therapy. Get what you want from them and get out."

"Um, how many times have I said I don't get down like that. I got to the store and forgot to bring money. I was anxious to get outta there before a crowd formed." She cleared her throat, regret coloring her voice. "I was sorta mean to him."

"Some guy at the store? You? Mean?" Luci inched closer to Emma, her eyes filled with a thousand questions Emma suddenly didn't want to answer. "Do tell."

"I took his Seven-Up." The six pack of soda sat on the kitchen counter where Emma had emptied the bags. Shane purchased her groceries and didn't even ask for a thank you. Who was that woman on the curb spewing insults at a stranger?

"You stole his Seven-Up?"

Emma absorbed the scathing look on Luci's face. She deserved it. "I was horrible."

"Hmmph." Luci picked up the remote control and pressed the stop button. "You apologized to him, right?"

"I kinda drove off first?" Emma dug into the popcorn bowl and popped the morsels into her mouth. "I had every intention of apologizing."

"And yet, you didn't."

"He paid for my groceries and I yelled at him like I was breaking up with someone. I kept seeing Jordyn and his stupid tabloid picture in my head. It made me mad just thinking about it again."

Luci scooped up a handful of popcorn. "He must've been cute."

"He tried to tell me the whole time I had his six pack of soda. And what did I do?" Emma grabbed one of the couch's toss pillows. "Drive off!" She pressed the pillow over her face and groaned into the cushiony fabric.

"Did he recognize you?"

"I wore the beanie and shades. I kept them on the whole time."

Luci let out a sigh of relief. "So, you were furious with him because he was cute, and you were attracted to him?"

Emma dropped the pillow. "I never said he was cute." Sexy. Gorgeous. Mind blowing. She could name a dozen more adjectives to describe Shane's killer smile, that clean-shaven face, and those intense green eyes.

"You never said he wasn't. What does this guy look like?"

"Black hair, green eyes, fit body. He smelled amazing."

"You should've jumped him."

"I've already explained how that's a bad idea. I might play some self-assured, sexy hero on screen, but in real life—" She shook her head. "I'm clumsy and awkward when it comes to stuff like that."

"What about sex with Jordyn?"

"It was nice."

"Nice?" Luci arched a brow. "It should be roll-your-eyes-back, body-tingling-when-you just-think-about-it kinda sex. You've never had that?"

"I guess not."

"You poor girl."

Emma threw the pillow at her. "Whatever. This isn't even up for discussion. He's some guy I met. And even if I ever considered someone like him, I couldn't."

"What? Why not?"

"We don't move in the same circles. He's not in the industry, and we're not the same color."

"Not the same color? What is he, white?"

Emma didn't answer.

"Does that bother you?"

"No, but I know people that would be bothered by it. There'd be too many complications."

"Since when did Emma Jacobs start worrying about what other people think? You battle your Mom practically every day because you won't do what she says. I thought we're out here because you wanted to clear your head about how *you* feel and what *you* wanna do? Without the outside world. And since when did a man need to be in the same Hollywood circles as you? How'd that work out last time?"

Ouch. Luci was right. It hadn't boded well in the past. Emma had only dated two other men before Jordyn, a sitcom writer and a TV producer. Their competing careers seemed to intervene each time. They'd been better friends than lovers.

Her mind flipped back to Shane. She imagined how it would feel, his fingertips across her skin, his lips gently pressed against hers. She barely knew the man and didn't understand why her thoughts drifted in a lust filled direction. A man she'd insulted and left standing on the corner.

"The Emma I know is way stronger than believing in what other people think." Luci waggled her brows. "Have you ever even slept with a white guy?"

Nope. Instead, Emma shot back, "Have you?"

"The whole rainbow, girl."

"Hoochie." She laughed and tossed another pillow at her.

"Hey, no judging." Luci threw the pillow back. "I'm not the one who stole someone's soda."

"I should've shut up and said thank you."

"It's too late now." Luci set the bowl of popcorn on the coffee table. "You don't have his last name, no number, no idea how to find this guy. We'll just chalk it up to a lesson learned."

Emma stared at the plastic green bottles on the kitchen counter. The man at the grocery store paid her bill and endured Emma's tirade. He deserved an apology. Shane, the schoolteacher. She rose from the couch and walked back to her room. "I've got a name, and I've got a pretty good idea where he is. I'll find him."

CHAPTER

Six

"So, you're not going?" Gabe Thompson poked his head into the room as a dozen high school students filed out of the classroom.

Shane slipped the stack of papers into his shoulder bag. Late afternoon sun splashed the white board behind him. He locked his desk drawer and looked up at his coworker. "I'm not going."

"It's a double date." Gabe put his hands together, pleading for Shane to change his mind.

Shane shook his head. "I've got papers to grade."

"It's Friday night, man. It can at least wait till Saturday." Gabe enjoyed the weekends, thrived on the bar scene. Beers and dancing, developing new "friendships." Gabe fed on all of it. He was twenty-nine and living the bachelor's dream.

Shane pushed his glasses up onto the bridge of his nose and slung the strap of his bag across his right shoulder. "What about Doug? He's always game for the double date thing."

Gabe's eyes widened. "Are you kidding me? I like the guy, but he's a klutz. He spilled beer on everyone last time and rambled on about some wizard game he likes to play on his tablet. The ladies hated it. He's a great teacher but a total buzzkill."

"I'm a great teacher and I'm a total buzzkill, too." Shane walked into the vacant, wide corridor lined with slate-colored lockers.

Three students, books in hand, hurried to the double exit doors at the end of the hall. The doors opened and banged shut. Shane locked his classroom and started down the corridor, Gabe close behind him.

"So, that's a no?"

Shane shook his head at his wild and crazy friend. "Yeah, Gabe. That's a no." He pushed open the double doors, chilled air nipping at his face. Only seven cars remained in the parking lot. Shane readjusted the strap of his shoulder bag, heaved in a deep breath, and hurried down the first set of concrete steps leading to the parking lot.

"Shane, you can't stay a hermit forever."

Shane chuckled. "You're stalking me now?"

Gabe walked beside him. "Not stalking, persuading. I would've made an excellent Wall Street broker."

"You *were* a Wall Street broker."

Gabe pondered the last statement. "You're right. And I was damn good at it. Just like you."

"Yes, we were." Shane walked down the next set of steps. "But I'm still not going. And I'm not a hermit."

Gabe held out his hand, counting the reasons on each finger. "No social life. No girlfriend. No late-night parties as a wing man for your buddy here. No phone calls. Hell, I'm lucky if you answer the phone. Your sister's calls are my only other lifeline."

"You talk to Sallie?"

"Yeah when she can't reach you. Which is all the time."

Gabe quickened his pace falling in line beside Shane. "When was the last time you went to the movies?"

"I don't do movies." Shane tried to think back to the last afternoon matinee or midnight showing of a film he just had to see. It'd been awhile. Heather, his ex-fiancée, didn't like going to the movies, considered it juvenile. Shane got into the habit of not going.

"When was the last time you went on a date?"

Shane remembered his conversation with Sallie days before and groaned. If only his lackluster love life didn't require so much attention from everyone. The memory of the woman in the oversized sunglasses and beanie hadn't escaped his thoughts. She was frustrated with him for helping her, as if she had never experienced sincere compassion. The idea of that made him sad.

"When was the last time you had a beer with the guys?"

"I don't drink like that."

"You used to."

"That was a long time ago."

"That was a year ago."

Shane reached the last step and spun on his heel to face his friend. "Gabe." His voice held a fierce edge to it that instantly caught Gabe's attention. "Drop it, okay?"

Gabe stepped back. His eyes flashed hurt at the coldness in Shane's tone. "Sure." He stalked across the parking lot toward his car.

"Gabe," Shane called out, regret tearing at his voice. "I didn't mean that."

Gabe unlocked his car and yanked open the door.

Shane cursed under his breath and started toward Gabe's truck. Gabe climbed into the driver's seat. Shane scowled at the roar of the truck's engine as Gabe pulled out of the lot.

"So, I'm not the only mean person in town today," a female voice quietly said behind him.

Shane whirled around. A woman sat on the waist-high brick wall separating the concrete sidewalk and the high school's massive, land-scaped lawn. He recognized the bumblebee sunglasses and black beanie. Silky, chocolate-colored skin. Gentle waves of brown hair peeking beneath the beanie. Soft full lips, now smiling at him.

He didn't return the cheery smile. "It's Emma, right? Did you come back to insult me some more?"

Emma cringed. "No, I'm sorry about that."

"Care to explain?"

"I'm going through a rough spot right now?"

He made small air circles near his temple with his pointed index finger. "Temporary insanity?"

She held up her index finger and thumb, an inch apart, to demon-strate her amount of craziness. "A little. It can't be helped right now. But I was rude, and I am sorry." She tapped the six pack of soda sitting beside her. "I brought your stuff back."

He glanced at the six pack, then back at Emma. "A thief with anger issues, who doesn't like anyone helping her. You must be a joy to be around."

"So, my mother tells me."

He leaned past her and grabbed the six pack. Fresh soap, the scent of rainfall wafted beneath his nose. He enjoyed the intoxicating scent of her, but quickly stepped back. If she could get angry that quickly at a complete stranger, then the emotional baggage she carried around was more than anyone could bear. And after his behavior with Gabe, his actions weren't any better. He needed to be alone. "Are you like this with everyone?"

She shook her head. "Nope. You're the first."

"Exactly how did you find me?" Their interaction at the grocery store had been odd, but Shane had become accustomed to city people. The island took a little while to get used to, but her actions were tame compared to some other incidents he'd observed.

Emma proudly raised her chin. "You said you taught at the high school, so I looked you up online. Your picture was on the school website. There's only one high school on this island?"

"It's a small town." The one burning question bubbled past his lips. "Those sunglasses aren't part of your face, are they?" The sun, once blazing in the afternoon light, hid behind graying clouds.

She instinctively touched her shades. "This? No." She fiddled with the beanie but kept it in place. "I don't know if taking them off is a good idea."

"Are you hiding from the cops?"

"No."

"Bad hangover? Tequila and rum?"

"You're funny." She laughed sweetly, angling her head to one side, her fingers resting on the edge of the brick wall. "Do I look like a tequila and rum kinda girl?"

Shane lifted his lips into a broad smile. It'd been awhile since he made a woman laugh. Gabe was right. There were benefits to being social, and Emma definitely was one of them. "Please, educate the educator." He swept one hand in front of her like a man introducing Emma to the world.

Emma's stomach twirled in nervous knots. Once she discarded the beanie and shades, her true image would be revealed. Emma the starlet, and not the person. Fantasy instead of reality. She stifled the frown;

he deserved to see her. Slowly, Emma removed the sunglasses from her face and slid the beanie off her head.

Shane took in her dark brown, doe shaped eyes, a lock of hair shifting slightly over her left eye. She tucked the wayward strands behind her ears, smiled faintly, and waited. Ready and yet dreading to hear that moment of recognition. When it didn't come, Emma tilted her head at him.

"Do you know who I am?" She analyzed the sudden arch in his brow, the purse of his lips, his eyes masked in sudden bewilderment. He had no idea who she was.

"Am I supposed to?"

Emma shook her head. She wasn't about to tell him. "I guess not."

"How do you feel about coffee?" Shane placed a hand over his chest. "With me. I'm really curious to know the story behind that little speech you gave me. Then, we'll be even."

Coffee and Shane. A volatile combination, possibly leading to more than she was willing to give. Or maybe not. His interest in her might be limited to only friendship; her luck with the opposite sex hadn't exactly been on a winning streak. He had no clue of her identity, her occupation or her fame. She dialed back the confidence. Whatever path she chose wouldn't end well. Still, her mouth was unable to form the word no.

"On two conditions." She skimmed his plaid shirt and tan pants. Shane's aloof, English teacher look didn't match the intensity in his eyes. An unexplainable conflict, like he tried hard to simmer down the man inside, the person people rarely glimpsed. A disguise, no different than her own. "Ditch the plaid shirts and brown pants."

He glanced over his outfit. "What's wrong with this?"

"I'd rather see you without them on." She clapped a hand over her mouth. *Did she just say that?*

"You'd rather see me naked?" He grinned.

Emma laughed. "You are full of yourself today. No plaid shirt, no Dockers. That's the deal. I'm sure you have other colors in your closet."

"I'll take it. Second condition?"

Emma sucked in a quiet breath and released it. "We go for coffee as friends. Acquaintances." The swirling knots in her belly and clammy hands disagreed.

"I'm okay with condition two." He surveyed his appearance again. "I don't think there's anything wrong with my clothes."

"That's the deal." Emma hopped off the brick wall. "You wanted to see the real Emma; I want to see the real Shane." She tugged at the sleeve of his shirt. "If you can't, I understand." His magnetic green eyes followed her every moment and Emma lowered her head to avoid them. "It was nice knowing you Shane." She backed away from him, turned and walked away.

CHAPTER

Seven

*I*N THE COVERED DECK IN THE BACKYARD, EMMA eased onto the chaise and fumbled with one arm as she slipped on a skimpy, pale blue, chenille sweater. The evening air chilled and the twinkling lights illuminated the backdrop of Seattle. Cell phone pressed hard against her ear, she listened to Jordyn's contentious tone on the other end of the line.

"Where exactly are you?" he demanded.

"It doesn't matter where I am."

He overlooked the snarky comment. "There are reporters everywhere, Em. We should come out together, show a united front."

"You can't be serious." Jordyn had an ego huge enough to do almost anything to keep his public image clean. His suggestion reached a new low. "United front? Are you kidding me?"

"I'm not a comedian, and this isn't a joke. You've got a responsibility to the public as do I."

"If you think—"

"This is not open for discussion. Get your ass back here and do your job."

Emma pressed the end button on her phone and shut the entire device off. She gazed across the vast amount of water separating her from Seattle and was tempted to pitch the cell phone into the darkened sky and listen as it plopped into the water.

Jordyn's ambition, his drive, had attracted her to him. They shared a passion for acting and he understood the media, a life she'd been hesitant to share with anyone else. If she dated someone within her social circle, the issue of fame was one less romantic relationship obstacle. Emma stared at her cell phone, remembering Jordyn's forceful tone. Jordyn Mars, who once professed his love.

The back door squeaked open and Luci poked her head out.

Emma heaved in a long breath. "I'm okay. What's up?"

"It's desert cactus."

Emma swung her legs off the chaise and sat up straight. She and Luci had created a secret code for her mother's incoming calls, an easy warning system whenever Emma needed to take the call in the public eye. "Desert cactus" was the code for when her mother Madeline called and would not be put off with any excuse. "Wildflower" meant mere annoyance at Emma's unavailability, requiring a return call as soon as possible. "Pink Rose" was Emma's favorite. A casual call from Madeline, no call back necessary.

"She's on mute." Luci handed Emma a second, red trimmed, cell phone.

The red phone was used for family only, the black phone in Emma's hand, for all others. Emma gave Luci the black phone and took the red one. She pressed the mute button on the small screen and held the phone to her ear. "Hey, Mom."

"Don't 'Hey Mom' me. Where the hell are you?"

Emma winced at the biting tone. "I was going to call you." She felt fifteen years old all over again. "Things just happened so fast."

"Are you bleeding to death?"

"No."

"Arms and legs broken?"

Emma looked down at her body parts. All limbs in place. "No."

"Fingers and hands okay?"

"Yes."

"But you couldn't call me?" Madeline breathed heavily and paused to collect herself. "I've seen the tabloids. The garbage being printed about you and Jordyn. I'm sure this has been very overwhelming for you. Press coverage needling into every area of your life. You have to let me know these things dear. I'm your mother. You just have to tell me."

"It's not garbage, it's fact. Jordyn and I have been separated for months."

"That's not possible," her mother said, returning from the devil incarnate to the overbearing, critical parent Emma remembered. "You're living with him."

"That's about to change."

"This is just a rough patch. Couples go through this."

"Mom, we're not in love, and we're not together."

Silence.

Emma waited for her mother's reaction.

More silence.

"Mom?"

"Jordyn is the best thing that's ever happened to you, both personally and professionally. Exactly what did you do?"

"Seriously?" Emma opened her mouth to say more but the words would not come. She knew her mother favored Jordyn, but over her own daughter? Sure, her mother had hinted daily that Emma's sarcasm and her rebellion against behaving in a ladylike manner was going to

scare the men away. Jordyn hadn't initially minded her jeans and tennis shoes, her laid back, stay at home demeanor. Her mother instantly latched onto Jordyn as the quintessential catch. Emma had been single for years until Jordyn, attending events alone, throwing herself into her work. Her mother swore Emma would be a rich spinster, unable to carry on the family line. "I can't talk about this."

"We should talk about it. You're nearing the peak of your career and it's good to have a man at your side. He'll protect and support you. Not too many men out there will. Jordyn has his own money, so that's one less thing to worry about. Be the bigger person and fix this."

"I gotta go." Tears stung her eyes.

"Once you've got your head straight, call me." her mother said gently. "We'll figure out how to get Jordyn back. It'll be alright." Madeline ended the call and Emma stared at Puget Sound, wishing the scream tearing at her throat would erupt from her mouth and echo across the blackened sky.

"You're really giving me the day off?" Luci stood at the end of the dining room table, hands on her hips, her vibrant red hair in its usual two ponytails, the ends of her pigtails barely scraping her shoulders. She wore jeans and a long-sleeved shirt. Sunglasses perched on her head, her eyes searched Emma's face for an explanation.

"We're on vacation. You deserve a break just as much as me." Emma bit into her toast. Luci ached to go out. Emma wanted to stay in. Curiosity loomed at the city along the shoreline and the island's best attractions, parks, and the amazing views. Emma longed to see the sights and disappear into the crowd as a tourist.

"Go," Emma said and smiled, absently waving a hand at Luci. "Don't mind me. See the sights. Bring back pictures."

Luci's face broke into a wide smile. "Thanks, boss." She grabbed her parka off the back of the couch.

"I'm not just your boss you know," Emma called after her. "I'm your friend."

"Yeah, that too," Luci shouted back. The door creaked open, slammed shut and the screen door whined, then slapped closed against the doorframe.

Emma bit into her toast again, closing her eyes at the delicious taste of strawberry jam touching the roof of her mouth. She rose from the table, carrying her cup and saucer into the den, and paused at the front windows. Ivory curtains protected her and Luci from curious eyes peeking into the house, but Luci had pushed aside the two front curtains. Natural morning light flooded the formal living room.

The round, gold-framed clock hanging on the living room wall ticked ten minutes past eight. If Emma were home, she'd be in her basement gym right now, hammering the punching bag. The vacation house contained a small exercise room. Emma had already spent thirty minutes running full force on the treadmill, chasing away steamy thoughts of Shane. The confused look in those hypnotic green eyes when he accepted her apology.

Three hard knocks pounded the front door and Emma jumped, startled at the sound.

She cautiously made her way to the kitchen threshold, peering around the wall at the front door.

The three knocks came again. Knuckles against wood. A voice followed. "Emma?"

She walked to the door and peeked through one of the front windows. Shane stood on the porch in dark blue jeans, a moss-colored, V-neck pullover shirt, and a black parka. Head lowered, he waited for Emma to respond. When she didn't answer, he straightened, aimed his knuckles over the door and rapped three more times. "Emma?"

Despite herself, she smiled and yanked open the door. "What are you doing here?"

"You said two conditions." A corner of Shane's lips lifted. He backed away from the door so she could view his appearance. "No plaid, no Dockers. I know a great place for coffee."

Shane's eyes sparkled against the matching color of his shirt, mischief dancing in them, taunting her. His solid build defined the shirt, the structured chest of a man who kept in shape.

"How did you find me?" She held the door slightly ajar as she contemplated his request. Funny Shane was a yes, sexy Shane was a no. Just the slant of his lips in that boyish smile made her skin tingle and ache with need. Desires and thoughts she had no business imagining at a time like this, but she couldn't formulate the reasons not to see Shane at the moment.

He smirked. "You're not the only one that can ask around. It's a small town, remember?"

Small town giving away her address? Maybe it was time to relocate. "They knew my name?"

Shane shook his head. "No, but they do know a visitor just came to town. I got a partial description and since you were at the market, I only had to look for rentals on this side of town. It wasn't hard." His eyes pleaded with her. "Come out with me."

"That sounds creepy."

"I'm not creepy." He put three fingers up of his right hand. "Scouts honor."

Emma searched his face searching for deceit but found none. "Let me get my coat."

Jordyn expected her to be at the airport, racing back home to repair their tattered image tarnished by scandal—not casually sharing coffee with a strange man. Emma jerked her parka from the closet, hurried into it and dug her hands into the pockets. Cash, her driver's license, a beanie, sunglasses, and a stick of gum. Perfect.

She stepped outside onto the porch, and closed and locked the door, the screen bouncing against the frame as it shut. She pulled her beanie and sunglasses from one of the parka's pockets and concealed herself behind the shades. She slid the beanie over her head, pushing wisps of hair away from her face.

Shane studied her for a moment.

"What?"

He shrugged. "Just trying to decide if I want to aid a fugitive."

Emma laughed. "Is that the best you've got?"

"Witness protection?"

"No."

"Former mob boss?"

She shook her head, her lips spread in a wide grin as she held her hand out toward the gravel driveway. "Lead the way."

Eight

SHANE'S GAZE SKIMMED OVER EMMA'S UNDEC-
orated fingers, reaching the implication she wasn't married;
her flirty nature hinted at the absence of a boyfriend. At least he hoped.
No husband, and hopefully, no boyfriend. He'd noticed the interest
in her eyes when her gaze lingered on him longer than it should've,
yet she continued to remind him this burgeoning connection could
go no farther than friendship. He wanted to know why.

He stood on the ferry, gazing at Emma from several feet away as
she held onto the rail and watched Seattle grow closer. Wisps of her
wavy hair whipped around her face and she shifted her head away from
the wrath of the wind. Her jeans hugged the round curve of her hips,
pausing at her slim waist. He'd caught only a glimpse of her slender
frame when she opened the door for him. Long legs, slim arms, how
her soft brown eyes stared back at him worriedly as she removed her
sunglasses for the first time. She seemed so surprised, and almost

relieved, when he said he didn't recognize her. He searched his memories, wondering if they'd ever met before, but no, they hadn't. He was sure of it. Emma was not someone easily forgotten.

She released the rail and walked toward him. She tilted her head toward the entrance leading to rows of seats inside. Shane followed her through the threshold and Emma slid into one of the few booths alongside the windows. Sunlight blared across the linoleum tabletop, and Emma took off her shades. Several people sat in the bucket seats, reading newspapers, listening to their iPods. Others stood outside, braving the wind, gazing at the city skyline as the ferry approached Seattle.

Emma placed her sunglasses on the table. Shane smiled and the corner of Emma's full lips curved upward. "What?"

"Nothing." She wanted answers, and he had none to give. He could not explain his fascination with her, only that he needed to know her. "Have you ever been to Seattle?"

"No." She stared out the window.

"Well, I'm taking you to a place I go to when I really want to be alone." He leaned back against the hard-plastic back of the seat. "And you look like someone who needs alone time."

Emma glanced at him, then back at the window.

"So, what's his name?" Shane asked, not fully prepared for the response.

She turned from the window, the shock on her face evident by her open mouth and enlarged eyes. "What?"

He shrugged. "That speech you gave me the day we met was meant for someone else. What's his name?"

"Jordyn."

He scanned the hunch in her shoulders, misery in her eyes. Unspoken words of betrayal. "I'm sorry."

She opened her mouth to speak, then closed it. She finally answered, "What's happening between Jordyn and me is more like a coming out event."

"Coming out event?"

"We haven't been together for a while. No one knew. Not even my mother."

At last, a crack in the wall. Shane leaned forward, his elbows on the table and his chin in the palm of his hand. "Didn't want to disappoint your parents?" Shane remembered his mother's expression when he told her that he and Heather had broken their engagement. Terror and panic had struck her face. He was amazed she didn't suffer a heart attack right there in the massive formal living room of his parents' million-dollar home.

His fiancée at the time, Heather, argued that Shane had transformed into the man she no longer wanted and needed. Shane welcomed the end of their engagement. Her assumption correct, he'd awakened from a dream, truth glaring back at him. Money. Status. Lack of substance. Up until two years ago, he thought he and Heather would be long married by now. His sudden life changes had strained the relationship and eventually Heather let go. "So, did you tell them or did someone else figure it out?"

"Multiple *someones* figured it out." She toyed with the ends of her shades. "Then the calls came."

"Parents?"

She nodded.

"Friends?"

"Yes. Nobody could believe it. Neither could I. But it is what it is."

"What's that?"

"Over." Emma withdrew her hand from her shades and sat back.

Shane recognized the finality in her voice; her body looked defeated by both the breakup and the realization the bond she'd believed in was over. The stinging reality of her dead relationship being dug up again by meddling, but concerned, family and friends must've been painful.

"What about you?" she asked. "Ever been married?"

"Almost." There'd been many gifts to return, hundreds of people to notify in the two days before the wedding when Heather cancelled. "It was a long time ago." He cleared his throat and straightened up in his seat. "This topic is too heavy for a first date, right?"

"This isn't a date, remember?"

Shane scanned the room as if divulging his deepest secrets. "No? This isn't a date?"

Emma shook her head slowly. "No."

"We're going for coffee?"

"As friends."

Shane leaned back. Emma had been clear from the start they would be friends. Acquaintances. Friendship. Her eyes, the shaky confidence in her voice belied more than she was willing to tell him. The reason she insisted on keeping him at a distance. She could hide all she wanted, but Shane was a patient man. Friendship was a beginning. He could build on that.

Shane gazed out the window. The intricate designs of tall buildings, that had once been specks, formed the Seattle horizon. The ferry pushed into the dock and a male voice boomed across the intercom. They'd arrived.

Emma snatched the sunglasses from the table and slid them onto her face. She adjusted her beanie. "Shane, I don't know if this is a good idea."

Torn from his thoughts, he rose from his chair and held out his hand. "Trust me."

Her smile dimmed, but she looked up at him with humor. "Trust you? I don't even know you."

"I don't know you either, but I'm willing to take a chance." He kept his hand extended toward her. "Even if you are a vampire."

She stood up. "A what?"

"Vampire." He pointed at her shades. "That's the reason for the sunglasses? Too much sun."

"You are one strange man."

"You have no idea."

Emma gazed at the hand he offered, inhaled, and took it.

Gently squeezing her hand, Shane led her through the exit doors.

Emma walked through Pike's marketplace, a lengthy arrangement of fruits, vegetables, and seafood, all types of items for sale. Tourists and locals chattered, comingled voices coming together like an all-day talk radio station. The heat of hundreds of visitors crowded together under the shade of the covered marketplace warmed Emma's cold skin. She paused at a vendor selling candy and bought a small bag of miniature chocolate squares. Shane walked beside her, her hand no longer clasped within his. When their hands were together, fingers entwined, his touch ignited Emma in places she'd long forgotten. She politely and quickly removed her hand from his grasp once they reached solid ground. *No reason to give him the wrong impression.*

What was the wrong impression? That skin-to-skin contact between them was electric and filled her mind with endless images of them together.

Lust, she told herself. *All lust.*

And trouble.

The instant stimulation from Shane's touch hadn't been present when she first met Jordyn. Not even close. Emma would have to keep her thoughts away from Shane.

"This is where you go when you wanna be alone?" She approached a new vendor, one offering cheaply constructed toys at an inflated price. She reviewed the selection and bought a tiny yellow bottle of bubble mix.

Shane sauntered over to the next merchant. "No one knows me here. It's my safe haven."

Emma followed behind him. "You said you were almost married?"

Shane sifted over a rack of sentimental tourist souvenirs. "I was a different person back then." He grabbed a pair of orange star shaped glasses off a white plastic carousel and put them on his face. "I'm not that person anymore." He looked at Emma and quirked his lips in an odd way, emulating the crazed appearance of a grown man wearing a pair of bright orange star glasses.

Emma laughed as Shane poked fun at himself. "What was that guy like?" She unscrewed the small yellow container and blew bubbles through the purple wand.

"You mean the old Shane?" Bubbles of all sizes floated over his head. "He was an arrogant, vain, money hungry, not a care in the world kinda guy. Selfish, too."

Emma was about to blow another set of bubbles over his head but paused. "That old Shane sounded like an ass."

"He was." He took off the sunglasses and positioned them back on the carousel.

"I'm sorry for your ex-fiancée."

"Don't be." Shane browsed the selection of mangos and kiwi at the next fruit stand. He picked up a plum instead. "She liked Shane the ass."

"The old Shane sounded a lot like my ex." Emma blew bubbles around him and Shane popped the ones closest to his face.

He threw Emma a stern look, lacking any bite. "Does it look like I'm a man who likes bubbles?"

"Depends on where they're at." She put the wand back in the bottle of bubble mix and twisted it shut, avoiding the suddenly amused look on his face. How did those words come from her lips? "Please don't respond to that."

"Why not? I think it's an invitation."

"I don't know why I keep saying things like that around you. I don't know you and you don't know me like that." Emma unwrapped a tiny piece of candy, slipping a small square of milk chocolate into her mouth.

Shane watched the chocolate morsel slide onto her tongue and disappear into her mouth. "You keep saying that." He chose three plums, bagged them and paid the vendor. "So, I'm going to give you your full life story. Free of charge."

"My life story?" She popped another chocolate square into her mouth.

"Yes. You're single and a hermit, just like me. You're in some kind of trouble, but I know you're not going to tell me, which explains the shades and the beanie. And I bet you just love movies. Whatever you do for work is creative. The way you mimicked that young guy's dialogue outside the store was way too good for an amateur like myself. Maybe you're a writer, an actress, something like that."

Emma choked on the food in her mouth. She coughed, her eyes stinging. A writer, an actress, Shane had captured a major portion of her life in the short span of time they'd known each other.

He patted her on the back, his hand gently wrapped around her arm. "You okay?"

His green eyes glittered down at her, concerned, then smug. He knew he'd come close to her truth.

She swallowed and cleared her throat. "I'm good."

"You sure?

"Yeah. Tell me the rest of my story."

Shane studied her a moment, then released her arm. He turned away from her, perusing an arrangement of fruit. Oranges, melons, kumquats. "You don't settle in one place for a long time because you haven't found the right place, or the right person." He glanced back at a speechless Emma and arched a brow, emphasizing his final three words. "*The right person.*" Shane spun around and wandered along a row of coffee mugs, trinkets, keychains and shot glasses, the perfect venue for tourists. "The house you're in right now is a rental, and it goes for a lot of money. So whatever work you're doing either pays well, you're secretly a lottery winner, or you're a relative of the woman who owns it."

"How did you do that?" Emma asked. He was so observant yet could not place her true identity.

"Do what? Tell your story?" He grinned. "I'm just good at paying attention."

Not good enough. She yearned to tell him who she really was. Emma Jacobs, the famous actress. No matter the various manners in which she revealed herself, it felt pretentious. She opted instead for silence.

They reached an area ripe with the smell of fish. Emma's nostrils flared at the odor.

Shane stepped to the edge of the shaded marketplace. There was a bistro two blocks down. "Now we get coffee." He grabbed her hand and led her across the street.

Emma looked down at her hand, and this time, she didn't remove it from within Shane's grasp.

Nine

BY THE TIME THEY RETURNED TO THE ISLAND, the sea blue sky had faded into night and the weather had dropped down to a chilly forty-eight degrees. Emma bundled herself into a jacket. She followed Shane to his parked car, the orange glow of streetlamps lighting the sidewalk. Passengers exited the ferry, hustling past them, anxious to seek shelter from the icy air.

Shane first unlocked the passenger door of his navy blue, mid-sized SUV. He held the door open for Emma and she smiled. "Thank you."

Emma climbed into the seat and Shane gently shut the door. He walked around the back of the car and opened his own door.

Emma glanced at the rear of the car, noticing the pile of mail on the back seat. An index card rested on top, the words "*Conquer your fear (Noboru)*" printed on the surface. "What is Noboru?"

"It's a long story." He gripped the steering wheel with one hand, his gaze steady on the road. "I'd rather not talk about it."

"It doesn't seem like much scares you." The sudden tension piqued her interest.

"Huh?" Shane rounded a corner, and another, cruising along the road to her house.

He turned to look at her briefly, then back at the road.

"Conquering your fear? What fear is that?"

"It's hard to explain."Shane veered the car onto her gravel driveway and switched off the ignition. "And I really don't want to talk about it."

"At all?"

"Ever."

"Tell me anyway?" She hoped her light tone lessened the uneasiness brewing in his eyes. "I promise I'm a good listener when I'm not insulting strangers."

Shane didn't speak.

After what felt like minutes when it had only been seconds, Shane said quietly, "I'll answer three questions about this and then we talk about something else."

"Deal. What is Noboru?"

He lowered his eyes and cleared his throat. "It's part of a bigger picture. A list of things my best friend Liam mapped out for me to do."

"Like a bucket a list?" Emma's eyes grew wide. "I've always wanted to create my own bucket list. Go the Coliseum in Greece, eat dinner in Paris. Ride a motorbike through the streets of Brazil, lounge on the beach in Nice. I've just never had the time for any of it." Her grueling work schedule left little play time.

"It's not a bucket list. It's supposed to help me become more social with the opposite sex."

Shane didn't supply any details and Emma pressed on. "You don't exactly look like someone who has a problem with women."

"That's what I told him. It just wasn't the right time."

"Or maybe it wasn't the right woman. How many items are on the list?"

"Eleven. I'll get a card each week with a new task to complete."

"Who's sending it?"

"I don't know. I just got my first card a few days ago."

"Have you completed any of them yet?"

"No, and that's five questions, not three."

"Okay, I promise, this is the last one. So, this whole thing is to help integrate you back into society. Are you hiding?"

"Maybe."

Intrigued, Emma leaned forward in her seat, her lips parting into a wide smile. Funny how they were both hiding from the world for vastly different reasons. She was lying low due to her celebrity status and scandal. Shane isolated himself for a past he refused to mention. Her heart broke at the pain in his voice. "That was thoughtful of your friend, Liam. He's dragging you out of your comfort zone. If you are hiding, we should get you back into the world." She settled into her seat. Soon, she'd have to exit the car. The heat from the vents soothed her freezing hands. With the engine off, the icy air returned, and she rubbed her hands together. "That wouldn't be such a bad thing, right?"

Silence.

"You really don't wanna talk about this."

"I don't want to discuss this with you or anyone else."

She noted his clipped, icy tone, the way his back straightened and his chin lifted slightly in defiance. He'd squashed the idea of being pulled from his loner status. Her voice was gentle, barely audible, but resolute. "I appreciate you helping me like you did the other day. I forgot what it's like for strangers to be kind to me for no reason at all." Managing a small smile, Emma flung open the car door. Shane's complications didn't need to be tangled up with hers.

He grabbed the door handle to get out on his side, but Emma clamored from the car. She hurried to the porch steps, then turned and gazed back at him. "Thank you for today. Take care."

"Emma," Shane started, but she unlocked the door and disappeared into the house.

Shane flipped through paper after paper. B-. C. D. Another C. B+. Red ink from his pen splashed the pages in long strokes as he scribbled a grade on each paper. No A's, barely any B's. Clearly, his class didn't understand the fundamentals of imagery as it related to Romeo and Juliet. The story of the two tragic lovers was a difficult read for anyone, yet Shane had expected better. He tossed the stack of graded papers onto his coffee table and blew out an exasperated breath of air. He dragged his hands over his face and scratched his head.

Maybe it wasn't the topic, it was the teacher.

In the last year, his tolerance for less than stellar assignments had earned him the reputation as the *ogre*. A few teenage girls with high school crushes still batted their eyes at him, although Shane paid little attention. Most of his students were terrified of him, scared of each assignment, inquiry, or project. Blank faces stared back at him.

He flopped back against the couch, angled his head back. Teaching was the only talent he had. A gift he'd almost wasted until the day he woke up and decided to change. He returned to college, earned a teaching degree, and found his way back to Bainbridge Island. His mother thought it was another one of his phases that would pass. Like a cycle, the old Shane would come back around again. Liam was impressed and proud of his best friend. His encouragement kept Shane going.

Shane, once the easygoing, mild-mannered teacher. The class every-one eagerly hoped to attend. Now he forced himself to control the irritation in his voice during class.

His sister's words drifted over him.

Not talking about it is like not dealing with it. You'll never heal unless you deal with this.

He closed his eyes, the memories of that tragic night flooding back. He heard the sound of crushing metal, tires screeching, the strong stench of gas smothering him.

There was silence from the backseat.

Sallie'd whimpered, her arms dangling upside down, scratches on her face, her right cheek beginning to swell.

And more silence from the backseat.

He'd unbuckled his seatbelt, dropped onto his left shoulder, wincing at the pain radiating from his shoulder to his arm, pressure building in his chest. He twisted his body, reaching toward the back seat.

Say something, Liam. Anything.

Shane opened his eyes and gazed at the ceiling.

What would Liam say now?

Go big, win big.

Finish the list.

Shane snatched the index card off the coffee table, the place he'd dropped it after his poor behavior with Emma. He stared at the first task.

Conquer your fear (Noboru).

He picked up a second index card that he'd received a week after the first.

Task two. *Learn another language.*

His sister had called Amari who insisted she hadn't mailed him anything either. He was left with the index cards and his anonymous sender.

His cell phone rang, and he raised his head at the sudden shrill ring. He reached over with one hand, snatched up the phone and pressed the accept button. "Hello?"

The voice on the other end of the line boomed excitedly. "Shane, come to the window, man."

Shane stood up and walked over to his window, staring down at Gabe's black Toyota Tundra. "Tonight is the night, man. Come on down."

"Gabe, look I'm sorry about the other day."

"It's all good. You can make it up to me and I won't take no for an answer."

"Gabe, no."

"C'mon! I haven't even asked yet."

Shane laughed. "You want to go over to the Yard for happy hour." The Yard was a neighborhood bar most of the residents visited after a long day of work. The hangout included some of his colleagues. Tourists hit it during the peak summer months.

"It's the happiest hour." Gabe honked the horn. "And you haven't been there in ages. Now get down here or I'll keep banging on this damn thing and make your neighbors hate you."

"I only have one neighbor and she already hates me."

"Her loss." Gabe honked again. "Get down here, already."

Shane frowned. He headed for the door, the phone still clutched to his ear. Emma drifted to the front of his thoughts. He glanced down at his outfit. Black plaid, black dockers. He looked toward his bedroom, the French doors slightly open.

Gabe honked, the horn wailing long and loud for a third time.

"Do you really want me to come down and kick your ass?"

Gabe laughed. "You can try, but wait until we get to the Yard first."

Shane walked into his bedroom and flung open his closet door. He thumbed through the clothes hanging at the back of his closet, a col-

lection of barely used outfits. "Give me five minutes and I'll be right down."

———————

Shane sat at the bar as his friend whispered into the ear of a woman at a table ten feet away. Her long chestnut hair shook as she giggled. She glanced at her friend and giggled again. Even in the dim light with crowds pushing to the bar, Shane watched as Gabe looked up at him with pleading eyes. Begging for Shane to be his wingman and finish what Gabe had begun. A brief, shallow conversation with both women would trail back to Gabe's place. A nightcap to follow, Gabe tumbling into bed with the raven-haired beauty while Shane sat in another room, uninterested in the brunette beside him. Not because she didn't have an angelic face, silky skin and a body ripe for naughty behavior. Not that she wouldn't be ready for a dose of heavy petting, hands everywhere. It's just that Shane wished the woman staring at him from across the room was Emma.

He turned away from Gabe and wrapped his hand around his mug of beer. Shane raised the glass in his hand to his lips and drank.

A woman slid on to the empty stool beside him and called out to the bartender. She glanced at Shane and smiled. "Shane Rawlings. I didn't think you'd ever come out of your cave." The bartender walked over, and the woman ordered a Cosmopolitan. She shifted in her seat, faced Shane, and held out her hand. "Delia Rose."

Shane slowly accepted the handshake. He studied Delia, trying to place where they met before. Parent teacher conference? Another sudden member of his sister's wedding party? He pried his brain, but her face didn't register. He managed a smile. "Have we met?"

Delia crossed her legs, a surprising accomplishment, considering the number of people packed at the bar, squeezing up against one another as they fought for the bartender's attention. She seemed at ease in a black skirt that rose above her knees and revealed long, slender legs. She wore an ivory camisole. Her slim arms rested neatly on the counter, her brown eyes working over his haggard appearance. She'd pinned her dark brown hair into a bun at the back of her head. Small diamond studs adorned her ears and she wore just a hint of makeup, her tanned skin and natural beauty catching a few male eyes seated at the bar near them.

The bartender placed her drink on the counter. She paid him and sipped the drink. "Not officially." She studied Shane, rotating her right foot, her three-inch heels accentuating the length of her legs. "I'm the new biology teacher."

Shane remembered the rumor of a new teacher in town. Whispers started after Jack Miscone up and quit. Substitutes followed until a permanent replacement could be found. He'd heard the rumors but didn't really listen much.

Shane glanced down at her bare fingers. "Welcome to Bainbridge Island, Ms. Rose."

Delia tilted her head. "Thank you, Mr. Rawlings." She tipped her glass at him. "I'm surprised you're here. I heard you don't get out much."

Shane frowned. He didn't need prying eyes reaching into every crevice of his private life. He craved his solitude.

He thought of Emma's beanie and her sunglasses, the constant need for a disguise. What had he missed about her identity? What did he not understand? He searched his mind, thumbing through images of every woman he could remember. Her face was vaguely familiar, as if he'd seen her in passing.

"So, what's Bainbridge like?" Delia swirled toward him on the stool, her back erected in a proper pose, her bare legs bumping against his.

The posture, the hair, the clean lines of her outfit distinctly reminded him of Heather, his ex.

Shane glanced down at her legs touching his. He wanted the feel of a woman's skin against his own but not from this woman. Shane stood up. "Bainbridge is a nice place. It was good to meet you, but I have somewhere I need to be." He hurried to the door before Delia could respond.

Shane stood outside in the frigid night air and felt a tap on his shoulder. He spun around.

"Where the hell you goin', man?" Gabe scowled.

Shane stepped back. "Thanks for bringing me out here, but I gotta go."

"Where are you going?" Gabe held his arms out. "You didn't drive, remember?"

"I don't need a ride." Shane turned around and headed down the street. "I'll be fine."

*E*MMA WATCHED LUCI SQUINT AT THE IMAGE SCRIB-bled on the large white notepad. Sketched in thirty seconds, Emma captured on paper what the game's playing card instructed her to draw.

Luci rotated the picture several times, lifting the pad closer to her eyes. "What the hell is this?"

The final sliver of sand sifted from the top to the bottom of the plastic egg timer.

Emma thrust her arms in the air. "I win. It was a vacuum."

"You cheated." Luci dropped her pencil on the table and held up the large white notepad. "That's not a vacuum."

"It is, too." Emma jabbed her finger at the picture. "You just have to look deeper."

"This isn't an abstract painting Em," Luci griped, stifling a laugh. "That line and circle, oval, whatever it is, it's not a vacuum. And who's the stick guy?"

"He's vacuuming." Okay, so the black dot the size of a penny and the attached long lines were supposed to be the outline of a body reaching for a round circle linked to another long black line. Far from any Monet. She laughed, and Luci followed. Doubling over, Emma fought to catch her breath. She grabbed the wineglass from the mantel and sipped her white wine. "Okay." She raised the glass and suppressed another laugh. "I suck. Big time. But I'm an actress, not a painter."

Luci snorted, tossing the notepad on to the coffee table. "Yeah, don't quit your day job."

Emma chuckled, sipping more wine. It'd been awhile since she laughed about anything. Work, work, work was her mantra. Her career came before all else, and Jordyn had preferred it that way. Both of them vanished into the movie scene, film premieres, interviews, and press junkets, any place her agent told her to go. No vacations. No sightseeing. Nothing. Emma created her own vortex, her own hell, never giving herself the chance to breathe.

Luci gathered up the notepads and pencils and put them back into the box. They'd played Pictionary for the last two hours and Luci had won every game.

Emma thought about the vacuum drawing. So, her visual art skills lacked talent, but she could recite a line from a screenplay as though her life depended on it. As if it were worth millions. She shook her head. She *was* worth millions but couldn't draw a damn vacuum cleaner.

"What about you Luci? When you gonna get that idiot Ron to get your own show? Your photos should be up on the walls for the world to see. And buy."

"I don't know if they're good enough."

"They're good. Did you even call Ron or Darnell?"

"No, do I really need an agent?"

"If you want your work to be shown." Emma groaned. "Luci, I gave you both their numbers because they're the best in the business. You have talent. I don't want you working for me forever. This is your 'day job.' And as your friend I'm telling you, call the guy."

"Okay, okay. I'll call him when we get back. I'll admit though, you picked a beautiful location, perfect for my camera." Luci stood up, box in hand as she left the room to put the game away on a shelf in one of the guest bedrooms.

Emma gazed at the flames flickering in the gas fireplace. She placed her glass on the table and plopped down onto the carpet. She needed the break, even for a few minutes a few days, a few months. A few months? Emma wasn't sure she wanted a sabbatical that extensive. Spend too much time away from the entertainment industry and she'd lose all the opportunities she'd earned. Hollywood wasn't exactly forgiving for a leave of absence.

"Are you okay?"

Emma half smiled, her thoughts lingering over an unsure future. She wasn't yet ready to return to the photographers' flashes and the fast-paced world attached to her occupation. She took in a long breath, her gaze fixed on the fireplace. "I'm fine. Just thinking."

"Of what you're gonna do?" Luci sat down on the couch, settling into the comfort of the plush square pillows.

"Yeah, I guess." Emma sipped her wine. "Did I ever tell you I wrote a script a long time ago?"

"No." Luci pulled her feet to her lap and curled into the couch, hugging the pillow. "What happened to it?"

"Never finished it. Here I am lecturing you about following your dreams and look at me. Not following my own advice. I was trying to get it out there and somehow I landed the actress gig first."

"Think you'll ever finish it?"

"One day." Emma carried their glasses to the kitchen and placed them in the sink. "When I have time."

"You have time now."

Emma's cell phone rang, a country twang from an old song Luci did not recognize.

"Country this time?" Luci shot Emma a disapproving look. "Really? Tim McGraw?"

Emma scrunched her eyebrows together and shook her head at Luci's limited knowledge of the non-rock genre. The man crooning as Emma's ringtone was not Tim McGraw. "That's Blake Shelton singing, thank you very much. I might switch to 50 Cent next week."

"You, and your ringtones." Luci scurried to the large oak dining room table where they left Emma's black phone. "You're an awesome actress. I'm sure your writing has the same high caliber. But you and I are gonna have to talk about your music choices."

Emma blushed at the half compliment. "Thank you, I think? And again, buttering me up isn't getting you another raise."

"I thought that was gonna be the one to show me the money."

Emma laughed. She'd increased Luci's salary several months ago, grateful for her assistant's attention to detail and her ability to keep Emma on track with her professional obligations.

Luci made a face at her boss and picked up the phone on the second ring. "Hello? Yes, Jordyn. Just one moment please." Her face reddened, fire simmering in her eyes. "I'm getting her right now if you'd—no, I'm not incompetent, I'm—"

Luci met Emma's gaze, belligerence captured in the delicate features of her face. She gripped the phone, her knuckles white as she held on to the device.

Emma took the phone from Luci and held it up to her ear. "What the hell did you say to Luci?"

"Emma?" He quieted at her snippy tone, but followed quickly with, "Listen. I get it. You needed space and I've given you that, but now it's time to come home."

"Not gonna happen."

"You owe me that much."

Emma wanted to slam the phone down on the table, but she'd only destroy her own belongings. "I don't owe you a damn thing. Stop calling me."

He softened his voice to a deep baritone. "Emma, we only have each other to lean on right now. This is a critical time for us. We should be facing this together."

"We wouldn't be in this position if you'd let me make a statement about our status from the beginning."

"That wasn't a wise decision. It wouldn't have helped either one of us."

"Either of us? Or you?"

"What does that mean?"

"Figure it out. And don't ever talk to Luci like that again." She pressed the end button and looked up at Luci.

Luci leaned against the rear glass door and peered out into the darkness.

Emma tossed the phone onto a side table. "You okay?"

Luci nodded. "I'm gonna call it a night, if that's okay."

"I'm really sorry." She'd never approved of the way Jordyn talked to the house staff or to his own assistant. His voice always carried superiority with them, their status holding no purpose for him.

"Don't be," Luci said and half-smiled. "You're not the ass, he is." She disappeared down the maze of hallways leading to her bedroom.

Emma frowned. Damn that Jordyn for his foul mouth and disrespect of women. The longer this scandal played out, the more her eyes awakened to the real Jordyn Mars. An emotional lady killer. Weak.

Pathetic. Selfish. She could think of a thousand more adjectives, but a knock on the door tore her from the list of colorful words.

"Emma?" Shane called out from the porch.

Emma walked to the front door and peered around the side curtain. Shane stood in front of the door, his head down.

"Emma," he said softly.

The sound of her name, so gentle across his lips, made her shiver with pure joy. She pushed away the feeling and opened the door. "What are you doin' here? A man who shows up this late to see a woman could be called strange."

"I am strange, remember? And it's not late, it's only nine o'clock."

"What do you want, Shane?"

"I wanted to apologize." Pain shadowed his eyes, coupled with regret.

"You don't have—"

He held her gaze, his voice low, gentle. "I'm sorry. I shouldn't have acted like that."

"Shane, it doesn't—"

"Are you hungry?"

"I ate already."

"So, dinner is a no, then?"

Emma smiled. "It would seem so. I get the impression you don't get out much." She leaned against the edge of the door.

"Neither do you."

Emma opened her mouth to spew a witty response but couldn't think of any. Her ventures beyond work were just as limited as his. Without quick words to slaughter his correct accusation, Emma had nothing to say.

Finding an opening, Shane said, "I go out."

"Where?"

"To my sister's wedding, when that happens."

"And when is that?"

"Two months from now." He glanced beyond Emma to the core of the house, the living room, and the flicker of light from the flames in the fireplace. "May I come in?"

"Oh, sorry." Emma pulled open the screen door and Shane stepped inside brushing past her. She caught a whiff of his aftershave and closed her eyes, remembering what it'd been like to be in such proximity to a man she desired. She opened her eyes.

Shane glanced back at her for unspoken permission to further enter her living space. Emma held her arm out, inviting him into the center of the house. He walked into the living room and she followed, plopping down onto the couch.

Taking her lead, Shane peeled out of his jacket and sat down on the opposite end of the couch. "So, what about dinner tomorrow?"

"I don't think it's a good idea." She drew her legs to her chest and rested her chin on her knees. Every inch of her screamed yes, but her mind produced a solid no. Additional visits with Shane would potentially lead to a path of chaos. Tabloids disrupting an innocent teacher due to his association with her, shredding his life into pieces for public entertainment. Shane deserved better, and Emma couldn't bear to be the cause of the commotion.

"You're not going to be hungry tomorrow?" Shane appeared to be unfazed by the hesitation on Emma's face. "I doubt that."

"I'm sure I'll be hungry tomorrow." Emma forced herself to suppress the smile creeping across her lips. In a black sweater with dark rugged blue jeans, and the way his eyes grazed over her, made her stomach flop nervously, her hands clammy, her heart race. Shane Rawlings was a force to be reckoned with. "It's still not a good idea."

"Eating is not a good idea?" Shane said.

"You're not gonna let this go, are you?"

He narrowed his eyes at her, his chin set; declining his offer wouldn't stop the questions. "Are you going to say yes?"

Emma mulled over his response. "Ask me tomorrow."

"Ask you tomorrow?" He gave her another lopsided grin and Emma bit her lip, fighting the urge to laugh.

"Okay." Satisfied, Shane scooted back into the couch. "This is a really nice place. I meant to tell you that earlier."

"Thanks." Emma picked at the edge of the pillow. "What made you become a high school English teacher?" She remembered the photo of him on the school's website, with the subject he taught listed below the picture.

He cupped his hands together. "I wanted to shape young minds. What creative job did you say you have?"

"I didn't." Emma shifted her legs on to the couch, tucking them under her. "I'm an actress."

His eyebrows lifted with the news and Emma waited for the recognition to settle across his face. It didn't.

He wagged his finger at her. "I knew it. How long?"

"Awhile." Her wineglass was empty, and she suddenly craved more. Instead she kept herself pressed into the sofa, curious at Shane's inquiries.

"It pays well?"

"It pays decent."

"You look like you enjoy it and you're probably good at it."

"I've been thinking about writing instead." Emma was surprised at her small confession. To Luci, it'd been okay, but telling Shane? It made no sense.

Shane leaned forward, his arms on his legs. "Writing? I think you'd be great at that too."

"You don't know that."

"I know you. I gave you your life story, remember?"

Emma did remember. He'd described the major details in her life, yet he did not recognize her face. She grinned, thankful that he didn't know the famous Emma Jacobs. Just the Emma in jeans and an over-sized mustard yellow sweater. "You're right. You did. Why don't you tell me yours?"

His voice was calm and deep, the velvety sound partially distract-ing. "Nothing to tell, really. I've isolated myself because I enjoy the silence. Everything on this island for me is simple, uncomplicated. The exact opposite of who I used to be." His gaze held hers, but Emma averted her eyes, easing into the comfort of the sofa and the sooth-ing sound of his voice. Blue and orange flames danced over the stone logs in the fireplace.

He smirked. "But enough about my story. Do you miss L.A.?"

She sat upright, stared hard at him. "How do you know I live in L.A.? Maybe I live in New York."

"Isn't L.A. the mecca for acting gigs?"

"I guess you could say that. Do I miss L.A.? I miss it. There's so much energy there, but sometimes it's too much. I miss swimming in the ocean." Emma relaxed, her arms falling to her side, her gaze steady on the flames licking the stacked logs. She hugged herself, fighting the chilly edge in the room. "Something about the water is so calming."

"How many auditions have you been on?" Shane watched Emma swirl the last bit of wine in her glass.

Emma lifted the glass, swallowed the remaining bit of wine. "At least forty." She remembered the cattle calls, the last-minute call backs, the rejections. And, finally, acceptance. She stretched her legs, resting them across Shane's lap. "How long have you been on the island?"

He glanced down at her legs, gazing over her bare feet, and looked back at her. "A few years." He placed one hand on her lower leg, his fingers still. "Small towns are pretty quiet. The downside, of course, is the gossip. People hear everything."

"Gossip, huh?" Emma wondered how long before the gossipers learned her true identity. "Anything on me, yet?"

Shane smiled. "The mysterious loner that rode into town, in the middle of the night? I've only heard bits and pieces. Mostly questions, with no answers."

"Such as?"

He shrugged, clearly accustomed to the town's longstanding curiosity. "Who is she? Where'd she come from? And my personal favorite, from a few of the guys in town, is she single?"

"Am I single?" Emma repeated, laughing. "A beanie and sunglasses don't exactly scream attractive."

"*You* caught my attention."

She gulped. Flames crackled in the fireplace, flickering shadows across the walls. Heat radiated from the center of her body to the tips of her fingers. Not from the fire, but the determined, hungry look in those intense emerald eyes. A look promising more than fireworks if their lips met.

An explosion.

An awakening.

Shane leaned forward, his gaze locked with hers, then lowering to her mouth. "I should probably go home."

She nodded as his lips closed in on hers. "You should."

Shane paused, a breath away, struggle looming over his face. He kissed her cheek. "I don't want you to get the wrong impression of me. And it is late." He leaned back. "I should go."

Rationale returned to her brain. If his lips found hers would they have been able to stop before it progressed beyond the couch? Shane was right, but she hated to see him leave.

Shane stood up and Emma rose from the couch, stretching her arms and legs with a feline grace. She noticed Shane studying her, his eyes filled with emotion. Terrified he'd catch the exact look in her eyes, she escorted him to the front door.

Shane shoved his arms into his jacket, gave her a small nod and stepped out on to the porch. "Night, Emma."

"Night, Shane."

She closed the door but didn't hear the screen door whine shut.

Shane knocked on the door.

Emma looked around the side curtain. Shane still stood on the porch. She cracked the door ajar. "Did you forget something?"

"Have dinner with me?"

"Shane, ask me tomorrow."

Shane peeked into the house. "The clock in there says twelve-eleven. So, it's already tomorrow."

Emma glanced at the clock hanging on the wall near the corridor. Twelve-twelve. She shook her head and grinned at his persistence. "Fine. Lunch. You pick the place."

"You know what? Forget dinner. Come on an adventure with me. To make up for how I acted before."

"An adventure?"

"Nothing extravagant. And I'll explain what Noboru means."

"No crowds?"

"No."

"I don't know."

"I'll be back here at noon. Just be ready." Shane stepped back from the door. "And wear a good pair of tennis shoes."

Tennis shoes?

"Wait," Emma said. "Where are we going?"

"It's a surprise. I'll see you tomorrow, Emma."

Shane hurried down the steps and Emma shut the door. Tennis shoes and an adventure? What the hell had she gotten herself into?

CHAPTER

Eleven

"I KNOW YOU SAID ADVENTURE, BUT THIS WASN'T what I had in mind." Emma followed Shane into the dense growth of towering trees that blocked out the midday sun. She hoisted the straps of her backpack on her shoulders, tilting her head back to stare up at the tops of the trees. "This is massive."

"It's a national park," Shane said. "Liam and I used to come here when we were in high school."

They ventured further into the forest, the view of the parking lot diminishing, cackling birds and the hum of other flighty creatures she couldn't name surrounding them. Soft, spongy moss squished beneath her foot as she stepped over a fallen tree trunk. "You guys came out here?"

"During the summer." He glanced over at her. "So how come you don't like crowds?"

Emma scrambled for words. *I'm an actress with millions of fans? My last movie grossed over a hundred million, increasing my popularity?* A half-truth was better than a full lie. "Sometimes I just want the quiet."

"Quiet is good. I understand that."

"It's nice to slow down."

"Yup." Shane continued along the dirt trail, Emma beside him.

Fresh, damp air filled her nostrils, tinged with the distinctive scent of Douglas firs. "Where are we going exactly?"

"There's a waterfall not far from here. I thought you might like the scenery."

Emma gripped the straps of her bookbag with both hands, a small smirk on her lips. At least they were away from the public for the moment, the sounds of the forest awakening around them. The perfect location for their date.

Wait. Not a date. Was it a date?

Her grin faded. She wanted it to be a date, the public didn't need to know everything.

"What's L.A. like?"

Shane's voice cut through her meandering thoughts. "It's the complete opposite of quiet."

"I'm sure there are some places where you can hear yourself think."

"There are a few, but not like this." She charged ahead of him, gazing at the large ferns sprouting up from the base of the trees, moss cloaking the trunks. Sunlight streaked through clusters of branches. "Tell me about teaching. Dealing with high schoolers? I admire that."

He laughed. "They're not that bad. They just need direction. And every year, whenever we go over Romeo and Juliet, I usually get a round of glossy-eyed looks."

"Because they love it?"

"Because they don't get it."

"Switch it up. Explain it on their terms."

"Their terms?"

"Show them in 'teenager' terms. Stuff teenagers will relate to." Twigs crackled under her feet, her legs burning at their moderate pace. They'd been hiking for at least thirty minutes. "So, this list is all about you meeting women?"

The trail curved and Shane edged ahead of Emma. "Not all women. Just one. As he called it the 'right one.'" He veered off the path, holding his hand out for Emma as he stood behind another larger tree trunk on its side.

She accepted his hand, a current of electricity rushing through her. His mere touch sent tingles up her spine. Why was her body responding so viscerally? Emma stepped up on the trunk, her foot twisting at an awkward angle and she stumbled. She wildly flung her other arm upward as she tried to regain her balance. She tumbled off the log instead, her entire body descending toward the ground. Shane gripped her hand and grabbed her waist, her shoulder slamming into the hard planes of his chest. He swayed back from the momentum of her body, but his feet remained rooted in place.

"Sorry," she mumbled, his woodsy scent lingering beneath her nose. She grasped his arms, his tight muscles bunched beneath her fingers and stood upright. The tingling in her pelvis rang incessantly like an unanswered dinner bell. How long had it been since she craved any man this way? She tried to remember, but the memories were lost.

"You okay?"

Not really. "Yeah."

Water babbled from a small brook, winding through the host of trees. Soft strips of sunlight peeked through the branches, offering little warmth. Emma gazed up at the sky, the tops of the trees bunched together, their branches entwined. She heard sounds of insects buzzing, frogs croaking, the gurgling stream growing louder as they trekked deeper into the forest.

Shane walked a foot ahead of her, rambling on about his previous summers at the park. Emma couldn't stop wondering how this might turn out if she could keep everything between her and Shane a secret. Yet, she wasn't a one-night-stand girl and didn't engage in brief affairs. Her personality had never been that way.

You're overthinking this Emma.

Dammit.

Emma scrunched her eyes shut then opened them.

"Emma," Shane said. "You okay?"

"Uh-huh."

They reached the tree line, the gushing sound of water almost deafening. A burst of sunlight flashed in her face, and she squinted. The stream of water emptied into a wide pond, spilling over an embankment roughly fifty feet high.

"This," he said gazing up at the waterfall, "is Noboru."

"That's what it's called?"

"That's not its real name. But Liam renamed it Noboru after he jumped off of it. Noboru means to ascend or rise in Japanese. And Liam always said the day he dived off this cliff, he'd risen above his fears, grown somehow, into something better. He felt invincible."

"Sounds like he was invincible before."

Shane chuckled. "Yes, he was."

"So, am I to assume that 'conquering your fear' meant diving off this thing?"

"As Liam said, 'to get my mojo back.'"

"Like you have mojo?"

"What?" He looked at her incredulously. "You said I don't look like the kind of guy that has a problem with women."

She smirked. "I reconsidered. Maybe you should take a leap off Noboru."

"Harsh critic."

"I mean, it sounds like we've both had some pretty messy past relationships. Noboru is a new start, right? According to Liam?"

"Rising above your fears. Letting go. Reclaiming your mojo."

"I guess my 'mojo' could use a boost," Emma said. "Let's make a deal. You go, I go. Start fresh."

Shane stared at the cliff, then back at Emma. "Deal." He took off his glasses and slipped them into his jacket pocket. "There's a dry spot over here we can use to jump off." He shrugged out of his jacket, then tugged the t-shirt over his head, the sculpted muscles of his broad, bare chest and carved abdomen on full display. He absently scratched his head, his round bicep shifting up and down as he turned around and studied the waterfall. A tribal tattoo inked his left arm and a vertical Celtic tattoo followed the middle of his muscled back; the image aligned with his spine.

Whoa. Emma fantasized how Shane would look without clothes and her dreams paled against reality. She folded her arms across her chest, restraining her hands from reaching out to touch his smooth skin. "What? I was kidding."

"You jump, I jump."

"I didn't mean it. That's a high drop and I'm not undressing in front of a man I barely know." *I'd rather watch you do it.*

"You know more of me than some people. Trust me, you'll be fine up there. This is a perfect icebreaker for our first date."

"This is so *not* a date."

"It feels like one." He grinned at her.

Emma tried to keep her eyes level with his, but they kept drifting to his chest.

"I'll keep my pants on, you keep on whatever you want."

Shane *not* taking off his pants? She'd half hoped to ogle the bottom half of his gloriously toned body. Disappointment dropped in her stomach. "People will see us."

"No one's around." He kicked off his shoes and pulled off his socks. "You're right, we both need a fresh start."

"I didn't know what I was saying."

"You sure sounded confident. We could go up there together."

"How about you first?"

Shane eyed her closely then disappeared through the trees, reappearing moments later at the top of the cliff.

"You really don't have to do this, Emma called out. What if the water wasn't deep enough? Or he banged his head on the jagged rocks on the way down? The gravity of his actions suddenly weighed on her, but before she could protest further Shane stood on the strip of dry rock. He dashed forward, a serious expression on his face as he raised his arms in the air and leapt off the edge.

She covered her mouth with one hand, neared the edge and peeked over the side.

He plunged into the water feet first, with a loud splash then popped up to the surface.

Emma inhaled a relieved breath. Shane stared at Emma expectantly.

She considered the pros and cons of throwing herself off the waterfall. She and Shane were isolated. No cameras, no agents, no publicist, no fans. She followed the edge of the pond, climbing up small rocks, around overgrown ferns, the moss squishing underneath her shoes. At the top of the embankment she gazed out at the array of Douglas Firs, the rich green landscape sparkling under the sunlight.

"Emma?" Shane called out.

"I'm okay." No Jordyn, no expectations. She envisioned her world simplified, without tabloids, filled with true friends like Luci and authentic men like Shane.

I have the power to change things.

I'm gonna get my mojo back.

Emma slid out of her jacket and peeled out of her jeans. Her socks and shoes followed. She kept on her pink t-shirt, her bra, and red bikini panties. She wanted to keep at least one major article of clothing dry. She thought about Shane seeing her in her undies. Embarrassing, but Luci would say it was the same as wearing a bikini bottom and urge her to be adventurous. No need to be shy. *Adventurous?* She could do that. Chilled air attacked Emma's skin, and she shivered.

"Emma." Shane's voice grew louder, his tone more concerned. "You okay?"

"If I do this, we do all ten tasks together."

"*All of them?* You haven't seen the whole list."

"Have you?"

"Some of it, but that was a long time ago."

"Did you see anything about killing anyone?"

"Uh, no."

"Good. Any whips and chains?"

Shane's laughter echoed the forest walls. "Nope."

"Awesome. Let's get that mojo back. Agreed?"

"Agreed."

Emma heaved in a sharp breath, backed farther from the edge then ran full force toward it. Heart pounding in her ears, the forest quieted as if waiting for the moment to pass. Emma dove off the embankment with a single scream, her body soaring into the air. All the responsibilities, the heartache, dissipated and she was the Emma who worked as a waitress all those years ago, who sat in front of her laptop typing up scripts, hoping to be the next big screenwriter.

She crashed into the freezing water, then burst upward, gulping in air.

"It's colder than I thought it would be."

"I know." Shane stood at the edge of the pond, his jeans soaked, droplets dotting his face. "That's why I got out."

She squinted at him. "You didn't tell me that."

"You looked great up there. I'll get your clothes."

Emma swam to the shallow end of the pond, smiling, adrenaline flowing through her, her heart still racing. She'd taken a leap of faith—let go with Shane. And she wasn't wearing any pants. Maybe this was a date.

HANE FOLLOWED EMMA UP TO THE STEPS OF her house, the wood creaking, fierce rain pounding upon them. His brain twisted with all the reasons he dove off the waterfall, a feat he couldn't accomplish as a teen. He remembered the other females, in their small colorful bikinis, staring at the dorky, skinny kid who froze at the top of the Noboru, unable to conquer his fears. Too risky, too shy, wearing gym shorts and a t-shirt, he'd gazed at the scenery, his feet stuck at the top of the embankment. They'd laughed at him, but Liam shut them all down with a warning look.

After all these years, he'd at last jumped, releasing some of the confusion and frustration at how and why his world unraveled in the last ten months.

Emma adjusted the hoodie on her head, clothing Shane had purchased from the gift store on their way out of the park. He'd bought sweatpants for himself.

She swung open the screen door, and it whined louder than the rain's banter. She looked back at him. "Thanks for the sweatshirt. And thanks for today. That was fun."

"Best day in a long time."

She paused at the tenderness in his tone. Neither of them spoke. He ached for her lips

to be joined with his. As hard as she fought to mask it, he'd witnessed the same hunger in her eyes.

"Think you got your mojo back?" she asked.

Shane stepped closer to her, invading her personal space and absorbed the questions in her honey-colored eyes. "I think so. What do you think?"

"Feels like it."

"Is that a good thing?"

"Yeah?"

"Is that a question?" He placed his hands on the door beside her head, the gap between them mere inches. He zeroed in on her mouth, lush, full, anticipating how sweet she would taste.

"No." Emma pressed her back into the door. "I mean yes, it's a good thing." She stared up at him, her breath quickening, her glossy eyes responding to the request he so desperately wanted.

Yes.

Shane dropped his hands from the door, slipping one arm around her waist. He lowered his head, tilting slightly to one side and leaned in, their lips a breath apart.

The door swung open. "Emma?" The woman glanced from Emma to Shane and back to Emma. "Oh, sorry. I thought you were alone."

"It's okay, Luci." Emma dropped her chin to her chest releasing a long breath. "I was just coming inside."

Emma was grateful for the disruption, seconds from inventing a new mess, another mistake. Without Luci's interruption, all control abandoned, Emma would've tackled Shane and that rippled body. Whatever followed would be completely and happily out of her hands. She needed level-headed thinking and reeled in raging thoughts of her and Shane together.

Shane released her, and she stepped back.

"I can close the door and we can all pretend this never happened," Luci said. "And you two can get back to whatever you were doing."

"Luci, really. It's alright." She waved a hand between Luci and Shane. "Luci, meet Shane. Shane, meet Luci."

He extended his hand to Luci, a wide smile on his face. "Nice to meet you."

"Shane, the schoolteacher?" Luci shook his hand. "Nice to meet *you*." She shot Emma an expression that said, "damn girl, good job."

Shane glanced at Emma. *So, you've been talking about me?*

Emma cringed. "I better go." She spun around, quickly hurrying inside. She turned back and caught a final look of longing in Shane's eyes.

If anything happened between them…if the press ever found out… She shut her eyes tightly. Shane was the toy she couldn't have, the forbidden candy she couldn't eat. Acting on the firestorm that raced from her pelvis to her chest at the sight and the sound of his voice, wasn't worth the price he'd pay if the press discovered the two of them together.

Her temporary reality was quiet, secure from prying eyes. One day that would end. Once Shane knew her true identity and the paparazzi found her, there'd be nowhere to hide, no secret place to hide. His teaching, his students, his life unveiled to a world of strangers. He was normal. She was a different kind of normal, and the two wouldn't mix well, unless she found a way to keep her "dates" with him hidden. Kept herself concealed. Maybe there was a chance.

"You ladies have a good rest of the day." Shane turned to leave.

"Wait, Shane?" Emma took a step toward him and Shane paused. "How good is your memory?"

"Not bad. Why?" The unclear reason for her question lingered in his eyes.

"I'm only gonna say this once, and I'm not writing it down." She rattled off ten numbers.

Shane easily repeated them, a big smile on his face. "Bye, Emma."

"Bye, Shane."

His descended the porch steps then rushed across the yard toward his car.

"Emma," Luci said. "I hope you know what you're doing. You just gave him the red cell phone number."

"I know." The red cell phone number. Reserved for close friends and family. Only four people knew the red cell phone number. Not even Jordyn had the number. She pondered why she'd never given it to him. She thought of Shane, her lips tilting into a satisfied smile. "Let's see if he remembers it."

Thirteen

SHANE WAITED FOR HIS QUESTION TO BE ANSWERED. *What had been the reason for Mercutio's untimely demise? Misunderstanding, a rush for vengeance without gathering all the facts.* The sea of faces stared back at him. Baffled. Scared. Awkward.

Shane stood at the head of the class, his eyes seeking acknowledgement that someone, anyone, understood the day's lesson. His room was filled with the usual assortment of students. One of the three football players shifted nervously in his seat. A few others looked down at their notebooks or doodled on their papers. Most of the class avoided eye contact.

The final bell rang, and the students scrambled from their desks.

"Don't forget about tonight's homework," Shane called out as students hurried past him. The door slammed shut and the last student rushed into the corridor. Shane picked up a stack of papers from the previous night's homework. He shuffled the papers together, tapping the edges against the desk to align the sheets and stuffed them into his shoulder bag.

Liam's list came to mind.

Number one, conquer Noboru.

Completed.

He dug into his back pocket, retrieving the third index he'd received from his "concerned citizen."

Task Three.

Play a musical instrument to an audience.

Play to an audience? He'd rather bite his fingers off. He'd told Emma about the third task and she sounded determined to help him. Maybe she could calm his nerves and they could devise a plan to play at least one song in front of an unsuspecting crowd. In a bar? On the street? Shane frowned; he didn't even own a musical instrument.

The classroom door opened. "Rough day?"

Shane looked up at the female in a black pencil skirt and teal camisole that hugged her curvy figure. The name instantly came to him. "Delia Rose." He slid the card into his back pocket.

"Sometimes I ask myself why I still do it." Delia paused just inside the classroom, her slender fingers curled around the door handle.

"Do what?" Shane hoisted the bag onto his shoulder.

"Teach." She sauntered toward him. "How do you feel about catching a drink with me? I think today we've earned it."

"I can't." He took his cell phone from his front pants pocket. In the week since Emma gave him her telephone number, he'd called the first time just to see if it was real. After that, they spoke by phone every day. Once, he'd called her minutes before leaving for work, just so he could hear the sound of her voice. Half asleep, groggy, and confused at his early call, the inflection in her tone had been happy. That instead of trying to rid herself of him, she welcomed the sound of his voice. It was progress, and worth it. The old Shane refused this much excitement over any woman, even with Heather. Always holding back, not exhibiting his honest, raw emotions. The new Shane swam nervously in uncharted territory.

"No?" Delia blinked at him.

He thumbed through the contacts on his cell phone screen and located Emma's number. "I'm sorry, Delia. I really have to be somewhere right now." He hurried to the door, his eyes silently asking her to step back.

Delia gave him a tight smile. She spun around, her black high heels clacking across the tile floor as she returned to her classroom.

"Shane." Gabe passed Delia she exited the room. He glanced back at Delia, a wide smirk on his face before he turned to Shane. "Did I just interrupt something?"

"I'm on my way out."

Gabe continued his rant. "What the hell, man? Where did you go the other night? You don't seem to be yourself. Cutting out of here as soon as the last bell sounds? That's not your style."

"I've been busy."

"Busy taking French lessons with Mrs. Loutiere? Rumor has it you're serious about learning French. What's going on?"

"Long story Gabe, but I have to go." He shuffled Gabe out into the hall, then pressed the button to call Emma and held the phone up to his ear.

She answered on the first ring. "Hello?"

"Hey." Shane smiled, seeing absolute bewilderment on Gabe's face. "Hold on a sec, Em." He locked the classroom door. "I promise I'll call you later, Gabe."

"Who's Em?"

"Later, Gabe," Shane repeated, swiftly reaching the corridor exit. He pushed open the doors and stepped out into the frigid, early evening air.

"Emma, you still there?"

"Yeah, Shane," she said gently. "I'm here."

———

Emma settled into the huge leather chair of the massive mahogany desk in the home office of their vacation rental and sighed with satisfaction. The walls were painted olive green, books were packed into built-in shelves, and two square windows faced the street. The curtains were drawn, and sunlight splashed across the room.

After five minutes on the phone with Shane, she stared at the screen of her silver laptop and powered it down. Eighteen pages, four hours straight. She intended to finish the script, even if her agent thought she'd lost every bit of her brain cells.

Her gaze flickered to the red cell phone. Shane had been keeping his physical distance at her request. Emma wanted to, needed to complete the script. She lowered the laptop monitor and clicked it shut. She had a surprise for Shane and was ready to meet him in the designated location in twenty minutes.

Luci tapped the side of the doorframe, wrenching Emma from her thoughts. "You're going out with him again aren't you? Do you know what you're doing?"

"Nope." Emma tucked her laptop under one arm. She grabbed the red cell phone with the other hand.

"But you're doing it anyway?" Luci folded her arms and leaned back against the door.

Emma handed Luci the red cell phone and rushed to her bedroom to change. "Yup."

"I'm so proud of you," Luci said as she patted Emma on the back as she passed by.

"Proud of me?"

"You're back to the Emma I know. Not doing what's expected of you and not caring what anyone else thinks. I think this guy really likes you. And you like him."

Emma smiled. Every time the red cell phone vibrated, her insides curled with excitement, knowing it was Shane. They spent hours talking about almost anything and everything. Except Shane didn't explain what'd caused the major shift in his life, and she'd avoided letting him know how successful an actress she'd become.

She pinned her hair up into a soft bun, a strip of wavy hair falling near her eyes. She slipped her arms into a golden scoop-neck top and dark blue jeans. She opted for matching flats instead of her casual boots. She applied a little makeup, just a small amount of eye shadow and lip gloss. Hoop earrings, no costume jewelry, Emma was set for her meeting with Shane.

Her cell phone rang, the distinctive melody of her mother. Alanis Morrisette's infamous song playing, "*Uninvited*." Luci appeared at the bedroom door. "It's desert cactus. I put her on hold. What do you wanna do?"

Desert cactus. A discussion with her mother was required immediately. She wished the code meant a real emergency. Like being admitted to the hospital. Or receiving terrible news that required sympathy and comfort.

Her mother's so-called emergency call meant a lecture, words she wanted to scream at Emma directly. Emma studied the phone in Luci's hand. If she lied, said she was in the bathroom, her mother would wait on the line for her to finish.

If Luci advised her mother that Emma was sleeping, her mother would demand that Luci wake her up. If Emma took the call now, it might alter her mood when she met up with Shane. Or she might be late meeting him. Emma didn't want the airy, cheery feeling coursing through her veins to be disrupted.

She glanced from the phone to Luci then back to the phone and held out her hand.

Luci released a long breath and dropped the cell phone into the middle of Emma's palm.

Emma pressed the mute button and held the device to her ear. "Hello?"

Madeline's firm, irritated voice belted out a single question. "Please tell me you're not avoiding Jordyn's calls?"

Emma stifled a long drawn out breath. Back to the same old conversation. Jordyn Mars. Not exactly the name she wanted to hear before her meeting with Shane. "What's there to say mom? We're not together anymore."

"He wants to reconcile. You're not even giving him a chance to make it up to you."

Jordyn and her mother were having far better discussions than she was with her own mother at the moment. Her mother and Jordyn had formed a bond from their first introduction. Madeline wanted them to marry, the glow in her hazel eyes approving the union.

"Mom, he cheated on me."

Her mother huffed as if Emma were being silly. "It happens. He tried to apologize."

"When?"

"Every time he's called. Check your voicemail."

"Mom," Emma said, trying a soft approach, her tone gentle. "He's only looking out for himself and his career."

"There's nothing wrong with that," Madeline shot back. "Your careers *are* important."

To you. Emma stuffed the words back down her throat, knowing there'd be no way to win this argument. Since she was five years old, her mother entered Emma in pageants and a variety of other activities, the foundation for what she believed would become the basis for Emma's success. In competition with the other moms in Maple Grove, a small, but wealthy suburb outside of Los Angeles, each mother used to brag about all the activities her child participated in. There were foreign languages to learn, music, ballet, tap, and piano lessons to master. Then came tennis, which her mother considered to be a lady's sport, swimming, and track. By adulthood, she'd created her own path in life, but it hadn't stopped Madeline from throwing rocks at her along each trail.

Madeline took Emma's hesitation as agreement. "Good, it's settled. Jordyn will call you around six-thirty tonight, so you two can talk this out. Bye, hon. If you keep avoiding his calls though, I'll have to give him the red cell phone number."

"Mom—"

Her mother's voice dropped from the line.

Emma stared down at the red cell phone's screen.

"Want me to change the number?" Luci asked quietly.

"It's better if I block his," Emma said, fiddling with the phone, searching the options to block Jordyn's number once. "But changing my number might not be a bad idea either." Her eyes caught sight of the time on the small screen. "Damn, I'm gonna be late." She dropped the black phone into her handbag. "I'll block him later."

"Yeah, drama later, because right now, you look awesome." Luci examined Emma's image in the full-length mirror behind the bedroom door. "Shane's gonna think you're a hottie."

Emma scrutinized her reflection. Hair in place, outfit complete. She pulled the shades out of her purse and slid them onto her face. "That's a compliment, right?"

"Yeah, so go get your man, girl." She swatted Emma on the butt, like a football player boosting his teammate's confidence before the big play.

"He's not my man," Emma said with a smirk, scurrying down the hall to the front door.

"Don't worry," Luci called out. "He will be."

CHAPTER

Fourteen

"AH, BACK TO THE BEANIE AND SHADES," SHANE said as he glanced at Emma standing beside him on the sidewalk.

Emma shrugged. "It's the new style. It's called 'Disguise.'"

Shane chuckled. He looked up at the neon blue sign glowing above the store's large pane glass window. "Something tells me this has to do with the list?"

"Did Liam play an instrument?"

"The clarinet."

"That's sexy."

"It was. The females loved him." He laughed lightly, then sighed, lowering his head, as if rehashing his childhood memories brought more pain than joy.

Emma wondered about the sadness that flashed in Shane's eyes. Had he and Liam suffered a falling out? Or had a tragedy struck him somehow? A conversation Emma tucked away for later. She sucked in a deep breath, flashed him her best smile, slipped her hand into his, and gently tugged him toward the door. "He might've been onto something."

Shane looked down at their joined hands and up at Emma.

Emma pulled harder. *Good, he's distracted.* "Shane. You agreed we'd complete everything on the list."

Shane took a few steps toward the glass double door entrance. He tilted his head, flashing a puzzled look, but silently followed her inside the shop.

The music store's lights beamed brightly. Guitars hung upright along one extended side wall and saxophones lined the back wall. Keyboards and a few upright pianos lined the middle of the store. Customers milled through the shop, several rattling the keys of the piano, others examining various guitars hanging on the side wall. Emma soaked in the array of musical instruments. Violins. Guitars. Saxophones. Clarinets. Pianos. Drums. She sauntered to the racks of musical books, classical, movie soundtracks, pop music sheets. Shane stood beside her and thumbed through a shelf of pop music books, his expression that of a man wanting answers, but patient enough to wait for them. She wondered how long that patience would last.

A skinny man with glasses and short blond hair approached them. "Can I help you with anything?"

"Yes." Emma pushed the sunglasses up onto her face and gazed at each guitar on the wall. There were electric guitars in all colors. Black, red, auburn. White straps, blue straps, dark brown. She pointed to a six-string acoustic guitar hanging on the top row with a mahogany body and a spruce top. "May I see that one, please?"

"Sure." The man carefully removed the guitar from the wall and handed it to her. "Do you have any questions about it?"

"Oh no but thank you." Emma located three small rooms toward the right wall, each compact space lacking doors and only able to uncomfortably fit four people. The middle room was vacant. Emma wandered inside and sat down on a black stool. She hoisted the strap of the guitar over her head, positioning it across her left shoulder.

Shane studied her closely, his eyes flickering from her face to the guitar, her hands, and her face again. "You know how to play the guitar?"

Emma scanned the strings, the fretboard and knobs. "Since I was eleven. My mother insisted I learn an instrument. She preferred the piano, but I learned the guitar out of spite."

Beyond Shane's shoulder Emma saw a sliver of the store's front entrance. The sound of electric guitars and pianos diminished.

Emma angled the shades on top of her head. She slid a blue guitar pick from her right jean pocket. "Turns out I really liked it."

She relaxed her arms and poised her fingers over the strings. She slowly strummed the guitar, finding the right pitch, playing a soothing melody, her fingers moving with ease. She held the last note and smiled triumphantly.

Shane shook his head in disbelief. "Actress, writer, musician. Is there anything you can't do?"

The inability to shake her mother's phone calls and rid herself of Jordyn's advances instantly sprang to mind. She rested one hand on the side of the guitar. "I can't cook." She stood up and lifted the strap over her head. "Okay, your turn."

"Excuse me?"

"It's your turn now." Emma handed him the guitar and placed both her hands on his arms.

"Emma…"

"You're gonna learn to play the guitar today. Remember your mojo?"

"How could I forget?" He eased on to the stool. "You're really going to make me do this?"

"Someone has to." She adjusted the guitar across his body, arranging his fingertips in the correct position. She put the pick in his hand. "Now try it."

Shane lightly stroked the guitar and smiled at the harmonious sound.

Pleased, Emma put her hands on her hips. "Good. Do it again."

He replayed the tune, his fingers tripping across two notes as he maneuvered his hand on the fretboard.

"Slowly," Emma said. "You don't wanna rush something like this."

He suddenly looked up from the guitar and she realized the double meaning behind what she'd said. Neither of them spoke. Emma finally said, "Why don't we just stop dancing around this?"

"Okay." Shane placed the guitar upright against the barstool.

She bit her lip and thought of the proper approach to a discussion about a relationship they didn't have. "Shane, if you knew the real Emma—"

"This isn't the real Emma?" He sized up Emma from her ballet flats to the beanie on her head.

"This is the vacation Emma. The real Emma in L.A. is a lot different."

"Okay." Shane folded his arms across his chest. "So, the real Emma doesn't play the guitar, doesn't like movies and doesn't normally hide from everyone?"

"I play the guitar and I love movies, but it's different in L.A."

"Different?"

"Well yeah, it's sorta complicated."

"You-have-a-secret-boyfriend-complicated?"

I wish you were. "No."

"You have a husband stashed somewhere?"

"I'm not married, remember?"

His lips curved into a wry, challenging smile. "So, what other excuse are you going to give me? And don't say the race thing because I really don't care what people think."

"Other people care."

"I'm not other people." He stood up and surveyed the area around her legs as if she harbored a huge trunk behind her. "What else you got?"

"We're different. In a lot of ways."

"We complement each other. It's simple. Everything else can be figured out."

She searched for the words and couldn't find them. The knots in her belly wound up tight inside her. Shane had become attached to her new reality, something she wasn't ready to change. "Shane, I like you, but—"

Her cell phone rang. She rummaged through her handbag, located her black cell phone and frowned at the flashing screen. Jordyn. If she didn't answer, her mother would eventually call with another one-sided discussion. Her strength to deal with mommy dearest wouldn't hold for the evening. She needed to replenish her power to handle her mother another day once she'd actually blocked Jordyn's number.

Shane glanced at the cell phone clutched in her hand. "What's wrong?"

"I wish he would just go away." The phone rang a second time.

"Who?"

She held up the phone so he could see the name. "I've already told him to stop calling me. It's really starting to piss me off."

"Old boyfriend?" Recognition settled on Shane's face.

"Very old," she emphasized. "We are not together."

"You want my help, huh?"

"Not sure how else to drop the hint." The sound of a male voice might cease all further communication with Jordyn Mars. "I told you.

Complicated." Jordyn would be outraged, the message clear. Emma had moved on.

Shane inched closer to Emma, the hint of soap tickling her nostrils. She stretched her fingers to avoid flattening her hands across his chest. Shane held out his hand and Emma carefully placed her phone in his palm.

He pressed the button and raised the phone to his ear. "Hello, Jordyn."

Emma heard the muffled sounds of Jordyn's surprised and infuriated voice on the other end. "Who the hell is this?"

"Hi. Jordyn? Emma can't talk right now." Shane pressed the button, ending the call and tossed the phone into her purse. Smoldering green eyes burned through her. "Was that okay?" His gaze shifted to her lips. He nudged the shades and beanie off her head, gripping both objects in one hand.

"That was good," she said, her heart racing, her breath quickening. *Now he's going to kiss me.* No Luci to interrupt, no internal struggle on his face. She tried composing her alternative that they remain friends but couldn't piece together an explanation.

Shane touched her cheek with his free hand and lowered his mouth to hers. "Emma."

Unable to stop him, Emma angled her mouth upward to meet his. Shane dropped the shades and beanie and they clattered to the floor. He cupped her face with both hands, parted her lips, his tongue sweeping the inside of her mouth. Every part of her body suddenly ached for him and she softly moaned. He deepened the kiss, hungrily tasting her, ravishing her like a man possessed. Emma grasped the hem of his shirt, groaning into his mouth, shivering. Shane leaned back, grazed her lips, and reluctantly released her.

Someone behind them coughed.

Emma's eyes fluttered open.

"Everything okay?" The store clerk peeked in the doorway.

Emma looked up to see Shane watching her. As if he'd expected her to angrily slap him and end their date.

"Perfect," Shane said. "Everything's perfect." He reached down, picked up her shades and beanie, and handed them to her.

Emma gratefully accepted them. The store clerk hadn't seen her face, not that it mattered at the moment. Her mind numb, her body raged for Shane's touch.

The unexpected throbbing between her thighs diminished when Shane looked at her, his eyes intense and said, "I have a confession to make."

———

"A confession?"

Shane gazed down at her. He could still taste her on his lips. Sweet, minty. He wondered if she'd knock him on his ass after that kiss, instead she'd stared up at him with swollen lips and glossy eyes. Her whimpers, her fingers clutching his shirt nearly drove him off the edge and he'd fought with every fiber of his being to release her. "I know how to play a musical instrument already."

"Really? The guitar?"

"No. I'll let you guess."

Emma squinted at him, slid her shades back on and tugged her beanie over her head. "Okay mystery man. I'm good at guessing games." She stalked out into the main area of the store and assessed the dozens of instruments positioned in the center of the room. She started toward the side of the store and brushed her fingertips across a clarinet. "Clarinet, maybe?"

"No."

"It has to be something unusual. You seem like a guy who does the unexpected."

"Was that a compliment?"

She lightly beat a pair of conga drums with her palms.

Shane chuckled and shook his head.

"No?" Emma placed a hand on her chest, feigning surprise. "I thought that would've been the one. Maybe it's these drums?" She grabbed a pair of wooden drumsticks and gently tapped the crash cymbal and the snare drum.

"Nope."

She eyed each instrument carefully then pressed one finger and another on the white and black keys of a Privia digital piano. "Could it be possible, the old Shane learned something as classic as the piano?"

"You're just showering me with compliments today." Shane walked to the piano. "Yes. My mother made me take lessons for years when I was a kid." His adrenaline was building within him at the prospect of playing the piano again, especially in front of someone. Several customers milled throughout the store; no one was paying attention to him or Emma. The last person to see him play had been Liam, but Shane had never played in the presence of anyone else, not even Sallie.

Emma invaded his space, smirking up at him. She lifted her glasses so he could see the mischievous glint in her eyes. "Your mojo will take a huge leap if you can actually play a song. I might even give you a reward."

A reward? He sat down on the bench. "What kind of reward?"

She shrugged and lowered her shades, her eyes once again covered. "I don't know. I haven't heard you play yet."

"I'll think of something." He positioned his fingers over the keys then began to play a soft melody.

"That's good." She appeared genuinely impressed. "Did you write that?"

"It's a Dalton Matthews song," Shane said. "What you'd consider Indie rock. He actually plays the guitar, but I like the sound of it under the piano."

"Nicely done." She signaled for the cashier and asked for the guitar she'd been playing earlier. He handed it to her, and she began to strum the guitar in tune with his song.

Customers turned and watched them. Shane continued to play with tenderness and ease, Emma accompanying him with her guitar. He finished the last note and Emma struck the final chord, the song ending.

The customers applauded and Emma just smiled at him. "Playing a musical instrument in front of an audience? Well done. Now we have to go back to learning a new language. We missed that one. Do you know how to speak another language?"

"Do you?"

She rattled off several sentences in Spanish.

His jaw dropped. What the hell didn't this woman know how to do?

She set the guitar down. "Roughly translated I said, 'if you want to go out with me again, you'll have to ask me in another language.'"

Shane watched her walk away, her hips swaying. She paused at the exit doors and turned to look at him. Emma had no idea he'd been taking lessons from the French teacher, Mrs. Loutiere for the last two weeks. Learn a new language in order to see her again? Not a problem.

Fifteen

EMMA ROLLED OVER AND CLUTCHED HER PILLOW. She blinked, fully opening her eyes, welcoming the morning light. The ivory curtains partially open, dense fog lingered outside her bedroom window. She lifted her head slightly, peeking at the thick trunks of the trees blocking her view of Puget Sound. Mist drifted across the water, filtering among the trees.

"So, this is what you look like when you wake up."

Emma snapped her head up.

Shane leaned against the doorframe; arms folded across his chest.

Emma instinctively drew the covers up to her neck. Dressed in a gray tank top and navy boxers, she felt naked with Shane this close to her bed. Her mind traced back to the night of their first and only kiss, the kind of kiss that made her forget words, time and all common sense. Shane was definitely a bad influence.

"I'm a little creeped out that you're standing in my bedroom right now."

"I'm not in it." He analyzed the room and the doorframe. "I'm at the edge of it." He pointed at her clothes. "Is that a Max the Mouse shirt?"

Her top was imprinted with the image of Max the Mouse, her favorite childhood cartoon character. "How did you get in here?"

Shane jabbed his thumb over his shoulder. "Luci. I thought you'd be up by now."

"What time is it?"

"Almost twelve."

Emma glanced at the red cell phone charging on her nightstand. Fifteen minutes to one o'clock. She'd overslept. Staying up until nearly 4 a.m. left her in a deeper sleep than she'd hoped. For several days she'd tended to her manuscript, writing early into the a.m. She and Shane spoke by phone but hadn't seen each other since their impromptu band session at the music store.

"Luci," Emma called out.

Luci appeared in the doorway and pointed at Shane. "Oh, yeah. Shane's here." Her eyes wide with amusement, her mischievous smile said she'd knowingly allowed Shane inside to witness a half-asleep Emma.

He held up an index card, the print identical to the others.

Task Four.

He flipped the card over.

Take a two wheeled ride to the Pass.

What was *the Pass*?

Emma rubbed her eyes with both hands, not caring how odd she looked. Hair tussled, eyelids dragging, voice earthy. "I've never heard of 'the Pass' but I told you Shane, I'm not going out with you again until you can ask me out in another language."

If Shane was appalled by her late morning bedroom appearance, he didn't show it. His gaze roamed over her with bemusement. Placing his hands together and tipping the edge of his fingers against his lips like a man in prayer, he gave a small bow and looked up at her. Straightening, he let his arms fall to his sides. "*Bonjour belle. Voulez-vous sortir avec moi? Je tu m'as tellement manqué. Je vais attendre.*" He stepped back from the doorway as Luci and Emma both gaped at him, their mouths unabashedly open. Shane glanced at Luci, then Emma. He broke into a wide grin and casually strolled down the narrow corridor to the living room.

Luci marched into the bedroom and shut the door behind her.

Emma raised up on her knees, the covers sliding away. She pointed at the place Shane had stood. "Was he just speaking French?"

"I believe he was, and it sounded really good."

"What do you think he said?"

Luci tore through Emma's closet, scanning the hanging shirts for an appropriate outfit. "I think he said, get your ass up, put some clothes on, and meet me out front."

Emma laughed. "That's not what he said."

"Close enough." Luci dragged a short sleeved white button blouse and a charcoal colored vest from the closet. She jerked open the second drawer of Emma's dresser and thumbed through the stack of jeans. She held up a pair of dark blue jeans with the button shirt and vest. "Perfect." Luci tossed them at Emma. "Put them on. You don't have a lot of time."

Emma rammed her body into the clothes, the jeans hugging her hips, the shirt and vest outlining her curves. The top button, unfastened, displayed a small bit of cleavage. Emma looked down at her chest. "I feel naked."

"They're breasts, get over it." Luci tousled Emma's hair, waving her hands around her head like a stylist putting the image together.

Emma brushed her teeth while slapping Luci's hands away. Small wisps of hair drifted near her eyes and she pushed them aside. The face she put on for the cameras was Emma at work, but Emma at home loved jeans, sneakers, less makeup and no-fuss hair. It infuriated her mother whenever she caught Emma in downtime. Hair pulled into a ponytail, clothes no more than jeans and a t-shirt. Jeans were for boys, Madeline liked to say.

Emma brushed her teeth, gargled with mouthwash, and stared at herself in the full-length mirror behind the closet door. She definitely did not look like a boy, and the jeans fit her well— not too tight, and just loose just enough to capitalize on the forty-five minutes spent on the treadmill three times a week.

Emma grabbed the red cell phone from her nightstand and dropped it into the purse. She flung open the bedroom door and started down the hall.

Shane waited in front of the fireplace. Utter amazement glazed his eyes when he saw her. Delight. Admiration. As though she could wear a garbage bag and look just as enchanting.

"I'm not dressed up, you know." She squirmed under his flaming green eyes. She wanted to get lost in those eyes, run her fingers through his hair, lose herself completely for a couple of hours.

Shane handed her a brown shopping bag. "You're going to need to put this on. Over your clothes."

She peeked in the bag and looked at Shane. "What is this?"

"A rain suit. You'll want to wear it before we get there."

"It's not raining." The fog had lifted, the sun stripping away gray skies, streaks of light crossing the hardwood floor.

"It's not raining *now*." Shane followed her gaze to the window. "But it will be. Trust me, you'll need it."

"A rain suit." She whirled around and headed back down the hallway. She shut the door to her bedroom, realizing Shane was wearing a rain suit similar to the one he'd given her. She climbed into the nylon pants, which fit easily over her jeans, and slid her arms into the matching jacket, zipping it to the apex of her neck. She returned to the living room and found Shane still standing in front of the fireplace.

He picked up a bookbag she hadn't noticed sitting on the floor and slung the right strap over his shoulder. "You ready?"

"I guess."

Shane opened the door and pushed the screen ajar. He held it open as Emma stepped into the late morning air. A red motorcycle was parked in her driveway. Emma turned back to Shane, and he pressed one hand softly on the small of her back, easing her toward the cycle. She stopped, and Shane strode ahead of her as if a red motorcycle in her driveway was a regular event.

The sleepy part of her brain fully awakened.

A two wheeled ride.

A motorcycle.

"You want me to get on that?" She pointed to the bike.

"*That,* is a 646 Monster Ducati."

"Monster?" She blinked, staring at the bike as if it were the devil incarnate.

Shane chuckled. "She's easy to ride, don't worry. You've never ridden on a motorcycle, have you?"

"Clearly, you have."

"You'll be fine." He handed her the bookbag and swung his leg over the seat of the Ducati. "You agreed, we'd do these tasks together. Put this on for me. We'll need it later."

She hooked her arms through the shoulder straps of the bookbag. She'd never been on a motorcycle. If she received a script requiring a bike ride, Emma would've happily done so under the guidance of a stunt man or woman. Yet no script with a bike ride ever came, and there were no stuntmen around in case she screwed up. No stuntmen, just Shane. Shane, who straddled the bike, adjusted his head into a black helmet and handed one back to her.

Emma took the helmet, put it over her head and was unable to take another step toward Shane's outstretched hand.

Buck up Emma, she told herself. *Get on the bike. You jumped off a waterfall. You can do this.*

Emma accepted his hand and swung her leg over the seat of the bike. He helped her adjust her legs and feet, and she wrapped her arms snug around his waist. Shane turned the key in the ignition, the engine roared to life, and he carefully maneuvered them to the end of the driveway. At the edge of the property, Shane charged out into the vacant street, easily accelerating through the winding roads at a steady pace.

Trees, the lush green landscape, passed by them in a blur, and Emma smiled. Her future plans were mired in uncertainty; the only thing she knew as fact, she wasn't leaving Shane or Bainbridge Island, any time soon.

———

As Shane had predicted, by the time they reached the ferry, rain drizzled upon them. After the ferry ride, sun blazed through cracks in the clouds. Speeding up along Interstate 90 and approaching the first bridge, droplets pelted her suit. Thunder crackled the sky, but Shane rode with ease, shifting in and out of lanes as they reached the second bridge. She pressed herself against his back, her arms relaxed around his waist.

He drove into the parking lot of an old-style diner, built like a long silver trailer, red neon lights cutting through the overcast sky. He pulled into a space, turned off the engine and pushed the kickstand down. He took off his helmet and Emma did the same. The storm diminished, water sprinkling her face and she stared up at the glowing red letters above the restaurant entrance. *Island Diner.*

She looked at Shane. "Where are we?"

He glanced over the half-empty parking lot. "We're in Everett." He took her helmet, placing both helmets on the bike. "I used to come here a lot."

"You lived here?"

"Used to." He stepped back to soak in the image of Emma, strands of her hair plastered to her face. "You look so beautiful."

"Don't change the subject."

Shane slid a strand of hair from her cheek. "I'm not." He gently lifted her chin and lowered his head, teasing as his lips brushed hers. His tongue invaded her mouth, caressing her with promises of tenderness and an urge for more. She held him tightly, her arms around his waist, head tilted back. He pulled back, captured her mouth in another quick, tender kiss and released her.

Emma fought the strong desire to reach up and find his mouth again. "You're trying to distract me."

"A little." He took her hand and led her toward the entrance. "C'mon. You've got to try the peach pie."

Emma fumbled with one hand in the bottom pocket of the bookbag for her bumblebee sunglasses. Feeling the hard frames, she yanked the shades from her purse and slid them on her face.

The restaurant contained only a few customers. Shane and Emma quickly slid into a booth toward the back. Linoleum gray tables with orange colored leather seats. Shane sat across from her and frowned at the shades on her face. "The sunglasses? Again?"

Their outings, so far, kept Emma in disguise. Always the shades and beanie. She forgot the beanie this time, with only her sunglasses to shield her from public view. She prayed the waitress wouldn't notice or any of the restaurant's customers. Shane needed to know the whole truth about her identity, but she couldn't bring herself to tell him. Not yet. She just wanted to enjoy her limited time with him before it exploded.

Someone would eventually recognize her, and the paparazzi, everyone, would be upon them. Emma didn't want anything or anyone to disrupt the connection between her and Shane, but irritation simmered behind his eyes. The kiss in the parking lot was a declaration. He didn't care who knew, or who saw them.

"Just humor me? Please?" She held the square plastic menu up, covering her face and scanned the lunch items listed.

The waitress appeared at their booth. She was a petite, older woman, wearing a white dress, the hemline an inch above her knees, and a purple smock. Her silver and gray hair was tied tightly in a ponytail, her bangs neatly cut at the brow line.

Emma dipped her head behind the menu but glimpsed the small square black nametag on the woman's uniform. *Macy.*

"What'll it be?" Macy raised her pen and paper, poised to take their orders.

"Coffee, please." Emma peeked over the top of the menu.

"Make that two coffees," Shane added. "And two slices of peach pie."

The waitress repeated his instructions and wrote down their orders. She spun on her heel, scurrying off, her tennis shoes squeaking as she hurried to the silver counter where two men cooked the day's orders.

Shane leaned back in his seat and studied Emma closely. "When are we going to talk about the disguise?"

"Not right now." Emma set her menu on the table, averting Shane's questioning gaze. "I'll tell you later." Reality threatened to fall from her lips and once revealed, she wouldn't be able to take it back. How would Shane view her then? As a pariah? As a trophy? She shoved the thoughts aside. "How long has your family lived here?"

Shane's gaze lingered over her a minute longer. He inhaled a long breath, released it. "Most of my life. Liam and I used to come here."

"Liam, the ladies' man?"

Shane smiled. "He did love the ladies." He fiddled with the edge of the menu. "But so did I. Up until Heather."

"Did Liam settle down?"

Only one corner of his lips slanted upward. "Yeah, he did. Amari. Sweet lady. I think everyone knew I'd follow in his footsteps. I almost did." He turned his attention to the window where the downpour increased to hail. Ice chips tapped the window, begging to get in. The edges of Shane's eyes creased, his brows furrowed downward, his mouth set in a grim line.

Emma recognized the sudden transformation from annoyance to sadness. "He sounds like a really good friend."

"He was my *best* friend."

"What happened?"

"He's dead." Shane looked at Emma and she no longer saw the Shane that kissed her with so much warmth and gentleness minutes ago. He disintegrated into a different Shane, lost, angry, lacking words or an explanation. He pushed the menu away.

"I'm sorry," she said quietly. "What happened to him?"

"Car accident."

The waitress returned and placed two ceramic mugs on the table filled with hot coffee, swirls of steam rising from the surface. Emma mumbled her thanks, and the waitress gave a small nod, moving on to a packed booth three seats away.

Shane tore open a small creamer container and poured the white liquid into his coffee. He glanced up at Emma, and the Shane she remembered from the parking lot resurfaced. "Liam was like a brother to me. He and my sister Sallie never treated me different, even after I 'fell out' with my family who I see only about once a month." He ripped open two sugar packets and emptied them into the mug. "My mother still has that look of disappointment on her face any time she sees me. I only go because I know Sallie will be there and I do miss her."

"You and Sallie sound close." Emma poured three creamer packets into her coffee.

Shane raised the mug to his lips. "We were, I mean, we are." He took a small sip and set the mug on the table. "I should call her more often."

"You're lucky to have siblings. I don't have any."

"Only child?"

"My mother wasn't keen on siblings."

"That's rough. She didn't like kids?"

"No, she didn't. She wanted to make sure there was one sufficient offspring to carry the bloodline. And for my mother, one was enough."

"How did your dad feel about that?"

Emma sipped her coffee. "My father wanted a house full of kids. They argued a lot about it. My mother looks at babies like they're toxic, but I think she loves me in her own way. She wanted to keep the essentials, her figure, her free time. She did charity work, raising money for underprivileged schools. She traveled a lot, sometimes co-developing new, non-profit organizations."

"She sounds like a saint."

"Yes, to the public. Especially to the jealous other elite moms she was trying to one up. I spent a great deal of time with nannies. My mother firmly believes a woman should be married to a man with a respectable income. A man with a sizable fortune would allow me the opportunity and freedom she had to do all the things she wanted. As she says, there's the hard path and the easy one. I disagree, so she and I butt heads quite often."

"She loved your dad?"

Emma thought on that. She remembered loving looks passing between her parents when they didn't think anyone was watching. "I think she did. My parents always had this physical connection with each other. Mom would have her hand on his shoulder, or he'd have his palm gently against her back. They had a ritual of kissing each other goodbye every morning. Not a peck on the lips, and not a slobbery X-rated one either. Just this intimate kiss between them before he went to work. One day, my dad forgot, and my mother had a fit." She cupped her mug with both hands, heat warming her skin and she lowered her eyes. "Right after he died, she locked herself away in her bedroom for a whole week. I'd bring her food and could hear her crying on the other side, but she refused to open the door for me. Didn't think it was 'ladylike' for me to see her like that."

"I'm sorry, Em."

"That's okay. It was a long time ago." She faintly smiled. "Mom enrolled me in every activity imaginable to keep up with the neighbors' kids, but my dad sometimes snuck me away to do normal kid stuff."

"Like?"

"Like teaching me how to play basketball. Taking me to the fair when it was in town. He'd go on all the rides with me and Mom never knew. She'd never allow it, also considered it 'unladylike.'"

"Sounds like she has a long list of 'unladylike' items."

Emma giggled. "She does."

The waitress reappeared, delivering two small plates, each with a slice of peach pie. "Anything else?" She glanced from Shane to Emma.

Emma propped her elbow on the table, dropping her head in her palm, her fingers shielding her eyes. She shifted her gaze away from the waitress. "No, thank you."

Shane shook his head, a signal that he too, had no further instructions for Macy.

The waitress left the table.

"Bank robber?" Shane asked.

"What?"

124

He nodded at her hands. "I'm not one to judge. You hid the money and you're lying low, right?"

"You might be on to something."

"How about we share the loot, fifty-fifty split?"

"Money's all mine. *If* I were a bank robber, which I'm not."

"An assassin, maybe?"

She laughed. "Shouldn't you be afraid of me then?"

"I like to live on the edge."

"So I've noticed."

He eyed her closely. "I think this is more than just enjoying the quiet. I'm gonna solve this little mystery of yours."

I hope not. Once he learned her identity, the famous Emma at last exposed, Shane might retreat to his solitude. Without Emma. She wasn't ready for any of it to end.

"So, what's the plan for today?" Emma cut a small portion of pie with her fork and lifted the piece to her mouth. She closed her eyes at the decadent taste of warm peaches on her tongue. Sweeping her tongue across her bottom lip, she opened her eyes to see Shane observing her, his fierce gaze following every movement of her mouth.

He shifted his focus to her eyes and smiled. "Do you know how hard it is to watch you eat?"

Emma laughed. "So, don't watch." She picked up her mug and drank her coffee. "Where are we going after this? What is this *Pass* thing?"

"You'll see." He raised his fork over his slice of pie. "Just hurry up and eat before you make me forget where we're going."

CHAPTER

Sixteen

*E*MMA TIGHTENED HER ARMS AROUND SHANE'S
waist as he smoothly wound through the curves, their bodies
tilting into the bend. The rain had dissipated, and the setting sun blazed
an orange glow. She inhaled damp air and gazed in awe at the surrounding mountains that were consumed with evergreens. The motorcycle's engine purred and Emma laced her fingers together just below
Shane's navel.

Shane hadn't revealed where he was taking her, and Emma didn't
care. They'd been riding at least another hour, further from Everett
and Seattle. Into the second hour, Shane finally maneuvered the bike
into a parking lot. He shut off the engine.

Emma glanced around. "Where are we?"

"You'll see."

She climbed off the bike and Shane followed. He took off his helmet.

Emma took off her helmet and stared at her new environment. Trees and more trees.

Shane pointed to a walkway beyond the parking lot. "We're going that way." He grabbed her hand and led her to a trail.

"Why?"

"It's a surprise, remember? I promise you'll like it."

They headed further along the path. Dusk settled over them.

"You seem to be good at everything," Shane said. "Tell me one thing you can't do."

"Cook."

"Cook?"

"I burn water."

Shane chuckled. "I didn't think that was possible."

"Well, it is. Are you gonna tell me you're an awesome cook?"

"I do alright."

"You seem to be a guy doing everything right."

He huffed. "Far from it. I worked on Wall Street for years, making obscene amounts of money and one day I realized I didn't like the person I'd become."

"So, you became a teacher."

"I quit my job, which my mother never forgave me for, and I already had my degree, so yes, I got my teaching certificate, and this is who you see now."

"Someone who's happy in his second life."

He paused, their walking ceased for the moment. He stared at her, confusion muddled across his face. "You surprise me."

"How so?"

"When I say I made *obscene amounts of money*, the first question most people ask me is *how much*."

Emma shrugged. "It's just money. And it satisfied your material needs but didn't make you emotionally happy, right?" Her statement stung with the truth of her own life. Professionally successful, but personally she struggled, uncertain where she fit in the normal world, if "normal" would ever apply to her. "This is the new Shane; the old Shane is gone."

They started walking. "Yeah, but that's what Liam's list is about. Parts of the old Shane weren't so bad. My sister says she misses the funny, sarcastic Shane. The extrovert. That's why Liam thought my mojo needed a boost."

"So, you could get a girl."

"So, I could wake up some parts of the old Shane." He turned to her and smiled. "Finding you was a plus."

Emma returned his smile. "Looks like I've been seeing parts of the old Shane."

"Looks like you have."

She knew she'd have to leave Bainbridge Island one day but there had to be a way to keep in touch with Shane. She had to figure out a way to keep this connection going. They reached the mouth of the trail, a large observation deck that overlooked the most amazing view Emma had ever witnessed.

"Wow," she whispered.

The shadow of a mountain shaped like a volcano lined the horizon and a narrow stretch of dense clouds mingled with the millions of stars peppering the dark sky.

"It looks like the Milky Way."

Shane came up behind her, wrapping his strong arms around her waist. She leaned her head back against his chest and he dropped a kiss into the crook of her neck.

"This is the Washington Pass," Shane said. "As the card said, *a two wheeled ride to the Pass*. Mission completed. Now on to the next surprise."

Seventeen

"Is it okay to be here?" Emma studied Shane anxiously, afraid that they might be trespassing.

Shane huffed. He gazed down at the water, beams of white light radiating beneath the surface. "It's okay. I know the owners and they're out of town." He pulled his shirt over his head. "I promise you we're not doing anything illegal."

Emma glanced from Shane to the pool. "Why did you bring me here?"

He shrugged, draping his shirt over one of the benches. "You said you missed swimming in the ocean." He nodded toward the pool. "It's not the ocean, but it is heated. We've got a few hours before the last ferry leaves and we're all alone, so your privacy is intact."

"And Luci snuck my bathing suit into the bag?"

"Yeah." He slid out of his rain suit, revealing a pair of jeans. "She put it in the bag when you went to put on the rain suit. She said she always packs a bathing suit for you no matter where you go." He paused, his hands on the buttons of his jeans. It occurred to him Luci had detailed knowledge of Emma's clothing and that Emma tended to travel often. "Does Luci always pack for you?"

"Sometimes. We go a lot of places together. She's my best friend."

"Hmm." Shane plopped down on the bench. Emma scrunched her face in concern. He rested his hands on his legs and looked up at her. "Look, I'm sorry if I overstepped my bounds. I just wanted to return the favor. Do something I thought you might like."

Emma clutched the bookbag in her hands. "It's all right. A heated pool is perfect. I'll go change."

"Are you sure?"

"I'm sure." She walked over to the small cabana, slipping behind the door.

Shane exhaled a long breath, thankful he didn't ruin the moment by stumbling through his explanation. No woman had ever been so thoughtful to do something as kind as Emma had in the last couple of weeks. She'd forced him from his exile, dared him, the two of them sharing not only laughs, but interesting memories. Leaping off Noboru. Strumming the acoustic guitar to a song Emma played so eloquently. High school French teacher Mrs. Loutiere had agreed to tutor Shane in conversational French. The motorcycle ride through town and along the highway was exhilarating.

And Island Diner.

The spot where he and Liam debated, ate peach pie, and where Liam announced his engagement. Where Shane confessed his disenchantment with Wall Street, and his plan to extricate himself from his old lifestyle. He and Liam celebrated his education certification and first teaching position. All at Island Diner. A place he hadn't visited since Liam's passing.

Shane gulped, fought back the tears that stung his eyes. Liam wasn't supposed to die. Fate had made a mistake.

Outside, the downpour of rain clawed at the massive windows encasing the Olympic sized indoor swimming pool. The wind howled and thunder clapped overhead like a classical harmony of violins and drums. He quickly stepped out of his jeans, already dressed in swim trunks and jumped headfirst into the pool. Lukewarm water enveloped him as he swam several feet then pushed to the surface. Small beads of water trickled down his face. He ran the palm of his hand across his eyes to clear his view of the woman suddenly standing at the edge of the pool.

Emma wore a cobalt blue, two-piece bathing suit, slender string tied together at the back of her neck, the bottom molding with the sensuous curves of her hips. Wavy locks of hair settled along her shoulders, surrounding her face, her lips parted in a wide smile. "Stop staring, Shane."

"I can't help it." He rubbed his eyes again, a lopsided grin on his face.

Emma peered cautiously at the surface of the water, before diving into the deep end. Seconds later, she drifted up to the surface.

Shane watched as she angled her head back to keep her unruly wet strands of hair away from her eyes. Drops of water gathered over her brow, dripping onto her cheeks. She was still smiling.

For a moment, words caught in his throat. He was going to find out the reason for her constant fear of public recognition and no matter what the reason, he wasn't going anywhere. He forced his brain to function. "So, tell me about the Max the Mouse pajamas."

Emma treaded lightly, small waves lapping against her chin. "It was my favorite cartoon and I like the shirts. No one but Luci has ever seen me in them."

"And me." Shane concentrated on Emma's graceful movements. Like a ballerina with an underwater stage.

Emma held his gaze. "Yes, and now you. You'd better not tell anyone either or I'll deny I ever knew you." She dove underwater then floated to the surface, a ten-foot distance between them.

"Should I be aware of any other secrets?"

"More? You sure are greedy."

"Yes I am." He coasted toward her. "Now spill it."

"Okay. I know Kenpo karate."

"Kenpo karate?"

"My mother considers any form of physical self-defense as 'unladylike.' She says that's what men and guns are for. My dad snuck me to the classes when I was a kid."

"So, you could hurt me if you wanted to?"

"Yup. I can break a man's bones in twenty different places. And if you ask me to share anything else, I'll be forced to demonstrate."

"You'd break my bones?"

"I'd hate doing it if that makes you feel better." She laughed and swam to the edge of the pool, gripping the siding. "What's your weird thing?"

Shane glided next to her, folding his arms over the smooth concrete. "Seven-Up."

"Seven-Up?"

"Instead of beer, I drink Seven-Up. I mean, I used to be the social drinker, the party guy. Frat boy, whatever you wanna call it." He gazed outside where rain poured down the windows. A ferocious wind whipped tree branches back and forth. "That was the old Shane. The new Shane just sticks with bottles of Seven-Up."

"How many cases do you go through in a week?"

The old Shane knocked down five tequila shots, three beers and a glass of Jack Daniels before he felt a buzz. He'd stayed up until 3 a.m. at parties all around town, surrounded by women he didn't know, women who flocked to him as he'd tossed hundred-dollar bills to bartenders.

When he'd decided on his transformation, reducing his alcohol intake had been priority one. "A case a week?"

Emma shoved away from the pool's siding and purposely splashed Shane. "You're a sodaholic?"

Shane followed Emma to the middle of the pool, steadying himself beside her. "And you are a Max the Mouse fanatic. We make the perfect couple."

"Who does this place belong to?" Emma waded toward the shallow end of the pool and sat on the bottom step, only the top half of her body exposed to the suddenly frigid air.

Her taut nipples poked against the fabric of her tiny bathing top. One pull of the string knotted behind her back and her plump breasts would be set free to be fondled and tasted. She smoothed her wet hair back, exposing the delicate features of her face. Round nose, warm brown eyes, cheeks pushed upwards as her full lips curled into a grin.

"Shane?"

"Huh?"

She wiped her face, glancing back at the expansive two-story beige home in front of the pool house. She bent her legs, rested her chin on her knees. "Whose house is this?"

Shane felt himself harden, every muscle in his body tightening. From Emma eating pie, to the feel of her arms snug against him as they rode through the maze of trees en route to the pool, Shane hadn't been able to think clearly. No lucid thoughts until he could taste her again, feel her again. Her every word, look, touch kept him sane. Her unknowing power over his reason and logic twisted him inside. Yet he could not keep himself from her.

He reminded the bulge growing in his trunks. *She wasn't ready, they weren't ready.* Emma would set the pace, lead the way. He fought to keep his hands in check as the urge to caress every part of her body threatened to overwhelm him.

He followed her gaze to the house twenty yards away. Hidden in the mass of towering trees, the five thousand square foot mansion boasted eight bedrooms and a garage for his father's ten classic cars.

He swam to her, joining her on the pool steps. "My parents live here."

"What?" Emma darted incredulous looks at Shane and back to the house. Spotlights surrounded the residence, glowing against the shrubbery and cascading across the siding. "Your parents live here?" She pointed at the house and straightened her legs. "Are they in there right now?"

During the few times Shane ever brought a woman to meet his parents he'd observed the "change." The oh-he-really-does-have-money look. An indication the relationship had reached its end. Working on Wall Street, Shane had funds at his disposal and rarely the free time to use it. His father's accumulation of money from investments and as the CEO of several companies had allowed him to furnish each of his children with a generous trust fund.

Shane paid for his living expenses through his teaching salary, never mentioning his trust fund. Whenever Shane brought a woman to meet his family at their extravagant home, Shane's burgeoning relationships crumbled. Shattered by looks of vanity, flashes of greed in their eyes. Shane became adept at catching that "look," no matter how blatant or subtle.

Subconsciously, he realized he wanted Emma to see the house. To believe she didn't care about any of it. A test. Especially after her confession about her mother's quest to find a suitable, rich husband.

He studied her as the reality of his family's wealth sunk in. Emma didn't look impressed. She folded her arms across her chest and swiftly inventoried each large, pitch black window. As if a light would flicker on and she'd catch his parents staring back at them. No, Emma wasn't impressed with his family's wealth. Instead, she appeared panicked.

"They're in Cabo," Shane said.

Emma dropped her arms to her sides. Shadows formed along the siding by darkened trees. She looked at Shane, hard fear lingering in her eyes. "They're not here?"

"Nope."

"And you knew that *before* you brought me here?"

"Yeah."

"And you really grew up in that house?"

"For eighteen years." Shane analyzed the leisurely expression on her face, her eyes no longer focused on the mansion but at the bushes and trees whipping fiercely back and forth outside. She did not have the "look" of a woman hungry for his money. Relief washed through him and he looked back at the house.

"Shane?"

"Yes?"

The words never came. Emma looked away from him, to the storm brewing outside, her eyes transfixed on the water gushing down their expansive glass cage. Indecision slid down her face, the urge to explain something hovering across her slightly parted lips.

———————

Tell him. Tell him. The words taunted her, resting on the tip of her tongue.

I'm Emma Jacobs, not a starving artist, but one of the highest paid actresses in the film circuit right now.

Shane liked regular Emma, not celebrity Emma with the flashing camera lights, the paparazzi shouting her name, the fans repeatedly asking for autographs everywhere she went. Her mother's demands coupled with the pressure to make every film better than the last, to hone her craft into an Oscar worthy performance were no longer firmly embedded at the front of her thoughts.

She was simply Emma, a decent actress from L.A. on vacation, sitting on the edge of the pool next to a man with rock hard abs. Her gaze drifted to the valley of his sculpted chest.

"Emma?" Shane said suddenly.

She quickly glanced away. Had he caught her ogling? She looked up and found him smirking at her.

That was a resounding *yes*.

Emma slid into the water and swam to the middle of the pool. She didn't do brief affairs, especially with the paparazzi bloodhounds sniffing out every lead. She had to protect Shane's privacy.

Shane dipped into the pool and reappeared moments later in front of her. "What is it?"

She ached to touch him everywhere, feel his skin against hers. A bead of water raced down his neck, trickling through the valley of his toned pecs.

"Emma, why are you holding back?"

Her nipples poked at the fabric, her center awakening at the huskiness in his voice.

She wanted him.

Damn her mother.

Damn the press.

Shane lowered his gaze to her mouth, and Emma inhaled a sharp breath. Before she could exhale, Shane covered her mouth with his own, his lips nipping at hers, pleading for an invitation. She accepted, his tongue invading her mouth, the taste of him deliciously sweet.

He stood upright in the pool and Emma clasped her legs around him. One of his hands molded to her bottom, the other cupped the back of her neck as he pushed the kiss further, his mouth demanding more.

Emma moaned, raked her nails through his hair, and gripped his shoulders. A burst of energy sprouted from her core, settled in her pelvis, screaming for release.

Shane dragged his mouth from hers and trailed kisses along the curve of her neck. He softly massaged her lower, then upper back. "I wouldn't do anything to hurt you." He brushed one palm across her breast.

Emma shivered.

Damn her mother.

Damn the press.

He pulled aside the small scrap of material covering her breast. Cold air tickled her flesh, replaced by the warmth of Shane's mouth.

Her fingernails dug into his shoulders. Her words came out in broken breaths. "I...don't do...one night...stands."

Shane looked up at her. "Do I look like the kind of guy who does one-night-stands?"

Emma just stared at him.

"Okay, by your response you think I am. I'm not that guy, Emma. I want to be with you, only you." He brushed his lips across hers, then claimed her mouth.

Emma tried to think rationally about their situation. Her residence in Los Angeles, his on the island, her hectic schedule, his not-so-hectic lifestyle, her celebrity status, his private existence.

She couldn't think, couldn't rationalize, couldn't explain how she felt. He kissed a path down between her breasts.

Her head fell back, and she cried out as his eager tongue explored one hardened peak, then the other.

Rain battered the windows, the wind howling incessantly.

She stared at the floor to ceiling windows. Easily accessible to paparazzi hoping for a shot of her, half naked making out in the pool owned by her boyfriend's parents.

Shane trailed his hand up her thigh. Her stomach flopped excitedly. Her brain registered reality.

Can't. Not here.

"Shane, wait."

Shane looked up at her. "What is it?"

"I can't." She recognized rejection and disappointment in his eyes and quickly followed with an explanation. "It's not anything you did. It's me. It's complicated."

"You said that before."

"And it's the truth." Emma uncurled her legs from his waist and dropped her feet to the ground. "This is your parents' house and we're sorta out in the open here. It's not the right place or the right time."

Shane heaved in a long breath. "You're sure you're not in witness protection?"

"No."

"And you're not working for the C.I.A.?"

"Not the last time I checked." Emma laughed. "Where do you come up with this stuff?"

"It rolls right off the top of my head."

"I can tell." She backed away from him. "We should get back."

"Yeah," Shane said.

Emma trudged toward the pool steps, inwardly cursing at herself. She wanted this, she wanted him. His patience, his kindness, every one of his rock-hard muscles tightening around her, his mouth plunging into hers, stirring a desperate need to take their relationship further. No, she couldn't have Shane. Not here at his parents' house. Not now, with the openness of the windows surrounding them. Not here, not now, but Emma made a promise to herself. No more insecurities or fears of public scrutiny.

Emma had her mojo back and Shane Rawlings would soon see the old Emma come to life.

CHAPTER

Eighteen

SHANE GLANCED AROUND THE EXTENSIVE TABLE draped in dazzling white cloth and seated for twelve. Each place setting included shiny silver utensils, porcelain plates, and a small glass of orange juice. Platters of eggs, bacon, biscuits, chicken fried steak, and red diced potatoes anchored the center of the table.

Sallie sat across from him, in blue jeans and a black turtleneck. Patrick sat beside her, engrossed in another conversation with his Uncle Phil. His mother occupied one end of the table, his father the other, his brother, cousins and uncles assembled in between. Everyone chatted, mostly about stocks and bonds, investments, and regulatory reform. His heart wasn't in the subject, just as his mother's ear for his daily musings on teaching high school students diminished in the span of five minutes.

His younger brother Mercer shared stories, laced with medical terminology his mother did not understand, yet she absorbed every detail. Enough to brag to the ladies from the country club about her doctor son and a daughter about to marry someone worthy of the Rawlings clan. No mention of the son working as a teacher. To his mother, Shane turned his back on the world he'd once known, a traitorous act, one not to be acknowledged publicly.

"Where ya been, Shane?" Sallie tapped his plate with her fork to get his attention. "Gabe says you leave right after school and not only are you harder to find, you're not even at home."

Shane stifled a smile. For the last few weeks since their swim in the pool, Shane dropped by Emma's house off and on after school, the two of them hanging out late into the evening. He left Emma each time with a kiss, swift, chaste, scared his mouth would betray him, knowing how much he ached to have her in his arms and in his bed. He recognized the same longing in her eyes, the same hunger and yet she continued to hold her back. Shane decided the next time he saw Emma they'd have to discuss her apprehensions with him. She had to trust him by now. He hoped.

"Shane?"

"Huh?" He looked up at his sister.

Sallie's brown eyes sparkled with curiosity. "Who is she?"

"What?"

"What's her name? You've been acting different, dressing different. Who is she?"

"What?"

A platter passed between them.

She shot him an all-knowing grin. "You haven't answered the question."

"I understand the question, maybe I'm just not answering it."

"Wow." Sallie pointed her fork at him. "I haven't seen you this mute since Heather, and even then, you didn't seem this guarded. You must really like her."

"Sallie." Shane poked at his scrambled eggs.

"Shane." Sallie drew out his name in one long breath.

He dropped his fork in his plate and shot his sister a spiteful look that lacked malice. She had a way of pulling anything out of him. "Her name is Emma."

"Pretty." Sallie raised her thinly penciled brows at her older brother. "When do I get to meet her?"

"I want her to keep liking me, Sallie," Shane joked, although he had considered an introduction.

Another platter, this time bacon, passed between them. Sallie snatched a piece off the plate.

Patrick finished his ongoing debate about the financial crisis with Uncle Phil and leaned over in his seat, inching closer to Sallie. He reached for the bacon on her plate and she playfully slapped his hands. Defeated and meatless, he withdrew his hand and smiled. He glanced from his fiancée to Shane. "Who are we meeting?"

"Shane's girlfriend," Sallie said gleefully.

Mercer, seated three chairs down, closest to their mother, stopped talking. Sallie, ecstatic by her older brother's confession carried her final word with not just exuberance, but volume. Loud enough to catch the attention of several people at the table, including his parents.

"Shane, you have a girlfriend?" Mercer asked.

Shane felt like a teenage boy being interrogated by his parents. He wasn't sixteen anymore, but a grown man, shrinking to the size of a pebble under the unexpected scrutiny of this new development. He shifted upright in his chair, his back straight, his chin slightly raised. He narrowed his eyes at Sallie, and she shriveled on the spot, her face instantly apologetic.

"I am seeing someone," Shane said quietly.

His cousin Luke peered around another relative to stare down the table at Shane. "Who is she? Is she from around here?"

"I heard it was Delia Rose," someone blurted.

"She comes from a good family," one of his uncles chimed in.

"No," Shane said, surprised that two conversations with Delia evolved into a twosome that didn't exist. "It's not Delia. Someone else I met back in Bainbridge."

"Well you must bring her over for brunch," his mother said in an eloquent voice that stopped all other chatter. Everyone focused on her and Shane. She smiled at her son, her curled lips looking more like a devilish cat than a concerned mom.

Shane returned the Cheshire smile. "Maybe." He shot his sister another accusatory look. "Just maybe."

SHANE STAYED LATE AT SCHOOL TO GRADE PAPERS. His students still struggled with the lesson, but he'd devised a new plan. He'd arrived home and found in his mailbox the DVD of the updated version of Romeo and Juliet he'd bought online. He modified his lesson plan for the next day, anxious the method Emma suggested would work and glanced at his wristwatch.

One-minute past six.

Emma would arrive at six-thirty. With no time to prepare, he rushed to the deli around the corner from his condo and ordered pastrami and cheese, her favorite, and a cheesesteak for himself.

At twenty minutes past six, Shane slid out of his plaid shirt and tan dockers. He put on a black, long sleeved button shirt and blue jeans, then rummaged through his cabinets for anything to drink. He had only orange juice and water.

At six twenty-nine, Shane heard Emma's footsteps on the stairs.

He unwrapped the sandwiches and set them on plates at the table. Three knocks vibrated his door.

He undid the lock and yanked open the door to find Emma standing before him. "Hey, you," he said softly.

Emma wore jeans, ballet flats and a sunset orange top, the wide collar resting at the tip of her shoulders, rounding out the delicate features of her collar bone and smooth skin. Large, soft waves outlined her face and tumbled along the edge of her back. Her full glossy lips smiled up at him and she wore a hint of shadow and eyeliner highlighting the whiskey color in her eyes.

"Hey, yourself." Emma peeked around him and stepped inside. "That smells good." She shrugged out of her jacket and handed it to Shane, venturing toward the kitchen table. "Is that pastrami and cheese?"

"Maybe." He hung her jacket on the coat rack. "Nothing to drink though."

"Water'll do." She jammed her hand into her purse and pulled out a DVD case. "Night of the Living Dead."

"No." He shook his head emphatically.

"It's a classic. Best horror movie ever."

"I'm not watching it." He walked to the kitchen, opening the upper cabinet doors for two glasses.

She batted her eyelids and pouted at him. "Pleaaaasse?"

"It's really that good?"

"It is." She bit her lip, glanced at the sandwiches on the table. "The food smells awesome."

He poured them both a glass of water from the pitcher in his refrigerator. "Speaking of food." Now was the time to introduce Emma to his sister. A chance meeting at a store. A casual drop by her house. A sit down over a meal at a restaurant. Sallie hadn't been introduced to any of Shane's female companions since Heather, and Sallie was less than excited about that meet up. Sallie and Emma would get along. Shane highly valued her opinion, but the last decision remained his. It had been with Heather; it would be with Emma.

Shane opened his mouth to suggest hosting a special dinner at his condo. He would cook and invite his sister and Patrick, Gabe and his date, and Luci. And maybe his brother. He lowered the pitcher, glanced at Emma standing at the end of the table and paused at the abrupt determination on her face. One corner of her lips tilted upward, her eyes chocolate pools, soft, hazy, sultry, telling him the DVD could wait, the food was about to get cold, and where they went next was completely unexpected.

Emma wasn't the type to seduce anyone. The man initiated what he wanted. Jordyn had always taken what he needed. He didn't hold her gaze as he'd attempted to satisfy them both, only stared at the bulge of his arms and the way his hips rolled over her. Jordyn had passed her fleeting glances of approval, not ones of passion and longing. He didn't call out her name, didn't call her anything, just grunted and finished.

Her interest in sex diminished as soon as her relationship with Jordyn ended. She'd once imagined taking control, seducing Jordyn, a simple glance or touch expressing an intense sexual need, but the urge to do so never came.

As Shane poured water into their glasses, that intense need washed over her. She wanted Shane.

Shane recognized the unspoken hunger in her eyes. "Emma?" He set the pitcher on the table.

The pit of her belly danced with anticipation. "Yes?"

Shane stepped back. "You don't want to watch the DVD?"

"Nope." Confidence high, she stripped out of the sweater and tossed it to the floor, exposing the black satin bra that encased her full chest. Inhaling a small breath, she reminded herself, *you can do this.*

His gaze flickered from her chest to her face. Restraint glossed his eyes, the edge of his mouth set firm as he desperately tried to give Emma an out. "You're not hungry?"

"It can wait." She slipped out of her ballet flats, hurling one shoe that landed near the coat rack. She threw the other, and it crashed into the lamp, knocking it over. The porcelain base tumbled to the floor, and the bulb broke.

She cringed. She really was rusty at this.

Shane stared at the fallen lamp and back at Emma. She took advantage of his hesitation by closing the three-foot gap between them. She chuckled, unwinding the nervous knots building in her belly and washing away the embarrassment flushing her face. "Sorry about that."

Shane smirked and grazed his hands over her partially naked body in the dim light, desire raging in his green eyes. He raised his hands to touch her arms and paused. Holding her gaze, his voice deep, he warned, "Whatever you start, I'll have to finish."

Emma unfastened two of the buttons on his shirt and stared up at him through half open lids. "Duly noted." Heart pounding in her throat, she finished the last three buttons, pushed the shirt over his shoulders, the material sliding past his arms and dropping into a crumpled heap on the floor. She pressed her lips against his smooth chest, her hands splayed across the hard ripples of his abdomen.

Shane tangled his fingers through Emma's hair, gently tugged with one hand and forced her to look up at him. His emerald eyes darkened, the promise of everything she ached for evident on his face. He lowered his head and captured her mouth, teasing, caressing her tongue.

Emma whimpered as he tugged her closer, one arm tight around her waist. He released her mouth, his lips tracing a path from the tip of her chin to the curve of her neck. Shane flicked the clasp of her bra and it glided from her arms to the floor. Her perky breasts freed, he closed his mouth over one nipple then the other, savoring the taste. She arched her back as his mouth tore through her body and Shane lifted her up, carrying her to his bedroom.

Depositing her on the soft mattress, Emma scrambled to unbutton her jeans. The incessant throbbing between her legs had proven too much and she could no longer wait.

Shane covered his hands with hers, ceasing all movement. She looked up at him and he slowly shook his head, chuckling at the blanket of confusion on her face. He guided her jeans over her hips and down her legs, taking her panties with it. Shane stilled her hands, positioning them on her belly as he gripped her wrists with one hand and took possession of her mouth. Her muscles tensed, her hips reflexively pushing upward but Shane kept her hands locked in place. Through his jeans she felt his erection push against her thighs. He lowered his lips to her ear and whispered, "Tell me what you want, Emma."

Emma could barely put two words together, let alone a whole sentence. Her body ached for more, the yearning fever pitch below her waist. Vulnerable beyond her naked skin, the touch of his hands ripped away the emotional barrier she'd fought so hard to maintain. Shane licked her breasts, feasting on each mound, licking and suckling the hard tips. She trembled against his nimble tongue, dizzy from intense pleasure, stifling the urge to cry out.

Shane saw the resistance in her eyes. He massaged her thighs then stroked the soft spot between them. She jerked back her head, quivering as he intimately caressed her. Emma wanted to lose herself in his touch, forget the cares of tomorrow. *Let go. She only had to let go.* Shane's jagged breathing was hot against the side of her cheek, his voice thick with need. "Emma, tell me what you want."

"You. You, Shane."

Shane softly kissed her cheek, and his lips traveled to her navel. Pressing his free hand flat on her belly he buried his head between her thighs.

Emma cried out, and he released her hands. She clawed at the sheets as he enjoyed her, tension rising within every muscle. Her behavior had ignited not schoolteacher Shane, wearing his black-framed glasses and plaid shirts. Not quiet Shane, who kept to himself, didn't laugh much, and whose heart weighed heavy with human loss. She'd awakened a different Shane, confident in every action, fierceness in his eyes both frightening and exhilarating. Like zip-lining from the highest cliff or diving out of a plane at fifty thousand feet.

Her arms and legs quaked, her mouth opened, but words were lost in a lightheaded haze. The trembling subsided, her breathing drifted to an even pace and she rolled her head to one side. Shane slid out of bed, then slipped out of his jeans and underwear. He switched on a single lamp, a yellow haze illuminating the room. His muscular back was to her, and she marveled again at the intricate Celtic design inked along his spine. Two shades of Shane and she was ecstatic about them both.

Rain sprinkled the windows then pounded the glass in a full range of rhythmic beats.

Shane quirked his lips into a wicked grin, his eyes sparkling. He shook his head, striding toward the bed, his full erection sheathed in a condom. "I'm not finished yet." His taut muscles flexed as he crawled on top of her, snaked one arm around her waist and shifted her upright so he lay flat on his back, Emma hovering over him.

He smiled up at her. "Hi."

"Hi." Emma glowed, her body on fire, skin tingling as she smiled back at him. Both of his hands planted across her back, he nudged her toward him. Emma leaned down, closing her mouth over his. She kissed him as he had with her, urgent, craving every bit of his mouth.

Shane moaned and sat up, threaded his fingers in her hair, his mouth exploring the curve of her neck. He kissed the tip of her shoulder and cupped her bottom. Emma lowered herself, sinking down, fully accepting him. He growled at the feel of her, tight, wet, ready for him.

Emma inhaled sharply at the hard length of him inside her. She pushed aside the nervousness quaking in her belly. Instinctively she rocked her hips back and forth and was rewarded when he shuddered.

"Emma."

She shifted her hips steadily and Shane matched her rhythm, crushing his mouth over hers.

She gripped his shoulders, bucking faster against him, and he held her tightly. Shane's breathing quickened, each thrust forceful, possessive, and Emma loved every bit. She threw her head back and electricity shot from her core, shaking her body uncontrollably. The tremors calmed, her breathing steadied, and she dropped her head down, catching mischief in Shane's eyes.

I'm not finished yet.

Her grin matched his as Shane flipped her onto her back. He absorbed the sight of her, the curve of her waist, her round hips, small bottom, and brushed his hand along her silky skin saturated with sweat.

She studied him, becoming self-conscious under his wondrous gaze. She opened her mouth to speak and Shane tenderly kissed away any doubts. He eased into her and Emma's breath caught as he released her mouth. He plunged deeper, slower, each tantalizing thrust bringing Emma closer to completion. Not yet. He wasn't finished yet. Shane groaned in pure ecstasy, marveled at her breasts, then closed his mouth over one globe and the other. His pace quickened, the vibrating heat between her legs gaining momentum.

Shane rubbed his thumb across her sensitive nub and a powerful wave of pleasure washed over her. She screamed out his name in broken breaths and Shane shivered with his final release.

Thunder rumbled low outside and rain pelted the windows. Emma rested her head sideways on the pillow and Shane collapsed, his head buried in the arch of her neck. Her wait had been extensive, for Shane, for this overwhelming amount of satisfaction, and her eyes watered. *Why did everything have to be so complicated?* Emma shoved aside the stark reality of what morning would bring. She turned her head to look at the man who left her vision blurry, her breathing ragged, and the soft spot between her thighs moist and still tingling.

"Finished now?" she asked.

Shane's panting slowed, and he raised his head to look at her. "Not even close, but I'm willing to give us a thirty-minute break."

Emma laughed. "Thirty minutes?"

He arched a brow. "Okay, fifteen."

"Twenty-five."

"Twenty."

He planted soft kisses on her neck, cheeks, chin, and smiled. "I can live with that."

CHAPTER

Twenty

"NIGHT OF THE LIVING DEAD. I CAN'T BELIEVE we're watching this." Shane shook his head at the black and white images on his flat screen TV, zombies slowly chasing the few remaining survivors up a hill.

Emma shifted her gaze from the TV to Shane. "It's a great movie." She lay across the couch, her head nestled comfortably in Shane's lap. They watched the survivors scramble to the safety of an old farmhouse.

Shane wore a pair of pale blue boxers, and Emma wore one of his long sleeved, button plaid shirts. "We're watching because you distracted me."

Emma grinned. "Distracted you?"

He gazed at the length of her slender, bare legs and Emma stretched them, shifting one over the other. Memories of her legs tangled with his, her soft moans against his ears, the way her lips trembled as her body shook under intense pleasure. "Yes, distracted me."

"Well, whatever works."

He leaned down, softly kissing her, murmuring against her lips, "You can distract me like that anytime." Shane was grateful and shocked Emma initiated the transformation. Emma coaxed him out of his shell, dared him, tilted his views on the way he lived. He hadn't been living, just as Sallie had told him weeks ago. She'd accused him of biding his time until he passed away, the accident nearly a year ago dictating the direction of his personal life.

Emma turned toward the TV to watch the end of the movie.

Credits rolled up the screen. Shane lightly kissed Emma's temple. She sat up and he stood up. "Bath time."

"Bath time?"

He disappeared into the bedroom. Seconds later water gushed from the bathtub faucet in the en suite bath. Shane wanted to do a thousand things for Emma, to thank her for forcing him to breathe and live again. He returned to the living room and Emma stood up. He held out his hand to her. She looked at it and glanced at the bedroom doorway. She couldn't possibly be unsure of his intentions, not after the last several hours? Shane had seen that same uncertainty shadowing her face as she lay exposed beneath him hours before. Self-conscious. Unsteady about the image of her body.

"You're not worried about me seeing you naked, are you? It's a little late for that."

Emma bit her lip in that delectable way Shane loved. He fought the urge to reach down and cover her mouth with his own.

She nodded but said, "No."

"You're beautiful."

"I'm not perfect."

"Neither am I." Shane held out his hand again. "Come with me."

She studied him, tentatively reaching for his hand. He took it, gently squeezed and tugged her up from the couch. "Okay."

Emma dropped her head and closed her eyes. Warm water slapped at her chest as she swayed forward from the feel of Shane's knuckles kneading the muscles of her lower back. Dressed in a pair of boxers, he'd perched himself on the narrow, marble edge of the deep soaking tub, his bare legs penetrating the water.

When Shane offered a "bath," she'd expected something more… involved. Arms and limbs tangled in a confined ceramic space, submerged in heated water. Instead, Shane seemed content massaging the sore muscles of her arms and back.

He shifted his hands upward, pressing circles into the base of her neck. "So is your dream to be the big film star or is theater more your style?"

Emma lowered her head and closed her eyes, the sound of an alternative rock band crooning a love ballad she didn't recognize in the background. "Film. Although, I wouldn't mind acting in a play every now and then."

"Film huh?" Shane rubbed her shoulders, his fingers squeezing and releasing the muscles. "Been in anything I've seen?"

His question hit her square in the chest, her breath hitched, her eyes flew open. How did she explain? Since Shane wasn't a big movie buff, she had a fifty-fifty chance he'd never seen her in a movie. No film teasers. No clips of her nights out splashed in the tabloids. Then again, if she revealed small pieces, clues that unveiled the extent of her fame, how exactly would Shane handle it?

Emma didn't want the risk. Not with the feel of his hands manipulating her shoulders. She didn't want the feeling to stop. Physically and emotionally. Better to keep quiet.

She lifted her head, straightened her shoulders, the water swishing against the sides of the tub. "Where'd you learn to do that?"

"What?" Shane's warm fingertips disappeared from her shoulders, her skin instantly chilled.

She turned her head, glimpsing his naked chest, his sculpted abdomen eye level. Like a teacher by day, stripper by night, his body still awed and amazed her. All that hidden beneath plaid shirts and Dockers combined with the intellect and patience. She lowered her gaze to the floor, pretended his finely tuned muscles were no big deal. "Your massage technique. Let me guess, you were a masseuse in another life? I'm sure this worked on the popular girls when you were in high school."

Shane threw his head back and laughed, a hearty rumble from his chest. "I wish. I was the dorky skinny kid, remember? Tall, lean, like a beanpole. I had acne all over my face."

She grinned, skeptical that Shane referred to himself as dorky. She was the dorky one, sheltered, naïve, so trusting as a teen. Her hair always pulled into one of those neat buns at the crown of her head. A woman has grace, elegance, Madeline would say. Never free and flowing. Never wild and spontaneous. Always scheduled, prepared for anything. Boys called her pretty, despite the bland schoolgirl uniform she was forced to wear every day at the academy. Girls, she rarely got along with.

"And the tattoos?" Emma trailed her fingers across the tribal tattoo on Shane's upper left arm.

"I got that at eighteen, trying to be cool. Liam got one too. Thought it would help with the ladies." He chuckled, then his voice softened. "But the one on my back, I got that the day I received my teaching certification. It took a while, it hurt like hell, but it was a symbol about me growing into my own man. Not under my parents rule anymore."

His parents vehemently disapproved of his lifestyle changes. She understood, empathized with his plight. Her heart called out to him— she admired his firm stance to be his own person, follow his own dreams. "You did good." Her head fell forward, the soft sound of the guitar lulling her eyes closed. "Who's this playing?"

"Dalton Matthews." He traced his knuckles from the center of her lower back to the base of her neck. "One of my favorite artists. Speaking of which, I got a new card today. I'm supposed to see my favorite band play live."

Emma listened to the singer's raspy baritone voice, belting out his confession to be a better man through Shane's wireless speaker. Dalton strummed the guitar sharply, each note crisp and in tune with the melody.

"You're lying."

"I'm not." He stood up, cold air clawing at her back. He walked out of the room then returned with an index card in his grasp. He handed the card to her.

Emma read the front of the card.

Task Six.

"We're halfway through the list," she said.

"Yes, we are."

She flipped the card over and read the back.

Watch your favorite artist sing live.

"Who are your favorite artists?"

Shane returned to his seat on the tub's ledge, resting his palms on her shoulders. "I have three. Dalton Matthews, Light of Day, Serious Motion."

Emma recognized only one band. Light of Day. They'd won two Grammys. An indie rock band comprised of three young guys and one blonde who sang and played the piano. She'd seen one of their videos, a rolling image of the blonde and her bandmates running through several rooms as she and the male lead sang about life's mysteries.

"Have you seen any of them play live?"

Shane smoothed his hands down her back and Emma moaned. His thumbs circled her shoulder blades. "No."

"Hmmm." Out of the three bands, one of them had to be performing somewhere. Hopefully somewhere close. But it was becoming increasingly difficult to concentrate with Shane's hands caressing her back.

"Hmmm what?" he asked quietly.

She draped her arms on both sides of the tub's ledge, water dripping from her skin. "I can't think with you doing that."

Shane ran his knuckles up her spine again, applied a small amount of pressure. "Doing what?"

"Hmmm." Emma arched her back. "That. Feels. So. Good."

He leaned down, swept the wisps of hair that escaped her messy bun to one side and brushed his lips across her moist neck. "I'm trying to behave, but every time you make that little noise…" He planted an open mouth kiss on her neck, slid his palms down her arms. "You're tempting me."

She dropped her head back, raised one arm and cupped the back of his head. His breath warmed her skin. "I don't want you to behave."

"Emma." He grunted as though restraining himself, torturing himself to stay back. "You called me greedy once. I'm trying not to be an animal."

An animal after two amazing times in his bed? They'd rested, eaten some food and now Emma's body rallied for more. The feel of his mouth fused with hers, his fingertips trailing along her arms, touching her as he was now. And he was suppressing the urge, trying not to scare her with his voracious appetite. Well, she had one too, but she'd give him his out, his rest, until the next time. And there would be a next time.

Sighing, she let her arm flop into the tub, water sprinkling upward. "So, what do you suggest as an alternative to all this wonderful sexual tension?"

"I don't know. What else do you wanna do?"

Emma thought of the list. The one item Shane already experienced. "Teach me how to ride that pretty bike of yours?"

Twenty-One

"I'M NOT SURE I CAN DO THIS." EMMA FLIPPED THE visor up, frost instantly prickling her cheeks. Fresh air filled her lungs as she inhaled, her nervous breath released in a small puff of smoke. "I don't wanna break anything."

Shane stood beside his Ducati and spread one of his arms out, showcasing the vast, deserted parking lot. Cream colored buildings with darkened windows and unlit signs lined the edge of the lot. "It's three in the morning. There's no one out here but me and you."

Emma took another tentative look around the empty parking lot. Streetlamps glowed milky white, slicing through the still black sky. Shane pushed the "start" button on the compact console and the Ducati's engine tore into the silence.

Straddled across the Ducati, Emma jumped, her bottom vibrating with the engine's merciless growl. Shane rode this thing? Daily? Weekly? Riding on the seat behind him, her arms locked around him, was exciting, freeing. But Emma sat upfront, completely in control of this red beast, her heart hammering wildly. Sure, she'd imagined driving a motorcycle, the rebel female on an amazing bike. Reality kicked her swiftly in the ass.

Shane placed his palms downward, his eyes reviewing her carefully. "You can do this Emma. We'll go step by step."

He seemed so calm for a man with an extremely inexperienced driver seated on his, at a minimum, ten-thousand-dollar bike. His shoulders relaxed, his gaze studious, the teacher in him on full display. His raven hair was a tangled mess, his glasses pushed to the bridge of his nose. His plain white t-shirt and blue jeans conformed to the muscled physique she'd witnessed naked earlier in the evening.

Shane mapped out several instructions to get the bike moving. The clutch? Which gear? Where did her feet go?

"Why are we out here again?"

"Because you asked me to show you."

"And you said yes?" Emma gripped the throttle hard. "I was drunk right?"

Shane placed one hand over hers, softly rubbing her tense fingers. "I'm right here. I promise you'll be fine."

She stared at him, studied the way his emerald eyes sparkled at her, believed in her. She stuffed the fear down her throat and gave him a shaky smile. "Okay, rebel Emma is ready."

He gave her further instructions, holding the throttle, disengaging the clutch, shifting gears. She heeded his words, tried not to think of the way his chest flexed as he demonstrated his directions and how the commanding sound of his voice elicited memories of their previous hours together.

In his condo.

In his bed.

His mouth, his hands.

She shivered as the images flooded back, the engine's steady rumble amplifying the firestorm that simmered low into her pelvis.

"Emma?" Shane peered at her closely.

She blinked away the lascivious thoughts. "Got it. Make sure I'm in neutral. Let go of the clutch, use my left foot to changes gears, rotate throttle toward me, put my feet up."

He stepped back. "So, you were listening?"

She blinked again, nodded, tried to sound like her hormones weren't raging maniacally out of control. "Uh-huh." Emma's desire for Shane frightened and surprised her. She'd been waiting for the moment of annoyance, when her body called for enough. Except it demanded, ached for more of Shane. Just the look of him sent her core into a frenzy.

Emma focused straight ahead, averting the curious expression on Shane's face, and lifted the kickstand. Dropping the visor down over her eyes, she pressed her fingers against the thin, cold metal and released the clutch. She pushed down on the lever with her left foot until she found the first gear. Her hands twisted the throttle slowly, and the bike began to move.

Emma raised her feet, resting them on the pegs. "Omigosh, omigosh, omigosh." She looked back at Shane. "I'm moving!"

He trotted after her, pointing ahead. "Yes, you are! Keep looking that way."

"Oh yeah." Emma turned her head, rotating the throttle a little more. The bike sped faster, the engine kicking up, whining impatiently for the next gear as she approached the end of the parking lot.

"Emma, brake!" Shane called out.

She skimmed the console. Brake. Brake. Where was that again? She gently pulled back the lever on her right side. The bike jerked a bit, then stopped, her torso lurching forward. She found neutral, lowered the kickstand, and disengaged the clutch.

Shane caught up to her, bent over, panting heavily.

Emma took off her helmet and glanced backward to the spot where they'd started. A football field away. "Did I really ride that far? How did I do?"

Shane put one hand on his leg and raised his index finger until his rapid breaths slowed. He grinned, straightened, and shook his head. "That was great." Shane cupped her face with both hands and covered her mouth with his own, his tongue possessing her, driving a moan from her throat. Tiny licks, long strokes, easing back, brushing, nibbling his lips across hers. Their mouths still connected, he took the helmet from her and hooked it on the rear of the bike.

Her hands free, Emma wrapped her arms around his waist, tugging him closer, hungry for more of his mouth.

He groaned and released her, his arms dropping to his sides, his emerald eyes darkening. "You did amazing."

"Was that my reward?"

"Yeah."

She smiled. She could get used to those kinds of kisses on a daily basis. "Want me to go again?"

———

"How come you're not tired?" Emma picked up the acoustic guitar and strummed the strings. The sound echoed off Shane's bedroom walls.

After Emma's riding lesson, Shane drove them back to his condo. It was almost five in the morning. They should've slept but Shane couldn't get his eyes to shut, couldn't wrap his mind around how lucky he felt that he and Emma's relationship changed. Beyond acquaintances, well beyond friendship.

"How come you're not tired?" Lying on his side, he dug one elbow into the mattress and rested his head in his palm.

Emma settled her fingers across the strings and glanced up at him, mischief in her eyes. "Someone won't let me sleep."

Shane flopped his free hand in the air. "Whoever this guy is, he's pretty selfish keeping you awake like this."

"He is, you're right." She stroked the guitar, a comforting melody floating over the room, the kind of song reminding Shane of lost love and a hopeful future.

He watched her fingers intently. "Are there lyrics to that song?"

"Nope."

"Do you sing?"

She paused and smirked up at him. "That is something I don't do. I know my limits."

"I bet you've got the voice of an angel."

"More like a wildebeest. Or Bigfoot screaming in pain. Or a hundred crows squawking at once."

He laughed. "It can't be that bad."

Emma nodded, locks of hair falling across her brow, her good-natured smile widening, her fingers back to playing what sounded like a calming lullaby. "Shane, there are many things I can do. Act. Smile pretty. Break a man's bones. But the one thing I know I can't do is sing. No Grammys, no platinum record sales." She shook her head. "Nada. Can you sing?"

"I can try." He sat up, pressed his back against the headboard, cleared his throat and tried a few lines in a deep voice. "I met this girl named Emma. She glowed like the evening sun."

Emma covered his mouth with one hand, laughter just beneath the surface of her studious expression. "We'll just stop you right there."

"You didn't like it?" He pretended to be in shock by her none too thrilled reaction. "I've been practicing."

"You've got a long way to go." She chuckled and strummed the guitar again, returning to the song. "When did you buy this thing?"

"A few days ago." He stared at the acoustic guitar, its honey glazed face and cherry outline, the same guitar Emma played the night of their first kiss. Shane hadn't felt so sentimental before, but he couldn't pass up the one item present the day they'd moved past the first step in their relationship. "I thought you'd help me with more lessons."

"Lessons?"

"Yeah." His gaze dropped to her hands. "Where did you learn this song?"

"Sort of made it up. I play it whenever I'm really stressed and I wanna refocus."

"I can see why it works." He inched closer to her. "Can I show you how I de-stress?"

Emma opened her mouth to speak, her eyes catching his, the words stuck.

Her gaze fell over him, her need for him just as all-consuming as he was for her. Watching her play the guitar, so at ease with him, dressed in nothing but a tank top and boxer shorts, ribbons of wavy dark brown hair wavering slightly, her eyes smiling at him. Shane hardened. He'd been fighting, forcing himself not to be greedy, to not overwhelm her so she wouldn't rethink her decision to be with him. He didn't want her scared off by how much his body craved hers or believing all he wanted was sex. Their physical attraction was off the charts, but Shane desired Emma beyond their tussle between the sheets.

Her eyes didn't reflect fear or regret, only hunger, and her breathing quickened. "Are you gonna be an animal now? Or—"

He crushed his lips with hers before she could finish, tasting her thoroughly, ravishing her mouth, sliding the guitar aside, and hauling her firmly against him. Her arms slipped down his shoulders, her fingers digging into the muscles of his back as he deepened the kiss.

Emma shuddered, and Shane growled against her lips. "Yes," He nipped at her top lip. "Yes I am." He jerked the tank top over her head. She fumbled with the button of his jeans.

Emma was a tourist, her stay temporary. One day soon she'd have to leave him. Return to her true home. He tossed her tank top to the floor, and she tugged at his sleeves. He peeled out of his t-shirt, the strength of how he felt about Emma astounding him and his breath caught, his mouth finding hers again.

Shane decided in that moment. Their connection was not a mistake, not temporary. Unlike anything he'd ever known. He'd have to convince her they would find a way to work it out. Despite the geographical distance, despite their differences. He'd find a way.

Twenty-Two

EMMA STOOD ON THE FRONT LAWN, BAREFOOT, holding her ballet flats with one hand. Her sunglasses and beanie were stuffed into the purse slung over her shoulder. Sunlight beamed across her face and she squinted at the early afternoon light. Smiling, she skipped up the porch steps and yanked the screen door ajar. She grabbed the knob and opened the front door.

"When do you think she'll be here?" Suzanne Darling sat in one of the sofa chairs in the formal living room.

Luci's trademark red pigtails were replaced by one ponytail high at the crown of her head. Her square-framed glasses shifted down her nose and she pushed them up with one finger. "Emma," she said, relief evident in her voice. Her tone held a hint of melancholy as if their ride as unknown tourists was about to end. "Suzanne is here."

Suzanne Darling—who kept Emma's career going even in her absence and the tabloids at bay.

Suzanne wore a tan pants suit, her three-inch matching Jimmy Choo's blending in with the color of the couch. "Emma sweetie, you look well!" She stood and hugged Emma, her raven bob bouncing as she gave Emma an air kiss on each cheek. The scent of her expensive floral perfume lingered under Emma's nose. "How was your walk?"

Emma glanced at her assistant, grateful for the partial lie. After her all-night adventure with Shane and several hours asleep snug against his warm body, she'd awakened to the midday chill and took two walks. One from Shane's condo to her car. The other from her car to the door of her temporary residence. "It was nice, thank you."

Suzanne gazed in awe at the transformation of the vacation home. "This place looks so lived in." She turned back to Emma. "And that's a compliment."

"Yeah," Emma agreed. "It is beautiful and thank you so much. The peace and quiet helped me clear my head. I've started writing again."

"Writing?" Suzanne eased down on the couch, disappearing into the colors again.

"Yes." Emma plopped down in the nearby loveseat. "I wrote a script."

"Honey you are a wonderful actress, not a writer."

"Yes Suzanne." Emma bit her tongue, tempted to lash out at the words Suzanne barely registered as offensive. "But I think I've acted in enough films to be taken seriously. With the right director, financing—"

Suzanne angled her head sideways and plastered her best I'm-here-to-help-you-smile on her face that Emma was all too familiar with for a subject better left alone. "Emma, I'm here to see how you are and get you back to work."

"I like my vacation," Emma said. "It's been surreal to just relax."

"I know, but this isn't a vacation anymore, it's a sabbatical. And I don't do sabbaticals."

Emma shifted forward on the chair, her patience thinning. Collecting her thoughts, she redirected her rising anger and flashed Suzanne a fake smile. If Suzanne was here, the paparazzi wouldn't be far behind. "How soon are you looking for me to return?"

"Well, the scandal has died down some but more importantly, the editor of *MaryJane* magazine called." Suzanne shimmied her shoulders with excitement. "You've been voted the number one most beautiful person! I mean there are fifty beautiful named in the issue, but you, my dear, will be on the cover."

"You're kidding."

"Is humor one of my best qualities?"

Suzanne didn't laugh much in the five years Emma knew her and she certainly didn't crack jokes. "You're not kidding." *MaryJane* was a highly respected and popular magazine. Entertainment insiders used the magazine as a temperature gauge on the hottest trends, catapulting careers.

Emma leaned back in her seat. Most beautiful person? Emma consistently wore jeans and tennis shoes, her hair in ponytails and loose buns. Suzanne practically shoved Emma into designer clothes and form fitting couture dresses for every charity event, movie premiere and press junket. Her makeup remained light; even Suzanne felt Emma carried a natural beauty that needn't hide under a barrage of foundation and blush. With a stacked work schedule and the recent scandal, Emma was surprised to hear the words voted most beautiful anything.

"What does this mean?" she asked slowly.

Suzanne gave her a thousand-watt, sincere smile. "It means that you have a photo shoot and interview in two days. You need to get back to work. I have meetings already set up for you. I brought a couple of scripts for you to peruse. *Paris at Night* has set a release date, and it's almost press junket time."

Emma groaned. Press junkets and interviews, weeks in hotels. Emma loved acting, the publicity she could do without, but she understood the need for it. *Paris at Night* had been filmed prior to the recently finished *Cry Unheard* and with everything else going on, the break after back-to-back filming was welcome, even if temporarily.

"You know the drill. Late night and morning talk show circuit. Besides it's getting a lot of buzz." Suzanne raised her brow. "A lot of Oscar buzz if you know what I mean."

Normally Emma would've been thrilled at the sound of Oscar anything. Upon the film's release, the critics would share their own opinions. Emma's first thought was Shane. Promoting a movie was like a band going on tour. Constant traveling. Stops in different cities, countries. Many interviews, minus the performing live. She didn't mind so much. Sometimes the press scene gave her the feel of a mini vacation from Hollywood. That was before Shane.

"Emma? Did you hear me? There's Oscar buzz for your movie and you've just been voted *MaryJane*'s most beautiful person."

"Suzanne, the movie's not even out yet, so I think Oscar anything is a bit premature." If she was about to grace the cover of *MaryJane* her fame would skyrocket beyond her current status. More exposure equaled more power. She knew it and Suzanne did too. Emma kept her voice firm as she dictated the new terms of her career. "I'll do the interviews and press junkets. I'll read the scripts you brought and if I like them, I'll go for it. I'd appreciate it if you have someone take a look at my script when it's ready because I'm extremely serious about this. If you can't help me find a backer for my script, I'll find someone who can. As far as the magazine cover, I'm grateful and I'll be there for the interview and the photo shoot."

Suzanne looked surprised, her eyes widening in concern. "Is everything okay?"

"It's great. Better than ever."

Suzanne glanced back at Luci who stood by the edge of the corridor, leaning against the wall. Suzanne bent forward, assessing Emma closely. "What's his name?"

"What?"

"His name," Suzanne repeated. "You practically skipped in here. That robust, manly scent is all over you. Should we release another statement before the press gets wind of this?"

Emma waved her off and suppressed the impulse to smell herself. Being cloaked in Shane's scent wasn't exactly a bad thing. "Suzanne, I'm good."

Suzanne eyed her, crossed one leg over the other. "How does your mother feel about this?"

Emma snorted and shook her head. "My mother wants me back with Jordyn. I've stopped answering those calls. I'm sure there'll be hell to pay for that."

Suzanne grinned. "Honey, whatever he's giving you must be good. I mention your mother and you mention Jordyn and you're still smiling ear to ear. Where is the other Emma and what did you do with her?"

Emma laughed. "I'm fine, really."

"Well after your mother sees you on the cover of *MaryJane* she'll come around and stop the Jordyn talk."

Emma didn't care either way. Her mother's approval fell to the bottom of the list. Suzanne stood up and Emma followed. She hoisted her designer tote over her shoulder. "I'm only in town for the day. I have a flight out tonight to Kansas, don't ask, and I have to take care of a few things before I go." She started for the door but whirled around and faced Emma. "I'll expect you in L.A. tomorrow?"

"Yeah."

"Good. I'll send Luci the details. And try to stay out of trouble. At least before the cover." She scanned the room again. "It's absolutely beautiful in here. Worth every penny." The door opened, then shut, followed by the whine of the screen and the click of Suzanne's heels on the porch.

Emma hung her head at the realization of what was coming. Her real identity revealed. Luci wandered over, tightening her arm around Emma's shoulders. "You knew this would happen right? He has to find out sometime."

Emma nodded somberly.

"You've gotta tell him. Before he sees you on the cover of anything."

"I know." Emma threw her arms up letting them fall to her sides. "I just don't know what's gonna happen after that."

Twenty-Three

LUCI HANDED EMMA ANOTHER TISSUE, AND SHE blew her nose. A couple of first-class passengers shot Emma disapproving looks, but she didn't care. The commercial plane began its descent toward LAX. She called Shane from the airport, explaining she had business out of town and would return in a few days. The hesitation in Shane's voice when he'd said "okay," had Emma nearly spilling the important details of her full identity. She wanted to calm him, assure him his uncertainty was unfounded. Instead they said their goodbyes, both of them promising to call while she was away.

Los Angeles appeared thirty thousand feet below them and Emma glanced down at her red cell phone. She felt cowardly for not telling Shane the truth, that eventually reporters would crash his private life because of his relationship with her.

She blew her nose again. "I better not be comin' down with a cold."

Luci didn't comment, saying little since they left Seattle. She handed Emma another tissue.

The plane landed in fifteen minutes. They debarked and filtered into the airport terminal.

"I'll get the bags, you get the car," Luci ordered.

Emma frowned. "I can grab my bags."

"You know how crazy it can get with the fans and the paps. They're like bloodhounds. The less time you're in here, the better."

Emma grunted. Luci pointed toward the exit signs.

"Fine. I'll get the damn taxi. Next time, I get the bags." She headed for the airport exit but was stopped four times by fans to sign autographs. The rapid click and flash of cameras told her hidden paparazzi garnered several snapshots.

Outside, Emma stood at the curb, prepared to hail a cab as a black limousine pulled up. The driver hurried out of the vehicle and over to Emma. "Emma Jacobs." He held open the rear door. "I apologize for my tardiness."

"Don't worry about it." A limo, Suzanne's handiwork no doubt. Emma preferred an economical vehicle to a limousine. She glanced back at the baggage claim area, heard the repeated click of cameras. Faces turned in her direction as recognition dawned, some people pointing, others smiling excitedly. Luci exited through the double glass doors, two suitcases in hand.

The driver took their luggage and situated them in the trunk. Luci jumped into the limo beside Emma just as a small crowd started to gather around them. She snuggled into the leather seats and stared at a movie playing on the DVD player, the screen anchored in the middle of the limo's ceiling.

"I'll never get used to this," Luci said dreamily.

Emma half chuckled, her eyes wandering to the window. She had a full day and little time to think of anything else. Photo shoot. Interview. Read a script. The other Emma had returned to L.A. Time to dive back into acting and the publicity functions. Studio lots. Lunch meetings. Evening fashion and charity events. She focused on the Los Angeles skyline, her voice soft. "Time to get back to work."

"Tired yet?" Luci gave Emma a bottle of water that she unscrewed and happily gulped down. When the bottle reached halfway Emma stopped and screwed the cap back on. Four hours at the photo shoot, and two hours interviewing with various magazine reporters, Emma finally completed her commitments for the day. She and Luci hurried to the exit door at the back of the building, more than ready to disappear for the evening. The limousine waited in the alley. The driver jumped out of the car and held the door open for them. Emma and Luci climbed inside.

Emma leaned her head back on the leather seat as he maneuvered them into traffic.

"You promised Suzanne you would read at least the first twenty pages of this script." Luci lifted the stack of pages for Emma to view. "That's before we go back to Seattle."

"Twenty pages. Got it." Her body begged for a hot bath and images of sharing one with Shane immediately flashed before her eyes.

"I don't think I've ever seen a goofy smile like that on your face. What the hell did you two do that night?" Luci leaned back in her seat. "I mean, does he have a brother?"

Emma froze. Had she been smiling like that during the photo shoot? Her shoulders relaxed, her lips lifting upward. She wouldn't trade that night with Shane for anything.

Luci patiently waited for a response. Emma figured the question was rhetorical, not literal. Their time together in his bed was precious, not to be discussed, even if Luci was like family.

"Yes, a younger brother," Emma said. "I think he's single."

"And the answer to my first question?"

First question? Emma flipped through their conversation. *What the hell did you two do that night?* Emma searched for words, the lopsided smile on her face practically permanent. "No comment."

It was five o'clock on a Monday and she wondered how well Shane's lesson plan had gone that day. Emma grew accustomed to hearing about Shane's high school adventures, his tales of good and not so good days. She'd offer suggestions or just listen.

Her red cell phone rang and Emma glimpsed the screen.

Madeline.

The phone rang a second time, flashing Madeline's name.

Luci glanced at the phone. "You're not gonna answer?"

Emma sighed. Her mood was high, no sense in allowing Madeline to drag it all down. "Not today."

"I'm sure she knows you're back in L.A."

"Of course, she does."

The driver dropped them off at one of the five-star hotels in Beverly Hills. The bell hop carried their luggage up ten floors to a room at the end of the hall. Opening the double, ivory doors, Emma and Luci wandered into the two thousand square foot suite. Earth tones colored the walls, the carpeted suite divided into a living room and a dining area with an extensive table for eight and full-service kitchen. Emma sauntered through each area, noting the gas fireplace, the modern black chairs, forest green couches and the three separate windows, two with balconies and panoramic views of the city.

Luci moseyed beside Emma, gazing at the luxury accommodations. "I don't know how you ever get used to this."

Emma reached the master bedroom, pushing open the double doors to a massive king-sized bed and spectacular landscape views. She fell across the mattress, cloaked in clouds of blankets and pillows so soft her eyes closed upon impact.

"Emma, you okay?" Luci neared the bedroom door, awaiting her boss's instructions.

Emma turned her head, mumbled to Luci to go home, she deserved time away. Luci took a step from the door, then hesitated.

"It's okay. Take the night off and relax."

Luci stared at Emma for a while before she at last turned and left. The front door clicked shut and Emma rose from the bed, strolling out to the balcony and nestled into the deck chair. The sun slowly descended among the horizon. Her mind flickered back to Shane, her small smile fading as reality crept in. Eventually Shane would discover her full identity.

The orange glow of the setting sun blazed the balcony and Emma averted her eyes. She cared too much to see Shane's teaching career, friendships, and family jeopardized because of her. Overcoming her separation with Jordyn hadn't been easy, but she'd achieved it. If required, she would leave Shane, even if it was for his own good.

———————

It took two days to finish the MTV version of *Romeo and Juliet* with each class. Shane reviewed imagery and metaphors, the class enthusiastically participating in the discussions. He relayed the storyline as it would happen in modern times. There were giggles, smiling, involvement.

"We know there is a connection to hate and violence in Romeo and Juliet. Is there a connection between love and violence as well as it relates to this story?"

Several hands shot into the air, some with fingers wiggling to be chosen. Shane picked a girl seated at the back of the class, her strawberry blond hair falling past her shoulder blades. She was skinny and pale, her eyes as green as his and she smiled a look of flirtation rather than innocence.

"Sela?" He pointed at her.

She leaned back in her chair and tossed part of her hair over her left shoulder. "Yes, Mr. Rawlings. They loved each other so much that they used violence to prove it."

Shane nodded at her answer and opened his mouth to say more when the last bell sounded. Students rushed from their seats, gathering their books, slipping binders into bookbags. They chatted quickly, shuffling from the room.

"Pop quiz tomorrow," Shane called after them. Several students groaned and Shane waited by his desk, a smile on his face. His students finally latched on to Romeo and Juliet, just as enthralled by the tragic love story as he was. The MTV version of *Romeo and Juliet* was Emma's idea and a successful one. He couldn't wait to share the good news. Emma had been gone for only a week but her absence felt like three weeks. Further appointments kept her busy back in L.A.

"Everything okay in here?" Gabe peeked into the room.

Shane glanced up at his friend. "I'm okay." He walked around the back of his desk and gathered up his papers to put in his bag.

"You've been moping around here for days now."

Shane missed Emma and her absence left him with spurts of a foul disposition. "I'm not moping."

"That puppy-dog-I'm-sad look? I don't think I've ever seen that one on you before."

"Gabe." Shane slipped the papers in his bag and paused at the harshness of his tone. Maybe he had been moping the last few days. Maybe his lack of carnal intimacy and the feel of Emma affected him more than he originally thought. "Sorry." He dropped the irritation from his voice. "You're right, I've been a little out of it lately."

"I am right." Gabe stepped forward and glanced around the room. "I saw a lot of happy faces leave your class today."

Shane smiled at the memory of his enthusiastic students. "Yeah, they are."

"New tactic?"

"Emma's idea." The words were out before he could stop himself.

"Emma?" Gabe analyzed his friend like someone he'd never met. He sat down in a student desk and dropped his satchel on the floor. "Oh please, enlighten me. I remember no Emma."

Shane exhaled a long breath. No one except Luci knew how they met, where they went, what they were like together. Bainbridge carried a small population, under twenty thousand people, but in certain circles people paid attention to new residents. Emma seemed so intent on keeping herself secret from the world, Shane hesitated to divulge any facts about the two of them together. Still, he couldn't bring himself to keep it a secret and didn't fully understand why he needed to. Another discussion set aside for when Emma returned.

Gabe rested his chin in the palm of one hand, his elbow propped up on the desktop. He used his other hand to coax Shane for information. "Waiting."

"Okay." Why shouldn't he reveal his happiness? "Her name is Emma."

"I got that. And?"

"And, she's great. She's beautiful, intelligent, and so out of my league."

"Give yourself some credit bud." Gabe straightened. "So, what's the real problem?"

"Problem?"

"There's always a problem."

Shane slung his bag over his right shoulder. "Gabe, you're a cynic. You always see a problem."

"There always is one."

"Isn't that called a relationship?" As much as Gabe pushed Shane into the dating world he had yet to see his friend in a single relationship. Gabe frolicked in one-night stands. Flirting with tourists. Most "relationships" lasting thirty days maximum. What spawned his distrust with women? A parent? Old girlfriend?

"I'm really sorry about her." Shane piled together the last of his papers on his desk.

Gabe looked confused. "Sorry about who?"

"Whatever woman made you like this."

"Oh, there is nothing wrong with this." He swept one hand over his body to demonstrate. "I was born a beautiful male."

Shane laughed and mimicked Gabe's hand gesture. "Beautiful male? You can add insanity to that list of yours."

Gabe rose from the student desk and followed Shane to the door. "Crazy is my aphrodisiac. That thing still at your place tonight?"

The smile fell from Shane's lips. He was hosting a "gathering" at his condo for the mixed martial arts fight on his fifty-inch flat screen television. His brother-in-law, younger brother, and several cousins and uncles would be there for the main event. He'd bought cases of beer and his sister promised to bring appetizers. In a school day immersed in the world of Romeo and Juliet he almost forgot about the dreaded small party.

Shane agreed, only to appease his sister. "Yeah, Gabe. Tonight. My house. Fight starts at seven." He glanced at his watch. Four hours to prep everything before visitors arrived. Check the beer. Call his sister. Set up the fight on pay-per-view.

"Don't worry bud." Gabe slapped him on the back. "I'll be there."

All of the worry didn't drain from Shane's face but he appreciated having someone there who knew him. Not old financial whiz Shane, but new, teacher Shane. "Thanks man."

Shane opened the door and Gabe stepped into the hall first. Shane locked the door. Banners hovered from the ceiling displaying the year's prom theme. With prom on the horizon, graduation followed, the end of the school year fast approaching.

Gabe noticed the banner too. "You takin' Emma to the prom?"

Shane strayed from chaperoning school events. Especially dances. Emma accompanying him to the prom put a new smile on his face. His stomach tied in knots at the prospect of asking her. He felt like a teenager all over again. "Maybe."

Twenty-Four

"You're late." Shane held the door open and Sallie stood in the hall, two trays of food stacked in her hand.

Sallie blew out a breath of air and offered him the food. "I know. I'm sorry."

Shane took the trays from her and hurriedly placed them on the kitchen counter. He glanced at his watch again. Ten minutes to go and the first guests would come knocking.

Sallie noted the distressed look on her older brother's face. "Shane, it'll be fine." She pointed at the doorway. "I have more bags in the car."

Shane's scowl deepened, and he opened his mouth to scold her, then shut it. No time for debates, he had a party he didn't want to host that was about to begin. He rushed down the stairs and brought the remaining groceries from her car inside.

Sallie helped him arrange trays of appetizers on the long, bar counter. She prepped the couches and Shane put three cases of beer in the refrigerator. He poured two separate bags of chips in two large bowls, situating them beside her trays, and lined up several two-liter soda bottles next to a stack of red plastic cups.

Sallie reviewed the selection of food on the counter. The TV blared with scenes of an impending fight. Not the title match, but the first of two bouts by other fighters before the main event.

Someone knocked on the door.

"I got it," Sallie shouted and answered the knock. Patrick and Dorian waited in the hall. She lightly kissed Patrick and gave Dorian a fleeting glance.

If Dorian was bothered by Sallie's dismissive nature, he didn't show it. Dorian gazed around the massive condo. He snorted. "Nice place man."

"Thanks." Shane narrowed his gaze at the man standing in the middle of the living room. He couldn't tell when Dorian was being sincere or an ass, and he didn't have the time to decipher which. Easier to treat him like an ass.

The door swung open several more times as people filled the loft. Uncle Phil, his brother Mercer, four cousins who brought along their three buddies, and two other uncles he rarely spoke to. Gabe was the last to arrive.

By six-thirty, the loft was packed with people and Shane wished he could disappear in the safety of his bedroom. He agreed to this little shindig only to keep his promise to Sallie. Gabe settled into a conversation with Dorian, and Mercer was in the kitchen, telling wild medical stories to one of their cousins.

Sallie walked over and nudged Shane's arm. "You okay?"

He folded his arms across his chest. Nope, he was far from okay, but he nodded anyway. "I'm fine. I'm the older brother remember? I don't need taking care of."

"Touchy." Focused on the television, she lowered her voice. "Fight with the girlfriend?"

"No," Shane whispered back. "Everything's good. She's just out of town."

"Oh." She grinned. "So, you miss her?"

That was an understatement. He missed the sweet scent of Emma in the morning. The touch of her skin, the sound of her voice beside him. Their late-night phone calls did not compete to what he'd become accustomed to in person.

Shane didn't answer Sally's question, finding the perfect opportunity to avoid the topic altogether. "I forgot about the Seven-Up." He started for the door.

"Wait!" Sallie called out. "The main event is about to start."

"It's okay." Shane flung open the front door, his lips quirking up at the memory of him and Emma at the M.M.A. match not long ago. "I've seen one of these fights live before and once you've seen that, the TV version is just not the same."

A couple of the conversations in the room paused and several eyes turned in his direction. "You went to a live match?" someone asked.

Shane grinned. "Sure did." He shut the door and dashed down the steps.

At the grocery store downstairs, he grabbed two six packs of Seven-Up and waited in line behind a woman who rummaged in her oversized handbag for her credit card. His eyes wandered to the large pane window and the spot outside where the two lovelorn teenagers verbally sparred and later, where he and Emma did the same. Nearly two months ago still seemed like yesterday. He tore his gaze from the window and glanced at the rack of magazines neatly displayed above the conveyer belt.

One of the magazines, *MaryJane,* titled its issue the "Fifty Most Beautiful People." Shane did a double take at the cover of the magazine.

Emma graced the cover, wearing a long, white skirt and matching halter top, her hair blown slightly away from her face. Makeup enhanced the natural beauty of her face, playfulness sparkling her cocoa colored eyes as she smiled at the camera. Shane blinked, concentrating on the image. Emma. The yellow caption beside her picture gave her full name.

Emma Jacobs.

———

"You're really going?" Luci stood by the hotel room's double doors.

Emma hoisted the backpack over both of her shoulders. In blue jean capris, a pink sweater and tennis shoes, she looked like a teenager ready for her first day of school. She tucked a wayward curl of hair behind her ear, the mass of waves resting along her shoulders. "I'm ready."

"You've got clean underwear?"

Emma chuckled. "Yes."

"Toothbrush?"

"Yes mom."

"Bathing suit?"

The image of her and Shane swimming in the pool beyond his parents' home flashed in her thoughts, and she smiled. "There won't be time for that." Emma had twelve free hours before her next round of interviews. She wanted those hours to be with Shane, minus the swimming pool, maybe something more intimate.

"Pajamas?"

Emma packed her lucky Max the Mouse PJs. "Yes, but I don't think I'll need them."

The tight line of Luci's lips broadened into a satisfactory smile. "Got your speech ready then?"

Emma bit her lip. "Not really." She toyed with how to tell Shane. If he hadn't already seen the magazine cover. Hopefully he was confined to the loft, shutting out the world, preparing for finals week. Shane filled their phone conversations with student stories and she continued dodging specifics about her acting career. She told him she attended work, and she did. A meeting with the producers of a new film they tapped her to play in. Two brief meetings with her agent, the rest interviews. She omitted they were television interviews. Shane didn't watch much TV anyway. Emma adjusted the backpack. "I don't know how to tell him."

Luci placed both hands on Emma's shoulders. "Just tell him." She looked at Emma's backpack. "Got your ticket?"

"Yes." Her smile faded and her shoulders drooped. "Think he's gonna be mad at me?"

"I don't know."

Emma appreciated the honesty. Dragging her optimism to the front of her thoughts, she heaved in a long breath and released it. "Okay, I'm gonna get going. My flight leaves at—"

"Eight-thirty. I know." Luci stepped back and grabbed the door handle. "You'd better go. I'll meet you in Atlanta."

A radio interview, another talk show. Less sleep, less food. Twelve hours of Shane would be enough to get through the rest of the week. A quick flight and she'd arrive in Bainbridge with enough hours to spare before leaving for Atlanta, the day after that, to New York.

Luci flung open the door. Jordyn Mars stood in the threshold, his fist raised midair to knock on a door that was no longer there.

"What are you doing here?" Emma brushed past him, hurrying into the hall and toward the elevator.

Jordyn followed her, taking off his black shades and hanging them at the apex of his black V-neck shirt. "You're not taking my calls." He soaked in her overall appearance. "Are you gaining weight?"

Emma's mouth dropped open. In Bainbridge, she'd lost five pounds. She'd have to eat more as fuel to sustain another marathon session in Shane's bed. But Jordyn saw weight gain? He'd always noted the change in her curves, pointed out facial blemishes, commented if her skin wasn't sleek and regal looking. It made her aware of every flaw on her body, uneven skin tones, tiny beauty marks, bad hair days. "I'm not having this conversation with you. Shouldn't you be moving out?"

"Who's the guy that answered the phone?"

Emma jabbed her index finger on the down arrow button for the elevator. Only two suites occupied the top floor but she suddenly wished the hall was crowded with hotel guests, any distraction away from Jordyn. "It's none of your business."

"Are you seeing him?"

"Still none of your business."

He stepped in close, invading her space and Emma leaned her head back. "We need a statement to the press. Something that says we're working through this. A plan for when we get back together."

Not if. Not possibly. *When.* A plan for *when* we get back together. Emma groaned inwardly. What part of not-a-chance-in-hell did Jordyn not understand?

The elevator doors silently opened. Emma hurried inside and spun around to face him. She pushed the lobby button on the inside panel. "When do you plan on getting out of my house?"

"*Your* house?" Jordyn followed her into the elevator. "How about it's *our* house?"

Emma remembered shaking the realtor's hand, signing the paperwork, writing the check for the Tuscan style mansion. She couldn't recollect Jordyn's signature on any of the official documents. "Did you pay for it? Any of it?"

He pressed a hand to his chest, offended by what her question implied. "Is that what we're doing now? Trading whose salary's bigger?"

He tapped his chest again and a wave of strong cologne bombarded her senses. "I'm Jordyn Mars, makin' millions. When you bought that house, I was just getting off the ground."

"And now you're flying high." She wrinkled her nose at his overpowering scent. Jordyn didn't buy cologne, and she certainly hadn't paid for the pungent smell. Probably his newest female, yet to be unveiled to the public. "You and I aren't getting back together."

"I haven't heard a good enough reason why not."

A good enough reason? Emma blinked in pure disbelief. She stared up at the green numbers on the overhead display. The elevator stopped on floor eight. A couple entered, dressed in tank tops and gym shorts. Probably going to the hotel's gym on the seventh floor.

The doors shut and Jordyn scooted closer to her. "Do you think this guy really cares about you?"

Emma didn't respond.

"He just wants to be famous. And what better way than to use you to get there."

Was he kidding? Emma crossed her hands over her chest. Did Jordyn actually hear himself when he spoke? Had those stupid square sunglasses made him blind? He'd been using her for the last year to catapult his own career.

The elevator doors slid open. Seventh floor.

The couple exited, the woman glancing back sadly at the two of them as she followed her boyfriend down the corridor to the gym.

The metal doors shut, the pinging sound signaling their descent once again.

"Have you checked a mirror lately?" She glared at him then turned back to the doors.

Jordyn narrowed his eyes at her, his voice tight. "Don't twist this into something else. We should be working on us Em."

"And who have you been working on?"

"No one but you. We have history together. We shouldn't throw that away." He reached for her arm but Emma shook it away.

For a brief second, Emma swore she heard regret in his voice, his arrogance subdued. The old Jordyn, the one who'd made her feel special, wanted, beautiful, appeared before her. His eyes saying the words his mouth couldn't form. The image was mere fantasy, another one of Jordyn's mind games. They did have history together. History of his infidelity. History of lies and betrayal. History of her naivete. Not to be revisited twice.

She slipped her oversized sunglasses on her face. "We're over Jordyn."

The elevator stopped at the fourth floor. A family of four entered first, husband, wife, one son standing beside his dad, the other snuggled and sleeping in a monstrous stroller. Three young women came second, looking barely twenty in their cutoff jeans and toddler sized tank tops, their hair pinned up in loose knots.

Emma stepped back, allowing the influx of people to squeeze inside. Jordyn shifted to her side, their arms nearly touching as the doors closed and the elevator descended to the lobby, overhead eighties wave music escorting them the entire way. Neither of them spoke, Jordyn's head lowered, Emma focusing on the upper display of green numbers as they advanced down each level. She couldn't hear anymore, couldn't engage in any more battles with Jordyn. He was draining all the joy she carried on her way to see Shane again.

Jordyn opened his mouth to speak.

"Omigosh!" Emma shrieked, her voice heightened, mocking excitement as she faced him. "You're Jordyn Mars!"

The other occupants turned, staring at him, the husband from the family of four suddenly smiling. "It is you." He extended his hand. "You do good work man."

"Thanks." Jordyn shook the man's hand.

The three young women glanced eagerly among each other, before showering Jordyn with that look of amazement. A look all too familiar to Emma. Seeing not the person, but the celebrity. Recognition followed by stunned disbelief.

The elevator doors opened and Emma rushed out. She had a plane to catch and a man to see.

———————

"Emma Jacobs?" Shane said to himself. The same Emma who played the guitar and learned to sew a button. Who made him peanut butter and strawberry jam sandwiches. Who wore Max the Mouse pajamas to bed and loved classic horror movies.

"That'll be six twenty-nine," The cashier said.

Shane looked up at Tim the cashier. He hadn't noticed the woman ahead of him had left, and two people fell into line behind him.

"Shane?" Tim waited.

Shane slapped the magazine on the counter. "This too."

Tim scanned the magazine and placed it in a plastic bag.

Shane snatched it out of the bag, his eyes drawn to the magazine cover. He withdrew a twenty-dollar bill from his back pocket and handed it to Tim.

The cash register pinged, zipped, the drawer opened, and Tim handed the change to Shane. He studied him closely. "You okay man?"

Shane didn't take his eyes off the magazine. "Yeah." He gathered up the case of soda, the magazine gripped in his other hand.

He trudged up the stairs to his condo and opened the door to screams and shouts. The main event began and Sallie settled on the arm of his couch, leaning against Patrick, watching the fight.

Shane shut the door, dropped the soda on the counter, and rushed to his room. He needed to breathe, to understand. His Emma was on a magazine cover listed as the most beautiful person. He wasn't sure if he should be happy she was voted the top person, flattered someone as recognizable as her picked him as a mate, or bothered every other man would be looking at his woman with salacious thoughts. All three feelings ripped through him. He plopped down on the bed, holding the magazine up, examining the cover. It was an illusion, some kind of trick. Yet there were stacks of the same issue in the rack at the store. No illusion. Reality.

He recognized the curves of her hips, the smoothness of her skin, the way her brown eyes danced back at him. Emma. On the cover of *MaryJane*.

"Is everything okay?" Sallie peered through the opening of his bedroom door. Finding him seated on the bed, she came in and softly closed the door behind her. "You looked pale when you came back. Like you saw a ghost or something."

"Or something," he said absently.

Sallie stared at the magazine in his hand. "I didn't know you read *MaryJane*."

"I don't."

"So, you got that for me?" Sallie dropped down on the bed beside him. "It's their Fifty Most Beautiful People issue. I love that one." She took the magazine from Shane, his grip barely loosening to let her have it. "Emma Jacobs." Sallie crooned. "She's so pretty."

Shane jerked his head up at his sister. "You know her?"

Sallie recoiled. "No." She held her hand up over her head. "Emma Jacobs is way up here." Sallie lowered her hand to waist level. "I'm like right here. We might be rich and she is too, but we don't exactly move in the same circles. She's uber-famous and a really good actress. I just love her movies. According to the tabloids, she's been hiding out somewhere in Italy." She waved him off. "You don't even watch movies. Why are you asking about her?"

Shane scratched his head, uncertain how to respond. For weeks his time with Emma involved back-and-forth conversation, engaging in activities he hadn't ever done or revisited.

She didn't lie to him about her vocation, only omitted the extent of her success. He now understood the reason she asked if he recognized her. The reason she wore huge sunglasses and a beanie. Why she avoided public places.

He glanced back at the magazine cover, feeling foolish. "That, that's Emma."

Sallie nodded, baffled her brother might need mental counseling more than what she already wanted him to get. "Uh-huh. Her name is Emma."

"No that's Emma. *My* Emma. She's not in Italy."

"Your Em—" Sallie's eyes widened. "Your Emma as in Emma Jacobs?"

"I guess so." He took in a long, deep breath, stood up, and paced back and forth. "She said she was an actress, we just never really talked about it."

Sallie bounced on the bed excitedly. "She told you she's an actress but you never asked about it?" She put the magazine aside and clapped her hands. "Oh my goodness, I'm going to get to meet her, right?"

"We've been seeing each other almost two months, and I never paid attention to the signs." Shane avoided asking much about her acting career, realizing how uncomfortable it made her. She commented her acting gigs paid decent. An actress on the cover of this magazine didn't get paid "decent," her salary was more likely astronomical. What the hell did she want with a high school English teacher compared against the fast-paced world of Los Angeles? "I'm such an idiot."

"You've been dating her for two months and you didn't tell me?" Sallie picked up the magazine and thumbed through the pages until she found the article on Emma.

"I told you we were dating."

"Not for two months! And not with Emma Jacobs." Sallie scanned the article. "They asked her relationship status."

Shane paused and looked down at the open pages. He hadn't seen Emma in anything other than jeans and tennis shoes. The second image of her was just as dramatic and startling as the first. She wore a Japanese inspired, black two-piece skirt and sleeveless top, outlined in cherry red with black stilettos, the double ankle straps red. Her hair was loosely pinned up, wispy strands framing her face, her expression studious and appealing.

To see her in a skirt outlining the lithe body he knew beneath her clothes was breathtaking. It didn't matter what she wore. Both her mind and her body captured him and it was too late to turn back now.

Sallie continued reading. "She wouldn't comment."

Shane closed his eyes, thankful not to be under the public light. He tried to process all the information coming at him.

Sallie eagerly read aloud. "She loves horror movies and swimming. She talks a lot about film, not too much about herself except that she's a private person." Sallie lowered the magazine to stare at her brother. "When do I get to meet her?"

"I don't know." Shane paced again. Meeting Sallie? Meeting his family? She was so famous if anyone ever found out the press would have their hands full with his parents and his siblings. He didn't want them under a microscope any more than himself. "Sallie, please don't tell anyone."

"Are you serious?" Disappointment marked her face.

Patrick softly knocked once and peeked in the room. "Everything okay in here?"

"We're good," Sallie snapped.

Surprised at her curt tone, Patrick didn't respond but closed the door, his lips, eyes, ears vanishing from view.

"I'm serious Sallie. You can't tell anyone."

"Alright, alright." Sallie rolled her eyes. "But it has to come out at some point."

"I know." Shane didn't look forward to the day their union shined in the spotlight. Highlighted on entertainment shows. Snapshots on the cover of tabloid magazines. Reporters camped out at the house of anyone associated with her.

Sallie glanced back at the photo. "She's gorgeous. Too bad she got suckered by the last guy."

Shane stopped pacing and peered down at the magazine again. The thought of Emma with anyone else made his stomach curl. "What last guy?"

Sallie turned the page to several small photos of Emma over the years. One showed her standing with a man, brown skin, bald head, solid build. In his early thirties. He held one arm possessively around Emma. The knots in Shane's belly twisted, and he balled his hands into tight fists. Emma's smile was faint. "That's Jordyn isn't it?"

Sallie pointed to the picture. "Jordyn Mars, yeah. Jordyn stars in a lot of action flicks. Not the greatest actor, but he looks good kickin' butt."

Shane snatched the magazine from his sister, held it up to view and analyzed his competition. Jordyn Mars. The name of the man that answered the phone the night of Shane's guitar lesson. The same person Emma referred to as the "stalker." "So, they're not together?"

Sallie shook her head emphatically. "No! He was caught a couple of months ago cheating on her. It was a huge scandal in all the tabloids. They'd been together one or two years, I think. Jordyn was caught with someone else. That's why she 'supposedly' fled to Italy." She glanced at the magazine and up at Shane. "So, she was here, the whole time, hiding out after the scandal broke. And you're the rebound guy."

"I'm the what?"

Sallie held her hands up, regret flickering her eyes. "I didn't mean it the way it sounded." She frowned. "What are you gonna do?"

"I don't know." He sighed and sat down on the bed beside Sallie. A confrontation of this magnitude would have to wait for Emma's return. He'd know by then exactly what he wanted to say.

Twenty-Five

I'M AN ACTRESS. I'VE STARRED IN OVER A DOZEN successful films. I'm on the cover of MaryJane magazine. I have a house worth ten million dollars but I'm currently living in a Beverly Hills penthouse suite.

No matter how many times Emma chanted the words in her head, her mouth wouldn't open to speak them. She rehearsed the lines a hundred times, the explanation to Shane stuck to the roof of her mouth. She gave speeches at charity functions and awards shows. Words flowing from her lips, smooth and easy. Simple. Her words to Shane? Lost.

The voice over the intercom announced the arrival to Bainbridge Island, drowning out the chanting rain overhead. Seated at a table facing the window, Emma stared out at the pitch blackness of the water below. Fluorescent lights flooded the large inside cabin where several other passengers sought shelter. Emma wondered what the hell she would do if Shane decided her stardom was too much. Threatened by her success in the spotlight. Jordyn was jealous, envious, angry her notoriety far exceeded his own. She didn't realize it then, but long before their separation she recognized it in his eyes every time they passed each other in the house.

Her red cell phone blared the time in big, white numbers.

Eleven-twelve.

Her surprise visit to Shane was tricky. Late Friday night most single people gathered at bars, clubs, or attended parties. She'd be lucky to find him at home. Part of her knew he would be home since the bar scene, nightclubs and large crowds weren't his style. He preferred low key activities, home based fun. The way he maneuvered that Ducati reminded her Shane wasn't always the closed in, low key kind of guy.

Eyes glued to the window, she avoided the gaze of other passengers. Tugging down her beanie and slipping her shades on her face, she followed the remaining group to the exit. Rain battered the cars, people, droplets bouncing off the asphalt. Emma flipped her hood over her head. A yellow cab waited by the curb, one that she'd called in advance.

Emma lowered her head and hurried through the rain to the taxi. Her body shivered but not from the icy cold drops of water beating her windbreaker. She could only guess Shane's reaction to her news and none of them with a positive outcome.

The taxi ride lasted less than fifteen minutes. She paid the cab driver and jumped out, gazing up at the well-lit windows of Shane's residence. He was home. The driver pulled away and Emma, raindrops pelting her face, slowly took the steps up to his front door. She reached the top of the landing and knocked twice.

"Who is it?" His voice bellowed from the other side.

"Emma."

Silence followed. Longer than it should have been. Emma inhaled a deep breath.

Shane unlocked the deadbolt and opened the door. His brows creased, his mouth that once tasted her body, melted her into puddles, was closed. Not a "hi" or "welcome back." His eyes held a look of doubt and awareness. He knew her identity. Somehow. He shifted to one side to allow Emma entrance.

She cautiously entered the condo. "Let me explain." She spun around and he shut the door.

A mixture of hurt and frustration crossed his face. A five-foot distance separated them and Shane appeared in no hurry to close the gap.

"How did you find out?" she asked.

He held up the *MaryJane* magazine cover.

"Oh." She strolled to the couch and sat down. "I was hoping I could talk to you before you saw that."

"Why didn't you tell me?"

Fear, laziness, selfishness, the list kept growing. "I didn't know how to tell you. I mean, I told you I was an actress."

Some of the anger diminished, and he tilted his head at her. "You did. But you didn't tell me you're *Emma Jacobs*."

"I didn't think it mattered." He'd come to know Emma. Without the cameras, the scripts, the fans. Her quirky habits, her goals in life. Intimate details no one, not even Jordyn knew. "That's a real person on the cover of that magazine." She flattened her hand across her chest. "I, am a real person."

"But not ordinary."

"I am ordinary."

Shane huffed. "You're anything but ordinary."

"That's a compliment." She managed a small smile.

"It's a complication," Shane said tight-lipped. "I'm not sure how I feel about that."

Emma raised her chin. Tears stung her eyes, and she blinked them back. "It's too much, I get it."

"You were on some vacation and I was just a fling?" Shane folded his arms across his chest. "You told me you and Jordyn hadn't been together for a while. Is that true? Or am I just the rebound guy?"

Emma leaned her head back, surprised by the question. "Rebound guy?" It never occurred to her Shane perceived their relationship as a cushion from her former one. "I told you the truth. Jordyn and I have been apart for some time." Her eyes held his. "You are not a rebound guy."

She rose from the couch and narrowed her eyes at Shane. The prospect of cameras, reporters, questions proved too much. His ability to remain tolerant to her level of public scrutiny was nearly nonexistent. She'd been silly to believe they could work through this one major part of her life. Her voice came out low, controlled. "You're right. It's a lot to take in. You met the vacation Emma, and this vacation is over."

She stepped past him, opened the front door and shut it behind her.

Shane did not follow, did not call out, did not reach for her. Emma walked three blocks in the rain, called a cab and returned to the ferry. After a short wait it reappeared, taking her back to Seattle and away from the place she temporarily called home.

Thoughts flashed to Shane trying to sew a button, chatting animatedly about his students. The motorcycle ride, browsing through the marketplace, swimming in the pool while the storm brewed around their glass cage. Her skin tingled at the memory of his fingers trailing along her skin.

Shane was right about her world. Too complicated. His job might be impacted by the publicity if anyone ever found out. Fellow teachers, family and friends bombarded with questions. The small town of Bainbridge overrun with tabloid hounds. She couldn't expect him to deal with the type of life she learned to handle. So, the vacation was over. They were over.

The ferry reached the middle of Puget Sound, sloshing against the dark waves. Emma lowered her head and cried.

"So, what are my two favorite teachers doing in here?" Delia stood by the door, her dark brown hair pinned in its usual tight bun, pearl earrings adorning her ears.

Shane shoved his stack of papers into his bag. He flipped it closed and clasped it shut. "Working hard. Right Gabe?"

Gabe waited near one of the student desks, his bag hooked across one shoulder. He studied Delia who didn't smile at him, but gave Shane a wide grin.

"You've been working late this week." Delia leaned against the doorframe, one perfectly manicured hand on her hip. "Kids come out of your classes all smiles. What's going on in here? No one should be that excited over finals."

"Nothing." Shane slung the strap of the bag over his shoulder. "Inspiration maybe."

Gabe watched the exchange between Shane and Delia, his expression marking complete bewilderment. She started stopping by after school to chat about classroom activities. Shane learned more about Delia in the last few days than in the last couple of weeks. They avoided personal relationship questions, and he had no inclination to start now.

Shane glanced down at his watch. "My sister's having me fitted for a tux and I don't wanna be late." He scurried both Delia and Gabe out of the classroom, before either of them could object.

Shane didn't want to be a groomsman but his sister's insistence far outweighed his objections. Four groomsmen, four bridesmaids, a couple hundred guests, the wedding became the upcoming summer event. Less than two months to go and his sister would officially be married.

At the tux shop Shane followed his sister's instructions. Stand on the brown carpeted pedestal and allow the man with the black slacks and white shirt to stick pins into his tuxedo. Shane hadn't worn a tuxedo in years with no desire to put one back on. The attendant glared at Shane, asked him to hold out his arms. Shane held out both his arms, his body in the shape of a T.

Sallie crossed her legs, leaning back in the long buttery leather seat. She flipped back to Shane's overall appearance when he first arrived at the shop. "Solid colored shirts? Blue jeans? You look good bro. I really, really, like this girl."

Shane huffed. "I'm still the same person."

"No." Sallie rocked her leg back and forth absorbing her brother's updated appearance. "You are a newer Shane. And I'm loving it."

Shane shook his head. He spent nights wondering about the changes in himself. And Emma's whereabouts. What she was up to and how she was doing. He repeated that final night together, wishing he'd caught her arm, stopped her from leaving. Instead he let her go because he didn't know what else to do.

"She's not talking to me anymore." The confession pained him to say aloud and his sister took note of his hurt tone.

Sallie sat upright. "What happened?"

"She went back to L.A." The man knelt down, placing pins an inch up at the hemline of his suit pants. "Her vacation was over."

"What does that mean?"

"It means I was the rebound guy." How many times had Jordyn Mars called Emma trying to reconcile? Before Shane talked with him? She and Jordyn were from the same planet. His world was smaller, different. He couldn't compare with a megastar like Jordyn Mars.

Sallie winced at the word "rebound." "I should've never said that. Are you sure you're not? Because I don't think you are."

"Sallie, he called her while she was here, trying to get back with her. I finally talked to him and that got him to stop."

"You talked to Jordyn Mars?"

His outstretched arms faltered. "Yes, I did, for ten seconds. This thing is too complicated. I shouldn't be dating anyway, it's not right."

The man at his feet huffed. "Stay still please."

Shane looked down at the man. "Sorry." He raised his arms, assuming his T position and caught his reflection in the full-length mirror. Hardened features creased his face from the absence of sleep. Weary eyes, his voice gruff, he refused to regret his time with Emma. His fury at their separation eventually brought resolution Emma would not come back. *The vacation was over.*

Sallie frowned. "You shouldn't be dating because of what? Because you lived and Liam died? Because I lost a foot?" She held up her left foot, the titanium metal peeking from beneath her blue jeans but snug in her modified tennis shoe. "It was an accident."

"I don't wanna talk about it." There was an edge to his voice that normally backed others away from the subject.

Sallie matched the icy clip in his tone. "You will not use me or Liam's death as your crutch for not living." She raised her voice and even the attendant paused to look up at her.

Shane didn't know what to say. He'd never seen Sallie so wound up not even when he told her the doctors amputated her foot. She joked about still having the other one, not displaying any evidence of anger until now. "I don't know how you do that."

"What?"

"You're never mad about it. You should be furious with me."

"Why? Because you were driving? It was an accident Shane."

"I walked away with minor scratches. You lost a part of yourself. Liam lost his life. I could've turned the wheel faster or something, anything."

Sallie counted the reasons on each finger. "You weren't drunk, you weren't speeding, you weren't at fault. The other guy was. Was I angry? Yeah. Did it change anything? No." Her voice lowered, her eyes holding his with contempt. "So, don't you dare use us as your excuse for not living. I don't pity myself and I won't pity you."

Shane opened his mouth to speak but Sallie cut him off with one hand. "You are not the rebound guy and this woman really likes you. So, fix it."

Shane closed his mouth. He wanted Emma, needed her. Searching for her in Los Angeles held major challenges. No one just showed up in L.A. and found a celebrity's home with ease. "I don't know how to fix it." Shane lowered his arms.

"Sir!"

"Sorry." Shane was ready to step off the pedestal and go with any tuxedo off the rack. "I wish she was here right now, but it's complicated. She'll be away most of the time, she's got all this money. She doesn't need me. She's this huge star with men drooling all over her. She could have any man she wants."

"Probably." Sallie slowly nodded, her gaze on the floor as she thought through her brother's comments. "From everything I've read, she and Jordyn were 'quietly' separated for a while. She hasn't been linked to anyone." Sallie raised her head, her eyes burning the truth into Shane's skull. "Until now. And even though she probably has tons of men lined up that wanna be with her, she chose you older brother."

Sallie leaned back, the plush leather flexing under her weight. "Nothing is complicated that you can't work through." She lifted one leg over the other and relaxed in her seat. "You better figure out how to fix this. Because she is definitely invited to my wedding, but your attendance is seriously in question right now."

CHAPTER

Twenty-Six

EMMA STRUCK THE RED PUNCHING BAG. LEFT JAB, right hook, cross. She bounced back and forth fluidly, her gloved fists landing viciously on the bag again. Right jab. Left jab. Left hook. She eyed the swaying punching bag, struck it a third time with a barrage of combinations. Her breathing quick, sweat raced down the sides of her face.

One week passed since she last saw Shane. Seven days from the moment she left his apartment, chin up, eyes glossy. Shane was confused, and the decision had to be made for him. She'd learned to handle the chaos. She couldn't ask him to.

She hit the bag. Left hook. Right hook. Left jab. Right jab.

Sunlight filtered through the small, square basement window. She returned to her house in the Hollywood hills but only for a brief one hour, boxing workout. The basement of her home had been converted to an exercise room instead of a wine cellar, one of the few things she and Jordyn agreed on. It afforded Emma the opportunity to burn off calories and stay fit in private. Jordyn was on location for two days filming part of his yet to be titled movie and still hadn't moved out.

"It's almost six." Luci descended the steps and set an unopened water bottle on a small nearby table. "You've got a full day."

"I always have a full day." She punched the bag three more times. The week included a press junket, another round of interviews and two meetings about future films. Thankfully calls diminished over the last twenty-four hours.

"Shane called again." Luci leaned against the back wall, her arms crossed over her chest. Emma felt the burn of Luci's gaze, tearing through her skin, telling her to call him. Emma struck the bag. "Did you answer it?"

"No." Luci huffed, disgusted at her instructions to ignore Shane's calls. No answer, no messages, delete all voicemails.

Emma decided that to get over Shane, the separation had to be clean. No contact or explanations. Her heart could not survive it any other way. She punched the bag harder, and it swayed sideways. "Good."

"Why are you doing this?"

"Doing what?"

"Pretending he doesn't exist."

"It's better this way." She delivered another right hook. The metal link chain above the bag squealed.

"You're lying to yourself."

"I didn't ask your opinion." Emma lowered her fists and spun around to face Luci. Her tone contained more bite than she intended. "I'm sorry to snap like that. I didn't mean it."

Luci heaved in a long breath. "It's okay. You haven't been yourself lately."

"I know. I haven't been sleeping."

"You miss him."

Emma wiped the perspiration on her forehead with the back of her arm. "I miss him a lot."

"So, answer his calls."

"Too complicated."

"Nothing is ever that difficult." She turned to leave. "I have to do some grocery shopping. I'll be by the hotel in an hour. And in case you forgot, your red cell phone is on silent. Don't forget to turn the sound on." Luci hustled up the stairs before Emma could say goodbye.

Luci hadn't said much to Emma since that fateful day in Shane's condo. At first, her silence was borne out of sympathy. Her sympathy later transformed to belligerence. Why did Shane deserve the silent treatment? His initial reaction? Maybe. Emma's full separation, her devotion to breaking off all ties to him didn't settle well with Luci.

Emma delivered a right hook. She jabbed, but the strength in her arms at last gave out and her gloved fist scraped the swinging bag instead of landing against it. She hugged the punching bag like two boxers too exhausted to continue in the ring. Emma was tired of her quiet battle with Shane and her attempts at a clean break. She wondered if her decision to leave that night was truly a mistake.

After a quick shower, Emma drove to the hotel in her black Lincoln Navigator. The side and rear windows were tinted. She wore a sky-blue baseball cap and black shades. Even so, in L.A. people saw movie stars all the time. On the streets. In their cars. At the store. It was part of her life to be recognized by the public. She couldn't ask Shane to participate in what sometimes descended into a mess.

She drove up to the curb in front of the lobby doors, parked, the engine running and the valet climbed in. Emma marched through the hotel doors and straight to the elevators, her gym bag hung over one shoulder. She pushed the elevator up button and waited.

The ride to the penthouse was quiet, even in a crowded space of ten people. Everyone focused on the door, anxious for it to open. Excited to get to their rooms. Exhausted at the beginning of the day. The elevator halted three times at other floors before reaching the penthouse. Emma trudged down the hall to her suite. She slid the card in and out of the reader. When the lock clicked, she opened the door and dropped her gym bag in the small foyer.

Her throat felt parched. Water. She needed water. She started for the kitchen, then paused.

Emma turned her head slowly at the figure seated on the green couch of the formal living room. "What are you doing here?"

Madeline Jacobs adjusted herself, her back ramrod straight, legs perfectly bent at the knee at a ninety-degree angle, hands clasped in her lap. "Hello, Emma."

———————

"Hello, mother." Emma wandered into the living room, eyes searching for Jordyn. She half expected him to walk out of her bedroom or saunter from the kitchen with that smug look on his face. As if gloating that her mother always got what she wanted and her mission for them to reconcile wasn't yet finished.

Madeline was alone in the suite, her fiery red skirt and cream blouse a contrast against the rich forest green color of the couch. She sat, poised like a painter's model. Chin up, legs crossed at the ankle.

Madeline glanced down at the wide brimmed elegantly curved firecracker red hat beside her. Emma noted the monstrosity Madeline claimed as her favorite hat was missing a feather.

"I'm assuming Luci let you in." Emma strolled past Madeline to the kitchen and grabbed a bottle of water from the refrigerator. In the normal world the appropriate response after a lengthy absence from a family member would be a giant loving hug. Emma did not live in a normal world and Madeline despised hugs and any form of affection. "How can I help you today?"

"How *may* I help you today?" her mother corrected.

"How may I help you today?"

"I had your assistant meet me here and let me in. I haven't seen you in months. Why haven't you returned my calls?"

Emma heaved out a long breath, relaxing her shoulders. "You're right. I'm sorry. How are you?"

"I'm fantastic. Charles has been taking good care of me."

Charles, Madeline's beautician and shopping buddy. The same man through creative hairstyles and recommendations for facial peels and weekly spa visits kept Madeline looking forty, instead of fifty-five years old. "How is Charles?"

"Excellent, but enough about him." She examined Emma's appearance, absorbing the black shorts and peach colored tank. Her examination paused when she reached Emma's face. "You look refreshed. Clearly wherever you went helped."

"You could say that."

Madeline scrutinized Emma a minute longer. Emma waited for her to ask questions about the mysterious man who answered the phone the night Jordyn called. Instead, Madeline switched topics. "They're throwing a huge birthday party for Renee on Saturday."

Emma wore evening gowns designed by Renee. Suzanne used his services more than once for televised awards ceremonies, after parties, or charity events. Emma liked his designs, sleek, graceful, classic, and Suzanne ensured Emma received his birthday invite.

"I haven't been back in town long enough to be invited anywhere."

"You've been back long enough." Her mother glanced at the doorway as if Luci would somehow appear. "Your assistant confirmed it."

Emma's scowl deepened. Her mother had yet to call Luci by name. Always assistant this, assistant that. In Madeline's eyes Luci was the help, never to be addressed informally.

Emma twisted the cap off the bottle and gulped down half of the water. She stared at her mother, wondering where all that unconditional love had gone. When did a mother lose that part of herself? All priorities centered on self-preservation rather than a child's best interest. Emma repeatedly asked her father if she'd been adopted. News she could handle. Her father always laughed it off, thinking her question was a joke. She was born in a hospital by Madeline, with pictures to prove it.

Emma replaced the cap on the top of the bottle. "You want to accompany me to the party?"

"Of course." Madeline's lips spread into a smile lacking any warmth or sincerity. "Why wouldn't you bring your mother to such a lavish occasion?"

Maybe because you weren't invited, Emma wanted to scream. Talking back would only result in an argument. A battle better saved for another day. She put the bottle on the counter, headed to the foyer and snatched up her gym bag.

"Charles will bring me home." Madeline scoffed at the sight of the bag. A woman shouldn't carry such dirty things. It was unladylike. "You'd have a date for the party if you'd just give the poor man a chance."

Memories of Shane suddenly flooded her thoughts. She forced them away, blinked back tears, looked away from her mother. "I'm meeting Suzanne at Torino's in about an hour so I really need to get ready."

Madeline watched the somber expression fall over Emma's face. "Why are you fighting this?"

"Why do you like him so much?"

"I want you to be happy. I want you to have all the best things in life. You deserve that and he can provide it."

"In case you didn't notice, I'm providing pretty well for the both of us on my own."

"Don't get smart." Madeline cut her eyes at her daughter. "Your looks will fade, all those acting opportunities will shrink as you get older. Sure, you'll be cast as someone's great aunt or grandma, or if you're lucky, a middle-aged vixen. But the money won't be the same. You need to think long term. Jordyn can handle it."

"I don't love him."

"Who said anything about love?" Madeline flicked a piece of lint from her skirt. "This is about taking care of yourself. Jordyn is handsome, wealthy, charming, enough qualities to open so many doors in the long run."

"Did you love Dad?" Emma said quietly. "Or was he just a 'long term' solution?"

Madeline's lips fell into a grim, angry line. "We haven't eaten together in a while. I've made reservations at Sans Restaurant at 7 p.m. on Sunday. Your assistant assures me you have no other obligations at that time." Madeline stood up and smoothed the wrinkles in her skirt. She adjusted the hat on her head.

Except for a trip back to Bainbridge Island, Emma thought. She'd ruined that opportunity. And Madeline hadn't answered the question about her father. "You know the way out mother."

"Yes, I do." Madeline adjusted the collars of her blouse, though every piece of clothing was in place. "I will see you tomorrow night for Renee's party. You can pick me up at six."

Shane stared at the index card in his hand that had arrived only a week ago.

Task Seven.

Crash a party and meet five new people.

Shane heaved in a long breath. Infiltrate a party? A wedding reception? An elaborate birthday party? Shane couldn't imagine bringing out the old Shane, the man that would drop into any event unannounced just to steal a client from the competition. The old Shane. Clearly, Liam hadn't seen this skill set as a negative but a positive attribute to get Shane socializing again. No pilfering clients, betraying coworkers, forcing his way into the executive offices. In his quest to get his "mojo" back, Shane would have to meet people outside his small circle.

Only he didn't want to complete the list anymore, not without Emma. He shoved the card into his back pocket.

"Moping again?" Gabe leaned against the doorframe of Shane's empty classroom. Shane settled into his chair, focused on three pieces of paper on the desk before him. He avoided the teacher's lounge and the main office. The students and class assignments kept him busy. Gabe knew of all the reasons Shane avoided the public. One reason stuck out the most.

"She stop talkin' to ya?" Gabe said quietly.

Shane didn't look up. Eyeglasses set firm on his face, he stared at the papers, picked one up, analyzed it, set it back down. "Who? What?"

"The girl. What happened between you two?"

Shane found a misspelled word on the paper. His unit exam was nearly complete. He reviewed the questions again, concentrating on each line. He attempted to reach Emma, but she refused to take any of his calls. He had no way of knowing where she was staying, what she was doing, who she was with. The vagueness of it all drove him crazy. He tried settling back into a normal routine but Emma haunted his dreams at night and memories of them together followed him everywhere.

"Besides," Gabe interrupted his thoughts. "You're back to wearing plaid. I'd gotten used to you with the solid colors."

Shane glanced down at his shirt. He had been wearing solid colors, bringing back the black, green, blue, and white-collar shirts that took residence in the back of his closet. Paired with jeans, the sleeves of his shirt sometimes rolled to his elbows, he quickly noticed not only more of his female students batted their eyes in his direction, but some of the other female teachers began talking to him. Delia shot them dagger eyes as if he belonged to her, but Shane paid little attention to any of them. He wanted Emma back.

"I have to finish this test." He leaned back in his seat, ran his hands over his head. "This is a big unit exam and I want to make sure I get it right."

"She broke it off didn't she?"

"The kids worked really hard on this Romeo and Juliet lesson."

"She didn't wanna commit?"

"Gabe—"

Gabe held up his hands defensively. "I know, I know. You don't wanna talk about it."

Shane slumped in his seat, shoulders hunched forward. He took off his glasses and rubbed his left eye. The words on the page blurred. "She won't take any of my calls."

Wide-eyed, Gabe sat on the corner of the desk. "What happened?"

Shane released a long breath of air. "I messed up." He leaned back in the chair. "I freaked out. I don't know what else to do."

"You love this girl," Gabe said firmly.

Shane looked up at him. His feelings for Emma were summed up in four words and he could no longer deny it. The moment she returned to Bainbridge Island and stood in front of him ready to explain herself, he'd known. There wouldn't be anybody else but Emma.

Shane smirked. "I do."

"Does she know this?"

"No. She's not taking my calls, remember?"

"Go see her."

If only it were that easy. Shane shifted in his chair. "She doesn't live out here."

"So?"

"So, I don't know where she lives." Shane frowned. "I mean, I know, but I don't know. I have a general idea."

"A general idea? You never talked about it?"

"Not really." Shane's cell phone vibrated. He glanced at the caller ID. The telephone number was unfamiliar, but he answered anyway. Instantly recognizing the voice on the other end of the line, he smiled, said a few "uh-huhs," scribbled a location on a scrap piece of paper, and hung up. He gave Gabe an incredulous look. "Did you do that?" he joked, pointing to his cell phone.

Gabe hunched his shoulders, staring at Shane's cell phone. "You're welcome?"

Shane quickly shuffled his papers into his shoulder bag and clasped it shut.

"Did you get her address?" Gabe glanced at Shane then back at the phone.

"No."

"Was that her on the phone?"

"No." Shane slung the strap of his bag over his right shoulder. He slapped Gabe on the back. "Something's come up."

"She's agreed to see you?"

"No." Shane strode quickly to the door, Gabe following behind him.

"I don't get it."

Shane smiled again, his face glowing, as he shut the door and locked it. "Gabe, my friend, I just caught a break."

Twenty-Seven

*E*MMA FELT A TAP ON HER SHOULDER AND SPUN around. Sasha Moore smiled brightly, his pearly white teeth gleaming, his muscular build and six-foot-five frame towering over her. She looked up at him and returned his cheerful disposition with a faint smile.

"Sasha, how are you?"

"Fine, and you?" he asked, every syllable soaked in his Australian accent. His ruffled blond hair and blue eyes caught the attention of multiple admirers standing outside by the pool. Sasha introduced the young, dark-haired woman attached to his arm. "This is Marianne."

"Marie." The epitome of a model, Marie's slinky burgundy dress curved with her slender figure, complimenting her bronze skin. She eyed him carefully and beamed at Emma. "Congratulations on your win."

"Win?" Emma asked.

"The most beautiful person?" Marie said elatedly. "That must be a dream, certainly a career maker."

Emma stopped short of rolling her eyes. She starred in films long enough to call it a career. "It was nice to meet you." She glanced from Marie to Sasha and held up her empty glass. "I'm going to get another drink."

Emma marched over to the bartender waiting behind a white cloth covered bar, wine and shot glasses at his disposal. The drinks were free. Renee, the man of the hour disappeared long ago in his three-level mansion, among crowds of friends, family and strangers to celebrate his forty-first birthday. At five-four, he was small in stature but compensated with amazing gown designs that found their way to nearly every red-carpet event. People paid thousands of dollars for him to create that one of a kind dress.

The bartender was a slim man, his slick hair erupting into a crest of curls at the nape of his neck. He stared at her. "Drink ma'am?"

"Yeah." She put her empty glass on a passing tray. Madeline was somewhere in the house, chasing down Renee as if the two were life-long friends. "Another coke please."

"Coke?" the man stepped back, her words confusing. "Just a coke?"

"Yes, please." She wanted rum and coke, something stronger, vodka maybe, but that could wait until later. Driving Madeline to the party was one of the most difficult tasks she'd ever completed. Madeline, complaining about the speed, chastising her for not quickly checking her side and rear mirrors, and rattling on about Jordyn. Their union was the best thing to happen for Emma. The right thing. Jordyn made grievous errors, but only wanted to make amends. Why not allow him the opportunity?

The bartender filled her glass with ice and coke. Emma accepted the glass and took a small sip.

The outside pool area harbored dozens of guests. Small circles of people chatted, some engaged in heated discussions about what Emma had no idea. She wandered to the waist high glass barrier and gazed at the rolling dark hills below. The chill of the evening air finally scratched at her skin. She shivered in her silver, sparkly, wide collar, short sleeved top, paired with a midnight black skirt that stopped mid-thigh. She wore black, skinny three-inch, peep toe heels with an ankle strap. Her straightened, sleek hair glowed a deep brown swaying with the small breeze.

Emma rested her forearms on the shiny metal rail and admired the twinkling lights spreading across the Los Angeles valley. Shoulders relaxed, she hunched slightly over and shifted her weight from the balls of her feet to the back of her heels.

"Not thinking of jumping are you?"

Startled, Emma turned her head to see Shane standing beside her. She blinked a few times, wondering if someone slipped a hallucinogenic in her soda. When he spoke again, she knew the image was real.

"I mean, it's a nice view and all but not worth the jump." He took in the view of the sparkling lights against the pitch-black landscape.

Emma straightened. "What are you doing here?"

"I was invited."

"You know Renee?"

He grinned. "I know Luci."

Getting Shane an invitation to one of the biggest parties of the year last minute with ease and coordination was a Luci trait. Emma was unclear if she wanted to shake Luci with joy or anger at the moment. "What are you doing here?"

Shane held a drink in his hand. Clear liquid filled with bubbles in a small glass. Emma smirked. Seven-Up, same old Shane.

Shane sipped his soda, his green eyes blazing at her. "You weren't answering my calls."

She noted a few people in the room noticed the two of them talking, hesitant at Shane's presence and unclear if he was connected to Emma.

Emma turned back to the landscape. "I was trying to protect both of us."

"From what?" A waiter passed and Shane put his unfinished drink on the tray.

She waved one hand absently to the skyline. "This. All of this. The press. The public. Photos of you everywhere."

"So?"

"I'm serious," she said sharply. Several faces glanced in their direction and Emma winced. She ached to place her hand over his, drown in those intense green eyes, feel the touch of his lips against hers. Shane was taken aback by her harsh tone.

Emma gripped the railing and lowered her voice to just above a whisper. "It will impact your life. A lot. I couldn't handle it if it made things way too difficult for you."

"Anything worth having isn't going to be easy right?"

"This isn't a game Shane."

He put his hands at his sides, his jaw twitching. "I've been calling you for a week without an answer. Luci figures out how to get me an invitation and I hop a flight at the last minute out here. I take a taxi to a party where I know no one but you." He searched her face, forcing her to see the sincerity in his eyes. "And with no guarantee you'd want to see me. This isn't a game Emma. You're not playing games and I'm not either. You're serious and so am I. I'm serious about you."

All of the fight drained from Emma's body. The confidence on his face reminded her of the first night he asked her to dinner. The determination in his voice said he required a better reason than the public for him to go away.

"I'm sorry I reacted the way I did," Shane said. "I panicked like an idiot."

"It's okay."

"It's not okay. I should've heard you out. We should've talked about it. Good or bad. We're in this together."

"Together, huh?" She thought of all her late nights, awake in bed, wondering. Had her leaving him been the wrong choice? He floated to the front of her thoughts whenever she was alone. She wasn't sure of anything except she didn't want Shane getting back on a plane to Bainbridge anytime soon. At least not for another twenty-four hours. "I'm serious about you too. And I'm sorry. I should've said something from the beginning about...me. I jumped to conclusions before you had a chance to digest all of this." She glanced back at the crowded patio.

"So, this is the part where we make up right?" Shane stepped closer to her.

Emma stifled the excitement of being with Shane again, tried to look calm, cool. She suppressed the curl of her lips but a smile peeked through and Shane instantly caught it. She heaved in a breath, released it and turned back to the view of the valley.

He grinned. "You want me to kiss you right now, don't you?"

"No. Maybe." Her voice lacked conviction. "Don't sound so cocky. Even if that was true, it wouldn't happen. Not here."

"You don't like K.I.P.?"

"K.I.P.?"

"I hear my students say it. Kissing in public. They have other little sayings too."

She laughed. "Please, you can keep those little sayings right in there." She patted his chest.

"Emma sweetie, what are you doing out here?" A small man with a shaved head approached her, his arms outstretched, a broad smile on his face.

Emma hugged him. "Renee." She air kissed him on each cheek. "Happy birthday, young man."

"Young man is right! Subtract twenty years and that's my real age."

"And you look wonderful." She examined his beige suit and white-collar shirt.

"And you." Renee pulled back to analyze Emma's appearance. "You are a stunning specimen. Your new title suits you."

"Title?"

"Most beautiful." He nodded emphatically. "I adore making clothes for you. We should get together next week. I hear you have an Academy Award in your future."

"It's too soon to talk about any of that." Emma didn't want anyone jinxing it. Even she wasn't getting her hopes up. There were other actresses far better than her.

Renee would hear none of it and the expression on his face told her so. "There are plenty of awards ceremonies to attend before then. We must have you ready."

"Renee that's months away."

"There is nothing wrong with preparation. Nothing." He gently squeezed her arms.

Remembering Shane stood next to her, Emma gave the introductions. "Renee this is Shane, Shane meet Renee."

Shane held out his hand and Renee shook it.

"Firm grip." Renee studied Shane closely. "I've started a men's collection. You would fit the clothes perfectly. You are a model, no?"

When Shane found Emma she immediately noticed he'd discarded his glasses for contacts. She'd been wrapped in their earlier discussion but now took in his full appearance. Black jeans, a green long-sleeved dress shirt, the top two buttons undone, the deep green fabric bounced off the color of his eyes.

Emma noticed several sets of female eyes darting interested looks his way.

Shane shook his head. "I'm not a model, but thank you. And happy birthday."

Renee looked confused but accepted the response. "Thank you." He started toward a cluster of guests huddled near the pool. "Terese, you came!"

Emma and Shane watched Renee swing his attention to the new crowd.

"That guy is a ball of energy."

Renee cackled and waved his hands animatedly as he spoke with Terese.

"Yeah."

"Academy award, impressive. I told you that whatever you did, you'd be the best at it."

"There's no guarantee I'll win anything." She downplayed the notion of garnering any coveted awards. She was good, but in five years it would be her second nomination. She hadn't won the last time either. "It's all just talk."

"No." He pointed a finger at her. "You're talented."

"Thank you."

"You're welcome."

"And now I only have to meet four more people."

"What?"

Shane pulled an index card from his hand and held it up.

She read the card then looked at him. "Crash a party and meet five people. So, you only did this to accomplish the seventh task?"

"Emma, I don't know how else to explain this. I can't be away from you too long. It tears me up inside when you're mad at me. That's the truth." He shrugged, a rogue smile playing on his lips. "The fact that I can apologize to you and accomplish the seventh task at the same time is a plus."

Emma's red cell phone rang. She dug into her purse, retrieved her phone and stared at the screen. She looked up at Shane apologetically. "I gotta take this."

He leaned in close, his cheek close to her, breath soft against her earlobe. "You want me to get you a drink?"

If Emma turned her head just slightly, their lips would touch. She missed the feel of his skin against hers and fought the urge to cover his mouth with her own. "Glass of white wine if that's alright."

Sly grin plastered on his face, Shane headed toward the bar.

Emma answered her cell phone, and a voice spoke before she could say hello. "Are you mad at me?"

Emma smiled. "No Luci, I'm not. I'm actually going to thank you."

"Have you been drinking?" Luci asked.

"Not yet, why?"

"You said thank you."

"Okay wise ass." Emma stared across the packed patio at Shane talking to the bartender. What had she been thinking to give him up? She was trying to be selfless, but watching him, she could only think how she was going to be deservedly selfish.

Two women stopped Shane as he lifted Emma's drink and turned around. The two females had dark brown hair and long big curly locks—they could've been twins. Slender frames, slinky, glittery dresses, three-inch heels shining against the dim light. Emma liked the shoes, but didn't care much for the expression on their faces. Determination. The same way Shane looked at her.

The women giggled and Shane nodded at something they said. He started to leave when a third woman appeared swishing her long blonde hair back and forth. She wore more clothing than the others, a black pencil skirt with a slit mid-thigh on the side. Her black tank top highlighted a full bosom that she effectively pushed upward against him as her key selling point.

Emma and Shane were separated for less than sixty seconds and it was as if the women nearby had waited for her to release him into the wild. No one knew of a relationship between them. Shane could've been a friend. A friend of a friend. Emma made no claim otherwise.

"Em, you still there?" Luci's voice boomed on the other line.

"Yeah."

"You okay? He showed up right?"

"He did."

"You guys made up?"

Emma smiled. "We did."

"So, what are you doin' talkin' to me? Tell him I said hi and get your ass back in the game."

"This isn't a game. I gotta go." She ended the call, slipped the phone in her purse and strode toward Shane.

Shane spun around, detangling himself from the blonde. "Hi. You are...?"

"Melanie," the blonde said.

He looked at the dark-haired woman. "And you?"

"Bunny."

"Seriously?"

"Yeah."

He turned to the second brunette, and she offered her name before he could ask.

"I'm Coral."

"It was very nice to meet you ladies. And now I have to go."

"No," Bunny whined. "Don't go. It's still early." Bunny looked to be in her early twenties and her cohorts the same.

Coral swept her hair over her shoulder. "You're not from around here are you?"

"No." Shane backed away. "I have somewhere I need to be."

"You don't have a girlfriend do you?" Melanie placed a hand on her hip and pouted.

"I do. Sorry." He turned and discovered Emma standing next to Bunny.

The women glanced at Emma, unaware she'd been standing there for a good two minutes. She mildly smiled at them.

Coral spoke first. "Emma Jacobs, it is so nice to finally meet you!" She reached out her hand and Emma barely shook it. "I've seen all your films."

Emma's eyes flitted from one woman to the next. "I see you've met Shane." She realized he was trying to fit in his task of meeting five people. Renee, and now these three females. She turned to Shane. "I'm assuming you've reached only four people?"

"Five," Shane said. "I introduced myself to the bartender."

Bunny playfully frowned. "I haven't seen this one around. And I've been to enough parties in this town to know just about everyone." She glanced at Emma. "Let me guess, he's an out-of-town visitor?"

Shane didn't answer. Emma didn't either.

"He a friend of yours?" Melanie ran one hand down the side of his arm and Shane carefully shook it away. "He told us he has a girl-friend. Is that true?"

Emma narrowed her eyes. "He has a girlfriend." She wanted to kick the blonde woman's teeth all the way down her pretty throat. Instead, she looked at Shane. He seemed unsure, but she wasn't worried about Shane, only the vultures. "Shane?"

"Yes?" he said.

"Remember what I said about K.I.P.?"

"Uh-huh."

"I don't have a problem with it."

Shane eyed her closely, ensuring she understood exactly what she was saying. "Are you sure?" He set her drink down on a nearby table.

"Absolutely."

The women glanced from Shane to Emma then back to Shane. Baffled, they tried to piece together what was happening.

In one fluid move, he slid one arm around Emma's waist and pulled her to him. He smiled at her, his dimple reappearing, his eyes shifting to her mouth. Shane lowered his lips to hers, capturing her mouth, kissing her softly. She leaned up to meet him, his touch so tender, every part of her body ached to have him. Her hands snaked through his hair, his arm tightened around her waist.

He released her mouth, and she smiled. Shane felt like home and that was exactly where she wanted to take him at this moment.

The pool area fell silent. All chatter ceased, even the waiters looked stunned. A multitude of eyes rested upon Shane and Emma. *And so, it begins*, Emma thought.

Melanie shook her head dubiously, her frown deepening, the teasing on her face replaced with disdain. "I guess he does have a girlfriend."

Twenty-Eight

ITH THE BEDROOM DOOR AJAR, A SLIVER OF light from the living room provided a clear view of Emma's sleeping silhouette. She lay flat on her back, the sheets high up across her chest. Arms relaxed at her sides, her face away from him, her neck exposed.

Shane hadn't been positive Emma would give them a second try. After his call from Luci, he'd dropped everything and flew out to Los Angeles. His reaction to Emma's confession wasn't his best moment, but not enough to cut him off completely.

Their shared kiss at the party would hit online videos and social media sites. At her insistence, they transformed from unknown couple, to instant fame. Emma knew fame, understood it. Shane hadn't a clue how to handle it, except keep his head low, and hope it died down eventually. Emma would be there beside him, to help him.

Together.

The words he used.

We're in this together.

Emma stirred and rolled on her side, her face toward him, soundly sleeping.

Shane traced the roundness of her shoulder, lightly stroked the length of her arm with his knuckles. She was a celebrated actress, named most beautiful by the American people. Emma graced the cover of magazines and movie posters. She attended famous events his sister read about in magazines and watched on entertainment shows. Based on her penthouse suite, Emma clearly had money. More than decent. Shane had little to offer in comparison. He was a high school English teacher living in a small town on an island where it rained most of the time. Ousted by his own wealthy family due to his choice in occupation. He couldn't compete with men like Jordyn Mars, worth millions and adored by fans everywhere.

His sister's words echoed at the front of his thoughts.

She chose you.

Shane shifted a lock of hair away from her eye, tucking it behind her ear.

"It's not morning is it?" Emma blinked a few times, her eyes slowly opening.

Shane laid his head on his pillow and faced her. "Not unless you count two a.m. as morning."

"Were you just watching me sleep?"

"No." He could watch her sleep all damn day but he wasn't about to admit it.

Emma nestled her head against the pillow and gazed at Shane. She looked rested, peaceful, and Shane grinned, knowing he had some part in that satisfied look on her face.

She slipped her hand beneath the pillow. "Just remember. Take away the lights, the camera, the fans, and it's just me."

"I know. 'Just you' is my favorite part." He recognized the conflict in her eyes, torn between knowing if Shane cared about the woman before him now, or the celebrity the world adored. "I love you Emma. The regular you."

Silence lingered between them, lasting only seconds but what seemed like forever to Shane. Emma opened her mouth to respond and Shane softly pressed a finger to her lips. "It's okay. You don't have to say anything back." Even if she didn't share his sentiment, he could wait. Losing Liam taught him second chances didn't happen often.

Emma closed her mouth. She didn't appear to be terrified by his confession. A smile crept across her lips and her eyes grazed over his face, pausing at his lips, telling him exactly what she wanted from him at the moment. Happily complying with her unspoken request, Shane leaned over and lightly kissed her. He returned to his pillow.

"Have dinner with me tonight."

She chuckled. "We are so past dinner right now."

"Hosting a dinner is on the list. I haven't done that one yet. I'll invite my sister and my friend Gabe. Maybe my brother. They're important to me. You're important to me. I just..." He trailed his palm down the curve of her hip and tugged her closer. "...want all my important people to meet each other."

"And your parents?"

He gently touched the side of her face. "We'll save that meeting for later."

"Hosting a dinner is on the list. Are you trying to get back into the social scene?"

"I'm working on it, but not without you. So how about tonight?"

"Okay."

"Okay." He tried to picture her on a film set. "Tell me how you got started in acting."

She thought about that. "My roommate at the time was an actress and asked me to come with her to one of her casting calls for support. The casting directors took one look at me and asked me to try out. I got the part and a lot more after that. Go figure."

"You have a natural talent."

Emma eyed him with sincere curiosity. "You believe in me so much."

"Why shouldn't I?"

She couldn't answer that. She looked down, smoothing her hands across his bare chest. "Maybe it's because I get really focused when I'm in character. It's hard to break my concentration."

"Total concentration?" Shane asked, as more of a challenge. He gambled on Wall Street, trading and raking in millions of dollars for his clients. He took risks that normally garnered him bonuses, accolades with his boss, and jealousy among his peers. No risk, no reward. He wasn't on the trading floor, but it didn't mean he didn't like a challenge.

He reached over to the nightstand and Emma caught a glimpse of the small foil package he ripped open. "Meaning, you don't get distracted easily?"

———

She quivered with anticipation, her skin throbbing for his touch. Again, and again. Just a look, the feel of his fingertips tracing a path up her arms and along the crook of her neck. She heaved out a breath at his question. "No, I don't."

With Jordyn it was easy to focus on anything other than his stilled hands and arms. She'd only been with two men before him and her tumble in the bed with each of them was less than memorable. Simple enough to narrow her vision on an object in the room and ponder about uncompleted tasks until it was all over. She could've held an entire conversation during the process if asked.

Shane maneuvered his hands beneath the sheets for a minute and propped himself up on one elbow. "I'd like to test that theory."

"What?"

"This concentration theory of yours."

Emma rolled her eyes. "It's not a theory." She stared hard at him. "It's a fact."

"So, tell me what life was like for Emma before the big break," Shane said.

Emma opened her mouth when Shane flung the sheets back, her naked body exposed, goosebumps prickling her flesh. His eyes shimmered with mischief and Emma wondered if daring him was a good idea.

"You're not distracted already are you?" Hooking one arm around her waist, he folded her into his embrace, shifting her body under his.

Emma shook her head. "After I got my degree, I wasn't sure what I wanted to do."

"Uh-huh."

"Pretty quickly I realized I loved writing stories, and it just evolved into screenwriting."

"How did that work out?" He kissed her hand, pausing at each fingertip.

She pushed aside the wonderful feel of his lips on her skin. "My mother was not happy. She cut me off completely."

Shane cupped her breasts, tenderly massaging each hardened peak and replaced his hands with his mouth.

Emma inhaled sharply.

Shane looked up, taunting her. "You were saying?"

Emma raised her chin, determined not to be outsmarted. "I wanted to make it on my own anyway."

"You and I are a lot alike Emma." He trailed his hands along her belly, found the source of pleasure below her waist. He caressed her, his other hand threading through her hair. She closed her eyes and he nipped at her earlobe whispering, "You distracted yet?"

Steadying her breathing, she opened her eyes. "I worked at a video store at night to pay the bills."

Shane gazed down at her as she spoke. He smiled, his lips brushing hers, coaxing her mouth open as he slid his tongue in and his hand intimately explored her, prepared her. He let go of her mouth just as quickly as he'd taken it and ravaged her neck. Emma trembled at the combination of his slow intimate caress and the urgency of his mouth across her skin.

He held her tight with one arm, her body arching upward, his tribal sleeve tattoo glinting in the light, rising as his bicep flexed.

"During the day I tried to…"

Shane entered her slowly, every long inch of him filling her. Her mouth opened again, but all comprehension to piece together words and complete her sentence was lost.

Each thrust deliberate, he entwined their fingers and buried his face in the curve of her neck. "Keep going," he said softly, his voice muffled.

Emma tried to remember what she'd been saying. *I tried to… I tried to… Sell my writing.* "I tried to…" Her eyelids fluttered as he plunged deeper, slower. "…sell my…writing." She exhaled the final word on a shaky breath.

Shane feasted on one nipple then the other, savoring, suckling as if he couldn't get enough of her. Indulging in her taste, her touch. Each measured thrust pushing her closer to the edge. She rocked her hips to match his steady pace.

Their fingers still tangled, he raised his head, their eyes locked, lips inches apart. He dared her to continue but something else lay behind the gleam of his emerald eyes. Love.

Emma lifted her head and touched his lips with her own, craving the feel of his mouth, his tongue dancing with hers. He released her hands and kissed her fervently, destroying her ability to say anything else.

SHANE STOOD IN FRONT OF THE OPEN FRIDGE and grabbed a bottle of water. His dark hair was damp, skin moist, after a shower and quick towel dry. He stared at the open bedroom door where Emma remained asleep.

He'd told Emma he loved her. She was still sleeping, not running from him screaming. That had to be a good sign. He shifted his gaze from the bedroom door to the panoramic view of the city skyline. Homes nestled in the crevices of the hillside. The sun would rise over the crest of the mountains, the perfect view from her suite.

Cell phone in hand, Shane flipped on the kitchen light and texted Sallie, Gabe and Mercer.

Dinner tonight. My house. 7 p.m. Bring Patrick. Sorry last minute. Hope you can attend.

He sent the message and put his phone on the counter.

Nearly 6 a.m. and the sun had yet to show. He twisted the cap off the bottle and gulped down the liquid. He glanced again at the bedroom door. Emma needed water. Shane replaced the cap and grabbed another bottle of water.

The front door to the suite clicked and opened. Hard footsteps pounded the small tile entryway. Two different sets of feet. One soft and squeaking, the other on a mission.

He quietly shut the fridge and straightened. Wearing only his blue plaid pajama pants and his black-framed glasses, he wasn't shy about attacking any intruder barefoot and barely clothed. The most precious thing to him slept soundly in the other room and he'd do anything to protect her. One full bottle and a half bottle of water would do enough damage if he threw it hard and hit his target.

He didn't call out but waited until the footsteps rounded the corner wall and stepped into the open area.

He recognized Luci first. Red pigtails, loose scoop tee, relaxed dark jeans and worn blue tennis shoes. She appeared nervous and Shane suddenly understood why. The woman standing next to her was a foot taller than Luci, her raven chin-length bob bouncing with each step. She wore an argyle black sweater, matching slacks and thick heeled, black boots. She appeared prepared for battle and skimmed over him quickly like data to be scanned as reference material later.

"You must be him." She narrowed her eyes at Shane suspiciously. "You really are good lookin'. What's your name, sweetie?"

He set the bottles of water on the counter. "Shane." He looked at Luci who remained silent.

"Shane what?" the woman pushed.

Shane realized Luci, although aware of his presence and his name, hadn't disclosed any of this to the tall woman in the battle gear. Good or bad? He leaned more toward appreciation Luci'd kept silent.

"Who are you?" he asked.

The woman placed both hands on her hips and regarded Shane with amusement. "I'm Suzanne Darling, Emma's agent. And I've already called Kevin, so we need to get started."

"Who's Kevin?" Shane turned to Luci, expecting an answer. Luci knew Emma closer than anyone else.

"Her publicist," Luci said.

"We need to clean this thing up quick." Suzanne sat down on the couch and glanced up at Luci. "Honey, you'll need to take notes."

Luci retrieved a small notepad and pencil from her back-jean pocket.

Shane instantly surmised the "cleaning up" involved him and Emma. Especially the kiss from last night at the party. He wasn't celebrity status but understood anything Emma did in the spotlight eventually found its way back to her agent. "Which part are you trying to clean up?"

Suzanne was about to give another set of instructions when she paused and stared hard at Shane. "You ask a lot of questions."

"I'm a teacher, it comes with the territory," he snapped.

"You're mad?" Suzanne leaned back into the couch. "You kissed Emma Jacobs, *MaryJane* magazine's most beautiful person in the middle of a party and you have reason to be mad?" She shook her head dubiously. "This is comedy. She was just done in by Jordyn Mars, forced into a vacation in the middle of nowhere, has a fling with one of the locals and returns with him?" She laughed but without any real humor. "A schoolteacher? Really? Is that your story?"

Shane thought about scooping up the full bottle of water and throwing it at her head. He didn't condone hitting a woman, but Suzanne really touched more than just a nerve. She gnawed at it, bit into it, tossed it aside.

He took a deep breath, counted to five in his head. "Yes, she picked me, the schoolteacher. And no, she didn't return with me, I came after her. I'm not going to tell you how we feel about each other because that's none of your damn business. And if you don't like that, I'm sure there's a broom somewhere around here you can use to ride your way back to hell."

Luci chuckled and got the stink eye from Suzanne. She held the pencil over her notebook, ready for instruction.

Suzanne placed a hand over her chest. "Well it appears you aren't spineless." She lowered her eyelids into slits.

Shane thought fire would charge out of her eyes and burn him where he stood.

She heaved a sigh and relaxed. "Alright, 'just Shane.' I like a man with a spine. We both know where we stand." She pointed an index finger at him. "But she's a good girl. So, if you hurt her, I will bury you."

"If I hurt her, I'll bury myself," he said.

Luci smiled, a happy glow spread across her face. "How is Emma?"

Shane returned her smile. "She's good."

"That dimple is adorable." Suzanne wagged a finger at Luci. "We can make this work. He's hot, she's gorgeous. The color thing won't matter too much." She scanned the room. "Sleeping beauty's still not up?" Suzanne glanced at her diamond crusted wristwatch. "It's almost six. She's usually awake by now." She eyed the bedroom door, then looked back at Shane. "What the hell did you do to her? I still need her to work you know?"

Luci laughed and Suzanne smiled. Shane didn't believe Suzanne capable of lifting the corners of her lips. He scratched his head, but didn't respond.

Emma suddenly stood in the doorway, dressed in her gray, Max the Mouse pajama tee and navy-blue bikini panties. She rubbed her eyes groggily and opened them wide. "Shane?"

———

Emma stared at three faces that stared back at her. Shane. Luci. Suzanne. She'd awakened to find the right side of her bed empty. Morning air chilled her skin, and Shane's absence forced her to rise and find him. She didn't expect two more visitors.

"Emma?" The tone of Suzanne's voice conveyed instant displeasure.

Emma realized she was missing pants. Shorts. Anything to cover herself. Emma popped behind the door, yanked a pair of gray shorts from her drawer, and hurried into them.

When she returned, everyone stood in the same position, as if time stilled until she was ready. She strutted into the open area, thin rays of blaring sunlight filtering across the living room.

Shane stood in the kitchen, two bottles of water on the counter behind him. One half full, the other unopened. Her throat felt parched. She wandered toward him, reaching around his waist for the unopened bottle.

"Good morning," she said softly.

He lowered his head, gently pressing his lips against hers. "Morning."

Neither of them spoke, Emma reluctant to tear herself from the wonderful feeling of his gaze washing over her.

Suzanne cleared her throat. "We have things to discuss."

Emma wanted to kiss him again. Instead, she heaved a sigh, and turned toward Suzanne. "Okay, you wanna talk about Shane."

"That would be a start." Suzanne glanced at Shane, then back at Emma. "Your little kiss incident is all over the net."

Shane's kisses were anything but little. Emma stifled her comments so Suzanne could continue.

"We need to make a statement."

"To say what?"

"What do you think Emma?" Suzanne waved her hands absently in the air. "You're sleeping with him. People are bound to notice."

"People are going to notice whatever I do." Sadness laced her voice and Shane ran a soothing hand down her back.

"We need to get ahead of this," Suzanne said.

Emma glanced at the faces around the room. If people were going to talk, what difference did it make with a statement? Her life was her own, despite the public eye. "No statement."

Suzanne opened her mouth to speak, then took in the reality of Emma's words. "No comment?"

"No comment." Emma's energy was returning fast and her mind cleared. She had Saturday night free and would spend those hours with Shane, not bickering over her love life to the press. Her love life. Butterflies jumbled in her belly at Shane's words.

I love you Emma.

Regular Emma away from the screen. With the beauty mark on her hip, the wild hair after one of their marathon lovemaking sessions. Emma, without makeup and fancy clothes. At home on the couch with popcorn and a rental DVD. Who couldn't sew a skirt worth a damn and didn't know much about cooking, but could play a dozen songs, or a beautiful lullaby on the guitar. Shane loved *that* Emma.

"Emma, are you listening to me?" Suzanne said in a clipped tone.

"We're sticking with 'no comment.'" She looked up at Shane. "Are we having dinner tonight?"

"We are. I'll have to see about an earlier flight," he said.

"I can help with that." Luci pointed her pencil at him.

"Dinner's at seven tonight at my place and you're both invited." He arched a brow at Luci.

Luci slowly smiled at Shane then Emma, scribbling on her notepad. "Emma, you have a photo shoot and an interview at the Beverly Hotel this afternoon."

Emma forgot about the shoot and the interview. At last the publicity surrounding her newest film was dying down.

"You're going back to the island?" Suzanne stood up. The revelation caught her off guard and her face showed it for about a second. She appeared displeased, not entirely angry.

Shane glimpsed the digital clock on the microwave. "That means we've only got a few hours before I have to go and you're off to your interview."

Emma recognized the expression on his face as he gazed down at her. Want. Need. For her. "You're not finished yet, are you?"

He shook his head. "Not even close."

Emma laughed as he grabbed her hand, leading her back toward the bedroom. She glanced back at the confusion masking Suzanne's face. "Don't worry. It'll be okay. Just keep with the 'no comment.' Meeting adjourned."

Suzanne dropped her arms to her sides. "Where are they going?"

Emma jerked her thumb at Shane and grinned. "He's not finished yet." They reached the bedroom, Shane lifted Emma in the air, and she swung the room door shut with one leg. He tossed her on to the mattress, and she scrambled to get away from him, spurts of her laughter echoing the hotel suite.

HANKS FOR COMING SIS. I KNOW IT WAS LAST minute." Shane surveyed the dining room table for eight. Burgundy cloth placemats beneath white porcelain plates lined the rich black contemporary table. "Thanks for coming early and helping me get this all together."

Sallie set the forks and knives in their proper spots beside the plates. "Are you kidding me?" She worked her way around the table. "You've never invited me to dinner at your place. Like ever."

"That's dramatic." Shane returned to the kitchen and analyzed the sticky lemon chicken simmering in the skillet. He turned the knob on the stove and the blue flames beneath the skillet vanished. The rice was complete, the chicken finished, and a bottle of white wine chilled in the refrigerator.

The table setting done, Sallie looked up at her brother. "That's fact. I think I've only seen you cook once."

Shane loved cooking but hadn't found a reason to spend more time in the kitchen until now. He yanked off his black apron, folded it in half and placed it on the counter. He straightened the small amount of mess in his house. Books stacked on the coffee table. Jackets slung across the couch, three pairs of shoes scattered on the floor resting exactly where he'd left them. He cleaned the kitchen and swept the floor.

"We had plans." Sallie put her hand on the back of one of the chairs and admired the place settings. "I cancelled them."

"Sallie, you didn't have to do that."

She put one hand up. "You're my brother. You don't voluntarily invite people to your house. Especially for dinner. And I didn't wanna go to that other thing anyway."

Shane smiled at his sister. Always blunt, always honest Sallie.

"Don't thank me just yet." She scowled. "Patrick invited Dorian. That was part of who we had plans with."

Shane frowned. Dorian was like an ant that just kept reappearing. Too late to cancel the dinner now.

"Yeah, I know. I don't like it either, but what's a bride to do? Patrick and I have been round and round on this subject. Let's talk about something else." She analyzed her brother from head to toe. "I saw you kissing Emma Jacobs online."

Shane pulled a green ceramic serving dish out of the upper cabinet and scooped the rice into it. "Has everyone in the world seen that?" He would never live that kiss down, but he definitely didn't regret it. Or anything that followed. He wished Emma followed him back to Bainbridge Island, but she had one more photo shoot.

"Yes." Sallie smirked. "You looked hot bro, gotta give it to you. That green shirt did you justice." She took the serving dish and put it in the middle of the table. "You really like this girl."

I love her. Shane kept the thought to himself. He retrieved another serving dish from the cabinet and carefully situated the chicken on it. He drizzled the sauce over the chicken and carried the dish to the table. "You ready?"

"Are you gonna give me some details on what happened or what?" She stared at him across the table and waited.

Someone knocked at the door. Shane's second guest of the evening. Eyes unflinching, he shot his sister a playful look that reinforced he would give no explanation. "Or what. Please answer the door."

She pouted but moved from around the table and headed for the door.

Shane heaved in a breath and crossed his arms across his chest. It would be a long night.

Standing in front of Shane's building, Emma adjusted her clothes one last time. Her stomach twirled in knots and she rubbed her hands to keep them from shaking.

"You are really freakin' out about this." Luci studied her boss closely then back at the orange yellow glow of his windows. She saw a few people she didn't recognize.

Emma saw it too. She inhaled a deep breath. "I'm not freakin' out."

"You are."

"I'm just nervous."

"You just spent eight hours holed up in your bedroom having the most incredible sex with this man and now you're nervous?"

Emma shivered at the memories. Luci hit the mark on that statement. Even after a hot bath she was sore, and her limbs ached, but she didn't regret a single minute. "His sister's up there."

"Yeah?"

"That's why I'm nervous." With Suzanne's help Emma made arrangements for a private jet that whisked her and Luci to Seattle. She didn't catch any reporters, no one knew Shane's last name or where he lived. Soon, someone would come forward, plunging Shane into the spotlight.

"Who's the only person up there that matters?" Luci stared up at Shane's window again.

"There'll be two. You and Shane." Emma gazed over Luci's appearance, jeans and a black fading t-shirt of a rock band Emma didn't know much about. Clad in tennis shoes, her fiery red hair was released from its normal two ponytails, free and flowing across her shoulder blades.

"Aaww. Thanks boss."

Emma chuckled. She was definitely upping Luci's salary but instead she answered, "Still not getting a second raise."

"Dammit!"

They laughed.

"Do I look okay?" Emma reviewed her outfit. Salmon colored short-sleeved shirt, the top two buttons unfastened, hinting cleavage, dark blue jeans and matching two-inch wedge sandals. Her hair hung in loose waves to her shoulders, her makeup light, her wrist and neck carrying the sweet scent of perfume.

Luci stepped back and examined Emma's clothing. "You look great. That's what eight hours with him clearly does to you."

"You're right." Emma grinned. "Let's do this." She charged up the steps before she lost her nerve. If she could act in front of millions of people, standing in a room with Shane's family would be a breeze.

Emma knocked on the door, Luci behind her. They heard the sound of people's voices talking and laughing.

A female voice called out. "I'll get it. It's my job remember?"

The door flung open and Emma stared at the woman before her. Creamy pale skin, brown eyes, long, midnight black hair, china bangs. An ivory cowl neck sweater and blue jeans outlined her slim frame. The angular shape of her face and eyes distinctly reminded Emma of Shane.

Luci nudged her shoulder, and Emma realized they stood in the hall facing this woman for at least fifteen seconds without speaking. Emma thrust her hand out and smiled. "Hello, I'm Emma—"

"Jacobs." The woman finished. "You're Emma Jacobs." She vigorously shook Emma's hand. "Oh wow, it's really you!"

"You're Sallie, right?" Emma stared down at their joined hands, still bobbing up and down and Emma wondered if she'd ever see the fingers of her right hand again.

The woman hastily let go of Emma's hand. "Oh, I'm so sorry." She smiled crookedly and introduced herself. "I'm Sallie."

Emma wasn't sure how she imagined meeting Shane's only sister. In front of his parents. On a summer day, at a park with no one around. At Sallie's wedding, shaking hands with the bridal party and groomsmen. Meeting Sallie was a step closer to meeting Shane's parents and Emma's belly rumbled nervously.

The chatter of voices engaged in small conversation beyond Sallie's shoulders paused.

"Emma?" Shane said.

Emma closed her eyes at the sound of Shane's voice, then opened them. His tone was calm, soothing.

Baked chicken with a touch of honey wafted into the hallway and Emma's stomach instinctively growled. Her only meal was a dozen wheat thins before the photo shoot.

Sallie stepped aside, gesturing for Emma and Luci to enter the loft. They peeled out of their jackets and Sallie instantly took them both, hanging them up. Several guests sat at the dining room table but Shane wasn't one of them. She spotted him in the kitchen, now strolling toward her.

Her face brightened and the knots in her stomach unwound.

He reached her in seconds, placed one hand on the small of her back, leaned down and pressed his lips across hers. "Hi."

The contact was gentle but gone too quickly. "Hi."

She'd almost forgotten Sallie standing in front of them. Emma faced his sister. "It's nice to meet you Sallie."

Sallie opened her mouth, but the words didn't come out. Finally, she stammered, "It is so nice to meet you."

Emma turned to the sea of confused faces at the dining room table. Shane leaned over and whispered in her ear, "You smell good enough to make me forget about dinner and send everyone home."

Emma chuckled and Shane pulled her closer to him. "Everyone meet Emma and Luci. Emma and Luci meet everyone." He began the individual introductions. His sister's fiancé, Patrick. Gabe, his friend and coworker. Dorian. Shane's younger brother Mercer.

Shane sat at the head of the table, Mercer at the other end. Emma slid into the empty chair next to Shane. Sallie cleared her throat and tried to regain her composure. Shane poured Emma a glass of wine and she sipped it slowly. Except for Shane and Luci, all eyes were focused on Emma.

"Well hi, Emma," a hearty voice said across the table.

She studied the man with closed cropped, dark brown hair and brown eyes seated across from her. The same man who charged across the parking lot the day she met Shane. "I'm assuming you're Gabe?"

"That I am." Gabe dramatically waved his hands in opposite circles to emphasize his point. "I'm glad we're finally meeting Shane's mystery woman."

Emma glanced at Shane. "Mystery woman?"

Shane shook his head, smiling. "He's crazy." He scooped rice on to Emma's plate and topped it with a chicken thigh. He set the plate back in front of her and she smiled at him.

"Thank you."

"You're welcome."

"Been crazy all my life," Gabe said. "But you." One elbow on the table, he rested his chin on the back of his knuckles. "Mystery solved."

Emma asked Gabe about teaching and he responded with hilarious anecdotes everyone laughed about. The table exploded with various lighthearted discussions with a few political debates sprinkled between. They talked about the world at large, the economy, young adults, dating or Gabe's lack of it, and new medical technology courtesy of Mercer.

Luci and Gabe engaged in a side conversation. Emma wondered if and when Luci would start dating. She hadn't seen Luci with anyone. Due to her occupation or a fear of commitment? Emma hoped it wasn't assisting duties keeping her out of the dating scene. She made a mental note that there had to be a balance, especially for Luci. Emma would find a way.

"So, my brother crashed your party?" Sallie's mocha colored eyes shimmered, her mouth set in a firm line of disbelief.

Snapped from her thoughts, Emma looked up at Sallie and nodded. "That wasn't my party but yes he did. And he met five people as required by the list."

Sallie shifted her gaze to Shane, the incredulous look on her face deepening. "She knows about Liam's list?"

Shane casually shrugged, playing the list off as an unimportant part of he and Liam's friendship. Humorous at the time, not taken seriously. Not something that would become the topic of dinner conversation twenty-years later. Except the list was vital for Shane, a doorway Emma opened.

Sallie instantly recognized Shane's poor attempt to mask the truth. The list was he and Emma's connection. Smirking, she lifted her chin, shifted her eyes from Shane and stared at Emma. "What else has he done?"

"What list?" Gabe asked.

"Just something Liam created to get Shane out of his shell," Sallie explained. "He gets a card once a week with a new task until he reaches the last one."

"How many things are on the list?" Mercer asked.

"Eleven," Shane and Sallie said simultaneously.

Emma lowered her head, eating a part of her meal. The attention in the room quickly diverted from Sallie to Emma. Emma swallowed the portion of food in her mouth relishing the taste of lemon and honey across her tongue. Shane was a damn good cook.

"Hosting a dinner is one of the tasks." Shane's eyes were practically glued to Emma's mouth. He tore his gaze from her lips, his face wrapped in amusement. *Do you know how hard it is to watch you eat?*

She shot back a response. *So, don't watch.*

Patrick overlooked their silent banter. "Hosting a dinner serves what purpose?"

"It forces me to interact with people older than seventeen." Shane glanced over at his soon to be brother-in-law. He pointed at Sallie. "Makes me less of a 'hermit' as my sister has said."

"Yeah." Sallie jokingly scowled at Shane. "He'd just go to school, go home. Sleep, eat maybe. The man was a robot. And look at him now. He's followed Liam's list, we're all here together, and my brother is smiling more than I've seen him in a while. Liam created the perfect plan for him and so far, it's working."

Silence followed and Emma understood the sudden quiet. Liam was the missing person in this little adventure. Had he ridden a motorcycle? Or seen his all-time favorite band play live? Did he host a dinner once? Emma knew about loss, her father's sudden passing from a heart attack was devastating. She'd felt numb, walking, talking in a zombie like status, as if she too died.

"Noboru was on the list." Sallie placed her elbows on the table folding them over one another and giving her brother a sly look. "Did he jump?"

"Yes, I did." Shane raised his hands, surrendering to what everyone believed impossible.

Dorian pointed at Emma but he shot Shane an incredulous look. "What is Noboru?"

"A waterfall," Sallie said.

"And he jumped?"

Emma held up her wine glass. "He jumped."

"She jumped too." Shane looked at Emma and smiled. "I was impressed."

"Diving off a waterfall? In this weather?" Dorian shook his head. "You two are crazy."

"Did he play an instrument in front of an audience?" Sallie asked.

"How do you even know this stuff?" Shane said. "I thought you weren't sending me the cards?"

"I'm not. But I caught a glance of the list back then."

"Playing an instrument is on the list?" Mercer said.

Emma was surprised to see Mercer engaged in non-medical conversation. The man had uptight written all over his face and every limb. His hair was trimmed low, his white shirt, crisp and gleaming. Gold cuff links, black slacks, she couldn't see his feet but was sure he wore shiny black shoes. Like a distinguished man presiding over a corporate empire rather than a doctor. He had the same chin as Shane's, and green eyes that didn't sparkle the way Shane's did. At talk of the list even Mercer perked up.

"I played the guitar." Shane held up one hand as Sallie opened her mouth to ask another question. "I suck at it."

Everyone laughed.

"But then he played the piano, very nicely I might add. In the middle of the store in front of everyone," Emma said.

Sallie glanced around the room as did Emma at all the smiling faces. Pleased with the response Sallie had no intention of stopping. "What else was on the list?"

"I'm supposed to see my favorite band play live."

"Have you?"

"Not yet," Shane said.

"And what else?"

He sighed. "I had to learn a new language."

"Did you?"

"*Bien sur. Je veux en savoir plus.*"

Sallie whipped her head back to Emma with a questioning look. Emma sipped her wine and shrugged. "He just does that now."

"Speaking French, jumping off cliffs, what the hell?" Dorian frowned.

Emma finished her meal. She placed her silverware on her empty plate as the room buzzed with more questions about the list.

Sallie put her hand up. "Was anything about his motorcycle on the list?"

Emma smirked at Shane, remembering how he'd taught her to ride and what followed after. "Yes, it was. He had to drive it to the Pass. It was an enjoyable ride."

"Wait a second, you have a motorcycle?" Gabe appeared just as surprised and Emma suddenly realized how private a person Shane really was. His invitation to all the people around the table, a major step in his otherwise quiet life. She gulped, thinking how all of that was about to change.

"A Ducati," Luci chimed in.

Shane shrugged. "It's just a bike."

"That's not just a bike," Gabe corrected. "That's a Lexus on two wheels." Luci laughed and Gabe looked at her. "You like my jokes?"

"You are funny," Luci said.

"Enough about me." Shane stared at his sister, daring her to continue, the gleam in his eyes half joking, half not.

Sallie relented, flopping back in her chair, the amused grin still etched on her face. "You're right. Enough about you Shane. I wanna talk girl talk with Emma."

Shane groaned.

Emma smiled. "What would you like to know?"

"Are you excited about your title as most beautiful? I mean you are very pretty."

The banter around the table settled.

"I'm honored I've been voted by the public as the most beautiful person, but I don't let that go to my head."

Dorian, who was hunched over his plate like a snake scoping out his prey, finally leaned back and asked, "How many movies have you played in?"

"A dozen," Emma said.

"You're an actress?" Mercer at last dove into the conversation.

"Mercer, do you live under a rock?" Sallie glared down at the opposite end of the table. "Maybe it's all those medical magazines. Yes, she is an actress, a very good one."

"Enough for me to keep the lights on," Emma said.

Mercer scratched his head. "Maybe I have been under a rock."

Patrick pointed one finger back and forth between Shane and Emma. "Where did you two meet?"

"The grocery store downstairs," Emma answered.

Sallie propped her elbow on the table and placed her chin in her palm. She looked at her brother thoughtfully. "My brother can be very charming but I'm sure he's no angel. What's the most irritating thing he does?"

"Man Sallie, give him a break!" Mercer joked.

"I'm only curious." She turned back to Emma. "For example, does he snore?"

Emma blinked. "I'm sorry?"

"In bed." She gave a silly smile to Shane who just looked at her like she was the most insane person in the world. "Does he snore?"

Emma didn't mind. Shane described Sallie as the tough one who chose some of the most interesting tasks on the list. No filter, bold, brave. Amused, Emma wasn't in the least offended by Sallie's inquisition. She'd answered worse questions from the press. Sallie asked certain things to give Shane a hard time. She was playing with him. Emma found it cute.

Shane sipped his wine but didn't speak.

Emma picked up her glass, eyeing Sallie over the rim. "Your brother doesn't sleep when he's in bed with me, so I can't really answer that question."

Most of the table laughed. Shane practically choked on his wine. Mercer's mouth fell into a grim line, decidedly not amused. Dorian grinned slyly. Gabe patted Shane on the back until he breathed normal again.

Sallie glanced at Shane then back at Emma and nodded her head. "I like this one, Shane. I like her a lot."

EMMA SUNK HER FEET INTO THE SOOTHING HOT water, the bubbles tickling her ankles. She leaned back into the couch and stretched her arms to the sky. Early afternoon sunlight enveloped the penthouse suite's living room. Emma wiggled her toes beneath the surface of the water. "Luci, it'll be fine."

Luci rocked her feet back and forth in the compact soaking tub. "It's all so cloak and dagger."

"It has to be. We don't have a choice."

The water gurgled, massive bubbles gathering around Luci's feet. "There's always a choice."

Two women in lavender smocks gripped nail files, smoothing down both Emma and Luci's fingernails. Their expressions intense, blue hair set in neat buns, their slim build and complexion exact. They were twins, Celia and Caty. Both excellent at giving pedicures and manicures.

"So, I have to ask." Luci shifted her feet in her own bubble of relaxation. "Are you sure about all this?"

"Tonight?"

"With Shane."

Emma eyed her assistant and friend suspiciously. Luci urged her to be bold, go beyond what was always expected of her. Now she seemed reluctant to give her a full blessing. "What are you saying?"

"He's not like Jordyn."

"Exactly."

"No," Luci explained. "I mean he hasn't had to deal with the press on a daily basis."

"Whose side are you on?" Yet Emma shared the same fears. Could Shane truly deal with the public scrutiny? Photographers stalking his every moment, camped out in front of his home, in front of the school? Shane had made it clear. They were in this, *together*. Despite public opinion, her agent's misgivings, and her mother's illusions. Time to take the reins, decide her own fate. And she'd chosen her path, no retreating now. "Whatever happens, he and I will deal with it. Together."

Luci sighed. "I'm always on your side, Emma. I'm your friend, which means giving you the do-you-know-what-you're-doing speech."

The irritation building in Emma's voice diminished at the concern in Luci's eyes. She was just as nervous as Emma felt about going public with Shane. "You've been a really good friend Luci. Thank you for that."

Luci smirked. "You're just buttering me up so I'll agree to this double date."

"Yes, because friends go on double dates."

"With Gabe? And this plan is really gonna work?"

"Gabe is hottie teacher number two." She held up two fingers. Gabe with his dark brown hair, his relaxed look, like a man going for a walk around town rather than a classroom. His worn t-shirts gave Emma and Luci glimpses of his athletic build and his dark brown eyes sought Luci out like a man on a mission. He and Shane could easily grace the cover of a calendar for sexy teacher of the year. "He likes you. And yes, of course it will work."

Luci waved her off. The lavender twins continued the manicures, the swishing sound of the nail files nearly matching the popping bubbles from the foot soak.

Emma didn't want to reveal her proposal in front of the lavender twins. They rarely spoke, but their hearing was still intact and a leak to the press could happen with anyone. She needed a solid line of attack, something creative to get her first double date underway without the press smothering them. "First, we get the makeovers, then you and I cover the plan one more time."

———

"Do you know what this is about?" Shane grabbed his jacket off the coat rack and slid his arms through the sleeves.

Gabe shrugged. "Can you explain how Luci got my phone number?" He arched a brow. "I mean I tried giving her my number at dinner last week and she politely declined. All of a sudden she calls me on a Saturday afternoon and tells me to be at your house by one o'clock?"

"I didn't give it to her, and I don't know what's going on. It's a surprise. She told me that we needed to be ready no later than one-thirty." Shane rotated his shoulders, strolled toward the window and peeked through the blinds at the sidewalk below. Dozens of men and women crowded the walkway, cameras aimed at his window. Constantly clicking, in sync with white lights blinding his eyes.

"There he is!" someone shouted.

Shane backed from the window, pinched his eyes with his finger and thumb until his vision settled. For the last week, photographers hounded him with a million questions. How long had they been together? Were they in love? Would he stop long enough for them to capture a decent shot? His parents hadn't been thrilled by the onslaught of press, but Sallie found the whole thing mesmerizing. That through her brother, she now personally knew a bonafide celebrity. Shane opened his eyes and glanced back at Gabe. "Crazy right?"

"Hey, you're the one dating the superstar." Gabe plopped down in the sofa chair. "I'm just along for this little adventure."

Shane's earlier call with Emma had been brief. She'd given no hints as to the surprise, hanging up before Shane fired off his own interrogation. What was she doing? Where were they going?

Gabe held up his wrist and stared at his watch. "I feel like we've just joined the C.I.A."

The C.I.A? That was far-fetched, but Emma's lack of information did have Shane on edge. Her actions left him completely out of his element. He wasn't sure whether to be excited or annoyed.

Two sharp knocks rattled the front door. Shane barely opened the door, peering through the narrow slit at the man standing at the entryway. He looked near his early thirties, his height and build similar to Shane's, his raven hair cut slightly shorter. He wore a navy-blue cap, white short sleeved button shirt and blue shorts.

The man tucked a slim white package under his arm and took off his sunglasses. Ice-blue eyes stared at him expectantly. "Shane Rawlings?"

"Yeah?"

"Emma sent me." He handed Shane the package.

Shane waited for the man to leave. He didn't. "Can I help you with something else?"

"I'm supposed to wait here until you've opened this."

Shane glanced down at the package. What exactly was Emma up to? He ripped open the parcel. Inside, was a note, scribbled in Emma's handwriting.

Hi Shane. Sorry for the confusion. Wyatt is your decoy, he will help you get to the next destination.

He looked up from the note at the man in front of him now known as Wyatt. "What is all this?"

Wyatt placed out his palm. "May I come in now?"

Shane stepped aside, allowing the man to enter. He shut the door, pointing the note at Wyatt. "What is going on?"

"My name is Wyatt." He took off his cap. "I'm hired to help celebrities out of sticky situations. Emma's a good girl and if I'm here, it's because she really likes you. She's trying to take a few hours off incognito. My job is to make that happen." He clapped his hands together. "So, here's how this works. You're gonna go out there as me, walk right by the paparazzi, and drive off in my delivery van. We're close to the same build, almost the same height, same hair color. We trade clothes, I can make it work." He pointed at Gabe. "You, my friend, will come outside with me while I pretend to be him. Then, I'll lose the paparazzi. I can send them around in circles easily."

"And where is the next destination?" Shane asked.

"Seattle. They'll be a car waiting for the both of you there. Do you have a hoodie and some shades?"

Gabe straightened. "What's in Seattle?"

"Don't know about that part." He turned back to Shane. "Your friend here can pack you a spare outfit. But the hoodie? You got one?"

Emma had devised a way to rid them away from the paparazzi, if only for a couple of hours. A complex web of disguises and deception for a moment's peace. Definitely inventive and complicated. Shane wasn't about to complain.

He huffed out a breath and took off his glasses. "Yeah, I do. Let's do this."

Emma tugged the baseball cap over her head, her synthetic locks of auburn hair flowing mid back. She kept her head low as she ducked through the back entrance of the nightclub, hurrying into the illuminated kitchen, squinting at the flood of bright fluorescent lights. Garlic mushrooms and steak smothered her nostrils and her stomach growled incessantly. She scurried past chefs shouting at one another, waiters and waitresses snagging prepared, porcelain plates from the long, metal counter. Anxious guests filled the darkened main floor, multicolored lights roamed over the large hall. Voices hummed excitedly, everyone waiting for the night's final performance. Glasses clinked at the packed bar, bartenders sliding from one customer to the next.

Emma yanked off her shades and rushed up the dimly lit stairs to the V.I.P. section in the corner of the second floor. Optimum view of the stage below, the corner position limited by only the flicker of several candles provided much needed privacy. She reached the landing, hesitated, one hand on the post, and adjusted her eyes to the darkness. If it hadn't been for another interview, Emma would've arrived at the same time as the others. Questions and more questions. She still declined inquiries into her love life, but it hadn't stopped people from asking.

She scoped the corner, the V.I.P. tables and instantly spotted Luci. Luci's red hair fell into soft waves around her face. Lip gloss gleaming, her sweater and leggings showcased her fit and curvy build. Gabe sat beside her, sneaking a glance at Luci, the upward tick of his lips and the way his gaze lingered, an obvious signal he was interested.

Emma smiled. Finally. Luci on a date.

She caught sight of Shane as he shifted in his chair, bouncing one loose fist off his leg. His sleeves were rolled to his elbows, the black V-neck sweater and jeans hinting at the muscled physique she still struggled to get used to.

He pushed the glasses up his nose, scratched his head, and peered down at the stage.

Emma hurried to the table. "You all made it." Her smile broadened at the stunned expressions on Gabe and Shane's faces. Luci appeared relieved, her shoulders relaxing. Emma yanked the cap off and pulled the auburn wig from her head, massaging her scalp, allowing her natural dark brown hair to drop to her shoulders in its usual beach like waves. She looked down at Shane, the man she hadn't seen in seven long days. "Hi."

He studied her closely, questions hovering in his eyes about the reason she'd brought them to this place, at this time. "Hi."

He rested his palm on the small of her back and Emma dipped her mouth to his, tasting his lips as his tongue slipped forward and found hers. He tightened his other arm around her waist, and she cupped the side of his face as he cocked his head to one side, demanding more of her mouth.

A groan rose in her chest, threatening to escape.

Gabe cleared his throat.

Shane reluctantly released Emma. She kept her hand on the side of his face, felt his cheeks push upward as a smile broke over his lips. That adorable dimple reappeared and Emma could only think of kissing him again.

"I missed you too." She gazed at the man who shifted in his seat, slightly uncomfortable at the sight of her standing between Shane's legs, with one of his arms around her waist. As though Gabe was just as nervous about the press catching them all seated together. "And thanks for coming Gabe."

Apprehension melted from Gabe's face, replaced with one of his boyish grins. "You're welcome. And you two can save that for later."

Luci giggled. "They're like teenagers right?"

"Horny teenagers." Gabe scrunched his brows inward. "I see I still make you laugh."

She tipped her chin. "Yes, you do."

"We're in San Francisco." Gabe turned his attention back to Emma. "I've never been to this city, I'm a little curious why we're here." He jabbed his thumb at Luci. "And this one here ain't talkin'. Although I do enjoy her company."

Luci wiggled in her chair, averted the piercing gaze Gabe shot her way. She toyed nervously with the ends of her hair and glanced at Emma. "I'm just glad you made it."

Emma eased into the chair beside Shane who also waited for her response. After the decoy successfully eluded the paparazzi, Wyatt was to drop Gabe at the ferry where he'd meet up with Shane. A black town car drove them to the airport, to a private jet with Luci waiting inside. Several hours in the air, and they landed in San Francisco, well ahead of Emma.

"So why are we here?"

She smiled. "I was thinking about your favorite musical artist, so I did some research and got lucky. Luci and Suzanne helped make the rest of this happen. He's only in town tonight."

Shane sat upright. "Who's in town?"

A man walked on to the stage below, the spotlight displaying his balding hair, his black shirt stretched by his burgeoning belly. He waved at the crowd. "Good evening ya'll. Most people call me Brick, and I'm here tonight to announce a very talented person. A magical man with a guitar who stepped in and offered to do an intimate show here when the previously scheduled band was unable to perform."

Shane looked at Emma, disbelief on his face. Her stomach fluttered nervously. *Please like the surprise, please like the surprise.*

"Emma," Shane said slowly. "Is that…"

"Please welcome Dalton Matthews!" The man clapped as did the crowd, and Dalton Matthews suddenly walked onstage, his guitar strapped to his side.

Shane stared in awe at the man on the stage. One of the three from his list of favorite bands that he'd never seen perform live.

He jerked his gaze from the stage to Emma, a look of pure shock and appreciation flush across his face. He leaned in close, whispered in her ear, "I love you, you know that?"

A wide smile touched her lips, and she nodded. Yup, she knew. The words in return were there, at the base of her throat, on the tip of her tongue but wouldn't come out.

I love you too.

CHAPTER

Thirty-Two

GET UP. GET UP.

Emma opened one eye, blinked, then fully opened both eyes. Her bedroom blinds were drawn, shielding her from the daylight. The red numbers from the digital clock on the nightstand glowed against the shadowy bedroom. Eleven-thirty-four. She had a magazine interview scheduled at one. According to Suzanne, the last interview for at least two weeks. Then, back to the grind.

Emma pushed aside unruly wisps of hair stuck to her face. She grappled with the remote, pushed the button and the floor to ceiling vertical blinds twisted half open. Sunlight streaked the carpet, raced in thin lines across the fluffy comforter. Emma wiggled her hips, inching closer toward the edge of the bed.

Shane groaned, the deep, sexy grumble of a man awakening. He tightened the arm draped over her waist and tucked her closer to him, the heat of his naked chest warming her back. His legs shifted against hers, locking her in a firm embrace. He planted a kiss at the nape of her neck. "Where you goin'?"

She instantly smiled, the previous evening inundating her thoughts. Dalton Matthews playing the guitar at K.D.'s Roadhouse. Shane's expression of astonishment rocked Emma to the core. As though no one had ever done these types of things for Shane, that few ever understood him. They'd returned to the penthouse suite, the two of them knocked out in a heavy dose of exhaustion as soon as their heads hit the pillow. "I need to get up."

"No, you don't."

Shane nuzzled her neck and Emma giggled, the tip of his nose tickling her skin. "I have an interview in about an hour."

"Another one?" He pressed his body closer, his rising arousal flush against her backside, her underwear, his boxers, their only barrier.

Emma leaned the back of her head into his broad shoulders. The night before was magical, unforgettable even, but reality awaited them. Emma, returning to her duties, fielding questions about that infamous *MaryJane* title and her current movie release, *Paris at Night*. Time to rise, face the day, force Shane from the bed. Her cell phone remained eerily silent. Luci would've called by now, like an alarm clock, alerting Emma to the new day's responsibilities. "Shane."

"Emma." Shane nudged aside thick strands of her hair, dusting the curve of her neck and the slope of her shoulders with small kisses. "I want you." He reached beneath her tank top, plucking her nipples to hardened peaks.

Her insides fluttered erratically and Shane lowered his hands, spread her legs slightly open and kneaded her inner thighs. He slowly rolled his hips, his full erection rubbing harder across her bottom.

She inhaled sharply. *Think straight. Get up. Get going. The interview. Can't be late.*

His cell phone vibrated on the nightstand.

"You should get that."

"No." He slipped his hand beneath the waistband of her panties, stroking her heated flesh. "It's probably Gabe, and he can wait. Damn, you're wet already." He gently raked his fingers through her hair with his other hand, angling her head so his mouth found hers.

His tongue teased and tortured her, his lush kisses explosive, begging.

Stay.

Better than candy. Soft and warm, pleading.

Stay.

Sparks surged from her core to the tips of her fingers. She'd heard females on film crews giggling about the men in their lives that made their toes curl, their eyes roll backward, the rational side of their brains melting into an incoherent string of thoughts. From a single kiss to a single night. Now, she understood.

Shane broke the kiss, smoothed his palms down her arms, flattening one hand across her belly. He licked and nibbled the planes of her back, lowered to the valley between her shoulder blades then shifted up to the nape of her neck. His lips were soft and subtle across her naked flesh, a promise of more to come. Stay in bed or get ready for the day? With Shane, Wall Street had cultivated an expert negotiator.

She ground her hips against Shane and he groaned.

"Emma," his voice dropped an octave, gravelly and rough. "Did I mention I didn't thank you for last night?"

"I think you did."

"No, I didn't." Shane dipped his fingers softly inside her and massaged her center with just enough pressure to keep her trembling on the edge of completion. "I think I should."

"I think you should," Emma repeated, her breathing rapid, his skilled fingers doing unspeakable, wondrous things. If Shane didn't continue her body might literally combust.

"Yeah?"

"Yeah."

His hands disappeared, his touch gone. Shane turned away from her, the heat of his body fading away.

Cold air chilled her skin, the room quiet, his voice gone, and strips of sunlight streaking the floor. Her mind cleared, the interview pushing to the front.

Shane rolled on his side, his warmth returning. He tucked her closer in his embrace, her back to his front, lying on her side, her head comfortably nestled against the pillow. She felt the tip of his sheathed erection at her entrance, his lips sweeping her neck as he thrust upward.

They moaned together, Shane dropping his forehead to her shoulder as he retreated, then drove deep inside her, the angle, the position, different than before. An ache burrowed deep in her pelvis, its intensity building. She shuddered, raised her arm, grasped a clump of Shane's hair, and arched her back.

He tightened his hands on her hips, spouting words between broken breaths. "Missed you...so much...thank you..." He tugged at the tight buds of her breasts and Emma leaned her head back, turning slightly toward him. Shane captured her lips, claiming her mouth with a fierce growl. She couldn't breathe without more, more of Shane, his drugging kisses, his husky voice, his touch so in tune with her body. How he recognized exactly what she needed.

Her inner walls gripped him and Shane's breathing hitched, a low rumble vibrating the base of his throat. Her lack of prior sexual experience hadn't prepared her for Shane Rawlings but power coursed through her veins each time he cried out. As if he'd die of pleasure from her touch.

He continued his deliberate thrusts until Emma at last screamed his name, drowning in a tidal wave of unbridled ecstasy that seized her limbs. Shane clamped his hands on her hips again and groaned against the nape of her neck, following her into the torrential sea of bliss.

———————

Emma averted her eyes. She knew why Luci gave her the all-knowing stare. One that said she understood the exact reason Emma arrived twenty minutes late to the interview.

The studio set drummed with activity, assistants organizing the scene, an ivory couch against a gleaming white curtain. Emma sat in a blue folding chair in front of a mirror. A makeup artist dusted a shimmering deep café au lait color across Emma's lips. The hair stylist released the messy, loose knot at the back of Emma's head. She fanned out her dark brown tresses, smoothed a wave of hair to one side, and tucked it behind her ear.

"You little slut." Luci arched a brow, her lips slanted in a wry grin. "Why were you late again?"

Emma narrowed her eyes at Luci, unable to wipe the grin from her lips. Well, yeah she was late, incapable of lying as to the reason, but Gabe was also missing from the set. He'd opted to stay at the hotel, sleeping off his "wild" night of music, booze and Luci? Emma had purposely booked Luci and Gabe at the same hotel. She wondered if her sneaky tactics finally yielded some unadulterated fun for her hardworking assistant. Emma wanted to engage in girl talk with Luci instead of the serious pending discussion with the magazine interviewer.

The makeup artist stepped back, admiring the applied mascara, the curl of Emma's lashes, the glossy lips. The hair stylist and makeup artist shared a small smile. One that said their artwork was complete. The makeup artist gave Emma a small nod and scurried to the interviewer, likely advising Emma was at last ready.

Emma heaved in a long breath. The set, the pictures, the flurry of bodies all around her, the moment when all eyes fell upon her—she still hadn't gotten quite used to all the fuss, despite her successes. Heart pounding in her ears, she tried to drown out the varying volumes of mingled voices. "What did I miss?"

Luci ran down the list of callers. Studio execs. Her publicist. Suzanne. And her mother. Five times.

"Five times." Emma shook her head. "Really?"

"Yeah. She wanted to talk about Jordyn. I told her you were unavailable. She threatened to fire me a couple of times."

"Sorry."

"Don't be. You were gettin' your freak on."

Emma laughed. "And where did you end up last night?" She hoped Luci and Gabe's clear attraction transgressed beyond the multiple "I'm interested" looks they'd thrown each other.

Luci blushed.

Bingo. Emma's smirk widened. "Who's the slut now?"

"We went out again. He...we..."

"Hi." A young woman marched toward them, holding out her hand, smiling. "I'm Majie, I'll be interviewing you today."

Emma shot Luci a look that said their little chat wasn't finished. She shook Majie's hand. "It's nice to meet you. I'm sorry for being late."

Majie peered down her square, red rimmed glasses at Emma. The woman was at least half a foot taller than Emma's five-foot six height, compounded by Majie's thick three-inch heeled boots. Her thin lips were set in a straight line, her makeup light, spirals of strawberry blonde hair tied into a tight ponytail. She loomed over Emma, like a schoolmarm ready to give a harsh lecture. Emma half expected to hold out her fists and wait for the vicious slap of a wooden ruler across her knuckles.

Instead, Majie's lips broke into a broad smile. She looked at Shane, who quietly stood at the edge of the set. "I'm sure you had a good reason. And may I say he is much hotter in person than on YouTube."

That was an understatement. Emma suppressed the girlish grin bubbling to the surface. After their romp in her bed, she and Shane took a shower, leading to a second, just as intense lovemaking session under the spray of steaming water.

Bright lights beamed at the couch in the center of the set and Donnell Grafton, the photographer and her longtime friend arranged his camera on a tripod in front of the staged scene.

"Donnell?"

Donnell glanced up, returned her smile with an array of perfectly aligned white teeth. His chocolate skin, shaved head and neat goatee drawing the interested eyes of several female admirers in the room. "Hey, lil' mama. They wanted the best on this, that's me."

She walked over and hugged him. He'd been calling her "lil' mama" since her first film role. The new girl in the industry achieved fame, but no real friends. Donnell had been her initial supporter, the one who'd looked out for her like an older brother, until she found her own feet.

"When did you get back? Weren't you in Tibet?"

He nodded. "Came back early. I heard you took a vacation after that Jordyn fiasco."

"That's a whole other story."

"I told you he was an ass."

Emma released an exasperated breath. Donnell warned her the moment she met Jordyn at a movie after party that his intentions weren't honorable. He'd recommended Luci as a potential assistant, resulting in an ideal business match. His advice had always been sound, even when Emma declined to listen. Donnell was like the brother she always wanted.

He stepped back, assessed her physical appearance. "Look at this. You look refreshed." His eyes flashed from her to Shane, his expression not exactly welcoming. Apprehensive at Shane's presence.

Shane held the man's searing stare, his back straightening, his silent response saying he wasn't going anywhere. Defiance stormed his emerald eyes, his button-down shirt stretching to accommodate his suddenly stiff shoulders. He would not cower to Donnell's intimidation, both men engaged in an unspoken standoff. Shane casually strolled toward them, stopping two feet in front of Donnell. He looked down at Emma.

That was her cue for introductions, but her eyes loitered at the place where the last button of Shane's polo shirt was unfastened, the way her fingers raked through his raven hair only hours before. The rebellion in his eyes sparked a longing that simmered at her core and radiated through her fingertips. Damn, she had it bad.

"Emma?"

Shane's voice yanked her from meandering thoughts. "Shane, this is Donnell." She pointed to Shane. "Donnell, this is Shane."

Shane extended his hand. Donnell accepted it, but their eyes didn't greet each other warmly. More like a quiet warning.

"We'll need to get started," Majie interrupted, notebook in hand. "If that's okay?"

Emma nodded emphatically. More than okay. She needed a little space from both of them. Away from Donnell's overprotective nature and Shane's heightened, brooding, alpha male on full display. "Yup, ready."

Thirty-Three

SHANE WATCHED THE SET COME ALIVE, STAFFERS bustling around. He'd been a tad curious at what a part photo shoot, part interview resembled and accompanied Emma to the set. He watched her as she plopped down on the ivory couch. Her dark brown locks framed the right side of her face, the left side exposed with her hair tucked behind one ear. She practically glowed in her black button blouse, her long legs accentuated by skinny jeans, tapering to black stilettos, her red painted toenails peeking out.

The bottom half of his body roused at the sight, the scent of her, memories of her slender legs wrapped around him, her small cries of his name brushing his ear, the fresh scent of soap twirling around them, hot water streaming down bare flesh. Shane blew out a breath and concentrated his thoughts to the current moment. Taking her again in the shower, guilt gnawed at his chest. She was late to her important appointment because of his actions, but he wanted her so much, unlike he'd wanted anyone. He was enthralled and petrified at the same time.

"So, I'll ask questions and Donnell will take the pictures as we go along." Majie slid into a chair diagonal from the couch and placed a recorder on the table in front of them. "Is that okay?"

"That's fine."

Her megawatt smile lit the room and Shane's breath caught in his throat. She was stunning, talented, a thousand levels higher than him. He was lucky she'd chosen him and he gulped at how his own insecurities nearly tore them apart. He saw her the way others didn't. Humming as she brushed her teeth, the black scarf she sometimes wore to bed, the small moans just before she came. She didn't swim as much as she wanted, couldn't bake to save her life, but considering her motorcycle lesson, she welcomed any challenge just the same.

The whole world loved Emma Jacobs. Their favorite actress, adoring fans.

Shane loved a woman he'd met in the grocery store, bantering with him about young, teenage love. Throwing a tantrum as she sped off with his Seven-Up. He was in love with ordinary Emma.

"Pretty girl, right?" Donnell asked. His voice was firm, his eyes trained on Emma as she answered several questions about her upcoming new movie release.

"She's amazing."

Majie asked another question.

Donnell snapped several shots of Emma before she answered. "So, what's your game?"

Shane cut Donnell a sideways glance. Game? He was too old to play games and never with Emma.

Donnell must've assumed Shane hadn't understood the question. He repeated the inquiry differently. "What angle are you playin'? You want your fifteen minutes of fame?"

"Excuse me?"

"I've known Emma a long time. She's a good girl, bit of a romantic, but she works hard, she's honest and she believes in people. It's the reason she gets hurt so much. And every time she hooks up with someone, the guy has some angle."

"Well, I don't."

Donnell leaned back, fiddled with the adjustments on his camera. "And that kiss all over the Internet? You're saying you're *not* trying to be famous?"

Had nearly everyone Emma knew really carried an ulterior motive? To be unable to trust anyone, not your parents, not your friends? A sting of sympathy pierced him and he drifted his gaze back to Emma. She looked at him, impatience festering in her eyes, the corners of her lips falling.

Donnell caught her hardened stare, her meaning clear to both of them.

Stop it.

His eyes fixed on Emma, Shane said sternly, "I wish it wasn't all over the Internet but I don't regret a minute of it."

"So, you are looking for fame?" Donnell peered through the lens of his camera, aiming it at Emma.

"I'd rather not be in the spotlight. I live on an island in a small town for a reason."

"Her money then?"

"I have my own money."

Donnell huffed and placed his camera on to the tripod. "You live on an island? In a small town? What are you, in witness protection or something?"

Shane chuckled, remembering Emma with her oversized sunglasses and beanie. Roaming through the marketplace, nearly every outing, her appearance concealed. He should've seen the signs, her reluctance to be immersed within massive crowds.

"What's so funny?" Donnell glared at Shane, offended by his laughter.

Shane smiled. "I asked her that the second time I saw her."

"Asked her what?"

"If she was in witness protection."

Emma chatted with the interviewer, completely engrossed in the discussion about her next movie. Her shoulders were rigid, her back straight, the gleam in her eyes shadowed by worry. She'd been at ease when they'd first arrived, explaining to him the studio set, the series of questions, the hustle of people trying to ensure every piece of clothing, makeup, hair, was perfect.

Donnell tilted his head at Shane. "You didn't know who she was?"

"I'm not big on movies. And I live on an island remember?"

"She didn't tell you?"

Shane shook his head slowly. "No, she didn't. We spent weeks talking, and she never mentioned it. Just said she was an actress, but she didn't go into detail and I didn't ask. I didn't find out until I saw that magazine cover."

"You thought she was an average tourist?"

"I did."

Emma darted another nervous glance in his direction. Their voices were low, so although Emma couldn't hear the words, she sensed the discord between them. Donnell seemed to be the big brother, the man looking out for her. Shane respected that. Emma deserved to have as many genuine people supporting her as possible. The one thing they both lacked from their own families in different ways. His smile widened, and he gave Emma a low thumbs up with one hand. He wasn't going anywhere and didn't scare easily. Better to make peace with Donnell.

Shane scrunched his face and crossed his eyes, purposely making Emma laugh. Her shoulders shook as she giggled and looked away.

"I'm sorry Majie, could you repeat the question?" She stifled another set of giggles. Several of the females on the set chuckled, their eyes lingering on Shane.

Majie turned in her seat and looked at Shane.

His expression normal, he shrugged, feigning innocence.

Emma cleared her throat, switching to her all business face. "Was your question about my costar?" The concern dropped from her eyes, her shoulders, her body relaxed, the easygoing happy Emma reappeared.

"Nicely done." Donnell gave Shane a small nod, an acknowledgement that even he didn't like the worrisome expression causing her stiff posture. Agitation at Shane and Donnell's friction. Donnell pointed his lens at Emma and secured dozens of images. "So, you're telling me you don't have a story here?"

Shane drew in a long breath, hoping Donnell heard the honesty in his voice. "I'm telling you I've never met anyone like her. She's the first thing I think about in the morning and the last vision in my head before I close my eyes at night. I didn't know who she was when I met her. And I get why she didn't want to tell me, but I don't care. There's no story, no angle. I just love her."

Donnell straightened, scrutinized Shane, matching his tense, yet calm expression. "Now that's one I haven't heard."

"Donnell, we okay?" Majie called out.

"Yeah." Donnell strode toward Emma and crouched down. "I wanna try something."

He gently grasped her leg and bent it, tucking her foot under her right leg. Her right leg remained free, her heel tapping the floor. He placed her hands in her lap, backed away, examined the image and returned to his camera.

"Can you give me a small kick with the right leg?"

Emma rocked her leg, her calf lightly bouncing on the bottom edge of the couch. "Okay, Miss I'm-about-to-win-an-Oscar. Show me that winning smile again."

She rolled her eyes and laughed. "Whatever."

It was the second time Shane heard the words "Oscar." The highest accolades an actor or actress could receive. The mere mention of her name as a nominee was another symbol of her brilliance, her hard work, and determination.

Donnell shot several photos, the camera clicking repeatedly. He raised the camera from the tripod, moving from one side of the set to the other, snapping multiple shots.

Emma stared at the lens, glanced away, chuckled at something Luci said, and Donnell captured another round of pictures. He migrated back beside Shane. "Emma is one of the best people I know and she looks happier than I've seen her in a long while. You really love her?"

"I do." Shane watched her head fall back, her sweet laughter rippling through him. "And I don't want a damn thing from her."

SHANE GATHERED UP THE REMAINING WOODEN bats and stuffed them into the black duffle bag. Tall metal lampposts beamed down white lights overhead, illuminating the playing field. The air had cooled considerably from a tolerable sixty degrees to an icy forty. His fingers chilled, and he had trouble zipping the bag close.

The field was vacant, no longer occupied with teenagers running drills, hitting fly balls, and trotting laps around the bases. Eager parents had vacated the stands, the silver slats shining under the glaring light.

Near the back chain-link fence, Gabe scooped up several remaining baseballs, dropping them into his equipment bag.

Shane carried the duffle bag to his car, opened the trunk and tossed the bag inside. Two men in dark clothes, jeans, and tennis shoes held up cameras, snapping pictures of him. The repeated squeal of Shane's whistle during baseball practice was now silent, replaced by the click, click, click of cameras.

Paparazzi. Capturing images of a man who desperately wanted out of the limelight. The four men maintained a ten-foot distance, shouting questions at him, questions that Shane would never answer in public.

"How serious are you and Ms. Jacobs? Are you two gonna get married? Does her fame bother you at all?"

Does her fame bother you at all? Shane had asked himself the same question more than once.

Gabe tossed the remaining practice equipment into the bed of his truck. He held up his cell phone, displaying a picture of Shane brushing his teeth, shirtless, as he shut his living room blinds. The caption below read, "Emma's Hottie knows the right way to get ready for bed."

"Damn, it was like eleven o'clock at night when they took this shot. Who the hell is up that late, taking pictures?"

Did they eat and sleep like normal people? Or were they aliens, out in the open, sent to spy on humans? To wait day and night, hours upon hours, for a single shot? How did Emma deal with it all?

Gabe switched to another picture of Shane at a store in Seattle, browsing a table of neatly folded shirts. The caption in bold white letters said, "CELEBRITIES SHOP TOO."

"I'm not a celebrity."

"In this country you can be one just by knowing a celebrity. I thought all this would die down."

"It has died down."

Gabe shoved his phone in his pocket and frowned at the four men loitering nearby. "Doesn't look that way to me, but if you say so. Have you asked her yet?"

Shane slammed the trunk shut. "To prom?"

"Yeah."

"No."

"What are you waitin' on?"

To not be rejected. To hear the word "yes." To know that, despite all the fame, Emma could still enjoy the simple things with him. Like a formal date to a prom that Shane was chaperoning along with several other teachers.

"So?" Gabe leaned back against his truck door, his arms folded across his chest, waiting for a plausible reason for Shane's procrastination.

Shane had no reason to give.

"I'll call her." He pointed at Gabe. "You just worry about your love life."

"What love life? I'm the guy—"

"Luci?"

Gabe closed his mouth.

"Uh-huh." Shane had intended to have a conversation with Gabe about Luci. Emma's best friend, the sister she never had. More than just an assistant and Shane hadn't missed the flicker of interest between the two of them. "Luci is a sweet girl. She's not one of those women you pick up at the Yard."

Gabe's voice softened. "You're right, she's different." He lowered his arms to his sides. "And I know you're playing matchmaker right now, but the timing is way off. She lives in L.A. and she's got big dreams out there. You know me, Shane. I'm a small-town guy."

"It shouldn't stop you, Gabe." Shane eyed his friend closely. Gabe appeared resolute about the state of his and Luci's relationship. Non relationship. Friendship? They hadn't exactly elaborated on their current status but the downward crease of Gabe's mouth was all the proof Shane needed. Gabe cared about Luci, their chemistry was strong, but was it enough to bind them, force them to find a way, despite their geographical proximities and professional differences?

Just as Shane was doing now with Emma. "When you really want something Gabe, nothing gets in your way."

The cameras continued clicking, sparks of light flashing in Shane's face. He squinted, held up his hand. "Enough!"

Gabe rushed toward the four men. "Get the hell outta here!"

The four men scattered, shooting image after image of Gabe's angry face.

He turned back to Shane. "Nothing gets in your way, huh? Not even these weasels?"

The original question Shane had asked himself, without a response.

Does her fame bother you at all?

The lights, the cameras, the smothering press.

The verdict was still out.

Gabe gave him a small nod. "I'll see you later." He jumped into his truck, the engine roaring to life minutes later.

Shane slid into his car, following Gabe out of the parking lot. He noted one of the photographers trailed behind them in a beat-up brown sedan. All Shane had to do was make it home. Away from the glares of residents bothered by the onslaught of nosy visitors. Not tourists, but those crowding the streets, just to get one picture of Emma.

At his condo, Shane locked all the doors and windows, shut the blinds and settled down onto the couch. He pulled out his cell phone and called Emma.

She answered on the second ring. "Hello?"

Her voice instantly erased the tangle of doubt worming through him. "Hey. How's it going?" Music mingled with conversation peppered the background noise. Male and female voices.

Hello, it's been awhile.

I can't believe he said that.

Should we go inside?

"Where are you?" Shane said before his brain jumped to the irrational side and drummed up all the negative pieces to go with the background chatter.

"Still in L.A. at another film premiere." She sighed heavily. "I'm not in the movie, but Suzanne thinks it's great publicity for me."

Heart racing, he stretched his fingers out to relax. Remind himself that he wasn't sixteen anymore, not some lovelorn teenager, but a grown man asking the woman he loved on a date to a formal event. It's not like he was proposing.

He sat upright. Proposing? Marriage? He hadn't given the idea a lot of thought and suddenly his brain latched onto the idea of Emma as his wife. Wife, kids, like a runaway train, his mind operated at eighty miles an hour. He dragged a hand down his face, cleared all thoughts and focused on his one mission.

"About prom."

"Prom?"

A male voice seemingly far away, increased in volume and Shane instantly recognized it. "Emma. How are you?"

"Jordyn?" She hadn't covered the phone with her hand, the startled sound of her voice crisp on the line. "What are you doing here?"

"I wanted to see the movie. Same as you. I would call this fate."

Shane clenched his teeth. Jordyn Mars. A prickly thorn he couldn't seem to get rid of. The man was everywhere. On TV in millions of homes, on hundreds of film screens across the globe, and now, at the theater with Emma. "Emma?"

"Shane." This time, she covered the phone, her voice muffled, but Shane could still make out the words. "I'm on the phone right now." The chatter reappeared, but Jordyn didn't seem to be talking. "Sorry Shane. It's almost time for me to go in. What did you wanna ask about prom?"

He wasn't going to let her skate past her ex-boyfriend's presence at a public event so easily. "Jordyn is there?"

She sighed again. "Yes. But I didn't invite him. I'm sure he found out I was gonna be here somehow. It doesn't matter. Was there something you wanted to ask me?"

"So, he just showed up? Out of the blue?"

"Are you seriously getting mad about this?"

"We have to hide pretty much everywhere we go, but Jordyn Mars shows up and he's in the spotlight with you?"

"It's not like that," she snapped. "And you and I hide because I know how much your privacy means to you."

"What privacy? I have people taking photos of me brushing my damn teeth."

"I can't help that Shane. I told you this would be hard."

"So, I sit here while you go to the movies with your ex-boyfriend? We haven't even been to the movies."

"You haven't asked."

"You probably wouldn't go."

"I'm not talking about this with you right now."

"You never wanna talk about this," Shane quipped. "Go ahead. Go to your little movie with your ex and all your celebrity friends. I don't fit in there anyway."

Emma paused for a long while and Shane wondered if she'd hung up. His screen showed the line was still open. His insecurities led them to this awkward silence. The illogical side of his brain had taken over and his mouth was unable to stop the garbage from spilling out. He trusted Emma, believed she loved him, even if she couldn't bring herself to say it out loud. He had few reasons to worry. Yet Shane felt left out. Her fast-paced world was vastly different than his slow, small town one. The paparazzi had invaded every aspect of his life and although he understood it wasn't directly Emma's fault, a sliver of anger and resentment somehow surfaced.

The photographer's question shot back at him.

Does her fame bother you at all?

His unequivocal answer.

Yes.

But this was not the way to handle it, they'd deal with it together.

He opened his mouth to apologize when finally, Emma spoke two words with such calm confidence, his heart thundered in his chest.

"Bye, Shane."

The call ended.

Shane lowered the phone. What the hell had he just done?

Thirty-Five

EMMA GAZED ABSENTLY AT THE SCREEN, THE actors saying their lines, moving through each scene, but she couldn't concentrate on their words, the sound like radio music merely playing in the background. Her mind kept flipping back to her argument with Shane, how infuriated he'd been at Jordyn's presence. It'd been more than Jordyn's unexpected arrival, Shane's responses hinted at stress. Reporters, paparazzi had camped out in front of his condo, followed him to school and around town. He couldn't go anywhere without someone snapping a photo of him. Buying groceries. At the pump, filling his car up with gas. Leaving school for the day. And yes, brushing his damn teeth.

To have so many strangers peeking into your life. Emma remembered the overwhelming feeling, the sadness that her world had changed. Daily tasks wouldn't be easy to accomplish, trips outside would be monumental.

In the darkness, seated beside her, Jordyn placed a hand on her knee. As though the phrase "ex" offered little meaning. Emma shoved his hand away.

Jordyn looked startled. "What's wrong?"

Did she need to say it in another language? Had she missed any syllables in her "hell no" response? Emma shifted in her seat. His presence was far from coincidental. The film was almost over, the climactic scene of the two fighters battling on the streets reaching its peak.

Emma stood up, excusing herself as she shuffled past a line of kneecaps on her way to the side aisle. She exited the theater, squinting at the soft glow of the lobby's lights, the smell of fresh popcorn slapping her in the face. She needed to think and definitely not in the presence of Jordyn.

The red theater door swung open and Jordyn stepped into the lobby. He stared at her questioningly. "Emma?"

Groaning, she stomped outside, hailed the first cab and headed to the hotel.

———

Emma scrutinized the two men seated across from her. Warren and Carl. Warren, the taller out of the two, swept strands of his blond hair from his forehead, perspiration forming at his hairline. They'd chosen a table on the outside patio of La Belle, a restaurant specializing in French Cuisine. Fifteen floors up, with an amazing view of the Las Vegas Strip would've been enjoyable for brunch if the morning temperature had been ten degrees less. Emma heaved in a long breath, the humid heat searing her throat. The blackened edges of her buttered toast tasted like sharp cardboard.

The second man, Carl, with a glistening white, thick head of hair, in his tan polo shirt and jeans, hemmed and hawed. "This is really good. You wrote this?"

Emma swallowed a bite of toast and placed the remaining slice back on her plate. Yup, like jagged rocks scraping exposed skin. "Yes, I did." She sipped her orange juice, thanking the heavens that Suzanne listened to even half of her speech in Seattle. Carl and Warren's films grossed a total of three hundred million combined. They were the action whisperers, the summer mega blockbuster kings, and Emma couldn't believe she'd scored a meeting with them.

"I'm glad Suzanne sent it to us." Warren tapped the stack of pages. "We were looking for something out of the ordinary, a script for the indie screen."

Independent films? Smaller screen, even smaller audience, but a start. The cars below crawled to a stop, red taillights clamoring together. A fender bender between a silver Lexus and a beat-up Honda halted the steady stream of vehicles passing through the traffic light. Several cars honked, one man, five vehicles from the light, poked his head out the driver's side window and unleashed a flurry of obscenities.

"We'd like to set up another meeting about this." Carl leaned back in his chair, one dark bushy eyebrow arching upward.

"Absolutely. I'll have my agent contact you Monday." Emma stood up and the two men rose from their chairs. "And thank you for taking the time to meet me. I know you've been busy on this last film."

"Thank you for coming out here to meet us." Warren extended his hand and Emma shook it. Warren's palm was half the size of her head, her hand practically disappearing within his firm grip.

"Suzanne said you were in Las Vegas, so I figured why not take a weekend getaway while I'm at it."

Carl smirked. "Not a bad idea."

His all-knowing tone gave the impression he assumed her weekend trip included the type of unspoken activities never to be revealed beyond the city limits.

Carl held out his hand and Emma shook it. His palm smaller, she could see her hand. "You've got a lot of talent, Ms. Jacobs."

"So, I've been told." She gave them a polite smile. "Thank you."

"Have a good day."

Emma returned to the cool, air-conditioned lobby, but charged ahead outside again, into the humid air. Her tank top clung to her skin, her jeans melted against her legs. She yearned for a shower as soon as she returned to the hotel.

A black town car pulled up to the curb, and the driver opened the door to get out.

Emma waved him off. "It's okay, I've got it." She opened the rear door and climbed inside.

The driver paused, his hand on the slightly open door, his head turned from her view. She

didn't mean to make him feel uncomfortable. "Really. You don't have to open the door for me. I'll just tell them you opened it. The Bellagio, please."

Another place of Suzanne's choosing. Two nights at the Bellagio will soothe anyone, Suzanne had remarked.

Soothe. Emma needed to have an in-depth discussion with Shane, and in the last twenty-four hours, since their phone spat, they hadn't spoken.

Emma plopped back against the seat as the car eased from the curb and into traffic. She watched the pedestrians stroll the sidewalks, glazed looks on some of their faces. Vegas. Another city that didn't sleep. Its lights, casinos, nightclubs, all-night diners, and shows kept tourists awake and spending money. The allure to engage in any of those activities was lost on Emma. She was going back to the hotel to sleep beneath eight hundred thread sheets, her head pressed against golden silk pillows, eyes closed for the next nine hours. She'd call Shane afterward, once her brain and her body was fully rested.

The town car rounded a corner in the opposite direction. Away from the Bellagio hotel.

"Excuse me? This is not the way to the hotel. Where are you going?" Alarmed, Emma bolted upright and studied the silhouette of her driver. White male, mid-thirties, dark hair, wearing shades and a limo cap. She rummaged through her compact purse, a tiny clutch capable of holding a few things.

An even tinier wallet.

A comb.

Breath spray.

Great, she could subdue her assailant with breath freshener.

The driver veered to the right, made a sharp turn up a ramp, and entered a parking garage.

Emma plucked her red cell phone from her pocket, her fingers shaking. "I'm calling 9-1-1." *Please operator, don't let me die. Find me in this colossal city, in a garage somewhere.*

The driver circled the first floor, then the second, maneuvering into a vacant parking spot. He shut off the engine and spun around in his seat to get a better look at her.

She jumped, scooting back with nowhere to go. In her peripheral vision, she kept an eye on the door, ready to leap out and start running.

The man took off the cap and shades.

"Emma."

Emma froze.

Shane. Her driver the entire time was Shane. It had to be a dream. *Wake up, wake up.*

She closed her eyes, opened them.

Nope, still Shane. And he was smiling with that adorable dimple.

"Dammit, Shane!" She held up her phone. "I almost called the cops on you."

He appeared only slightly remorseful, reigning in that sexy smile she enjoyed seeing so much. "I'm sorry. I wasn't trying to scare you. I thought you'd figure it out when I opened the door for you but..."

"I did it myself." Emma studied him, in shock that he sat a mere foot away from her. "How did you know I was going to be in Vegas?" She realized the answer before Shane responded. "Luci."

He nodded. "Luci."

She groaned and Shane pleaded with her.

"Don't blame Luci. I had to beg her to help me. I wanted to apologize in person for my lunatic behavior."

"Lunatic, huh?"

"Yeah." Regret glimmered in those green orbs. "I'm sorry. I haven't been handling all this press stuff very well, and that's not your fault. We're supposed to be in this together and I forgot that."

"It's my job to remind you."

"You shouldn't have to."

"We're a team." One corner of her lips lifted. "We have to remind each other."

That youthful expression emerged, the one that screamed K.I.P. They weren't exactly in public, but not necessarily behind closed doors. Shane leaned forward and Emma inched closer to him. He contorted his shoulders through the gap of the seat until his mouth found hers, the kiss more intense than she remembered. His tongue stroked hers, the bottom half of her cried out. Damn, she couldn't stay mad at him for long, her body, her mouth betraying her.

Shane tasted her thoroughly, a man with a voracious appetite who hadn't eaten in days. One hand cupped the nape of her neck while they hungrily explored one another. His low growl flamed the storm brewing at her core and a muffled moan escaped her throat. Pulling back, he searched her face, settling on her eyes. "I was an ass and I'm sorry."

"You were an ass and I accept."

He grinned. "Thank you. Now that that's out of the way, a little a birdie told me you've been through Vegas, stopped a few times, but you've never experienced it."

A birdie? Luci again. "No, I haven't."

"So, what would you like to do first?"

"What?"

"We're in Las Vegas. You're the tourist, and I'm your driver. So, where we going, boss?"

She laughed. Boss, she liked the sound of that. "I don't know. Are you sure about this?"

He turned in his seat, faced the steering wheel, and put the cap back on his head. "It's time you got the authentic Vegas experience. I've got a baseball cap and your favorite sunglasses. Which casino do you wanna start with?"

"No idea."

"What about a show?"

"Never been to one."

"How about the gondola ride at the Venetian, or the roller coaster ride at the Stratosphere?"

A Gondola ride? They had makeshift rivers in the hotel? She'd heard rumors but never actually saw it for herself. And wasn't the Stratosphere skinny and taller than a twenty-floor hotel? How exactly would a roller coaster work in a building designed like that?

Shane took her silence as no. "We could take a walk down Fremont Street, visit Shark Reef at Mandalay Bay, or eat at the Eiffel Tower restaurant at the Paris Hotel."

"You're speaking Greek to me right now."

"Sheltered much?"

"I work a lot."

"How about the Mob Museum downtown?"

Emma perked up. "That sounds interesting."

Shane slipped the shades on his face and started the engine. "Tell me again."

"What?"

"That I'm not harboring a fugitive."

She chuckled. "I'm not a criminal."

"Then buckle up, Ms. Jacobs. Today is gonna be one long ride."

SHANE SLID A THICK STACK OF PAPERS INTO HIS leather satchel, class handouts he had yet to grade. The classes moved on from *Romeo and Juliet*, venturing into another classic story. Depressing tales but accurately portraying the era of the tragic economic times during the Great Depression.

He clasped his satchel shut and gazed at the row of windows. The blinds were closed, blocking the multitude of eyes peering through the windows. Paparazzi continued to stake out his condo, toiling around the grocery store downstairs until he arrived home. Bob, the grocery store owner, loved every minute, telling Shane his profits increased since the press came to town.

"Mr. Rawlings?"

Fifteen-year-old Martin Rimdale stood at the back of the class with another one of his students, Chip Barnby. Martin slung the straps of his bookbag over both shoulders. He seemed taller than his already six-foot thin frame as he wandered up to Shane's desk. His brown hair whipped to one side, tapering at his neck.

Chip followed Martin to the front of the room, his stocky five-four build a contrast to Martin. Blond hair, brown eyes, his shirt hung off him like a curtain, baggy jeans barely over his waist. Martin studied Shane hard and gripped the straps of his bookbag.

"Can I help you two with something?" Shane waited, not wanting to press the issue. Martin clearly had something on his mind.

Martin slowly opened his mouth, the conflict of what to say raging in his eyes. Chip cast Martin an impatient glance.

"Is Emma Jacobs really your girlfriend?" Martin asked.

Shane looked first at Martin, then Chip. Both boys did not catch the question as personal, their expressions noted a required response. "I'll see you boys tomorrow. Have a good night."

Martin furrowed his brows, taken aback by Shane's lack of information. "Night Mr. Rawlings." He tugged at the shoulder straps, gave a small nod, and headed for the door.

Chip followed closely behind Martin. "See, I told you he's seein' her."

Shane shook his head as the door swung open and shut, leaving Shane alone in the room. His personal life became town gossip and rightfully so, since the men and women with the cameras wearing sunglasses arrived. He at least had the safety of his home. They couldn't get in or scale the wall to the second-story windows. Curtains closed, he'd zoned out the clicking sounds below, and the various faces staring at him from the street.

Shane hoisted the strap of his satchel across his shoulder. His cell phone vibrated, and he glanced down at the screen flashing. His mother. She used the monthly brunches to ensure her oldest son was alive. If she called his phone, it was serious.

"Shane?"

Gary Alders, the school's principal, stood in the doorway. Six-foot-five, he could have been a basketball player rather than a school principal. Except Gary wasn't the athletic type, he won all the academic decathlons. At fifty-one years old, his full head of hair whitened, wrinkles creased his eyes and lips. Square, thin, gold-rimmed glasses sat over the bridge of his nose.

He was dressed in his usual black slacks, his rotund belly testing the limits of the clear, plastic buttons of his tucked in, blue striped shirt.

"Mr. Alders, how can I help you?"

Gary looked around the room. Assured they were alone, he shut the door. His shoulders dropped, he rubbed his hands together and smiled weakly. "Shane you've been doing an awesome job. I know there was a rough patch for a moment there, but these last months the kids are just ecstatic about you."

Shane lifted his chin, waiting for the punchline. Was he getting a raise? Did someone make a complaint?

Gary took a few steps toward him. "Recently, as I'm sure you've noticed, it's been a bit disruptive around here. Parents have been calling us about the people with cameras hiding out on the lawn, accosting their children in the parking lot with questions about you." Gary dropped his hands to his sides. "You have a famous girlfriend." He nodded, emphasizing his points, envy marking his face. "It's all very distracting. I think you need a sabbatical."

Gary was asking him to leave? Shane didn't understand. "It's almost the end of the school year."

"I know, but I think it's best for everyone if you take some time off."

"Are you firing me?"

Gary put both hands up and emphatically shook his head. "Not at all. I'm just saying some time off would be good for you. Until things die down a bit."

"Exactly when would you like this time off to begin?"

"Immediately."

"The cameras won't be here forever. This'll all blow over."

"Not soon enough, unfortunately."

"I don't think it's a good idea." Sabbatical? The end of the school year was six weeks away. Shane marched to the door and reached for the handle.

"It's not a suggestion Shane."

The coldness in Gary's voice stopped Shane from opening the door. He slowly spun around.

Gary shoved his hands in his pockets. "You're a great teacher. No one doubts that. But that online video of you and Emma Jacobs has parents pretty concerned. They're wondering what kind of role model that makes you."

"I've been teaching here for four years. Without incident."

"I know," Gary said. "So, take the sabbatical. With the summer coming you'll have the time to sort this out."

"I'm teaching summer school this year."

"No, you're not." Gary scratched his forehead, searching for the words to put Shane at ease, but found none. "Figure this thing out before the board finds a way to put you out." He strode to the door, vanishing into the vacant hall.

Shane watched his boss leave feeling as though his career and sanity walked out the door with him.

———————

Shane stood in front of the pristine, white, intricately carved oak double doors, the nickel-plated handles shimmering in the early evening light. His mother requested his presence immediately and Shane drove to his parents' home in Newcastle directly from the school.

Principal Alder's comments still hung in the air.

Take a sabbatical. It's not a suggestion Shane. Sort this out.

He hoped the publicity would die down, and it had partly diminished. Not enough to allay the fears from concerned parents. The press didn't hound the hallways of the classroom, but they did wait in the parking lot and loiter around the windows. They followed him everywhere. Shane should've known the extra attention threatened his teaching position.

He pressed the oval button by the door releasing a chime that echoed within the interior of the house.

A woman answered in a gray maid's outfit. Middle aged, fair skinned, slim, a tight bun of dark brown hair rested at the base of her head. Her brown eyes flickered over him. "May I help you?"

Shane didn't recognize the woman, and she didn't recognize him. She was new, and it meant his mother fired yet another house staff member. "I'm here to see my mother." He held out his hand. "I'm her oldest son, Shane."

She studied him suspiciously and his hand, as if his fingers would transform into serpents. Lifting her eyes to his, she slowly accepted his handshake. "Serita."

"Hello, Serita. May I come in?"

"Oh yes." She pulled the door farther open and Shane stepped inside. "Mrs. Rawlings is in the music room."

"Thank you." Shane followed the wide corridor filled with hanging artwork, some original impressions of Renoir, Monet, and other artists he couldn't name. The white marble table and brass legs were made in France. The wine-colored rug, the intricate design embossed in gold, was imported from the Far East. Vases from Indonesia, the antique, six-foot-tall grandfather clock restored to its former glory, chimed four times as he reached the end of the hall.

The chocolate marble tile switched to fluffy cream-colored carpet. The living room came into view showcasing expensive ivory couches, an oval glass coffee table, and a brick fireplace.

Shane continued past the living room and the long oak table with ten black cloth covered chairs in the dining area until he reached the music room.

The music room contained vaulted ceilings, and four expansive windows, two stacked on top of each other. Various framed musician album covers and pictures lined the walls. Photos of Mercer, Sallie, and himself at different ages hung among the many images on the wall. The three of them as kids. Sallie at fifteen. Shane after his first paycheck on Wall Street in his gray suit and red tie, a lopsided grin on his face, holding a twenty-dollar bill in front of his chest. He stood on the concrete steps of the building he'd called home for the next three years. Liam had taken that picture.

"Shane?"

Shane tore his eyes from the image, shifting to his mother. She sat on the bench at the baby grand piano with its sleek and glossy black finish. "What did you want to talk about?" He asked the question but already knew the answer.

Emma. He knew by the scornful look in his mother's eyes. She wanted to talk about Emma.

She swept her slender arm toward the left, to one of the two couches in the room. "Would you like to sit down?"

"Not really."

"Please." She dropped her arm, the elegance in her poise disappearing as she restrained the annoyance in her voice. "Please, sit Shane."

Shane exhaled, turned from his mother, and plopped down on one of the couches. "You called?"

"And you came." She said quietly. "That's progress. I didn't want to talk about it on the phone."

Shane fought the sarcasm building in his throat. He and his mother hadn't seen eye to eye on much since leaving his days as the golden boy on Wall Street. She once touted her son as the man who flipped pocket change into millions. The neighborhood women were jealous and when Shane quit everything, envy switched to pity. Her friends shied away from her, a few comforting her as though Shane tragically died.

"So, tell me." She narrowed her eyes at Shane and shifted on the piano bench to face him. "Why this girl?"

Anyone else Shane would've taken the question as an inquiry into Emma's celebrity status. His mother's inquest was deeper than surface level. "I don't know." Inexplicably drawn to Emma, he wasn't about to detangle himself from her now. "But I know how I feel about her."

"How is that?"

"I love her."

Mrs. Rawlings widened her eyes and scowled. "You're joking."

"I'm not."

"Shane, be serious."

"I am."

"You're not thinking this through. She's not like us." She leveled her eyes with his, the look conveying every possible meaning to the statement. Not born into the status of families from old money. Not born with the complexion deemed compatible with Shane's. Heather had been acceptable. Long blond hair with big soft curls sparkling gold in the evening sun. Her sea-blue eyes and infectious laugh enraptured everyone in his family. Her attire always conservative, bland colored pumps, streamlined skirts just above the knee, neutral browns, pastel blues, blouses buttoned up just over the bust line.

It was clothing Heather wore to appease his mother, but he knew Heather in her tight dresses and stilettos. A woman who danced on bar counters and guzzled down five tequila shots before passing out. Who'd grind the dance floor with any man to capture Shane's attention and referred to Shane as less than nothing. Average. Pathetic. Not worth the effort to keep their relationship afloat.

Shane stood up. The last thing he wanted to hear was a speech on how he ruined his chances with the woman his mother felt was best suited for him and the family. Heather Strauss.

"If this is what you brought me here for, I'm not interested." He started for the door.

"I heard about your job. And that's not all. There's more bad news coming, but don't worry, we'll take care of it."

"What does that mean?"

His mother didn't answer, her hand resting against the edge of the piano.

Shane halted, inches from the doorway. His suspension only happened an hour ago, miles from his parents' doorstep. "What do you want from me?"

"I want you to stop seeing her." Mrs. Rawling shifted her upper body around to fully face Shane. The reflection of sunlight from the five-carat diamond ring on her index finger cast rainbow tinted squares on the wall behind him. "Your father and I forbid it."

"Forbid it?" Shane chuckled, his voice lacking humor. "I'm a grown man, mother."

"So, act like it." She narrowed her eyes at him, the hard edge of her threat evident on her face. "If you pursue this, your father and I will cut you off completely. No more end of the year bonuses."

Shane set aside his annual "bonuses" for years, his expenses primarily paid through his teaching salary. Even if he lost his position at the school, he'd find another school, another town, a fresh beginning with Emma. "I'm not worried about money."

"We'll make her public life a living hell," His mother warned, curling her wrinkled fingers together like knots on a branch. "We'll dig up any dirt we can on her, we'll leak everything to the press. Every event she goes to, anyone she talks to, we'll be there with more dirt. She'll be buried in it. We'll make it up if we have to. You know your father has that kind of power."

Shane knew his father had connections, and enough power to ruin a man's life and reputation. His father smeared names for the sake of a land deal or a company acquisition. Lives spiraled into chaos, families broken, careers derailed. His father didn't just go after a person, he worked his way through the entire family. Bankrupt the husband, have the house foreclosed, cause the wife to lose her job, get child protective services to take away the kids on bogus charges. Even have someone snatch the dog and put it in the pound. Like dropping a nuclear bomb on a target, his father obliterated a person's entire world in order to get what he wanted.

"He wouldn't."

"To save his son," she hissed. "In a heartbeat. Life can get more difficult for her than she could imagine. All I have to do is say the word."

"This discussion is over."

"I still love you." The bite in her voice softened. "I just despise what you've turned yourself into."

Shane headed through the open doorway, eyes focused on the empty corridor and wondered how the day could get any worse.

Thirty-Seven

EMMA SAT ON THE COUCH, HER LEFT FOOT planted on the floor, her right leg tucked beneath her. She eased onto the couch, lowered her head, and softly strummed the acoustic guitar strapped across her belly. Her left hand glided along the fret as she changed chords. The setting sun cast a bright orange glow across her silhouette and she shifted away from the open window. She played the melody of a slow song, then drummed the strings in a slightly, faster beat.

Shane had hunkered down over schoolwork and exams. Papers to grade and lessons to plan. Summer approached, marking the beginning of sun-filled days for swimming, barbecues, humid evenings. Her fingers rested on the strings of the guitar.

She hadn't seen Shane in over a week, hadn't talked to him in three days. Neither of them in contact. No texts. No emails. No calls.

Emma removed the strap over her head and set the guitar on the floor, leaning it upright against the couch. She reached over to the end table and grabbed the red cell phone. She dialed Shane's number and waited while it rang three times. Voicemail.

Emma ended the call without leaving a message. Her black cell phone rang, and she hurried to her bedroom, her purse on the dresser. She rumbled through the contents in her large tote, locating the cell phone at the bottom of her bag. The caller ID flashed Suzanne's name.

Releasing a long breath, she answered, "Hey Suzanne."

"Emma, we have a problem."

Emma fought back a thousand devastating scenarios. Had she been dropped from that new project she'd just signed on to? That would be humiliating. Another actor publicly blasted her acting skills? Wouldn't be the first time and not a game changer. Had she been swindled out of her fortune? She was careful to check her investments thoroughly. Whatever the reason for Suzanne's ominous call, she'd face it head on.

"What is it?" she asked.

"I got a call from more than one magazine today asking me for a comment on a story they're running tomorrow."

"And?"

"It's about Shane. He's a murderer?"

Emma pressed the button on her cell phone to end the call. Twenty minutes of Suzanne's explanation and Emma was left speechless. Suzanne advised her to find Shane so they could confront the headlines directly. Without hiding. Without a "no comment."

Emma placed her cell phone on the side table. She uncrossed her legs and pushed her palms against the top of her knees. How did she approach someone about a man murdered in a car accident? That

Shane was the assailant, drunk and behind the wheel, his actions costing a man his life? The magazine would paint Shane as a man with a wild lifestyle. Shane was a different man back then, and now Emma understood the transformation from the old Shane to the new one. The one she knew and loved.

Her red cell phone rang, and she stared at the name on the screen. She didn't want to answer, but not responding only meant more calls. She pressed the button and spoke softly.

"Hello, mother."

Madeline's normal, crisp voice came out slurred and breathless. "Emma, I just came from the doctor's office, I need to see you."

"Are you okay?" Emma rose from the couch. She glanced around for her jacket and found it lying across the kitchen bar.

"I can't talk about it over the phone. You have to come over. I'm at your house."

"At my house?" Emma slipped into her jacket. "Why are you there?"

"I thought you'd be here." Her mother's words sounded more difficult, each word held back with a stifled sob. "We really need to talk."

"About what?"

"What the doctors said. Can you come now?"

Emma's trip would have to wait. "I'm on my way." She snatched her purse from the couch and headed for the door.

Emma took a taxi to the exclusive suburb of Los Angeles she called home for nearly a year. She bought the lavish Mediterranean style monstrosity at Jordyn's suggestion. They'd been dating and at the time, his opinion mattered more than she cared to admit. Her home held an indoor swimming pool, a theater, too many bedrooms, countless living rooms and sitting areas she often found herself wandering through. An interior designer furnished the home. Pieces of furniture she recognized, others she couldn't recollect where they came from.

She paid the cabbie and stared up at the house now up for sale. She rushed past the black wrought-iron gates and up the long brick driveway.

Terrifying revelations invaded her mind, disconcerting thoughts about her mother. What could've happened? Madeline was aggressive and annoying but still her mother.

Fingers trembling, Emma shoved the key in the lock and pushed the door open. She shut the door behind her, quickly heading for the sitting area to the left of the house, a pale blue painted room with a gray modern couch and two chairs. She spotted Madeline seated on the couch.

Arms folded neatly across her lap, she turned and smiled at Emma. "You got here so fast."

Emma wasn't sure if she wanted to sit or if she had the strength to hear her mother's medical diagnosis. Madeline had always remained in near perfect health. Tennis lessons, constant walking, her mother stayed on the go, but only on things she deemed socially acceptable.

Emma sat down in the chair angled next to the couch, took in a long breath and released it. "Okay, what did the doctor say?"

"Still a picture of perfect health." She stood up and stared down at Emma. "But I brought you a surprise." She stepped aside and Jordyn entered the room, sitting down on the couch.

Emma blinked a few times and shook her head as if trying to wake herself from an odd dream. She pointed at Madeline. "So, you're not sick?"

"Oh no." Madeline said. "I'm just fine."

Jordyn took Emma's hand, his voice gentle. "Emma."

Emma looked back at Jordyn and a flash of light pierced the corner of her eye. She glanced back at Madeline. "Did you just take a picture?"

"It's going to be amazing." Her mother beamed proudly. "You two need to talk." Her footsteps quick, she disappeared into the great hall.

Emma started after her mother but felt the grip of a hand on her wrist. She turned and glared at his hand on her skin then at the distressed look of longing in his eyes, glossed over in arrogance. "I suggest you remove that hand, next time I won't be so nice."

Jordyn chuckled. "I'm the action star remember? It's my job to save the damsel in distress." He let go of her wrist.

Emma wanted to move but her feet wouldn't go, her voice stuck in her throat. She shed tears late at night alone, even faulted herself for his wandering eyes. No more, she thought.

Jordyn appeared undeterred, and he scratched his chin amused at her anger. "You're upset right now, and I get that. I messed up, I know. But you make me a better man. I haven't been with anyone else for months now."

"What's that supposed to mean to me?" Emma folded her arms across her chest.

Jordyn put one hand on her arm, tugging them free to dangle at her sides. "It means I want you. Just you. You're the one I've been waiting for. I just didn't know it at the time."

"At the time you were sleeping with other women?"

"I was stupid. Guys do stupid things. You've done stupid things."

"Excuse me?" If they were about to compare all the idiotic things she'd done against Jordyn's it would be a short list.

Jordyn held up two hands defensively. "I'm only talking about the guy you're with now. He's not good for you Emma."

Emma tilted her head to make sure she'd heard him correctly. A serial cheater passing judgment on a gentle, caring schoolteacher from a small town? Who kept his head low, didn't bother anyone and loved her unlike she'd ever known? "Are you kidding me?"

"He's a murderer." He took a step forward and Emma took a step back. "He's killed people."

Murderer. She'd heard that same word earlier from Suzanne, before the story hit the tabloids in the morning. Suzanne and Jordyn didn't speak to one another, didn't even like each other. Madeline and Suzanne barely shared a conversation. Jordyn could've had an inside man at the tabloids but that seemed unlikely. Jordyn didn't make allies, he offended people. Emma created the connections. How could he know about the pending scandal?

Emma looked at the floor briefly and suddenly raised her head, her piercing gaze intent upon his face. "You told the tabloids about Shane, didn't you? You found something on him and you leaked it to the press."

Jordyn was silent.

Emma opened her mouth, but no words came out. Jordyn was ready to ruin a man's career to win her back. The gesture was frightening and sad. "He has done nothing to you."

"He killed a man. He was drunk and driving. He maimed his sister too."

Drunk driving? Emma hadn't ever seen Shane with a drink. Maybe the old Shane had been the drinker, and the accident had been the reason for his Seven-Up obsession. Even at the impromptu concert Shane remained sober, drinking only water. "So, you dug up his background and found some report that said he was drunk driving and convicted of vehicular manslaughter?"

"Well," Jordyn rubbed his hands together. "I didn't find the report. I hired someone who did. And it didn't exactly say he was drunk, that was more of a gray area."

"So, he wasn't drunk?"

"I don't think he was over the legal limit," Jordyn pointed out. "But he was driving. And the guy died."

Emma could hear no more. She put both her hands up, warding off any further discussion. "Listen to me Jordyn. Who I choose to date and why is no longer your concern. You and I will never be a 'you and I' again, so you can stop trying. It makes you look bad, and it makes me feel bad. I love this man and I won't let you, my mother, or anyone else interfere with that."

"Emma."

"I'm selling the house. Consider this your sixty-day notice."

Emma turned and started for the hall when Jordyn grabbed her wrist. Instantly she took his wrist and swung both their arms upward which lurched Jordyn backward. His face and chest exposed she closed her fist and delivered a swift but fierce jab to his lower right abdomen. He hunched forward in pain, Emma finished with a palm strike to his nose and blood trickled down his nostrils.

"Have you lost your mind?" He cupped his nose, wincing at the unbearable sting.

Emma shook away the tingling in her hand. "I warned you." She left behind her mother who had raced back down the great hall to the blue room to view the damage. Her eyes skimmed Emma as though she were the daughter of someone else. A violent wretched child who should've been given away at birth. The eyes of her mother.

Emma shook away the image. If Madeline thought of her as an alien baby dropped from the sky so be it.

Pressed for time, Luci coordinated a private jet that flew Emma to Seattle. It took a bit of luck and Emma called in a few favors but hours later, she landed in Seattle, riding the ferry to Bainbridge Island. Blackness settled across the sky, the freezing air clawing at her thick down jacket, autumn orange scarf, and matching beanie. She hustled to the end of the block and molded her body to the side of the building. She peered around the wall, searching for paparazzi. The front of the grocery store remained empty.

At ten at night most of Bainbridge's small shops were closed, the grocery store included. Emma didn't see the shadows of curious heads seated in the few vehicles parked across the street. She was alone.

Emma hurried down the block toward Shane's residence. The grocery store windows were black, Shane's windows dark. She sprinted up the steps and banged on his door.

"Shane?" she whispered loudly.

She pounded her fist, knocking harder in case he was asleep.

"Shane!"

The door to the apartment across from Shane's creaked open. An elderly lady held the door slightly ajar, peeking through the thin opening. Her gray and silver hair was tangled past her shoulders, her brown eyes wide, her fingers curled over the edge of the door.

"He's not in there," the woman spat angrily. "Stop waking up the whole dang neighborhood." She pointed down the stairs. "Try his parents' house. Go wake them up."

Emma returned to Seattle, arrived in Newcastle and trudged up the gravel, U shaped driveway of a custom designed, beige two story expansive residence. On the side of the house three separate glass doors upstairs led to a fifteen-foot-long, four-foot-wide, black iron gated balcony. The balcony provided a view of the large yard, towering trees, shrubbery and Emma assumed another cement pathway to the Olympic size swimming pool in the back.

She dreaded every one of the brick porch steps up to the massive, oak double door entrance. It was late, but she had to find Shane. In the morning the tabloids would feast on his story. Gossip or fact? She needed the truth, the reality of what occurred the night Shane's life changed.

Her stomach fluttered at the thought of meeting his parents. Waking them late at night. Her reluctance was the same as anyone meeting their partner's parents. Being a movie star didn't make the introductions any easier.

It was late but necessary. She rapped softly on the door.

Footsteps tapped the floor, hesitated, and the door cracked opened.

The person standing before Emma was not his mother or father, but a familiar face. Raven hair, china bangs. Brown eyes, cheeks normally lifted upward in a teasing smile now held a frown.

Sallie.

"Hi." Emma said quietly. "Is Shane—"

"He's not here." Sallie held up one hand, cutting Emma off, her eyes sympathetic. She stepped outside and softly shut the door. "Trust me, you don't wanna meet my parents right now."

Emma heaved a long sigh. "I'm so sorry. I tried to avoid all this."

Sallie wandered to the edge of the porch, and leaned against the thick white pillar, her ocean blue skirt swaying with the small breeze. It was then Emma noticed Sallie's right foot. Curved metal inside a fitted shoe replaced flesh and bone. She looked up to see Sallie staring back at her.

"From the accident." Sallie tapped her artificial foot twice on the brick porch. "It's titanium."

Emma lost the ability to speak. Sallie was maimed in the accident involving Shane. Emma understood better why he'd transformed himself, how deeply the incident affected him. He hadn't been forthcoming about himself since his return to Bainbridge, creating a whole other world built behind a wall of shame and guilt. A place he refused to let Emma view.

Her shoulders dropped, exhaustion marking the edges of her face. Emma backed away from the porch. She was foolish not to gather all the details about what happened to Shane.

Her naivete shred at her emotions, but the strong desire to learn all the facts about Shane's past didn't diminish. Seeing Sallie only urged Emma for more. She needed to find Shane.

She turned from Sallie. "I'm sorry to have bothered you." Her steps quick and determined, she marched across the gravel driveway back toward the main road.

"Wait," Sallie called out.

Emma paused halfway to the street.

"Where's your car?" Sallie asked walking up behind her.

"I took a cab."

"You weren't going to call one?"

Emma spun around. "I was gonna call on my way to the end of the driveway."

"It's late." Sallie pointed to a black Mercedes parked on the left side of the driveway. "That's mine, and it's too dangerous for you to be walking around here at night. Let's get some peach pie and I'll tell you what happened to my brother."

ALLIE TAPPED THE EDGE OF HER PLASTIC MENU against the table.

Emma and Sallie occupied one of the booths ten feet from the same one Emma and Shane shared weeks before. The same waitress trotted over, pencil behind her ear, in her white uniform and purple smock, the absence of sleep deepening the wrinkles on her face. Her eyes wandered over both Sallie and Emma without any recognition. She took their orders, her voice unenthusiastic, and she hurried back behind the counter with two orders of peach pie and coffee.

Emma stilled her hands, desperately trying not to fidget. Time away from her search for Shane meant the harder it would be to find him. The idea struck her maybe Shane didn't want to be found.

"Emma?" Sallie looked at her thoughtfully. "You really do love him don't you?"

"I'm not good at words."

"You're an actress."

"That's pretend. Not in the real world."

Sallie drummed her fingers on the linoleum tabletop. "You didn't answer my question."

"Do you know where he is?"

"You two belong together. Both so evasive."

The waitress returned with their coffees. Sallie grabbed four sugar packets from the container at the end of the table and poured two cream containers into her mug. She sipped the coffee and closed her eyes. "That's better."

Emma dumped two sugar packets in her coffee, adding a small bit of cream.

Sallie placed her mug on the table. "Shane wasn't always like this."

"You mean the old Shane?" Emma stirred her cup.

Surprised, Sallie leaned back in her seat. "He told you about the old Shane?"

"A little." She thought back to Shane's references. The old Shane was focused on money and led a wild lifestyle. "I know he's jumped out of a plane. He used to drink, but now he just drinks Seven-Up." She smiled at the vision of him and his six pack of soda. "He loves that damn soda."

Sallie chuckled. "I know. The old Shane was reckless, all about prestige, status, and money. He has a weird talent for easily making money. Like a gift, it fit him well in the investment world." She took another sip of coffee. "It was all he cared about, and my mother loved it. She bragged to all her friends about her golden child, spinning hundreds off his fingers. He was engaged to Heather, a woman from another powerful, rich family."

"Sounded like a full life."

"One day he woke up, and just knew it wasn't what he wanted to do anymore. He quit his job and got his teaching certification. Next thing we know, he's teaching at the high school."

"That must have taken everyone by surprise." Emma couldn't imagine the difficulty Shane faced walking away from the cushy life-style he'd built for himself. And to just wake up one day and change?

"Heather left him, my mother wouldn't even look at him." Sallie sighed. "But Liam, he was so proud of him. We celebrated right here the day he got his certification."

"He told me that."

The pies arrived, and the waitress sat both plates on the table in front of them. Sallie stared down at her slice of pie. "I used to follow Liam and Shane everywhere as a kid. They were always trying to get rid of me, but as you can already tell, I'm pretty stubborn."

Sallie picked up her fork and poked at the pie. "We went to Vegas, my first time ever, and everything changed. We came out of the last casino, Liam was buzzed, I was too. Isn't that what you do in Vegas?"

Vegas? As in the same city Shane had joined her for a two-day adventure?

"Shane was the responsible one that night. He didn't drink anything. Normally, he'd drink like a whale, but that night was all about me. On the ride back to the hotel, a drunken asshole crossed the yellow line." Sallie used her fork to cut away a smaller piece of pie. "One minute we were all talking and laughing, the next Shane was trying to steer the car away from the blinding headlights. The driver hit us head on. Liam died, I lost a foot, but Shane came out of it with a few scratches."

Emma blinked back tears.

"Shane never got over that. That he walked away with scratches and bruising. He just shut down. I think he wished he died that night. He continued on but..." Sallie shrugged. "He wasn't the same. No girls.

No friends. Just work and home. I think he felt guilty, that he didn't deserve any kind of happiness after what happened to me and Liam."

Her eyes watered, her lips lifting in a cheerful smile. "And then he met you. You made him go out, do things, brought his sense of humor back. Using that list was a genius idea. And I heard about Vegas. My brother never went back after the accident. Until you. And he was your chauffeur for the day? Can you imagine how hard that was for him? He loves you."

The full implication of Shane's trip to Las Vegas to see her slammed Emma square in the chest. Vegas had stripped him of his best friend and his sister's foot. Still, he'd hopped a plane to see Emma, to apologize, and be her driver for the day. In a city strife with the tragic memory of two of the most important people in his life. Two people he'd lost while being the designated driver.

Sallie eyed Emma closely, that mama bear look on her face. "This isn't a fling is it?"

She blinked back tears and shook her head. "No."

Content with the response, Sallie cut a piece of pie off with her fork and held it up to her mouth. "Good, because I have a few places I think he might be."

———

Space, that's what he needed. Just a little space. Not a thousand-mile distance from Emma but somehow that's what happened. He stared at the tabloid magazine in his hand, and plopped down onto the lumpy, motel-room-queen-sized bed.

The five-by-seven photo showed Jordyn and Emma seated together, holding hands, staring into each other's eyes. Below the photo, two printed words stabbed Shane deep in the heart.

Together again.

Tabloids didn't always tell the truth, right? He considered several explanations. Doctored images, misconstrued captions. He frowned and tossed the paper to the floor. It had to be a lie, there had to be a reason.

He'd prepared for the public scrutiny, but he'd overestimated the power of the paparazzi. Now it appeared he had no job, and no Emma.

A knock on the door tore Shane from his thoughts. He shifted aside the curtain, peering through the blinds at the visitor outside. Gabe.

Shane opened the door and Gabe entered the small room. "Did you bring it?"

"Yeah, I brought it." He handed Shane a cell phone charger.

"Thanks."

Gabe caught sight of the tabloid magazine on the bed, his gaze lingering on the same image of Emma and Jordyn as what appeared to be the happy couple. "What the hell?" He snatched up the magazine and slumped down in the corner chair. "You know this is crap. I don't believe it. Tell me you don't believe it."

Shane barely glanced back at Gabe as he returned to the end of the bed. "No, but then again, even gossip holds a small amount of truth."

"Not like this." He cast the magazine to the carpet. "Have you talked to her about it?"

"I haven't talked to anyone."

Gabe released a long breath, a sign he was completely aware of Shane's sudden teaching sabbatical. "I'm sorry about the boss man. The guy's a dick." He offered an expression of annoyance. "Who just puts someone on an involuntary leave like that?"

"So, everyone knows?"

"Most of the teachers. Word traveled fast. Can't say what the students know. Parents have asked me to take over the youth softball team. All of this sucks." He raised his head, his eyes demanding answers. "What are you gonna do, Shane?"

Shane was still unable to comprehend the events happening at hyper speed. Swifter than he could keep up. Principal Alders' unbelievable decision. His mother's ultimatum, her threat so passionately expressed. He had no notion at the moment of what to do or say next.

Seeing there would be no response, Gabe pointed at Shane's cell phone. "Tell me you're not gonna blow her off."

Shane quickly recognized the hard edge to Gabe's voice. Gabe didn't want Shane leaving Emma either. "I'm not blowing her off. This is just getting real messy." He wanted to tell Gabe, explain his options and receive an honest opinion. His parents had the means, the money, and now motive to undo all of Emma's professional progress. His mother lacked remorse, empathy, mercy when it came to her children. In her warped reasoning, Emma was the risk to be neutralized because based on his mother's standards, she didn't fit. Her money, her complexion, her name. Like jamming the incorrect puzzle pieces together.

Shane didn't care if his parents didn't think he and Emma fit. He cared less what the world thought, the public's reaction at the bottom of the list. But his mother was like a pit bull and when her teeth sank into an idea about something she didn't let go until the job was done.

"You told me you love her."

Gabe's voice cut through Shane's meandering thoughts. "I do."

"So, act like it. This job, the press. Everybody's got an opinion. But the only opinion that should matter is hers and yours. If you really love her, that's all that matters."

How did he explain his mother's warning? Maybe love wouldn't be enough to stop how she would twist Emma's name, her reputation, into something tawdry. Maybe protecting Emma meant he didn't get what he wanted.

Gabe stood up. "You were lucky to find her."

Luck, Shane snorted. People called him lucky after the accident. Luck stripped him down and took away everything.

"It'll work out. You'll see." He left the room, morning light bouncing into the room briefly, then plunging back into a darkened haze as the door shut.

Shane stared down at his cell phone charging on the nightstand. He should've called her after his meeting with the principal and the talk with his mother, but he couldn't bring himself to return home. Not yet. Sallie's place was not an option. He hated bringing her under public scrutiny; she'd suffered enough.

Shane rubbed his eyes with the balls of his hands. He told Emma they were in this together. Every word spoken to her that night at the hotel was true. She'd awakened him, snapped him out of the sludge he called life, reminded him what it was like to laugh, to not take it all seriously. He could call his mother's bluff, fight through her anger, her malicious moves to separate him from the only woman, outside of his family, that he'd ever really loved.

He heaved in a long breath and released it. Shane hadn't liked being in the dark and she probably didn't either. He raised his cell phone up, stared at the name on the screen and called Emma.

"A lot more to take on than you thought?" Emma stood at the end of the pier and gazed across Puget Sound. She fought off the icy wind, bundled in a large black coat and jeans and adjusted the scarf around her neck.

Shane remained behind her, his outerwear less bulky. He shoved his hands in his pockets. "A little, I guess."

"I'm sorry about the press. I know being around me can sometimes be harmful to your health."

Shane huffed, but the corner of his lips tilted in a wry smile. "You? Harmful to my health? I don't think so."

"You know what I mean. We're in this together, right?"

"Are we together?" The image of Jordyn and Emma sprang to mind and his smile vanished. Tabloids could print exaggerated stories, but pictures didn't lie. Jordyn and Emma were in the same room together. Jordyn's never-ending quest to win Emma back was not fiction.

"Shane." Emma tugged on his arm and he pulled his hands out of his pockets. She grabbed both of his hands and tenderly squeezed them, gazing up at him with an unfamiliar look.

Love.

"Jordyn and I are not together." Her eyes didn't waver, her tone confident. "My mother called him over. I didn't know he was going to be there. He tried to kiss me, my mother secretly took the picture, and Jordyn learned the hard way that I know how to break a man's bones in twenty places."

Shane grinned. "You broke his bones?"

"I broke his nose. He thought I'd gone crazy. My mother won't even look at me, or take my calls right now. That's not such a bad thing."

"You are crazy." Shane brushed her cheek with the back of his hand and Emma closed her eyes. "So, no Jordyn?"

She opened her eyes and stared at him. "No Jordyn."

Shane cupped her face with both hands, leaned down and grazed his mouth with hers. Emma parted her lips, inviting him in and he savored the sweet taste of her. She returned the kiss, tangling her tongue with his, saying without words how much he'd been missed. She moaned sweetly, a familiar sound that had the lower half of his body springing to attention. He broke away and Emma's labored breathing matched his own, her eyes glistening with desire. "We have to talk."

She waited expectantly for an explanation. Her brows dipped slightly, the corners of her lush lips falling.

Shane gulped nervously and exhaled a long breath. His mother would make good on her promise and it wasn't fair to Emma. He struggled for the words, logic that would affect them both in surprising ways. "I've been suspended from my job."

Emma stepped back. "What?"

"Because of the publicity. It's disruptive."

"They shouldn't have—"

"You were right Emma. The paparazzi, the fans, your life. It's too much."

Emma, clouded in confusion, leaned back as recognition of his statement took hold of her face. Hurt and anger glossed her eyes and guilt twisted his gut. He couldn't bear to look at her, and yet he couldn't turn away. His mother's voice trickled to the surface of his thoughts. She would do everything in her power to make Emma a public outcast. An image no longer valuable, enough to affect Emma's career, everything she'd worked for. Shane couldn't allow his family to do that to Emma.

"We should take a break."

"A break?"

"Yeah." He kept his voice tight. Forced the words evenly from his throat. "See other people. Take time away from each other."

"You mean break *up*?" She said slowly. "You said we were in this together. No matter what. We're a team. Why did you go to Las Vegas?"

"I went to see you."

"I know what happened in Vegas. With your sister and Liam." She paced back and forth in front of him, her hair swinging fiercely with the breeze. The scarf dropped around her neck, her feet plodded on the wood, hard. "I know it was just an accident and I can't imagine why you would've brought yourself back to a place of such pain, just for me. Not unless you cared more about me than you're acting right now. So, what's really going on?"

Someone told her about the worst day of his life. He should've been the one to explain, to chart out the events of that night. His own shame had prevented the words from coming out. He gripped the rail of the pier and stared at the spot where small waves slapped the rocky shoreline. "Las Vegas was my idea. I told Sallie everyone has to have that Vegas experience once. I wanted the night to be about my sister. So, I didn't drink that night. I was going to drive them around, bar to bar, nightclub to nightclub."

He looked down at his hands and back to the water. "I took my eyes away for a second and the headlights came at us faster than I could react. I spun the wheel, but it slammed into us, mostly on Sallie's side. Liam died instantly."

"That wasn't your fault."

Shane gazed down at Emma. Her mouth was pursed defiantly, arms crossed at her chest, her eyes refusing to accept anything less than "I agree." He turned away. "A cut on my leg. That's all I got. Sallie's foot was crushed under the dashboard and Liam's spinal cord was severed upon impact. They didn't deserve that."

"None of you deserved that."

"I can't do this Emma." His gut wrenched, bile churning at the base of his throat. This wasn't what he wanted but it would keep Emma and her career safe. He couldn't explain that fear had gnawed at him the moment he'd stepped off the plane into Las Vegas to see Emma. All those catastrophic memories rushing him, nearly overpowering him. Emma was the reason he'd continued. He summoned the courage to do exactly what he'd almost done the year before, chauffeur the people he cared about around town. He hadn't wanted to lose Emma after their verbal spat and making amends far outweighed his fears. For forty-eight hours he'd let go of the guilt, the anger, the self-pity, so he could live in the moment with Emma. And now, because of his mother, he had no choice but to distinguish that bit of happiness. "You should go."

"Go? You're serious? All that talk about being a team? You made me trust you. I believed you. What was this, some kind of fling with a movie star?"

"Maybe." Ouch. A new low even for him, but necessary to break things cleanly. To protect what Emma treasured most. Her career.

She inhaled a sharp breath. "Maybe?"

"Emma, I'm—"

Her open palm flew hard across his right cheek. She covered her mouth with one hand, her eyes filled with tears.

The area where her hand connected with his face stung.

Exactly what I deserve.

He slowly turned his head to Emma. She removed her hand from her mouth, averted her gaze, and stomped past him toward the shore. He didn't follow, listening to the sound of her boots thump against the wood as she reached sand, and disappeared beyond the brush.

Thirty-Nine

*C*OLD AIR TICKLED **EMMA'S** LEGS AS HER BLANKET abruptly disappeared from her body. Eyes closed, she awkwardly grappled for her blanket. Lying in her four-poster bed in the penthouse suite, Emma kept the shades drawn. She discovered the blankets near her ankles and hurled them back over her body and up to her shoulders. She twisted on her side and curled herself into a fetal position.

"Emma." Luci's voice echoed against the darkened bedroom and she yanked on the covers again. "Emma, you've gotta get up. It's been almost a week."

"I'm not going anywhere." Emma tightened her grip on the covers. She'd barricaded herself in the suite for six days. No visitors, no press, no mother. Meetings were rescheduled, filming her new project wouldn't be for another month. The time for interviews ended.

Luci picked up a remote control on the night stand, pushed one of the buttons and the vertical blinds shifted to one side. Sunlight blared through the window.

Emma squinted. "Close the shades."

"You need to get up."

"I'm not going anywhere."

"When's the last time you had a shower?"

Emma scowled and shielded her face with the blanket. She couldn't believe her foolishness. Shane Rawlings wormed his way into her life, burrowing into her heart. She trusted him when he said he loved her. She revealed to him her deepest thoughts and gave him her body. In return, at the first sign of serious trouble, he turned his back on her.

"I'm not going anywhere."

"You're getting up." Luci gripped the blanket and the sheets, jerking them out of Emma's grasp.

Wearing only a long white t-shirt, the icy air nibbled at Emma's legs again. She opened her eyes and sat up. "What do you want from me?"

"I want you to get up. I want you to stop feeling sorry for yourself."

"Why? Because I got dumped? I was an idiot who got taken for a ride? Who wouldn't feel upset about that?" The story about Shane's unfortunate auto accident never made the tabloids. Emma wasn't sure if that had been Suzanne's doing, the Jordyn fake reconciliation story was juicier, or someone else made it vanish. Either way, Emma was grateful the story had gotten buried.

"No." Luci sat down at the end of the bed. "You have every right to be furious and sad, but it's gonna take time to get past this. You can't hole up in here for the rest of your life because of it."

Emma's eyes brimmed with tears and she fought to keep them from spilling down her cheeks. "Jordyn, Shane, I keep doing this to myself."

"No, you're not. It's them Emma, not you." Luci spoke in a tone that said no would not be an option. "Now go take a shower. I'm taking you to lunch."

Emma groaned and reached for the cover. Luci flung all the bed linen on the floor. She looked up at her assistant. "Am I that bad?"

"Right now? Yes, you are."

Emma hung her head. Her hair was a scatterbrained mess, her eyes sunken, arms and legs skinnier than normal due to her diminished appetite. Her skin was dry, she probably smelled two days old, and her teeth needed to be brushed. She raised her knees to her chest and rested her chin on them. "What am I supposed to do now?"

Luci plopped down onto the bed again beside Emma and wrapped one arm around Emma's shoulder. "Keep moving. That's all you can do." She scrunched her face and wiggled her nose. "First, take a shower, because you smell and I'm thinking about burning the sheets."

Emma grunted. "Funny." She swung both legs over the side of the bed, rubbed her eyes and stood up. A hot shower, a little sunlight and a bit of breakfast was a start.

Keep moving.

Shane sat at the round table covered in gleaming white cloth, and decorated with three tall, golden candle holders in the center. The back of the chairs surrounding the tables were framed with golden rods. Shane stared down at the slice of wedding cake before him. Two-layer cake, white buttercream frosting, fluffy yellow inside.

Music blared from overhead speakers, a fast song Shane didn't recognize. Many of the guests finished their cake and danced on the large square tiled floor in the middle of the vast carpeted reception hall.

Shane was the only person left at a table seated for six. Finding he had little conversation to offer, some moved to the dance floor, others migrated to nearby tables for quiet conversation. Sallie danced, her princess cut white gown swaying with every lively move. She discarded the veil and her three-inch heels for a pair of white slippers Shane bought her the night before. His former coworkers advised him high heels on a woman's wedding day were killer. Walking, dancing, greeting guests in them. Now, Sallie used his slippers with relief on her face.

In a few weeks, school would begin again. The summer passed fairly quickly, and Shane spent most of it indoors. Once public curiosity fizzled, the paparazzi faded from his front step. Sometimes Shane snuck away to Gazzam lake, soaking in the silence. Other times, he took a trip to Seattle, blending through the crowds at the market to clear his head and think.

He missed Emma so much, it physically hurt. Gabe stopped talking to him. He was lucky his sister didn't throw him out of the wedding. Shane rented several DVD's starring Emma. He watched her films intensely, remembering she was no longer in his life. *Night of the Living Dead* became a staple in his limited movie collection.

His parents' table was across the dance floor and he caught his mother's stern look. He narrowed his eyes at her and turned away.

"Hey, Shane." Heather slid into a seat beside him. She patted him on the leg. "I haven't seen you in forever. Your mother said you would be here."

Shane scanned the woman who'd almost become his wife so many years before. Her hair was more honey colored now, her skin fair and smooth. She wore a simple peach colored pencil skirt, rising just above the knee. Her V-neck floral top matched the color of the skirt accentuating the curves he remembered. She revealed a bit of cleavage as she leaned forward and smiled, the corners of her rouge lips tilting upward.

"I mean it's been years since we last spoke to each other."

Shane nodded. "Yes, it has. How've you been?"

Blue eyes blinked back at him seductively. Was she flirting with him?

"I opened my own salon downtown. It's been doing really well." She gazed with longing at his sister, twirling on the dance floor. "Weddings are such bliss, aren't they?"

"I wouldn't know," he said quietly. He'd have married Emma in a second if he'd taken the time to think through the dilemma with his family.

"That's right. You never got married."

"*We* never got married."

Heather cleared her throat. "I know."

"Did you find happiness?" Their last conversation was about Heather's happiness. With someone stable. Worldly and ambitious. Everything she felt Shane wasn't anymore.

She stumbled over her words. "I thought I did. For a little while. He was chief of the surgery department at Stanford Hospital."

"Good for him." Shane glanced at his sister. Surrounded by guests, Sallie threw her head back and laughed at something Patrick said.

"And then I caught him with one of the nurses." Heather softly sighed.

Shane looked at her incredulously. "What?"

"He was cheating."

"Oh. I'm sorry to hear that."

Heather patted his leg again. "I'm divorced now. Maybe you and I can go out for coffee, catch up on old times?"

Shane eyed the hand still resting on his leg. When they were together, that gesture would've put a smile on his face. Now he thought how one look from Emma could change everything.

Heather didn't wait for his response. "I know it's been awhile. You're single, I'm single."

"I'm still a teacher," he said firmly.

She removed her hand from his leg and leaned back in her chair. "I heard they gave you some time off. Your mother said you've been looking into the investment workforce again. Maybe starting your own firm. This is a great time for you."

Shane looked across the room at his mother, in her pink two-piece skirt outfit, her silver and gray hair tightly wound in a bun at the back of her head. Pearls circled her thin neck and decorated her earlobes. She chatted with a few people who stopped by the table, most of them former clients and societies well-to-do.

"Heather, could you excuse me one moment?" Shane rose from his seat before Heather could respond. He swiftly strode from one end of the great room to the other, taking care to go around the dance floor.

His mother smiled as he approached her. "Shane darling, I see you and Heather are getting along again."

He glanced around the table to see his mother as the only occupant. "You invited Heather?"

"I did." She appeared surprised at the way Heather's name slithered from his tongue. Like day old pizza or black coffee. "Why are you upset she's here? She's good for you."

"She's good for you," Shane shot back. He leaned down so she could hear him better. "I am a teacher. That is not going to change."

"You don't know if they're going to hire you back once the summer is over."

"It doesn't matter. If they don't, I'll teach somewhere else."

His mother frowned and placed both her hands on the table. "Shane, why don't you sit down?"

"I don't wanna sit."

"Sit," she said in a firm tone he hadn't heard since their ill-fated conversation in the music room.

Glaring, he sat down in the chair beside her.

"I'm doing what's best for you," she calmly explained. "Even if you don't know what that is. Now that the movie star mess is out of the way you can focus on other things. The one good thing that came out of all that nonsense is the loss of your job. Teaching is beneath you." She shook her head at the idea. "A Rawlings man doesn't teach."

"No, he blackmails," Shane finished. "He destroys, he cheats, he does whatever it takes."

"Shane," she said through clenched teeth. "Lower your voice."

"I'm not ten. You threatened Emma so you could get what you wanted and now this? I'm not going back to the way I was."

"Think how Liam would feel about this."

The fury behind Shane's eyes boiled over at the mention of Liam. He bolted out of his chair, towering over his mother. "You don't speak his name. You don't get to speak his name. He was ten times a better person than you will ever be. You know what Liam would say? He'd tell me to not let my mother blackmail me into not seeing the woman I love!"

"Shane!"

The music stopped, dancing ceased, all eyes were upon them.

Shane rapped the table with his knuckles. "You know what else? This family didn't get its money by being saints. I'm sure if I dig hard enough, I'll find dirt on this family to bury all of you. Stuff I can leak to the press."

"You wouldn't!"

"I'm a Rawlings man. I'll do whatever it takes." He was so concentrated on his mother's face, determined she see the seriousness in his own threats that when he finally looked away, Sallie was staring right at him. Her gaze shifted first to their mother, and again to Shane. Embarrassment flashed in her eyes, replaced with hurt.

Shane wasn't sure how to comfort Sallie and he suddenly felt guilty for the scene he created at his own sister's wedding. Certainly, a day she wouldn't forget and neither would the guests.

"Blackmail into not letting you see who?" Sallie stared hard at her brother. "Emma?" Her intense gaze switched to their mother. "Mother, what did you do?"

"Sorry Sallie for the disruption," Shane mumbled and marched from the tables, the guests, the dancing floor, rushing into the corridor and at last out in the open air. He meant every word spoken to his mother. She had her threats, and he had his. First, he had to find Emma.

CHAPTER

Forty

SHANE STARED DOWN AT THE TOMBSTONE. BRIGHT yellow daisies lay flat in front of the cement block, a contrast to gray, darkening sky. He studied the four words etched in stone that summed up Liam's thirty-two years.

Loving husband, father, friend.

Shane closed his eyes, the rush of the headlights invading his memories, the clear image of his sister dangling upside down, the ominous silence from the back seat. If he could've relived several minutes before the accident and driven a different route or delayed their departure a few hours later, how different their worlds might've been. Had they stayed in the bar longer, chatted more about what to see and do in Vegas, Liam's life might've been spared.

"I'm sorry," he said quietly.

He wished he'd bore the brunt of the collision, saving his sister's foot and his best friend's life.

He heard the sound of an engine in the distance and looked up at the familiar sight of Liam's black SUV cruising along the gravel road. As the car neared him and pulled off to the side of the road, Shane immediately recognized the driver.

Amari Blackwell.

She shut off the engine, then hopped out and strode toward him.

She looked as he remembered, her fair skin the color of butterscotch, her green eyes paler than his own. Dressed in jeans, boots, and a sweater, golden and brown spirals of hair framed her face. She stopped in front of him. "Hello, Shane."

He gave her a small nod. "Hi, Amari."

"It's been awhile."

"Yes, it has. How's Nicholas?"

"He's such a good little boy, looks just like his daddy," she said. "He's almost walking and already getting into everything. And work is just as crazy."

"I'm sorry I haven't been by to see you and Nicholas." Shane lowered his head, ashamed that his fury at the world, at fate, had prevented him from saying a final goodbye to his best friend. "I should've been at the funeral." He peered up at her.

He understood why Liam fell so hard for Amari. She was headstrong, smart, and beautiful. And she'd turned Liam down the first seven times he'd asked. His persistence and charisma finally paid off the eighth time he'd suggested a date. To his surprise and Shane's, she'd agreed. Two years later, they were married.

The zest in her eyes, the normal defiant set of her shoulders had dimmed since Shane had last seen her. Bogged down in grief.

"I heard about the cards," she said.

"Has everyone heard about that?"

"It was me."

"Wait, what?"

"You said it wasn't you. Sallie told me it wasn't you."

She shrugged. "I had my assistant send you the cards. So technically I wasn't physically sending them to you. But I did set the whole thing up."

"Why?"

"I asked Sallie about you from time to time. She told me you weren't getting better, just kept digging in, getting further and further away from your family and friends." Amari looked down at the gravesite. "Liam loved you like a brother. He'd want you to move on. Do all the things he didn't, say all the things he wouldn't, experience more than he had." She held up one last index card.

Forgive someone.

"Amari—" Shane said.

"I was going through his things and I found the list. Creating that list was genius. And you crawled right out of the hole you put yourself in. After you lit up the Internet with Emma Jacobs, I realized Liam's list worked almost too good. Excellent choice, by the way."

"I think Liam figured his list would help me get over Heather."

She grinned. "It became more than that, don't you think?"

Shane slowly nodded and stared hard at the card. "I miss him."

"I miss him too."

His eyes stung with tears and he blinked them back, lifting his eyes from the card to Amari.

"Let it go, Shane." She wrapped her arms around him and held tight. "It was never your fault."

He swallowed hard, tried to force the pain down his throat.

"Whatever you think you did," she whispered, "forgive yourself and let it go."

He raised his arms and drew her closer to him. He lowered his head to her shoulder. Forgive himself? Forgive his driving, forgive his choices? Move on? It was like leaving Liam behind. To continue sharing the best things in life without the one person who was like his brother since the sixth grade? No more celebratory peach pie at Island Diner. No after work calls to tell Shane to get off his butt after the Heather debacle. No jokes, no crazy Liam ideas to shake his head at. No best man at his wedding, when he had a wedding again.

Shane thought of Emma, the first woman to practically drag him out of his self-imposed exile. He'd royally screwed up the most precious thing he'd ever had, all out of fear.

What would Liam say?

Go big, win big.

He released Amari, and she smiled up at him. Her cheeks were wet with tears and she wiped away the moistness on his face with the pad of her thumb.

"Go," she said. "Find her. Make this right. Liam would be so happy for you."

Yes, Shane thought at last. *He would.*

Forty-One

MMA BLINKED, SHIELDING HER EYES FROM THE
sun with one hand as she peered across the yard to the back
door. The sweltering ninety-eight-degree weather caused her canary
yellow sundress to stick to her legs. Her eyelids felt moist with perspiration. The two-acre backyard held a small cabana and Jacuzzi big
enough for eight people. Attached to the house was a covered patio
large enough to fit two couches and tables and a brick enclosed grill.
Surprisingly, the only fixture missing from the backyard was a pool.
Trimmed green grass blanketed the expansive area. An oak tree, its
thick trunk and twisted branches shaded a corner of yard.

"Dreamy, right?" Luci appeared beside Emma and gazed over the
lawn.

Emma nodded. She especially adored the wooden swing, its long
ropes attached to the thick branch overhead. "It's beautiful." Until her
time at Bainbridge Island, Emma hadn't paid much attention to the

landscape. Now, she yearned for the view of grass, trees and flowers. She spun on her wedge heel and stepped under the covered patio. "We should be going."

Luci glanced at her watch. "You're right. No more houses for today."

Emma visited several other homes for sale and so far, this one was her favorite. A two story five-bedroom, deep green Tudor style home. Office, great room, living room, but the color of the house reminded her of Shane. His green eyes piercing her, wanting her. She'd have to change the color of the house if she decided to buy it.

The realtor stepped outside, a middle-aged man with brown, perfectly coiffed hair and an array of blinding white teeth when he smiled. "Wonderful isn't it?"

"It is," Emma said softly. "I'll let you know."

He adjusted his blue blazer, masking the disappointment in his eyes. "Okay. Well, you have my card."

"I do." Emma toyed with his business card in her hand, flipping it over. It was time to start over and that meant buying a new house. Someone already bought her old one. She put the business card into her purse. "We really have to go." Filming would begin again in the morning but tonight she'd attend the film premiere of *Paris at Night*.

Luci shook the realtor's hand. "It was nice meeting you, David. If she's interested, she'll give you a call."

Emma remained quiet on the ride back to the hotel suite. She dropped Luci off at home and drove straight to the hotel. The valet parked her car, and adjusting the strap of her purse across her shoulder, Emma strutted through the lobby to the elevators.

"Emma?"

Emma turned at the sound of her name. She searched the faces seated in the huge lobby for the female voice that called out. Sallie Rawlings stood up.

"Sallie?"

Sallie smiled. "You remember me."

Emma strode toward her. "Of course, I remember you. What are you doing here?"

"Luci told me where you'd be." Sallie glanced back at two red, gold embossed empty wingback chairs across from each other. "Mind if we sit a moment?"

"Sure." She eased into one chair and Sallie in the other. "How are you?"

"I'm good." Sallie held up her left hand, the oval cut, two-carat diamond gleaming in the light beside the titanium wedding band on her third finger. "I'm a married woman now."

"Congratulations."

Sallie laughed, her giddiness at being newly married glowed on her face. "Thank you. I just got back from my honeymoon in Bali and I knew I had to fix this."

Emma was about to ask fix what when she realized the direction of the conversation. "Sallie you don't have to fix anything. It's done. Your brother made his choice." It was difficult just to choke out her confession. That Shane left her. That she spent the week after curled in her bed crying her eyes out and when she thought she couldn't shed any more tears, she cried some more. Eyes dry, face neutral, Emma didn't have anything left besides acceptance.

Sallie hesitated, trying to find the proper words. "He...didn't think he had a choice. I mean it was our mother of all people."

"Your mother?" When had Shane's mother come into the picture? She hadn't even met the woman. "I don't understand."

"I know. My mother isn't the friendliest person, and she and Shane do not get along." Sallie crossed, then uncrossed her arms for effect. Like an umpire shouting she was out. "Ever since he changed, left Wall Street behind, they've just butted heads."

"Okay."

"She wants to see him happy I think, in her own way. But you made him happy. You brought him out of his shell, you made him better."

"I didn't do anything."

"You did!" Surprised at the passion in her own voice, Sallie skimmed the room, but no one was watching them.

Emma scanned the room as well. Two men read newspapers in chairs several feet from them, but didn't look up.

Sallie released a long breath. "Sorry. My mother blackmailed Shane so he would stop seeing you."

"What?!" What could anyone blackmail Shane with? The auto accident? What kind of parent blackmailed their own child? Emma shook her head at the revelation. "What the hell?"

Sallie put one hand up. "I know. I said the same thing. When the press got wind of you two, my mother was livid. She demanded he stop seeing you, but he wouldn't. When he lost his teaching job—"

"So, he did lose his job?"

"Yeah." Sallie lowered her eyes. "They didn't hire him back."

"Bastards."

"Never mind that. I think my mother had something to do with that too." She leaned forward. "She told Shane if he didn't cut off your relationship, she'd smear your name. Start this whole dirt campaign on you. My family's very good at that."

"I don't have anything for anyone to use."

"They would've found something. Trust me. And if they didn't, they'd find a way to twist things or just make it up. Either way, your reputation would be on the line."

"I'm not afraid of your mother."

"Shane didn't wanna take the chance of what she might do."

"So, he broke up with me," Emma said, more to herself than Sallie. Part of her was relieved, her affair with Shane hadn't been a fling, not some conquest to tell all his friends. He did love her, willing to give her up to protect her. The other part of Emma was furious. Shane didn't give her the whole truth, the opportunity for her to decide how she felt about his mother's threat. Not dealing with the situation head on, the exact same behavior Emma exhibited when Shane first discovered her celebrity status.

"She even tried to get him back with Heather."

The mention of Heather snapped Emma from wandering thoughts. "Heather the ex-fiancée?"

"Don't worry, it didn't work. Shane blew up at my wedding and put our mother in her place."

"Where is he now?"

Sallie grinned. "On his way here if he isn't already."

Emma quickly surveyed the lobby and Sallie laughed. "You do still love him!"

Emma shook away the excitement gnawing at her insides. She wanted to see Shane more than anything at the present moment and was angry with herself for feeling that way. "I'm just surprised."

"Well you shouldn't be, he still loves you. Unlike I've ever seen. He didn't tell you about the last three cards, did he?"

Emma shook her head.

"Fall in love, get married, and see a baby born." Sallie chuckled. "He's already got one out of three completed and I'm pretty sure he's on his way to mark the other two off his list."

"Sallie."

"Emma." She widened her eyes, her lips stuck in a broad smile that spoke volumes on how determined she was to see Shane get a second chance. "When I last talked to him, his place was packed up. He's riding that Ducati all the way out here. I took a flight to beat him here. To talk to you first and ask you to give him a second chance. My mother can be an evil woman and he didn't wanna see you hurt. It tore him up to do that."

"So, what changed?"

"I don't know." Sallie shrugged. "Something just clicked at my wedding. He was different after that, on a mission. That's why he hasn't called." Sallie scanned the room as if Shane would pop out from behind a chair, planter or counter. "Anyway, I should be going."

Sallie stood up and Emma followed.

"Don't tell him I came here okay? He doesn't know, he told me to stay out of it."

"Okay."

She grabbed Emma's hand and gently squeezed. "Just remember, I don't know when or where, but I do know he's coming to see you. To apologize, win you back, whatever you wanna call it. So, give it some thought?"

Sallie didn't look like she was going to let go of Emma's hand until an acknowledgment was made. Emma nodded and Sallie let go.

MMA PLASTERED ON HER BEST FAKE SMILE AS the flicker of white lights flashed in her face. Camera after camera captured her picture, and she paused every few feet for a quick pose. She kept her outfit simple, a black spaghetti strapped dress curving with her hips, stopping mid-thigh, with a short slit on one side. She wore strappy sandals, three-inch-high heels. Diamond stud earrings and a tennis bracelet completed her outfit. Her costars followed behind her, each of them striking poses and smiling for the camera. Emma sincerely smiled as she shook hands with fans and signed autographs. Her perfected phony smile reappeared during brief interviews by entertainment reporters, followed by more pictures.

Suzanne met her at the door. "Get enough photo ops?"

The corner of Emma's lips dropped once inside the lobby. "Yeah."

"You should be excited." Suzanne gently lifted Emma's chin. "This is your premiere."

Her plastic smile reappeared.

"That's better." Suzanne narrowed her eyes at Emma and the two headed further into the theater where the movie would shortly begin. "Is your mother still not speaking to you?"

Emma nodded. Madeline's every day calls diminished to once a week. She felt betrayed by Emma's shock and anger over the tabloid cover of her and Jordyn. She did not raise a violent child and breaking Jordyn's nose was the final straw. Madeline's short, two-minute calls were to ensure her one moneymaking child was still alive.

"Is she going to be here?" Suzanne asked.

"I don't know." Escorted to her seat in the front, Emma sat down and Suzanne went back to work the crowd of agents, producers, directors, and actors. There were a few writers present and Emma made a mental note to talk with them later. For now, she had the premiere, and later, rereading her lines for the scenes she'd shoot at the studio lot in the morning.

"Only you, Luci." Shane heaved in a deep breath. "You really are connected. To get me in here last minute again."

Luci nodded emphatically, red waves of hair lightly bouncing off her shoulders. "I'm pretty good at my job." She'd snuck Shane in the side door, hiding him until after Emma had arrived.

Shane inhaled another long breath. The last couple of weeks after Sallie's wedding were a mixture of job interviews and packing up his loft. He'd finally found an apartment on the outskirts of L.A. Only one part of his life was missing and she sat in the second row of the theater, staring up at a screen yet to play her soon to be released film.

Upon moving, his mother backed off completely. His behavior at Sallie's wedding completely rattled her. His parents shunned him, cutting him off from any money, which is how he'd rather have it. Shane saved enough money from his Wall Street days, his old teaching position, and his parents "annual bonuses" to live comfortably without working if required. At the moment, money was the least of his concerns. Talking to Emma was at the top of his list.

He rehearsed the plan in his head. Go sit next to Emma. Start talking. Apologize. Explain. Apologize again.

In the lobby of the theater sat a table full of small appetizers, foods Shane couldn't name and some that looked delicious. Knots twisted in his stomach; he shied away from the food.

Luci chomped down on diced tomatoes mixed with other stuff he didn't recognize on top of a golden round cracker. She chewed, swallowed, and gulped down a half a bottle of water. "Want a bottle of water?"

Shane shook his head. His palms felt clammy, and he wiped the sweat from his forehead with the back of his hand. "Are you sure about this?"

"She's crazy about you. If you could convince me, you can convince her." Luci adjusted the collars of his crisp white shirt, unfastening the top two buttons. Black tuxedo, white shirt, no tie, all at Luci's suggestion. She flattened the lapels of his black tux jacket. "I got you this far. Go big, or go home." She gave him two hard pats on the back.

Shane took in another breath. He wanted Emma back and would do anything. "Alright then." He started down the aisle toward Emma's row.

———

Emma wiggled in her seat, anxious to leave, but knew she had to stay. She thought about Sallie's visit that afternoon. *I don't know when or where, but I do know he's coming to see you. To apologize, win you back, whatever you wanna call it. So, give it some thought?*

Emma browsed through Sallie's words. Starting a relationship where two people left each other when life threw curveballs didn't seem like a solid beginning. Both Emma and Shane had reasons for their actions. If Sallie was serious, and Shane came to see her, asking for forgiveness, would she take him back? Why hadn't he stood up to his mother back then? Why now? Did it really matter that it was now?

Emma had more questions than answers. She wanted to drag her hands over her face but that would ruin her makeup, her lips painted a shimmering light brown, mascara and liner highlighting her eyes. Her makeup artist would freak.

Some of Emma's costars walked by, waving, or saying a quick hello. She politely smiled, joked with them about some of the antics from the set, and watched as they took their seats far from where she sat.

The film would start soon. Emma stood up, desperate for a moment alone, the ladies room the only place she could quietly think, if only for a few minutes. She slipped out of the row, turned around, and headed back up the aisle toward the reception area.

She instantly recognized the face standing ten feet from her.

"Shane?"

"Emma," he said quietly.

Emma froze, unable to take another step. Shane wore a black tux and white shirt, the top two buttons undone. She'd never seen him dressed in formal attire, his broad shoulders filling the tux, his sculpted body looked gorgeous in anything.

His green eyes latched on to her. "You look beautiful."

She moved her hand to touch her hair, forgetting most of it was swept up in a loose bun. Sallie's warning sprang to mind. *Don't tell him I was here.* "What are you doing here?"

"I came to find you." Hands in his pockets, he kept his eyes on Emma.

"Shane—"

"Wait." He put up both his hands, warding off any early rejections. "I'm so sorry about everything. I was trying to protect you. My mother—"

"I know about that."

"You know?"

"Yeah." She'd apologize to Sallie later.

"How did you find—" Questions filled his eyes on how Emma discovered his mother's hidden agenda. His curiosity faded, overshadowed by determination. "It doesn't matter how you found out. I shouldn't have let it come between us. All the public attention, it's not too much. It's just one part of you. I get to see all of you, the person outside of the lights and the cameras. If that means dealing with the paparazzi, or fans, or whatever, I don't care."

People crammed the theater, some seated, others standing, several faces turning their attention to Shane and Emma. Emma sensed the tide of the theater changing, dozens of eyes suddenly concentrated in her direction. The crowd murmured as recognition of Shane's identity sunk in.

"Are you sure you don't wanna talk about this in private?" she asked.

His voice was firm, but soft. "I wanna talk about it right here, right now."

He didn't care about the public's view, the press, the paparazzi? Who was this person? This private man stood before her in a nearly packed room of people attentive to his every word.

"I shouldn't have left."

"We left each other," Emma said lowly.

Shane took a step toward her. "And it was a mistake. One that I'm not going to make again."

"You lost your job because of me."

"That wasn't your fault." He took another step toward Emma. "And I found a new one."

Her thoughts flipped to her first night with Shane at his condo. How clumsy, but so comfortable she felt. Empowered and beautiful to be simple Emma. No camera, no film, no lights. Her connection with Shane, amazing and terrifying at the same time. And the press could tear that all away. "We're different."

He paused. "That's a good thing. We have a few things in common."

Emma chuckled. Their mothers. "Some things."

Shane noted her half smile as a positive sign. He took another three steps toward her. "I don't care about all that other stuff. I just want you."

"Shane."

"I love you."

There were faint gasps in the crowd.

Emma couldn't find her voice. She'd heard him say it before but never out loud in front of everyone. Her mouth opened, but the words wouldn't come out and Shane wasn't waiting for a response.

"I know you love me. Tell me you don't, and I'll leave right now."

Emma bit her lip, but didn't move.

Shane closed the gap between them. He looked down at her, his eyes leveling hers. "Finish the list with me."

Her eyes watered.

"Finish the list with me." Shane smiled, his dimple reappearing.

"Shane," she whispered back.

"Marry me Emma."

"What?" She blinked and wondered if Sallie's prediction about the list was true. If Shane really arrived to ask her this one question.

He retrieved a small, black velvet box from his pocket, knelt down on one knee, and opened the lid. "Please, marry me."

The three-diamond princess-cut, two-carat ring stared back at her from within the box. Emma still couldn't find her voice. Tears streamed down her face. "I do love you Shane." She nodded emphatically, smiling. "And yes, I will marry you."

Shane stood up and fervently claimed her mouth, the two of them lost in each other. The crowd erupted into thunderous applause, whistles, and cat calls. He released her and softly kissed her neck as they held each other.

He leaned back to look at her and Emma laughed. "I can't believe you did this."

"Believe it." He brushed her lips with his.

"I love you," she said and was rewarded with another kiss. "We'll finish the list Shane. Together."

Epilogue

EMMA SAT IN THE LOUNGE CHAIR ON THE COVERED deck and watched the waves of the Pacific Ocean crashing against the shoreline. Surfers rode in from the choppy water, holding their surfboards, wetsuits glistening as they trudged back to their cars. Gray clouds drifted across the sky, the sun a distant memory of hours before. A soft breeze brushed her face, and she hugged herself to ward away the chill of the early evening air.

Santa Cruz.

Relocating to a beach city wasn't difficult considering how much she loved the water. Her new beachfront property was a one story, four thousand square foot, five-bedroom home with hardwood floors, a gourmet kitchen and spacious rooms. A home she and Shane bought together.

"You're still out here?" Shane poked his head out the back door. He surveyed the sky and watched the ocean waves overlap with increasing intensity. "It's cold out here, you should really come inside."

Emma swung her legs over the side of the chaise and Shane held out one hand for her to grab to help her stand. He held a DVD case in his other hand and raised it up for Emma to view. "*Killer Klowns*? Who watches this stuff?"

She smirked. "Who doesn't?"

"You're kidding?" He followed her into the living room. When she didn't answer, his eyes grew wide in disbelief. "You're not. What is with you and horror movies?"

"We watched a drama last Friday, remember?" She narrowed her eyes at him. "All three movies. All night."

"I don't know. It looks pretty cheesy."

"It's a good flick."

Shane grinned. "Says the award-winning actress."

Emma opened her mouth to add more reasons why he should watch the movie when she paused. Her golden statue rested on a bookcase next to a set of books, behind glass with dim light overhead. Sometimes she forgot it was there, that she indeed won the coveted award.

Movie offers had poured in after her Oscar win, but Emma had politely declined them all, focusing on her screenplays. Shane found another job teaching high school English in town. Life slowed down a bit, exactly what Emma wanted. Luci enrolled in film school. She visited Emma every few months, but called every day.

Emma rested her hand on her round belly, a burgeoning habit whenever she was fully relaxed. Six months in and the vomiting finally ceased, her energy perked up, and her appetite returned. She wondered about the baby growing inside her, a boy or girl, part her, part Shane.

"Do you think we'll be like our parents?"

"No, crazy parenting isn't genetic. I think we'll be fine. And you're going to be a great mother." He tossed the DVD case onto a nearby table and strode toward her. "What is this about? Emma, you okay?"

Emma nodded slowly. Her energy had indeed returned. Her eyes flickered over him and Shane caught the intensity in them. A look he'd seen many times before.

"Don't try to pull the shirt trick to get me to watch this movie with you." He put one hand up to emphasize his point and leaned against the back of the couch. "I'm not falling for it."

A wide smile touched her lips as she approached him. "It's not just about the movie." She yanked the blue sweater over her head and tossed it on the nearby chair. Her eyes rested on his lips. She stood on tiptoe and eased her mouth over his.

Shane moaned and buried his fingers in her hair, his other hand roaming down her spine to her bottom, which had slightly increased in size along with the swelling of her breasts, parts of her body he found irresistible. She pushed him back lightly, and he slid down, falling onto the couch and bringing Emma with him. Her mouth found his again, and she kissed him with urgency, an unbridled need to have Shane right where they lay.

"Okay." He panted between breaths. "I'll watch the movie."

Emma laughed, sliding the t-shirt over his head. How her life had changed in one year. She glanced at the wedding band on his finger and the one on hers. A simple list brought them together and would be completed with the birth of their first child.

Maybe they could create a new list. A new bucket list for her, Shane, and the baby. She repositioned herself, straddling him, and Shane sat up facing her, his eyes lost in a haze of longing as she unbuttoned his jeans. His mouth caressed her neck, his hands slipped the straps of her bra off her shoulders.

In the midst of a scandal, she found peace.

The words echoed in her thoughts.

We're in this together.

The tabloid fodder lessened, there weren't any paparazzi at the moment, no meddling parents, just her and Shane.

Emma wouldn't have it any other way.

To John, Dominic and Laila –
without you, I am lost.

Katrina and Yolanda – thanks for
pushing me to do better. I'm forever
grateful.

Sincerely,

Yvette

SHOP BOOKS

CayellePublishing.com

CÁLIX LEIGH-REIGN

opaque

SCION SAGA BOOK 1

CÁLIX LEIGH-REIGN

split adam

SCION SAGA BOOK 2

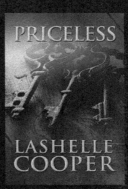

PRICELESS

LASHELLE COOPER

HUNTED

SARAH BIGLOW   MOLLY ZENK
USA TODAY BESTSELLING AUTHORS

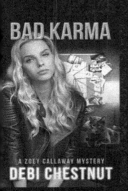

BAD KARMA

A ZOEY CALLAWAY MYSTERY
DEBI CHESTNUT

The List

YVETTE GEER

THE KILLING PLEDGE

ERIC NEHER

DREAMER

LORETTA KENDALL

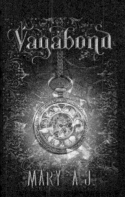

Vagabond

MARY A.J.

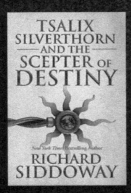

TSALIX SILVERTHORN AND THE SCEPTER OF DESTINY

New York Times Bestselling Author
RICHARD SIDDOWAY

Chameleons

ONYX GOLD

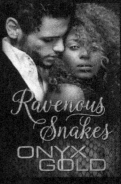

Ravenous Snakes

ONYX GOLD

amazon.com

COMING SOON